DEATH WHISPERS OF THE ETHERWAVE

C. B. Ash

Fabled Horizon Press

ISBN: 979-8-9947861-8-5

Published by Fabled Horizon Press

Death Whispers of the Etherwave is a work of pure, unabashed fiction. Actually, when it's not swinging off the rigging, or shivering some timbers, it's rather shy and retiring. Did I mention it enjoys baking?

Names of characters, places, events, organizations and locations are all creations of the author's imagination for this fictitious setting. So he really is all to blame here.

Any resemblance to persons living, dead, shoved overboard, or reanimated is coincidental. The opinions expressed are those of the characters and should not be confused with the author's, since the characters and the author tend to disagree a lot.

Cover by Leraynne S.

For more, Hoist the Colors see https://www.worldanvil.com/w/hoist-the-colors-kummer-wolfe or over on Substack at https://kummerwolfe.substack.com/!

For anyone who's wanted to catch that horizon.

Do it.

I'll see you there.

...and oh, the stories and tall tales we'll have to tell...

Contents

A Strange New Tide

The world ended in 1712. It happened all at once, and the next day no one knew what to expect. Nations, lands, even entire cultures were turned upside down overnight. Refugees from another world now call Earth home. Everything was changed, if not transformed - including people.

People like me.

There are those who plan to use what happened to their advantage, no matter who they hurt. They can try.

But they'll find us standing in their way.

- Doctor Pedro Sangre, Alchemist and Privateer

1

For want of a book

July 20, 1722. Ruins of the Silvashar Library of Lësarilis. Deep in a swamp on San Andrés Island, off the contested eastern coast of New Spain in the Caribbean Sea.

I love the smell of an old library, even one abandoned in a tropical swamp. The scent of linseed oil, aged leather, and old parchment lingered behind the swamp musk. It was somehow soothing. But the bitter smell of salty fungus and frustrated anger? That was a different story. I yanked the stained red leather book off the shelf in front of me, then jammed it into my battered canvas backpack.

"Run!" I yelled to the others.

A manic, staccato-like tapping sound from the floor-to-ceiling bookshelves flooded the gray, moist air. All around us, shadows shivered while forgotten papers rustled on their own across the wide, three-storey octagonal room. My blood ran cold.

"Pedro! The books! They have mouths with *shark teeth!*" A voice behind me yelped.

"They have razor-sharp claws and venom, too!" I shoved the gunner's mate ahead of me. "Thesaurus crabs! Everyone, run!"

Jonas didn't have to be told twice; neither did the rest of the landing party. I pulled a thin glass vial from my belt, then tossed it at the crabs. It shattered, spewing white-hot flame over the sinister swarm. The front line was scattered to bits, but the rest didn't seem bothered. Everything from room to crabs and their stained book cover shells were just too damp for my elixir to have much effect.

"Mierda!" I spat as I caught up to the others.

We ran for any exit we could out of the library. Narrow windows with their chestnut frames overlooked the swamp, which could have been a quick way out past the damp cobwebs. But the alarming wave of murderous tooth-filled books filled the entire space between us and those windows. That left the tall double oak doors we came in through on the far side of the room.

It was a desperate race across the tattered, wet carpet, rich with oily black mold. Partway to safety, someone slipped and fell with a muffled squish. Screaming erupted a second later.

I didn't look. None of us did. My chest went tight as I ran.

One—or even three—thesaurus crabs, a person could survive. This was at least thirty of the blue and orange book-armored monsters that rattled along with their poisonous promise of death. It was every inch a librarian's worst fever dream.

The rest of us reached the doors as the wet, gargled screams died away. Behind us, the crabs were on the move again. Their frantic scuttling over the wet carpet was a sloshing chorus of eager violence. Terror screamed that we needed to run faster. Who were we to argue?

We raced out of the main library and into a long entry hall. There wasn't much left of these ruins. This had once been part of a larger building. Now there were only four rooms here, including the library behind us, and a broken down entrance to the ruin itself. A long hallway connected all of them together. No sooner had we reached the hallway, than the Terrason brothers grabbed the library doors and slammed them shut. Crab claws scrambled for purchase on the other side. It was a manic hailstorm of muffled, lethal clattering.

Both brothers were your typical short, stout, dwarf-like grimlings with hard, work-honed blacksmith shoulders to match. They could keep the doors closed for a time, but even the brothers' strength had limits. Brass metal veins in the brothers' skin glowed from the strain. The doors' ancient wood splintered at the bottom with a dire crack from the press of the swarm. A tip of one blue claw peeked through. Durner Terrason stomped at it with a thick boot heel until the claw vanished back inside.

"We need to barricade the damn doors!" Skaldi Terrason yelled. "Use tables! Chairs! Anything!"

Several of us grabbed two thick, heavy oak tables from a nearby reading room and any other forgotten furniture we could find. We had a hasty barricade piled against the doors in moments. It wasn't well planned, but it would do for now. Thesaurus crabs were known for a lot of things, like fungal infections or brutal cleverness when hunting as a mob. Brute strength wasn't on that list. Still, we knew the swarm could eventually push through if enough of them battered at the time-worn doors.

I pulled off my black felt tricorn hat, then wiped the sweat from my face with a gray coat sleeve. Shadows along the hallway fought with the jungle-filtered light from outside while the humidity had us in a headlock.

My old friend and our navigator, Lysander Riverwind, appeared out of the long shadows next to me. I twitched, but at least I didn't throw a punch at him. The wiry, olive-skinned Nativan was as sweat-stained and covered in dust as I was from hair to clothes. His dark hair braid practically dripped with sweat.

"The *Codex Luminari?* You have it?" he asked, still out of breath.

"I grabbed it off the shelf before the murder crabs noticed us," I replied between deep breaths. "It looked intact, so Señor Argall should be able to find the maps and notes about Otherworld that he's looking for."

Lysander glanced around, tense as a bowstring. I watched his dark eyes dart to the broken windows along the hallway that overlooked the muggy swamp. After a hard scowl at those, he turned his attention to the half-broken, shadow-soaked entryway, at the far end of the hall.

"A doubloon says he'll just show it off in a display case in his shop," he said bitterly. "Better it was a compass that could show us a quick way out." Lysander pursed his lips. "Pedro, I've a bad feeling about all this."

I frowned. Lysander's 'feelings' sailed closer to being a true warning than just a bad case of nerves. That made me glance around uneasily before I squinted at him in the gloom.

"What do you mean, a bad feeling?"

Lysander toyed with the tiny pendant of a ship's wheel he wore around his neck before he shook his head slightly.

"Pedro, we're not safe here," he said. "It just feels wrong. The walls. They don't even feel safe."

The hallway was typical Silvashar thayan construction, which meant swooping, elegant Gothic archways that looked impossibly fragile. But despite their appearance, they were always made from a durable, gray-white speckled marble that defied almost any damage. The walls here weren't any different, with bricks set in graceful lines that sloped up to a gentle point in the ceiling.

But they had seen better days. Swamp water and humidity had eaten away at colorful tapestries and paint over the years since the library ruins appeared in 1712. Walls, and even some of the mosaic carpet, looked like a drunken madman had painted them with colored mushrooms and pond slime. I ran my fingers uneasily along the dark stitching in the brim of my hat, then slipped it back on.

"Fair enough. We've overstayed our welcome." I called to the others, who were fussing over the barricade. "All hands! Make for the ship before those crabs get at us!"

The eight of us ran for the swamp, our ship, and the welcome idea of freedom outside the ruins. We were only halfway to the exit when the west wall exploded into a storm of gravel. Burned marble chunks pelted us like a hellish hailstorm, even as the blast tossed us across the hall like worn-out rag dolls.

I bounced hard off the far wall before I hit the floor, gasping for air. The world around me was a muffled mess, filled with thin strands of gray-white smoke and marble dust woven into a light fog. Garbled shouts to attack rang out while shadowy figures raced through the blast hole in the west wall, weapons drawn. My crewmates hauled themselves upright, drawing their pistols and blades in reply.

A tall human in a blue-trimmed captain's coat followed close behind the invaders. I'd never met the man in person before, but his appearance matched the lurid description. His coat was smeared with streaks of soot and swamp water. Mysterious dark stains decorated his broad hat and the basket hilt of his cutlass.

Dull red streaks in his thick black beard complimented the lightning-shaped scar on his right cheek. The latter heavily accented his ruddy complexion, along with the nasty sneer that was most of his expression. A scrimshaw squirrel skull amulet completed the fashionable nightmare.

"Captain Dryden Storm," I coughed.

"The very same," the pirate captain replied in a chilly tone.

He arched an eyebrow at me, then widened his sneer. "An you'll be one Doctor Pedro Alejandro Sangre. If I'm not mistaken, you'll be having a book I want. Hand it over and I'll consider letting you and some of your crew keep your lives."

Those sinister, steel-gray eyes didn't hold a lick of mercy.

I answered him by smashing a cloudy glass vial from my belt on the floor between us. Alchemical thick, bitter fog exploded up, eager to swallow the air. I drew myself into a crouch and shot the pirate a sharp glare that would scald skin. Two seconds after, I tugged my hat down low, then melted into the smoke like a living shadow.

2

Best of bad choices

July 20, 1722. Ruins of the Silvashar Library of Lësarilis. In a duel of the Fates...

Smoke was everywhere, and I had melted into it.

I dashed to my right under the curtain of smoke when the captain lunged with his cutlass. The blade missed my arm by inches, but still managed a slice through my wool coat sleeve. Storm cut and hacked through any thick gray smoke or dark shadow that lurked nearby. I did my best to keep out of his way.

Clouded from view, I moved like a ghost running from its grave. The instant I stopped on Storm's right, that skull around his neck belched a sickly, glowing green vapor. The rolling steam poured out the eye sockets, then flowed up over the scrimshaw that writhed in the ghoulish gas. It rose around the captain's face.

"Very clever, Doctor!" Storm snarled.

He turned in the blink of an eye and lashed out at me. The slash toward my face was an alarming blur, almost too fast to follow. I stepped out of reach at the last second. His blade missed my nose by inches. At that moment, I regretted leaving my sword back aboard the

Silk Duchess. That was stupid. If I didn't die, I wouldn't make that mistake twice.

The captain pressed his attack with a wild ferocity. I dodged aside, but I couldn't keep that up forever. What bothered me was that he knew roughly where I was. The smoke should have clouded his senses, but he acted like it didn't. At least, not entirely. I saw him squint more than once before he tried to skewer me. It was as if he saw me as a faint blur or some suspicious shadow.

But I had something like a plan. When he tried for another stab at my throat, I went on the attack.

I ducked low, then batted his sword away with my left arm. Before he could recover, I followed up with a hard right fist smashed against his jaw. The captain's head jerked to the side, eyes crossed from the impact. I rubbed my hand to ease the sting from the punch.

The man stumbled backwards with a grunt and a bloody lip. Sinister steam boiled up around his face from that small skull at his neck. Storm blinked, then shook his head before he squinted in my direction. A glare of hot hate followed a second later. It really seemed he could see through the smoke. That was new. I suspected his amulet had something to do with it.

"I'll gut you and your crew, Doctor, then still get what I'm after! I'll hang your head and theirs from my ship's mast!"

I ignored the bait. There were worse things to worry about.

The smoke was almost gone, so I pulled a bit of power from the Etherwave Arcana to blend deeper into the shadows. Fatigue from the Arcana immediately haunted me, but the effect was worth it. Storm glanced around in a sudden panic while the small skull at his neck burned with a bright blaze of green fire.

The moment he turned his back, I let go of the power. It slid away while the enchanted smoke finally evaporated around me. I melted out of the darkness as Storm turned around. He instantly charged the second he locked eyes with me. I side-stepped, then smashed a quick kick into his gut. The pirate doubled over into a violent coughing fit while he dropped his cutlass.

I stepped in close to pound a right hook twice into his jaw before he could recover either air or wits. One punch might have been enough, but two were for good measure. Captain Dryden Storm collapsed to the worn down, weathered floor like an old sack of potatoes. I snatched up his cutlass, then reached for the uncanny amulet around his neck.

The thing burned me the instant I tried to touch it. I jerked back as a forked tongue of green flame leaped out of the eye sockets, hungry for my fingers. Once I stepped away, the fire slithered back into the skull. To my surprise, Captain Storm wasn't touched or burned at all.

That told me there was more to this amulet than I had time to understand. Besides, I needed to get my friends and crew out of these damn ruins alive. So, I left the captain and his strange amulet alone. Instead, I turned to help Lysander, Skaldi, and the others.

But they already had things well in hand.

Lysander had channeled power from the Etherwave Arcana to shove glistening, ghostly white shields between our crew and the pirates. This gave Skaldi and Durner a chance to grab a pair of heavy end tables, which they used to bash their way into the small mob of pirates. On their heels was the rest of our small group. They cut loose with a volley of pistol fire, then closed in with cutlass and dagger. I drew a deep breath, then raced over to join them.

The pirates didn't go quiet or easily. But it wasn't long before the whole nightmare came to a bloody, brutal, but thankfully short end. We lost another of our group, one of the new deck crew, but the pirates had lost more. The survivors had retreated with their dazed captain through the hole they had blasted in the west wall. Storm didn't yet have his wits back about him, but he looked none too happy about the retreat.

"The fight's gone out of them," Lysander cried out. "Make for the ship!"

We barely made it past the blast hole before a soul-splitting scream from the swamp stopped us dead still.

Outside the ruin, a swarm of books bearing claws dropped off the roof like an avalanche of knives. The nearest pirate shrieked and fell backwards into the swamp water, covered in a snapping blanket of crabs. His companions swatted desperately in all directions in an attempt to save their own skin. It was a losing battle that was difficult to watch. Fatigue from calling on the Etherwave Arcana to enhance the smoke clouded my thoughts, so instinct tried to take the wheel. I stepped toward the dying pirates.

Skaldi's grip on my left arm was like an iron vice.

"Doctor, no! They're dead already," he growled. "What the crabs won't get, their venom will. You *know* that."

"But..." I shook my head to clear my thoughts. "Yes, of course."

Skaldi nodded and released my arm. "After all, we've got our own problems."

The short blacksmith jerked his head toward the library's double doors we had barricaded. At least, the ones we thought we had barricaded.

I looked over in time to see the last of the unstable barricade fall apart. Time seemed to slow to crawl while the tall library double doors creaked open with a menacing moan. They parted just wide enough that a person could step through to the library, or a mob of thesaurus crabs could spill out into the hallway. Unfortunately, it was the latter.

A putrid wave of teeth, claws, and hungry death rushed out at us. I reached down to my belt for another vial, hoping to slow them down. There was only an empty belt loop.

"Hells! I'm out of elixir. Run for the outside!"

We raced down the hall with crabs hot on our heels. A good third of the murderous mob split off to rush out the blast hole for the pirates, but the rest were eager for us. Once we reached the ruin's entrance, a roar of anger, like a mad bear, exploded behind us. I spun around, cutlass at the ready.

Back the way we came, Captain Storm was in the hallway, slowly headed in our direction. His skull amulet burned like a sickly green signal lantern while he grabbed crab after crab to tear them apart with his bare hands. Raw fury tinted by a hint of bloodlust shone in his eyes. For each crab he killed, two more took their place to race onto the captain and bite down hard. The man was filthy with bite wounds in seconds.

Storm smashed a crab against a nearby wall, then stabbed a bloody finger in my direction with a savage snarl.

"You still have my book, Doctor. Mark my words, I'll have it, and your head!"

I glanced past the ruin's shattered front doors to a brown sandy clearing dotted with green, feather-topped clumps of pampas grass. The landing party survivors had gathered there, battered, bloody, but alive and whole. Not a single pirate or crab was in sight. That just left myself and the pirates inside the ruins. I turned and locked eyes with Captain Storm.

Anger seethed beneath his sinister, steel-gray eyes, boiling like a hot pot of soup while he methodically attacked the crabs. But there was something else, too. A dark predatory presence I could almost feel. It looked back out at the world, as if waiting for the right moment to strike. That wouldn't be today.

"Captain! Catch!"

I hurled the cutlass down the hallway. Captain Storm caught it easily in mid-air despite the crabs that desperately worked to tear him apart.

"Godspeed," I said, then ran out of the ruins.

Once I joined the others, I looked back. Captain Storm was right where I left him, fighting a desperate battle against the small swarm of thesaurus crabs. Between wicked slashes at the beasts during the middle of his fighting retreat, he shot a look of hellish rage at me. Crabs clung to him from boot to shoulder, chewing through to the man beneath the clothes. Throughout his fight, Storm never screamed or made a sound outside the occasional grunt, and a *crunch* when he severed a crab with his cutlass.

I let go of a shaky breath to steady my nerves. It didn't entirely work.

"Lysander? My friend, please tell me you've a path away from here," I asked quickly.

The navigator tilted his head a little to the right, then brushed a hand lightly over the feathery flowers of the pampas grass. He squinted at nothing in front of him, then frowned. In the past, he'd often told me it was like he could hear the rocks and trees whispering a bargain to him in exchange for suggestions. He glanced over at me a second later with a nod.

"I've got it."

He gestured to a faint path nearby that wound lazily through the jungle. It wasn't much more than a memory of a game trail.

"That way, follow me," he said, then trotted down the path.

The others hurried after him. Skaldi stopped next to me and rubbed the back of his neck.

"I'll be glad when we're back aboard the *Duchess.*"

"Won't we all?" I agreed, with a dark tone.

The last of the pirate screams thankfully died away by the time we lost sight of the ruins.

3

Matters At Hand

July 24, 1722. Harbor Street, Kingston, Jamaica. Brewed Gambit Alchemy Shop. Where the end was just the beginning.

"You were waiting for us, weren't you, Captain?" I murmured to the shadows in my shop. "Who sent you? How did you even know we would be there? That wasn't chance. You were too well prepared."

The scent of fresh jasmine mint tea was the warm hug I didn't know I needed. I took a slow, thoughtful sip of the hot drink, then set the cup down on the stained mixing table in front of me. After three days' sail across the Caribbean Sea, followed by a good night's sleep, I felt almost back to normal. Any nightmares of what happened would fade, given time, but there were some things not even a good, long rest could cure. I flexed my right hand and stared at the spiderweb of scars from where I touched Captain Storm's amulet.

Jagged, thread-thin dark lines wound around my hand like a manic lightning bolt. Emerald-green stains surrounded the blackened burns in patterns like elaborate Celtic knotwork. Pain had erupted in my hand the day after we sailed for Jamaica from San Andrés Island. Along the trip back, I brewed up a few healing elixirs to dull the feeling. They did ease the aches, but didn't do much for the rest. Those emerald-green stains, like swirls of sinister spilled ink, appeared right before the *Silk Duchess* reached Jamaica.

"You would think by now I would know better than to grab strange relics with my bare hands," I said grimly.

A disgruntled snort from my gargoyle, Sebastian, rumbled from the shadows on the far side of the room. Bright eyes blinked at me slowly, then looked away. I shook my head, then pulled on a black cotton glove to cover the marks on my hand.

"Snort all you want, but you weren't there," I replied. "You wanted to stay aboard the *Duchess* with Captain Blackwater. Which, honestly, was for the best. I'd rather not risk you against a lair of thesaurus crabs."

I desperately wanted to know what Storm's amulet was, but no matter what book in my collection I searched, I hadn't found a thing. That worried me. Was it a curse? It could be a curse, which would serve me right for trying to grab at it. I let go of a heavy sigh, then closed the gray canvas-covered recipe book next to my tea. After another sip, my eyes and thoughts wandered across the other well-worn books I kept on shelves between jars of powders, dried herbs, and more.

Not knowing what it was made me more curious than ever, and three times more worried.

A chaotic tumble of purple freckled sandstone—a gargoyle the size of a large bobcat—landed onto the worktable next to me. Sebastian was a flurry of large fruit bat wings, a tail, and a small whine when he landed. After a quick shake, he bumped his head softly against my left arm. I smiled as I scratched behind his pointed ears. This earned me a purr that sounded like a soft tumble of pebbles in a whiskey barrel. I glanced down and raised my eyebrows at him.

"Worried?" I nodded at the idea. "So am I. But I've sent a message to Lucien about it. If there's anything in the Marquee Brotherhood's records about that amulet, he'll find it."

Sebastian let out a short, soft bark, then rubbed the side of his miniature hippo snout against me. Then he took off in a lumbering flight over to his perch next to the front door. A door he fixed with a meaningful stare. I nodded a little at the dramatic display.

"Yes, yes, I know. It's time to meet the others and our employer. I'll get your leash."

Once I had my hat, coat, and the *Codex,* I set out with Sebastian in tow. A short walk later in the humid afternoon, we arrived at the east end of Tower Street outside the Word to the Wise bookshop. The others had already arrived, save for my captain, Elara Blackwater, of the *Silk Duchess*.

Elara appeared a moment later as she flew over the rooftops to land beside me. The captain had gone to some lengths to dress for the occasion, with her chestnut hair pulled back into a sensible braid. This was coiled up behind her head and secured with a wooden hair stick. She folded her shimmering dragonfly-like wings flat against her back like a cape, as would any thayan. Between coat, vest and more, she looked every inch the captain.

"Good to see you, Elara," I greeted her with a smile and a nod. "Ready?"

She smiled back, but a faint frown kept it away from her jade-gold eyes.

"Yes, but only to get it done. This warrant was harder than most to finish, and our employer is... ah..."

I raised an eyebrow as her words trailed off.

"Unusual?"

She grimaced and fidgeted with the pommel of her ghost blade.

"Uncomfortably focused," she replied with a terse look.

Hard to argue against the truth. So, without another word, we headed inside.

The back room of the shop was an office that had memories of its former life as a wide storage closet, complete with a faint musty smell. Sunlight eased in through a tall, dusty window across the room. Bowed, wooden tan shelves still held a few volumes, some new, others old. Gaps between the books contained maps, small statues, and jars with curious plants suspended in colorful liquids. Everything was labeled to a staggering degree.

A moment later, Argall's assistant drifted in to set a fresh pot of tea on a side table. She was slim, with ash-blonde hair, and the meticulous manner of someone who alphabetized their quills. She offered a quick smile to Elara, another to Sebastian, then vanished out of the office with a brisk motion.

"Thank you, Primrose," Argall replied absently to the young woman's retreating back.

I took the closest seat by the door next to Lysander, Elara, and the Terrason brothers. Sebastian made the rounds to greet them, before he settled down between Elara and myself on a worn spot in the carpet. The gargoyle eyed everyone curiously while he quietly gnawed on the iron bolt Elara had given him to eat. Meanwhile, I set the *Codex Luminari* on the battered wooden desk, then slid it over with a small flourish to our employer, and the shop's proprietor, Joshua Argall.

"As requested, señor. One *Codex Luminari*, intact and unharmed. At least, not harmed by us."

Argall leaned across his desk to clutch lovingly at the red book. He was a small human man, not so short and stout as a grimling but almost Elara's height at five foot four, if I had to guess. Topped with thinning sandy hair, he was dressed in a plain brown suit that hung on his rail-thin shape. Despite his frail, retiring appearance, his deep, watery blue eyes came alive behind his spectacles at the sight of the book.

"The *Codex Luminari,*" Argall said in a hushed voice. "Delightful, Doctor. Just delightful."

He lightly caressed the book's scarred cover with the tips of his pale fingers.

"You, all of you, have earned every coin I promised. It's taken five long years, but here it is." The man blinked as if a thought suddenly ambushed him. "Wait. Doctor, your message said there was some sort of trouble?"

I swapped an uneasy look with the others.

"Ah, yes. There was the expected trouble of wild animals that had decided to make themselves at home in the ruins. But the pirates that ambushed us? That was an unexpected trouble we didn't need. We lost crew, señor. Good people."

Argall's narrow eyebrows leaped up over the edge of his spectacles, then plunged into a scowl.

"Pirates?"

The word dripped with more panic than I expected. Also, it was hard to ignore that he didn't comment about anyone we lost. But that was sadly the life of a privateer. The sharp comments I wanted to say about this tasted like bitter oil when I swallowed them. Fortunately, Elara came to my rescue.

"Yes, pirates," she said with a smooth smile. "A pirate crew under the command of a very cruel man named Dryden Storm. We managed to deal with him and his cutthroats, but the fact they were there at all was a nasty surprise, sir."

I gestured to Argall and his mysterious book.

"Señor, it's very possible that someone else might be after your book. You might want to be careful for a few days. Perhaps you should contact the Marquee Brotherhood and see if they can spare a bounty hunter? You know, to fend off any sort of problems that might show up with a knife."

"Oh."

The man said the word with such weight that it was hard to overlook. A thousand thoughts raced across his eyes at that moment. None of them seemed good. He eventually nodded vigorously to us with another frown.

"Thank you, Doctor. That's a good idea. I think it would make me feel better."

I exchanged a quick, wary glance with my friends.

"Would you like us to stay until a hunter arrives to watch over you?" I asked.

Argall shook his head. "No, no, that's all right. I'm sure that I'll be safe here. Once all of you have left, I'll send a message to the Brotherhood. They'll get here quick enough. Thank you, though."

"You're very welcome," I replied carefully.

A sense of impending dread traced its sharp claws along my spine. I did my best to ignore it, but impending dread is nothing if not persistent. Something felt very wrong.

Once several seconds dragged themselves by without a sound, I swapped an uncomfortable look with the others, then cleared my throat. Joshua Argall had descended into a cloud of his own thoughts while he caressed the book with his fingertips again, as if he petted a cat. I half expected the book to purr at any moment. It was a little uncomfortable, but we couldn't leave yet. After all, we still had unfinished business.

Elara leaned forward in her chair. The squeak of wood was sharp in the quiet room.

"Pardon, Mr. Argall? I'm very sorry, but there's still a matter of payment. The price that was listed in the warrant to recover your book?"

Argall twitched. A confused look crossed his face, as if he hadn't seen us before. Then sharp understanding dawned in his eyes while his pale cheeks flushed pink. He nodded once more, then set the book down in front of him. Carefully, he rummaged through one of the lower drawers on his side of the desk. I heard the sound of a key meeting a metal lock.

"I'm terribly sorry," he said. "Please forgive me. I was entirely lost in thought, and I'm not used to hiring privateers." A pleasant smile lit up the man's face. "I have your money right here with extra to account for your lost crew members. Oh, your message also said something about unexpected expenses, along with the surprises?"

I returned the smile with a thin one of my own.

"It did, señor. You see, as I said, there were these animals. A nasty type of crab that prefers to wake up and choose violence in the morning..."

4

The Best Laid Plans

July 24, 1722. Outside the Word to the Wise bookshop, Kingston, Jamaica. Taking stock of the cost, only to learn we'd come up short...

By the time the story was finished and we concluded our business, afternoon light had aged to an orange sunset. I stopped on the footpath outside the bookshop to listen to the shriek of gulls over in the harbor. It was a soothing normal that helped pull me out of my dark thoughts. Nearby, lamplighters walked by on their way to ignite the lantern sparks that lined Tower Street for the night.

Elara walked out of the shop, then stopped on the footpath next to me. The bag of doubloons in her hand jingled as she toyed with it. I scowled at the shadows drawn out by the sunset.

"I know Argall said he felt safe at his shop, but I have a bad feeling about all this."

"So do I." Elara frowned.

I glanced at her. "We'll need to keep watch on him until someone arrives to protect him."

"Agreed." Elara's tone was terse. "I'm not sure he took your warning seriously."

"Once out of sight of his shop, we can set watch schedules," I said quietly.

There wasn't any more to say about that, so we didn't. Instead, we just listened to the sounds of Kingston in the evening. After a moment, Elara glanced over at me with a somber expression, then nodded at the bag of coins.

"There's plenty here for repairs to the *Duchess.* After that, there should be some left over in memory of the ones we lost in the ruins."

I blew out a soft sigh. This was never an easy conversation, no matter how often it happened.

"Lives are such a high price for anything. Especially for an old book of maps and notes." I watched the sunset and pursed my lips. "I'm ashamed to say it, but I didn't know the people we lost all that well. Any family?"

She shook her head as Lysander and the Terrasons joined us on the footpath. The five of us strolled town Tower Street to put some distance between the bookshop and its strange little owner. Then we'd plan out how to protect them.

"None that I know," Elara replied softly. "But they deserve a proper marker in Pauper's Field, or a vigil in the Proud Dog. Just something. They signed on with me. I owe them that. We owe them that."

"I knew one of the lads we lost. My vote's the Proud Dog Pub," Skaldi grunted with a shrug. "Bazel was as stubborn as a mule, but his heart was always in the right place. He always liked the Proud Dog."

"It would feel right," Lysander added quietly.

To be honest, I only half-heard the rest of the conversation as it dove into the details. I didn't realize it until Elara touched my arm.

"You've not heard a word we've said, have you?"

"Yes? No." I rubbed my eyes. "I have some. My mind's elsewhere."

Durner Terrason grunted. "Well, out with it, Pedro. If you hold it in, it'll eat you alive. What is it?"

The scars on my hand leaped to mind, but that was a conversation for later.

"The pirates. I have a feeling they knew we were there, waiting for us." I scowled and shook my head. "How did they know? We didn't even know that the island had the *Codex* until a day before we dropped anchor."

"Now, Captain Storm may have been after the book, but he could have also been after you," Lysander said. "He called you out by name."

That brought me to a dead stop on the footpath.

"What? No. I had the *Codex*. Storm was clear he was after it."

"Pedro, he acted like he knew you," he replied.

I replayed the fight again in my mind. If Lysander was right, or even half-right, it turned everything I had considered on its ear and wound my worries tighter.

"Storm was desperate to cut me apart, but I thought it was just to get the *Codex.*" I rubbed my chin. "But I see a little of what you mean."

The image of Captain Storm's skull amulet danced around in my thoughts. I rubbed my eyes, then shook my head.

"This is starting to sound like there's a bounty on me. Maybe even one on the book and myself? I understand the book, but I don't understand the other. Why put one on me?"

Durner shrugged. "If word leaked that Argall hired us, you'd be the likely one out of all of us to find and read the bloody thing." He scratched the side of his rust-red beard. "Hunt the book, get the book. Hunt you, still get the book."

The gearwright folded his massive arms over his chest. Brass veins in his skin glowed a soft golden hue. A sure sign he was concerned.

"When I worked as a hunter some years back, I ran into more than one contact like that. But! I'll tell you this." The look in his copper eyes turned brittle and hard. "Every one of those was always personal."

I glanced around in mild surprise.

"Now wait. Personal? Who? I don't mislead my clients with my alchemy. Not ever. I've also never met Captain Storm, or anyone that knew him that I was aware of. Not that he's a problem now. Either the crabs killed him, or their venom has."

Elara shook her head, dragonfly wings fluttering in agitation.

"No. Now wait, Durner. This all sounds too convenient. Yes, he took after Pedro, while the rest of the crew rushed all of you. But Pedro had the *Codex*."

"Yes, I did." A frown settled over me as I folded my arms over my chest. Thoughts turned over rapidly in my mind, sorting the pieces of the conversation. "But it was in my backpack, not visible at all. Storm and his cutthroats showed up after we left the main library, so they couldn't have seen me take it from the shelf."

Lysander raised his eyebrows at me with a serious expression. "The library had those tall windows overlooking the swamp. Could have been someone watching from out there."

I nodded. "Perhaps. We didn't exactly..."

Distant sounds of shattered glass and a muffled sharp shriek ripped through both the air and our debate. There wasn't any mistake where it came from.

"The bookshop!" I exclaimed.

We drew weapons while we ran.

"We've got the side," Durner said, then raced off around the building down a side street with Skaldi right behind him.

"Over and to the back?" I asked Elara.

"Yes. I'll meet you both in the back," she snapped off. Then she fixed me with a hard look. "Watch yourselves."

"You, too," I replied.

Elara's dragonfly wings snapped open, then she shot into the air. A faint stream of blue-white flames trailed after her ghost blade as she vanished out of sight above the building.

I glanced at Lysander before we yanked open the front door, swords at the ready. Sebastian raced in ahead of us, then stopped two paces inside, posture stiff, wings and ears tucked low. Then he rolled out a low hiss. Lysander and I stepped in to either side of the gargoyle, stunned.

"What in the nine hells happened?" Lysander whispered. "We weren't gone that long."

The place had been turned upside down.

Chairs, tables, even small bookcases had been tossed over. Books had been ransacked and scattered across the floor, spines bent and cracked from a quick heat. They looked like thick, twisted leaves ripped from a battered tree. Random, small wooden trinkets and other oddities lay forgotten among the debris. Dust clouds ran wild through the air.

I shook my head, stunned.

"Step carefully," I whispered as I eased past an overturned chair. A small field of black-smudged glass glimmered next to my boot. "Mind the broken glass."

Lysander slowly followed in my wake.

Caution went out the window when we heard a soft sobbing from across the room.

5

Unexpected Consequences

July 24, 1722. Word to the Wise bookshop. Where the shelves had become a battleground, and a mystery is planted like a poisonous seed...

Sebastian shot across the room like a harpoon with wings. Between two of the last bookshelves still upright, huddled on the floor against the wall, was Argall's assistant, Miss Primrose Stewart. A slim young human woman, who looked no older than twenty at most, and was absolutely not accustomed to what had happened.

Also, the young lady looked like she had been attacked by a wild chimney.

Her skin was covered in haphazard smudges. Soot stains were scattered across her once lively green and white dress and muted the colors. Bits of hair that hung loose from her once proper bun were singed at different lengths.

Miss Stewart nearly screamed when we appeared, but she recognized us at the last moment. Instead of a yell, she hugged her knees while she stared at us wide-eyed. Sebastian wasn't deterred. My gargoyle padded over, nudged her leg with his muzzle, then he looked at me with a worried whimper.

I knelt down in front of her. "Señorita Stewart, what happened? Who did this?"

The young woman shuddered like someone had stepped on her grave.

"I don't know! There were two men. Sailors, I think. They just rushed into the main room when I was shelving books. I don't know where they came from! Their blades glowed ... like their eyes." She touched her forehead to her knees while she shuddered again. "Oh god, their eyes were boiling out fire."

Lysander glanced out into the devastation, then swapped a concerned look with me.

"Señorita, please, go on. Are they still here?" I asked softly. "What about your employer, Señor Argall?"

Miss Stewart shook her head frantically. The young woman was at the end of her nerves, but to her credit, she took a deep breath to get her thoughts together. "I don't know, Doctor. Last I saw him, he was in his office. Those... men... they ransacked this room, then charged to the back for Mr. Argall. I tried to stop them."

She shuddered once more.

"They tried to stab me. Even the shadows clawed at me. There were just so many shadows. I ran over here and, for some reason, they left me alone."

"I'll check on Argall," I told Lysander, then stood and stepped away from the pair.

Something heavy hit the floor from the direction of Argall's office.

Lysander nodded toward the back room. "Go! I'll take care of her."

I tossed him a crimson vial from my belt.

"For any of her light injuries," I called over my shoulder, running out from between the bookshelves and down the hall. Sebastian was right on my heels.

If anything, the back room was worse than the front of the shop. Shadows dripped from the walls like a poisonous ink. Books and trinkets were scattered over the tattered carpet like the front room, only these came with a sharp, rancid smell.

Argall himself lay on the floor in a rumpled heap beside his overturned desk. Something was clutched to his chest, but I couldn't see what it was. The man's clothes were cut, even singed in places. Next to him lay his glasses, with one lens cracked. He didn't move.

I glanced to either side of the doorway, then rushed inside.

Sebastian barked to my right the instant I took a step. I dropped into a low crouch, just as a cutlass sliced across where I had been only a second ago.

The blade itself glowed with a sickly, green-white light, as if the metal burned with death's own eyes. I sidestepped to my left, while Sebastian spit a furious steaming ball of tar at the figure. It slapped the assassin in the side and ruined his charge. It also knocked him into view.

He wasn't quite human, thayan, or anything else. I wasn't sure he was even alive.

What was he? A problem. That was all I knew.

The assassin was human enough, male, and gaunt, with death-white skin, wearing the singed and torn clothes of a common sailor. Sickly green-white flames boiled out the man's eyes like a furnace as he swung for my neck with a rasping scream.

I sidestepped again with a shudder, then parried, even though my hands shook. Steel sparked against steel before I shoved his blade aside. The thing stumbled, and I stabbed him in the ribs. It felt like I had just stabbed a stack of wet paper. A black ichor oozed down around my blade.

At the same time, the scars under my glove burned like fire. I clutched my sword hand while I backed away.

"What in the hell are you?" I demanded.

I managed one more step before the thing moved. He was so fast, I barely noticed it before he backhanded me with the hilt of his sword. My world exploded into stars. The force of the blow slammed me back against the door frame, while sparks danced at the edge of my vision.

He, the creature, hissed at me, then tried to rush in and stab me. Another hot ball of tar into the thing's chest from Sebastian put an end to that.

"You're very fast, señor," I said in a low tone, rubbing my eyes.

Was it false bravado? Of course. I was desperate to get away with both Sebastian and Argall, but I needed more time and space for that. My vision was blurred, but I could still see the creature. His burning eyes made him hard to miss. The rest was a blurry, grinning ghoul eager to murder me.

I snatched a gray vial from my belt and smashed it onto the carpet. Fog and smoke swallowed the air as I melted into the smoke, then moved to my left.

The ghoul barreled right through it all at me like a supernatural mad bull, as if I hadn't done a thing. So much for that idea.

A quick parry knocked his cutlass aside, then a kick hurled him back against the door frame. The ghoul lunged at me again, only to get slapped in the face with hot tar. He staggered back, clawing at the tar with one hand while trying a wild swing at Sebastian with the other.

The ghoul was fast. Sebastian was faster. Another ball of hot tar slapped the ghoul in the face before my gargoyle bounced aside in a flurry of wings.

But it bought me the time I needed. As the ghoul staggered back to claw at the fresh tar, I got my feet under me and stabbed for the gut. He turned sideways, and I missed, but I was able to get a solid backhand across the side of the ghoul's face not painted with tar.

He shrieked the instant I hit him, wide-eyed, as emerald-green flames ran along his withered jaw. Before I could react, the ghoul raced out of the room for the shop's front. I tore after him.

"Lysander! Assassin!" I yelled out. There was a muffled reply, but I was too focused on running down the tattered figure in front of me to pay attention.

The creature burst through the doorway into the main room, just as one of Lysander's arcane shields snapped to life to partially block the space past the door. There was a sharp crunch and howl of rage. The shield held, but the ghoul didn't. He bounced off, then stumbled into the mess of books in the middle of the room. The creature turned to shriek at me when I hurried in a second later.

All at once, those scattered books around the creature rose off the floor, then spun around him like a tornado. Pages and binders glowed with an eerie storm of arcane power from blues and greens to a lurid red. Colored lightning snapped and danced between the books like an untethered storm.

"Know... you! Remember ... you!" the creature hissed at me, then cackled with jagged, broken teeth.

"A portal?" I yelled out over the storm, shielding my eyes with a free hand.

"Not possible!" Lysander yelled back, then pulled back his glowing shield to protect himself and Miss Stewart. "The Etherwave would have swallowed him for trying already!"

Then the giggling ghoul shot out a hand to grab at one of the bolts of power.

Why? I don't know. Didn't care. It just seemed like a bad idea.

"Oh, no you don't, señor!"

I snatched a vial from my belt and hurled it at the creature. Glass shattered as acid painted itself across the ghoul's outstretched hand with a hard sizzle. I followed right behind with a quick slice, but only landed a small cut. More black ooze splattered over my blade, and also my coat. The ghoul grabbed his hand and let out a shriek that could shatter the window panes while I stepped back.

Only I was a heartbeat too slow.

The ghoul's clammy hand lashed out in a blur and clamped down on my throat. I tried to stab him, but he caught my wrist. His grip on my throat was like an iron vise on my neck. I gasped, desperate to breathe.

"Know... you!" the ghoul repeated. His grip tightened as he dragged me closer.

White arcane constructs from Lysander flew at the thing, but couldn't penetrate the storm. My vision grew dim, as air became a precious memory.

Then a sword, hot with a blue-white aura, sliced into the creature from behind. The ghoul arched its back and shrieked in pain to shake both heaven and hell. It dropped me to the floor as I heard a sound like wet paper being severed. After that, the ghoul dropped to his knees.

Just behind the creature, at the edge of the arcane storm, Captain Elara Blackwater stood with her dragonfly wings out and ghost blade drawn. Black ichor from the ghoul burned away from her blade with a sharp sizzle like cooking bacon. Arcane winds stirred her captain's coat while she stalked toward the ghoul with a hard frown. There wasn't murder in her eyes, but righteous fury.

I crawled backwards, searching for my own sword with a free hand. Elara advanced on the ghoul like a mythical valkyrie in battle. One slice, then two, separated the ghoul's head from its body.

The storm, ghoul and all detonated like a ship's powder room on fire. Almost anyone, or anything not rooted to the spot, was thrown against the nearest wall or furniture. That is, except for Elara.

Captain Elara Blackwater stood firmly at the edge of a burned pile of ash on the ruined carpet.

"No one," she growled at the dust, "manhandles my alchemist! My crew!" She turned in a slow circle, eyes bright with determination to end any new threat that might appear.

The explosion had hurled me against the wall, then the floor, like a battered, discarded bag. I had done a lot of that lately, and worried it had become a habit.

Savaged books were tossed in all directions. Smoke from burnt pages, and the sharp smell of broiled skin, wandered the air with gleeful abandon. I dragged the back of a hand against my nose for all the good it did. No stench likes to be denied. They are stubborn that way. Across the room, I saw the glimmer of Lysander's arcane shield over himself and Miss Stewart.

Everyone seemed safe.

"Thank you," I croaked to Elara with a smile.

She sheathed her sword, then started straight for me, her face a mask of worry.

"Pedro, how bad are you hurt?"

"Enough," I sighed as I found my sword.

A groan from the back room caught my ears, followed by a frantic barking.

"Sebastian? Señor Argall!" I coughed as I hauled myself to my feet with a painful grunt.

"Pedro!" I heard Elara and Lysander call out behind me. But I kept running.

This time, when I ran into the back office, nothing tried to kill me. The novelty was nice.

Sebastian skidded across the floor to my feet, pawed at my boot, then raced back to Argall. I sheathed my own sword and hurried after.

The bookseller was still in a rumpled heap on the floor next to his desk. Only now, he was slightly more awake, but he still resembled a beaten sack of potatoes. I ignored the chorus of aches and knelt down to inspect the man's injuries. There were plenty, and none looked good. I saw at least a dozen cuts along his arms. What wasn't cut had been burned as if with acid.

"Señor, can you move?" I reached for one of the vials in a belt loop. "I have a curative that should help with the pain until..."

Argall cut off anything else I had to say.

"No! Listen!" he rasped, with a wild look on face.

The bookseller shoved a crumpled piece of paper into my hands. It looked like a page from a journal, filthy with scribbled notes in the margin. Argall gripped my hand and that page. His hands shuddered.

"The *Codex*," Argall wheezed. "You were right. Someone else wanted it. Please, get it back. He must not use it!"

"What?" A cold chill stabbed me in the chest. I tried again to reach for that vial. "Señor, we can talk later..."

"No!" he rasped at me. "Not later! Now! The *Codex* is more than just maps. It's an ancient blueprint! A guide for something terrible!"

I scowled at that.

"A guide? Who are you talking about? Who attacked you, señor?"

Argall's eyes went distant, haunted, and *just wrong*. He wheezed.

"The Wood-boned man!"

6

Questions for Answers

July 25, 1722. Brewed Gambit Alchemy Shop, Kingston, Jamaica. Connecting the dots... with more dots.

Argall's words haunted me most of the night. I felt I should've known what he meant, but I didn't. At least, not quite. That nagged at me while Elara and I spent the evening poring over the torn, yellowed page. The ghost of the man's words hovered around me the next morning while I worked. I was so preoccupied, I barely heard the bell for the front door to my shop.

"Ah. So, *that's* why Elara wanted me to check on you," Lysander said as he walked in. "Pedro, you know most people only do that to roast a chicken or a pig, don't you? Not a sword?"

I shot him a sour look from behind my goggles, then moved a glass vial on the iron stand next to me, a little to my right. Standing up, I stretched my back, then pulled off the yellow-tinted goggles to set them aside. My sword slowly rotated like a roasting spit over a fire in my raised stone fireplace. The ghoul's black blood on the blade glistened as the fire warmed it back to a liquid. I wrote down a few observations about it in my alchemist's notebook.

"Well, if you know of any way to remove black blood as hard as tar from metal, I'm all ears," I replied, and arched an eyebrow at him. "Water and soap didn't work."

That made my friend pause a bit as he walked across my shop toward me.

"It didn't?" Lysander squinted at the tar-like stains. "Are you sure it's blood?"

I shrugged. "No. But, when I stabbed the thing, that ichor came out. What else would you call it?"

The navigator shook his head and winced. "It makes a certain twisted sense."

"Speaking of theories," I raised a finger to highlight the moment, "I've another theory for you."

Lysander found a nearby wooden chair, chased Sebastian out of it, then pulled it over to the worktable to sit down. Sebastian grumbled and flew over to another chair to resume his nap. The navigator leaned forward to squint at my sword and the black stain on it, while both rotated over the fire.

"About which? This black blood? What Argall said? That page he gave you? Or what marinade to use on a sword?" A grin tugged at his mouth as he leaned back in the chair.

"Very funny," I replied. "I mean about the page. Also, I've no idea what Señor Argall meant about the 'wood-boned man'. How is Argall doing, by the way?"

Lysander let out a heavy sigh as he leaned back in the chair.

"The city watch put him in a hospital, and the nuns are caring for him now. Pedro... he's not all there." He ran a hand through his dark hair. "The man barely knew I was in the room. Instead, he kept muttering off at something I couldn't see. But at least he's someplace safe." Lysander watched me warily for a moment. "How are *you* feeling after the bookshop?"

I rubbed the hand-shaped bruises at the base of my neck. The ghoul's scream played out again in my head. A shadow of terror tickled my spine.

"I've been better." I pursed my lips, then gently sighed. "Rest and medicine to dull the pain helped." Then I shot him a dark glance. "I'm very lucky I walked away with just bruises. It was almost worse."

Neither of us spoke. We let the silence speak for us.

"What's your idea about the paper Argall shoved at you?" Lysander asked, changing the subject.

I slid the old journal page out of my notebook, then handed it to Lysander. He pursed his lips as he looked over the scribbles.

"So, the torn page." I flipped back a few pages in my alchemist's notebook, then slid that across the workbench. "With Elara's help, we translated a little of it. The whole thing is written in Zepheen."

Lysander frowned, then tugged at the navigator pendant around his neck. "Zepheen? That's a thayan language, isn't it? Elara's native language?"

I tapped my alchemist's notebook with its wild assortment of translations from last night.

"Zepheen? It is, yes. But that old journal page is written in an older dialect. Old enough that Elara couldn't read much of it."

I tapped two drawings tucked away in either corner of the rumpled page.

"But here, and here, are what's interesting. I think this whole thing is explaining a device. Señor Argall did mention a 'blueprint'."

Lysander squinted at the diagrams, then spread the page out on my workbench to smooth out the wrinkles.

"It looks like a pump mechanism." The navigator traced a finger over the old drawings. "Like from a bilge pump."

There was an odd movement to my right at the fireplace. I gave the gooey black blood a sideways glance; a dark tendril of it reached down off the metal. Almost like it was reaching for the glass vial below, which wasn't a comfort at all. Still, that seemed safe enough. I shook my head a little, then ignored the blood. With a sigh, I pulled over a chair, then flipped back a page in my notes.

"That's roughly what Elara and I translated." I took a deep breath, then tapped my notes again. "It is a type of pump, but not a bilge pump. Something smaller. What we've translated doesn't give any hints about what it's for. I've asked Skaldi and Durner to take a hard look at these designs. Maybe duplicate the parts to give us a better idea of what's so important here. They're off trying to build the real thing now."

Lysander gave me a cautious look.

"Is that wise?" he asked slowly.

"Probably not," I admitted with a small shrug. "But, my friend, we'll have a better idea of what we're dealing with. Maybe we'll have a better idea of why someone wants it so badly."

Lysander read over the translated notes, then glanced at the mysterious page from Argall. The frown on his face deepened.

"Why would Argall even have this?" He shook the wrinkled, yellowed page slightly. "This is something I expect a gearwright to have. Wasn't Mr. Argall more about maps and any odd bits of history about Otherworld?"

I gestured to the yellowed page. "I think it came from the *Codex.* Almost sure of it. Look at the torn edge on the left. There's a bit of thread binding there, just like from the *Codex.* The señor called the whole book a 'guide' and a 'blueprint'. This leans to that. For what?" I shrugged. "I have no idea, or how the ghoul we fought in the bookshop comes into any of this mess."

Abruptly, the fire to my right erupted with a loud pop and a shower of sparks. I jerked back as bright embers rained down across both the stone tile floor and the worktable with my notes. The table spouted flames.

Lysander yanked both my notebook and journal page to safety, while I snatched up a jar from a nearby shelf. I tossed a scoop of water from a nearby bucket over the sparks and a few tiny flames as they tried to ignite old powder stains on the table. A blast of gray smoke vomited up toward the ceiling.

I spun toward the raised fireplace and expected an inferno. Instead, I found a nightmare of ooze.

The black blood had warmed enough until it trailed off the metal in slow, stringy drops. Most of it collected in the glass vial like I wanted, but a few droplets hit the fire. A burst of blue-gray smoke erupted from the flames like a volcano's ghost with each splash. Hot sparks followed close behind, shooting up and out like a geyser.

I doused the workbench with more water, then yanked my sword off the roasting stand by the leather-wrapped hilt before another drop fell. A nearby cloth did the trick to remove the last of the wet black blood from the blade.

Searing, burning pain exploded through my right hand the instant I wiped off the blood. The sword fell to the floor with a sharp clang; the bloody cloth dropped under the table. I caught myself on the back of a chair before I fell over. My heart hammered in my chest and my hand shuddered.

"Pedro!"

Lysander launched himself out of the chair and raced around the table. I waved him away as he dug out a box of bandages and ointment from a cabinet next to the fireplace.

"No! Stay back," I hissed, struggling to yank off the cotton glove.

The glove hit the floor, and I shoved my right hand into a bucket of water on the other side of the fireplace. Faint smoke curled out of the glove in tiny gray columns, but I barely noticed. Lysander sure didn't. We were focused on the bucket.

Under the water, ghostly green flames burst to life like a lost lantern from a sunken ghost ship. Those flames danced along the scars seared into my right hand. I slowly turned my hand over, staring first at the flames, then at Lysander.

"There was some pain at first, but now? It's like casting an enchantment. I really don't feel a thing," I said, both amazed and shocked. To be honest, fear really wasn't that far behind. It didn't like being left out.

Slowly, I pulled my hand out of the bucket. The flames held on for a second in the air, then died with a soft fizzle as the water dripped off my hand.

Lysander blew out a low whistle. "Pedro, you don't need a surgeon for that hand. You need a wavebinder. Someone who understands casting."

I stared at my scars, as if they might turn into snakes and bite me. When they didn't, I dried my hands on a towel, then put away my sword in its scabbard by the closet.

Neither of us said a word for several long seconds. There was only the crackle of the fire in the stone fireplace.

"That was the same green, boiling fire from Captain Storm's amulet." I drew in a slow, deep breath. "Lysander, it was exactly the same. I just know it."

Lysander held up ointment and bandages and nodded to my scarred hand with raised eyebrows. I shook my head. The navigator returned both to the shelf where he got them.

"So, an acid?" he asked. "Surely not a poison. They don't catch fire, do they? Something on the amulet when you touched it?"

"No," I replied in a low voice. "Poison's don't catch fire."

I scowled at the scars that crisscrossed my hand, then snatched up my glove. A last few tendrils of smoke rose from inside, like it had been cooked just slightly. There were dark scorch marks along the lining that traced out the pattern of my scars.

Memories of Captain Storm's squirrel skull amulet leaped to mind. I showed the singed lining to Lysander.

"Those lines. My scars." I shook my head. "I should've seen this. The scars on my hand follow the same pattern of the scrimshaw on Captain Storm's skull amulet." My frown hardened into a scowl. "My friend, this isn't a poison or an acid. I think it's a *curse*, and a nasty one at that. But I'm no expert."

I tugged the glove back over my right hand to cover the scars. "This is well outside what I know of the Etherwave Arcana. We *do* need a wavebinder. Not just for my scars, but for that page from Señor Argall, and the black blood. We don't know nearly enough, and that's going to get us killed."

Lysander walked over to collect my journal and Argall's torn page. Not to be left out of everything, Sebastian flew over and landed on the worktable, leash in his jaws. I shook my head at him with a smile, and reached for the vial of black blood.

The moment his dark claws touched the table, he spit out the leash, then hissed at the vial. He barked maniacally, with the occasional angry growl or hiss.

"Sebastian? What..."

Lysander interrupted when he tackled me to the floor. Overhead, the black blood reached out desperately from the vial with two thick, wet tentacles. It swiped at the air where I had been only a moment before Lysander tackled me. The pair of tendrils oozed back into the vial, then vanished into the liquid.

I exchanged an uneasy look with Lysander, while Sebastian continued to bark at the vial.

My friend let out a heavy sigh, then helped me to my feet. “We don’t need a wavebinder, Pedro. We need an Archbinder. One who specializes in curses, and I know just the lady.”

The vial burped, and I ran a shuddering hand through my dark, wavy hair.

Lysander patted me on the shoulder. “I think I’ll carry the vial.”

7

A Slight Cause for Concern

July 25, 1722. Royal Academy of Arcanum and Science, Kingston, 2nd floor. Getting at the ugly truth.

It was just a quick stroll from south Kingston to Lyra Valtor's studio on West Queen Street. Her room in the Royal Academy building looked every inch a master wavebinder's workshop.

The late morning sun did its best to give the room a cozy feel through a lone dusty window. Books were neatly stacked between carved seashells, the odd shrunken skull, and other cheerful relics on the room's few shelves. Yellowed notes about curses were tacked to the faded brown wooden walls. The Archbinder herself was behind a wide sandalwood desk when we arrived. She cut a stern figure in her wine-red dress and silver-streaked black hair in a bun.

Archbinders are masters at channeling magic from the Etherwave, and Lyra Valtor was one of the best among them. Really, you'd have to be dead not to have heard of her, and death wasn't an excuse. After all, it hadn't slowed her down yet.

Fortunately, she was willing to see us as a favor to Lysander.

We explained what happened in my shop with my scars, the flames, and the blood after we arrived. That led to a brief examination for what the Archbinder called 'the usual signs of a curse'. I had no idea what that was, but apparently it could show up in my eyes.

After a pensive hum, Lyra sat down in the canvas padded chair behind her desk. For a moment, she tapped out a light rhythm against her gnarled oak cane. Frown lines creased the gray undead skin of her forehead as her eyes cut from me to the vial of black blood on her desk between us. Next to that lay the rumpled and yellowed journal page, along with my notebook.

She was stalling, and it made my scars itch.

"Doctor Sangre?" she said with a rough, melancholy sigh.

"Yes, Archbinder?" It was hard to keep the tension out of my voice.

"You're dying," she announced in a flat tone.

Sadly, her bedside manner needed a bit of work. Probably something that came with being a zombie.

Of all the things she could have said to me, that wasn't even on my list. I sat back in my chair, wide-eyed, staring at nothing. There was a bitter, metallic taste in my mouth and my right hand felt unusually warm. Over by the door behind me, I heard Lysander swallow a sputter of surprise.

"How long does he have?" Lysander asked in a horrified whisper.

She shrugged lightly. "Hard to say. Maybe as long as a wraith's curse? So a week? Maybe two."

"How am I dying, señora?" I sputtered out, voice rough. "What curse is killing me?"

Lyra leaned forward to tap on the side of the vial with a weathered pencil. The black blood burped back at her. It was an unusual conversation. She raised an eyebrow at me.

"One of three, Doctor. Of those, one might even be a wraith's curse, heaven help us." She narrowed her eyes at me over the top of the vial. "You both mentioned scars? Green flame? May I see it?"

Sebastian let out a soft snore where he slept by my feet as I swapped a glance with Lysander. With slow, deliberate movements, I pulled off my right glove to expose both burn scars and the emerald tattoo-like knotwork around them.

Using a thin pair of spectacles from a desk drawer, Lyra squinted at the scars. A few low hums later, she grabbed a book from a nearby shelf to consult a passage. That book ended up on the desk next to her, while she reached for my scarred hand.

I braced for pain or fire, but there wasn't any. Her gray-white fingers were dead cold against my skin. The ink-like stains around my scars faintly pulsed before they actively tried to avoid her. Slowly, she turned my right hand over to examine both sides.

"Ah," she said with a smile, as if everything somehow made sense.

Without a word, Lyra rose and rushed out of her office. She returned a moment later with a small porcelain cup of water, then added a pinch of salt to it as an afterthought. A few drops on my right hand brought the emerald-green flames to life for a moment. She raised her eyebrows and hummed at that.

"Water," she said. "I didn't expect that. The salt might not have mattered."

Placing the cup on her desk, Lyra settled back into her chair and steepled her fingers in front of her. Once again, she narrowed her eyes at my scars before she cleared her throat.

"This isn't your everyday curse, gentlemen. This one is ancient. Most certainly from Otherworld." She gave me a wry smile. "Seems you've stepped on some pretty nasty toes, Doctor."

"It wasn't intentional, señora."

"I imagine not," she replied brightly. "Most don't curse themselves on purpose. Though, if you need help with that, let me know."

Picking up the discarded book from her desk, she opened it to the page she had been reading. She turned the book around toward us, then tapped a series of symbols in a passage.

"This, right here," Lyra said briskly, "is what you're roughly dealing with. The Bindweaver's Curse. Quite a clever little thing. Normally, it compels a thief who steals a book with this curse to return said book to where it came from. Then they have to guard it, at least for a short time."

I felt my stomach twist into knots while I remembered the library and its murderous thesaurus crabs. Vaguely, I was aware of Lysander as he stepped over to look down at what Lyra indicated in the book.

"But," she added, "Bindweaver's Curse doesn't kill. Yours does, Doctor. Someone has made improvements, so it eats its victim away to powder, I believe. Nasty piece of work. I'm impressed. Now, why the water to ignite the flames?" Lyra raised a finger, then shook her head. "I've no idea."

"If all this is true, how was Pedro able to escape? Why wasn't I marked, too?" Lysander asked.

She raised an eyebrow at him. "Well, did you touch the book? This *Codex?*"

"No, only Pedro did," he shrugged. "I was busy helping the others deal with the thesaurus crabs, then the pirates."

"That's why," she said and shook a finger at Lysander. "He touched the *Codex.*"

That struck a chord in me.

"Wait."

I leaned forward to tap the passage about the Bindweaver's Curse. "Archbinder, would this affect anyone who touched the *Codex* after I took it?"

Lyra gave me a thoughtful look and nodded. "Yes, why?"

I glanced at Lysander. "Señor Argall touched the *Codex.* He actually held it for a long time. But he didn't have this happen." I held up my right hand to emphasize the point.

"Right, but the ghoul attacked him for the *Codex,*" Lysander replied. "Also, it said it knew you."

"Ghoul?" Lyra asked, gray zombie eyes fever bright with interest.

"Yes. That's where the black blood in the vial comes from," I explained. "But Captain Storm's skull amulet had scrimshaw that matched my scars, and the same green flames. I touched that amulet as well."

"Doctor, let me see your hand again," Lyra asked.

She leaned in close to study the scars and their green knotwork once more.

"Oh, how did I miss this?" Lyra muttered. "Those aren't true scars, are they? They're tattoos, Doctor. Someone has combined the Bindweaver's Curse with a vermin, like a flea, that made those tattoos. It wasn't meant for you, but it did imprint on you. Did you channel any Etherwave power for a relic? Spells?"

"Pedro, your fog potion," Lysander said quickly. "The one you often use to conceal yourself before you cloud someone's mind during a fight."

"I did use that one," I confessed.

She looked over the top of her spectacles at me.

"It seems this curse wanted a new home." She removed her spectacles, then shook them at me. "Apparently, it found one. You. Sadly, it's eating you inside out, Doctor Sangre. Almost certainly draining your life away and sending it somewhere. But to where?" She shook her head. "I've no idea."

"Storm had the same vermin curse then." I shot a tense glance at Lysander. "If this curse was on the *Codex*, and Storm was infected..."

Lysander nodded thoughtfully. "Then Storm had already found the *Codex*. Pedro, he wasn't trying to steal it. Captain Storm may have been trying to get you to put it back."

"Compelled by the curse?" I asked with a curious frown.

Lyra glanced up in consideration. "Possibly. I still don't understand what that vermin part is doing, though. Not yet."

Another thought hit me.

"Archbinder? When we last saw Captain Storm and his crew, they were being torn to bits by thesaurus crabs. Could that be another reason this curse jumped to me?" I asked, concerned.

Lyra nodded. "Absolutely. That means it needs someone who's alive."

Then she took a long breath with a serious expression.

"But, because you 'inherited' it though the late Captain Storm instead of the *Codex*, this Bindweaver's Curse hasn't taken effect yet." She fixed me with a hard stare. "Mind you, it eventually will."

I ran a hand through my dark hair, making it more unruly than normal. "I was afraid you'd say that, señora."

Lysander stood up from studying the book to point at the vial of black blood.

"This explains what happened with Captain Storm, but not this blood." He folded his arms over his chest. "Lyra, the blood attacked us. It reached for Pedro. In the bookshop, the ghoul, or whatever the hell it was, said it *knew* Pedro."

A storm of thoughts clouded the Archbinder's face. Her eyes glinted yellow-gold, a sure sign of channeling the power of the Etherwave

Arcana. Then she reached for the vial, her hand alive with soft yellow-gold magical power.

"Blood holds its own memories, gentlemen. Let's see what this one remembers."

8

Just a Little Bad Blood

July 25, 1722. Royal Academy of Arcanum and Science, Kingston, 2nd floor. Be careful of what you look for, it might find you...

Lyra passed her hand over the glass vial. Ghostly yellow-gold mist poured off her gray fingers and onto the dark fluid. The softly glowing magic collected on the surface of the black blood, then vanished. The air felt heavy, as if waiting in anticipation.

Both blood and vial were silent. Then, tiny bubbles formed on the surface of the blood, and the vial shook as if terrified.

Suddenly, books around the room glowed with a ghastly blue-white light. The blood's surface burned with a small flame of the same color. Lysander retreated while I jumped from my chair. Lyra tried to step back, but the blue-white power grabbed her hand in a glowing vise. We ran to help pull her free.

The room became a battlefield.

Books launched off the shelves like cannon shot, singed and smoking. Some hit the opposite wall, others circled around the desk, vial, and the Archbinder. Lysander dove for cover, while I ducked under two thick volumes aimed at my head.

Steaming black ichor streamed from the books to form a whirlwind over the vial of blood. At first, it was a glowing, spinning storm of paper and dust. Blue lightning danced everywhere as the debris formed a shape. A human body wearing ragged and torn sailor's clothing melted into view, complete with the thin, strained face of a ghoul. One with burning eyes of fire.

"Another ghoul!" Lysander exclaimed, before he dodged a thick book of anatomy.

It was the bookshop all over again. I clenched my jaw and kept moving toward the Archbinder. Lysander was right behind me.

The thing raced out of the maelstrom and reached for Lyra with a wordless shriek. She ducked with a grimace, avoiding its spectral, withered hands.

We reached Lyra's side a second later, grabbing her wrist. The instant we did, the ghoul recoiled in horror and hissed. It clawed at the air in front of us, like it wanted to lunge, but something kept it at bay.

Lyra's hand pulled free of the glow with our help, but she stumbled backwards, off balance. Lysander caught her before she hit the wall. At our feet, Sebastian was a mass of winged gargoyle anger, snarling furiously at the creature with his teeth bared.

I stumbled away from the desk as well, catching myself against a chair. The moment I did, bright green flame erupted from the scars on my right hand as the ghoul lunged for Lyra and Lysander.

They threw up large, round, glowing white shields of Etherwave power that knocked the creature aside. Cracks glistened in their shields a second later.

Undeterred, the creature rushed at them again.

Memories of how the ghoul in the bookshop reacted to my hand drove me forward. I threw myself between the ghoul and the magical shields.

The fiend pulled away and hissed, misshapen face twisted in a spitting snarl of rage.

"Doctor!" Lyra shouted over the magical maelstrom. "It's afraid of your hand! I can feel it!"

My throat felt tight at the memory of being choked by a creature like this the day before.

"Not this time," I growled, then slammed my burning fist across the ghoul's jaw.

It was like punching a bloated fish.

The ghoul's jaw cracked, and I grabbed its ragged collar, slamming my burning fist twice into its gut. It doubled over, then shrieked at me with decaying breath. All at once, as dramatically as it had appeared, the creature exploded in a flurry of what smelled like burned, rotten cloth and paper.

A second later, the blue glow around the books in the room shattered into bright crystal dust, then vanished. Bits of burned debris rained around the studio. Books collapsed to the floor, trailing tiny columns of gray smoke. In the center of it all, a sinister curl of blue mist coiled up from the black blood before the fluid burped softly.

"There's a ghoul in that blood?" Lysander exclaimed, while he gasped for air.

"No, Lysander, not even close," Lyra replied, far too giddy about this for my taste.

A pleased grin spread like butter over her gray face. She glanced around at her disheveled office and scattered books that steamed slightly.

"*That,* gentlemen, is a rare fiend called a Death Whisper. Which means your black blood isn't 'blood' at all. It's a type of ink charged with the darker aspects of the Etherwave. Cursed ink. It's what a Death Whisper bleeds when you cut them."

She picked up her oak cane, then leaned heavily against it while she caught her breath.

Lysander frowned uneasily at the blood-ink.

"So can a good sword or even pistol shot bring one of those down?"

The Archbinder shook her head.

"If only it were that easy. From what little I know, they *can* be destroyed that way. But! Some have said they'll put themselves back together in minutes. Fire causes them a lot of problems, though, and so does a ghost blade."

Then she shook a finger at me and pointed at the green fire on my right hand.

"But you! *You,* my good Doctor Sangre, are the first I've *ever* known who can dispel these horrid things with a touch," Lyra exclaimed.

I clenched my right hand and the emerald flames vanished in a soft burst of embers. The green stains around my scars slithered a bit, then went still. I leaned against the back of a chair with both hands, letting out a weary sigh.

"Touch? More like a fist, señora." I drank in deep breaths of bitter air to clear my head.

She tapped her cane against the floor with a grin. "Either way, it worked, which surprises me in a way."

Carefully, she walked over to her desk, frowning at the vial of dark liquid.

"You see, gentlemen, Death Whispers come from... let's call it 'corrupted'... ink. The original curse that is part of what's killing you, Doctor, is based on the idea to 'preserve'. Death Whispers rarely preserve. They're destructive stalkers pulled from the depths of the Etherwave Arcana."

Then she pointed at my hand.

"If I was to guess, your original curse, with its unique alterations, rubs out the corruption of a Death Whisper. Since that curse was altered to exhaust a creature's spirit and magic, you might actually be *consuming* them."

I made a sour face over that entire idea of eating mysterious fiends.

Lyra snapped her fingers. "But that gives me an idea about a way to keep you alive... more or less."

Snatching up a stray piece of paper, then an inkwell and pen, she scribbled out what looked like instructions and a list of ingredients.

Lysander glanced at me, then gave the disheveled room a pensive look.

"So they bleed ink?" he asked.

She paused in what she was writing, then nodded. "Yes, a type of it. I've never summoned one until now. But from what I've read, they 'build' a body using ink and pages of nearby books. Some even say that the emotion behind the written words is involved, too." Lyra gestured at the vial with her quill pen. "In any case, that means you have the remains of a Death Whisper in that vial! Delightful!"

Lysander wandered the room, recovering singed books from the floor to put them back on nearby shelves. Sebastian helped by sniffing nearby books suspiciously, teeth bared, in case anything else might appear.

I picked up a book from the floor myself, then flipped it open. Its edges were freshly burned. Inside, large, haphazard blotches of lettering were now faded. It was as if they'd become wet, then drained off the side of the page. I snapped the book shut, then placed it on the Archbinder's desk.

"That would mean the lightning storm we saw in the bookshop—and here—was some sort of 'summoning circle'?" I looked down uneasily for another book to help put away.

Lyra nodded. "A type of one, yes." After a moment, she stood up from her desk, pressed a fist against her lower back to work out a knot. Then she pointed her quill pen at me. "Doctor, you and Lysander said it knew you? The Death Whisper from the shop?"

"It did," I confirmed. "Also, it tried to choke me to death while dragging me into that 'summoning circle'."

She tapped the quill against her gray-white cheek.

"That's not good. Don't let it do that. There are some rumors that a Death Whisper can trap a victim in a book through their summoning storm. Supposedly, the victim can be let out later." The Archbinder shook her head sadly. "Provided they survived the whole thing."

Lysander returned two more books to the shelves while Lyra handed me the instructions she wrote. I looked over the list, blinking at some of the ingredients.

"Now, this is for a ritual I tend to use on graveyards that get unruly. Think of it as a type of purification ritual," she explained. "Lysander speaks highly of your skills as an alchemist. Make an elixir with those ingredients. One drink every three days should slow down the curse that's trying to kill you."

"Fire peppers? A rooster's foot?" I read slowly. "Powdered burial shawl? Hair of the..." I shook my head a little. "Señora, will enough of this eventually remove the curse? Or just delay it killing me?"

"... or make you immune to hangovers?" Lysander suggested in a low, wry tone while he continued to shelve books.

I ignored him. Lyra grinned and continued.

"Remove? No. Slow it down? Yes, a good deal. If we're lucky, it'll make the whole thing hibernate!"

"Curses can hibernate?" I asked, surprised.

Lyra waved a hand idly in front of her. "Oh, all the time. Especially the worst ones. It would help if we knew more about this *Codex Luminari*. This is a lot of curse for 'just an old book'."

The blood-ink in the vial bubbled for a moment, then went still. She gave the vial a sideways glance.

"Also, I'd like to keep your blood-ink, to see just how it's connected to your curse. That alone might give me a way to strip that curse out of you."

"The blood-ink is all yours, Archbinder." Fatigued relief underscored my words. I folded the paper she gave me, then put it away in a coat pocket for later.

A sharp pang of guilt gnawed at me over the mess in Lyra's studio. I reminded myself to repay her for the damage, once I knew the cost. When I turned to recover both the old journal page and my notebook, I noticed something interesting.

Neither one was singed.

It was almost like the Death Whisper avoided them entirely. Also, there was now a thin trail of pale brown letters in the margin of the torn journal paper. I stuffed the journal page into my notebook, then picked them up. It was all something to think about later.

"Señora, before we go, would you happen to know if these designs here on this paper and in my notebook are part of a ritual? Maybe one that involves Death Whispers?"

Lyra opened my notebook, then glanced over both designs and notes. I had no idea if she'd ever studied the old thayan language. Apparently she knew enough, since she soon shook her head with a frown.

"Not any ritual I know of, Death Whispers or otherwise." She traced a finger over one of the drawings. "To me, these look like something a surgeon would use. For what? I couldn't say."

I nodded thanks when she handed both back to me.

"Be careful." She fixed us both with a hard stare. "If someone is willing to use Death Whispers to get this *Codex* and secure its secrets, neither you, nor your companions, are safe."

"Thank you, Archbinder," I replied with a small nod. "We understand."

"Pedro? What about Argall's warning?" Lysander reminded me as I turned for the door.

"Oh, yes," I replied. "Señora? Would you happen to have heard the phrase 'wood-boned man' before?"

Lyra frowned and stared at the floor thoughtfully, hands clasped in front of her.

"Wood-boned man? No, I can't say that I have. It's an odd phrase."

"It is," I replied. "Well, thank you, Archbinder. You've been a great help."

We barely made it outside her door before Lyra called out to us one last time.

"Good hunting, gentlemen. Oh, and Doctor Sangre? Please try not to die before I find a cure for your curse?"

9

Dire Warnings and Malcontents

July 25, 1722. Kingston, Jamaica. Headed to the merchant row along Port Royal Street north of the docks, where trouble swarmed like flies...

We left behind the Archbinder's studio and her morbid interests and retraced our steps down the street.

"Where to from here?" Lysander asked, falling into step beside me.

"Waterfront," I sighed, then pulled out Lyra's ingredient list. "The booths and merchant shops are the best bet to find most of this." A grimace fell over me. "Except for the burial shawl. That has to come from a gravedigger at one of the graveyards."

"Look at it this way. Maybe you'll get one that's only slightly used," he joked, then his expression turned serious. "Pedro, do you think that this," Lysander waved a hand at the list, "will work? A potion made of all that, against your curse?"

I stared hard at the list, then nervously adjusted my shoulder bag that held my notebook and the journal paper while we walked through Kingston's square.

"Yes?" I replied, and winced. Slowly, I took a deep breath. "Really, I don't know, my friend. A lot of what Lyra's listed here would do fine to make a 'necromantic repellant'. Just not one I've ever thought of before."

We turned south toward the docks as Lysander said, "Well, the corrupted curse is eating you alive."

I folded the list, then pushed it into my satchel.

"Yes, so Lyra said. Which means some part of the curse is necromantic. But that makes me wonder what else this corrupted curse will react to?"

Thoughts of necromancy and corrupted curses from Otherworld kept us company on the walk. We reached the docks ten minutes later.

The docks just south of Port Royal Street and its warehouses were the main shipping point for the city. Ships from all over the world came in through the Kingston Arcane Gate a half-mile off-shore. It made Kingston's docks a hum of activity, with its exotic offerings and occasionally dubious back-alley bargains.

Port Royal Street itself held rich, memorable smells of spices mixed with the sharp stench of saltwater, dead fish, cooked meat, and sweat. Midday meant the morning crowd had thinned out considerably. There wasn't the constant press of people, just thick knots of visitors and dockworkers up and down the road. Booths, wagons, and tables, all shaded with brightly colored tarps, lined the roadside, hoping to separate customer from coin.

I drew in a deep breath of the abusive aroma while it assaulted my senses. Personally, I enjoyed a walk along Port Royal Street. It was a good place to think, and right then I had far too much to think about.

"It's almost noon," Lysander said with an uneasy glance at the clouded sky, then the line of merchant stalls. "Less crowd, but still plenty of pickpockets."

"More of the city watch is out, too," I reassured him. "They're always out in force at midday when the cargo offloads. It keeps most of the problems at bay."

We strolled down the weathered, dingy footpath along the north side of the street, opposite the warehouses and narrow roads to the wooden piers.

"Fine by me," he replied with a sour look. "We have enough on our list as it is."

"You're not the one having to make, then drink, a potion with rooster feet," I replied.

Lysander gave me a sympathetic smile.

"It'll keep you alive." He patted me on the shoulder. "Besides, your right hand catches fire with green flames on a whim, and we've been attacked twice now by book fiends called Death Whispers. Rooster feet potions seem pretty ordinary by comparison, Pedro."

I shook my head a little at that.

"Lysander, if that's our new measurement of 'ordinary'? My friend, I think we have a problem."

"Pedro, you worry too much. I'm sure it'll taste like chicken."

"Feet," I corrected him. "Feet, my friend. Chicken feet."

"Staves off death," he countered.

Our debate continued over the elixir's future flavor while we mingled with the crowd and searched the merchant booths. The first three weren't any help, but our luck changed with the fourth.

"That'll be three pieces of silver," a stout woman with gray-black hair at one booth told me with a broad grin.

She was broad-shouldered and square built, with thin lines of brass running through her deep olive-tan skin. Those thread-thin metal veins were like any other I've seen on grimlings I knew. Her clothing was a brightly colored style I last saw back in Córdoba. It was a nice reminder of home.

Now, was her price highway robbery? Oh, of course it was. But given my morning so far, I didn't feel up to the customary haggling.

I handed over the coins with a sigh for a small bag of fire peppers and two rooster feet. Before I could drop the feet into the bag to join the peppers, the woman snatched up my right hand in hers. She stared intently at my glove, then fixed me with a stern, piercing look. I tried to pull my hand away, but her grip was like an iron vise.

"What is this?" I snapped in alarm while I struggled.

Lysander noticed my problem and lunged forward to help me. The woman made him back off with a ferocious glare. The wind off the bay blew with a sharp chill.

"Back away, Navigator," she spit out at him. "This isn't for you, and you've seen why."

I waved a hand at Lysander to keep back, then glared at the woman. "What do you want, señora?"

"Your time's running short, Doctor!" My spine stiffened while I watched her brushed-silver-colored eyes deepen, then burn with a bright green flame. "You lost the book. Get it, and put it back where it came from."

I tried to jerk my hand free, but her grip only tightened.

"The wood-boned man has it," she snarled, shaking her head slowly. "He's building the device and needs that page you have. The bloody fool doesn't understand what he's about to do. Mark my words, Doctor, keep it away from him. Do not let him build it!"

While she talked, her voice took on a lower tone. A smooth, polished sneer I had heard once before, in a lone ruin on San Andrés Island, in a swamp. Dread sank its talons into my back and skittered up my spine. A mist obscured the woman's face for a moment. Then it changed into the ghostly appearance of Captain Dryden Storm, complete with a ghostly, red-streaked black beard. His sinister, steel-gray eyes stared holes into me.

"You!" I breathed, wide-eyed. "It can't be..."

I scowled, then tried to jerk my hand free. It would've been easier to overturn a ship with a spoon.

"Oh, it can be, Doctor," Storm's voice sneered out the woman's mouth. "We're connected, you and I. Joined at the hand, it would seem. Don't let the master of the book get what he wants. Get the book. Put it back where it came from, and free my crew."

The grimling woman possessed by Dryden Storm practically jerked me across the booth, scattering some fruits and other produce in the process.

"If you don't," Storm's sneer dropped to a gravel tone, "I'll kill you myself. That is, if the curse doesn't take you. Then you'll be a fine addition to my crew. I could use a good alchemist. Mark my words, Doctor. You've little time."

The woman let go of my hand, and I nearly stumbled into Lysander. I glared back into the booth, but the older woman had stepped aside to sort an overfilled crate behind her. In her place, a square-built grimling man about the same age walked over to us. He brushed his hands against his worn blue coat, draped over ordinary, brown common clothes. Sunlight danced over the silver veins shot through his dark skin and his slicked back, cobalt blue hair.

"That all for you gents?" he asked brightly.

Lysander started for the booth with a scowl, but I quickly grabbed his arm.

"No. Wait. Look around," I warned him.

Lysander did just that.

"At what, Pedro? It's just the docks and people. But that woman... it was Captain Storm! We saw him die!"

I scowled at him.

"Look again, my friend. No one's staring. That woman almost pulled me over the top of that booth. No one noticed. Not even the people in the next booth. They act like nothing ever happened, and they were two steps away."

Lysander looked around again, while I glanced back at the booth in front of us. The blue-haired man squinted at us curiously, worry lines traced over his forehead.

I noticed not a single vegetable or fruit was out of place on the booth. But when the woman, or really Dryden Storm, yanked me forward, several had been knocked aside.

"Nothing's out of place," I whispered low enough that only Lysander could hear. "Not even Sebastian is bothered. It's as if nothing happened."

Then the woman at the crate stood up to press her fists against her hips. Her eyes had returned to a polished silver, without a hint of what she had just done. At least, what Lysander and I *thought* she had done.

"But Pedro, how...?" Lysander stammered for words.

"I don't know how Storm did that, or what happened," I told him with a frown. "But Storm sent us a message. Now isn't the time to figure it out, my friend. Not here. Not now."

Down the road, I saw three of the Kingston city watch eyeing us warily. I shook my head at Lysander, then smiled at the merchant.

"No, señor, it's fine. This is all we needed."

I pulled Lysander away before anything else happened, or the city watch decided to get involved. Once we escaped past the next booth, a young man raced over. Sidwell "Buttons" McGee was human, thirteen at best, in a slightly oversized and worn-out, dirty long coat. He was one of the many ‘street rats' that lived in the area.

“Doctor! I was headed for your shop. Got a message for you.” He thrust a stained, folded piece of paper at me.

“*Gracias,* Buttons. I appreciate it.” I dropped two silver *reales* into the boy's hand, then patted him on the shoulder. “Get something to eat. Share it with the rest of your Rat Runners.”

Buttons bit the coins, then tipped his battered black felt hat.

“Anytime, Doctor!” he replied with a cheerful grin, then raced off through the crowd.

I dropped the bird feet into the bag of peppers, then tied that dubious mix closed. After that, I unfolded the note.

“Lucien has information about the *Codex.*” I looked up and down Port Royal Street, past the scattered crowds at the colorful booths and wagons. “He's here among the booths. Says he'll meet us past Jasper Finnegan's Freakish Delights.”

“Fitting,” Lysander replied with a shake of his head.

I lightly tapped the note against my hand before I folded it closed, then put it away in an inner pocket of my long coat.

“At least there's no mistake where to meet him.”

“How do we know this isn't Captain Storm all over again?” Lysander asked, eyebrows knitted in concern.

“That's just it, we don't,” I replied after a deep breath. "But I think Storm could've killed us right then if he wanted to. Just be ready, and hope this really was from Lucien. We could use the winds blowing in our favor for once today.”

We picked up our pace, heading down the street.

10

Dubious Elixirs and Dire Information

July 25, 1722. Port Royal Street, Kingston, Jamaica. Seeing help in low places...

"Jasper's wagon is just ahead on the right. I can see his acrobats over the crowd," I said, peering past the people ahead of us. "Lucien has to be here somewhere."

"It looks like Jasper is in rare form today, too," Lysander commented with a nod to the brightly decorated wagon.

I looked past the modest crowd at a wood-covered wagon sheltered by a set of striped red, gold, and green sun tarps. A blue-lettered wooden sign for Jasper Finnegan's Freakish Delights gleamed in the Caribbean sun. The merchant's wares were set out on portable weathered, wooden shelves where they could also catch the light, giving each bottle, brass-trimmed chest, and more, a golden glimmer.

"He usually is," I replied as I glanced over the crowd. After a moment, my expression melted into a faint grimace. "I don't see Lucien in the audience, but that doesn't mean he isn't there."

"Maybe he's waiting until we pass by?" Lysander asked while we skirted the edge of the crowd.

"Most likely," I nodded slightly. The tension knit my eyebrows tighter. "It makes me wonder if he's being watched or followed?"

Lysander shook his head. "No idea. You know him better than I do."

I glanced at the crowd one more time, then over at Finnegan's Freakish Delights as we walked past. Jasper and I exchanged a polite, but subtle, nod to one another across the audience. A bit of professional courtesy, since we were both alchemists.

Jasper Finnegan then gestured to his wares, stirring up the crowd with his practiced, energetic speech. From his groomed beard and mustache to his bright clothing, he was every bit the showman. Even the gray in his beard was carefully doctored. All of it was done to present the picture of a stately, eye-catching, older human 'man of the world'.

Performing on either side of Jasper were his two employees. One was a tawny-haired thayan man in bright, red-trimmed clothes, who was an expert knife juggler. The other was a short human woman with olive-tan skin, dressed in loose-fitting sailor's clothing. She was an acrobatic expert with a staff.

They both were extra entertainment and help. Mostly, they kept an eye on the crowd for anyone who might want to buy something, or cause a problem.

Jasper's cheerful speech dove into questionable, daring tales around his bottles and potions while we passed by.

"I really can't tell if the crowd is interested in his tonic, or just enjoys his wild stories." I grinned over the display. "He gives quite a show."

Lysander squinted at a nearby bottle of something yellow-brown and cloudy on Jasper's shelves.

"Apparently, this month he's using spiced rum in his tonic?" Lysander commented with an amused expression.

"The day one of Jasper Finnegan's rum lotions works to soothe my old joint pain, I'll bathe in it," came a soft voice behind us.

We had found Lucien, or rather he'd found us.

My old friend and mentor, Lucien Massena, looked far less dangerous than he really was, which was just how he preferred it. He was a thin, older human man with brownish-gray hair, who dressed painfully average, and was easily forgettable. Someone who always looked faintly amused by the world around him, no matter what.

Most would never guess that he was one of the most skilled poisoners that the Marquee Brotherhood had.

He greeted us with a brief nod, then gave Sebastian a scratch behind the horns.

I smiled. "It's good to see you, Lucien. So, you have something on the *Codex?*"

"Yes, but I doubt you'll like it." His face tensed with a faint grimace. "The Brotherhood has precious little on the *Codex Luminari*. What they do have is unsettling. The *Codex* was written by one Tristam Greenholm, about a century ago in Otherworld. He was a Silvashar thayan wavebinder who was delving into how the Etherwave Arcana touched the world, and people, at a deep level. Why some could shape it better than others."

"So, it's a just record of his studies?" Lysander asked curiously.

"It would seem so," Lucien nodded. "But the *nature* of those studies is what's unsettling. Experiments around how the Etherwave Arcana connects to a person—either alive, or mostly dead. Then how to tap into that, or so I've been told. Particularly the mostly dead part."

"Lucien, are you serious? That sounds like spectral alchemy." I scowled. "Necromancy. The darker side of the Etherwave." I shook my head bitterly. "That's playing with fire and an illegal keg of powder at best."

That made me wonder about the parts Skaldi and Durner were making, and the device they're meant to work with. It gave me ideas, and I didn't like any of them.

"My friend, did you hear or read anything about the *Codex* having a set of plans for a device? Perhaps some sort of 'arcane pump' or engine?"

Lucien shook his head.

"No. There's been no mention of anything of the sort. But all of this so far? That's only the half of it," the poisoner said with a warning look.

"There was a quiet hunt for your *Codex Luminari* about three years ago. Several assassins and hunters went after it. Most didn't come back. Those that did weren't quite in one piece."

Lucien then held up a finger in emphasis.

"Once the Brotherhood's Council of Five discovered *how* those assassins died, they quickly marked the *Codex* off limits to all Marquee Houses. No exceptions." He shook his head. "Rumor has it they were given a stern order to stop looking."

I swapped a puzzled look with Lysander, then touched Lucien's arm to interrupt him. We stopped outside a basket weaver's booth with a wide assortment of rainbow-colored wicker baskets. The crowd was much thinner here, with less chance of us being overheard.

"Wait. You mean to say someone *ordered* the ruling leadership of the Marquee Brotherhood to stop looking for the *Codex* and they just... obeyed?" I shook my head in disbelief. "Lucien, monarchies have tried that for years, and paid in blood for it. Who has that sort of influence?"

I felt a sharp chill along my spine when my old mentor folded his arms over his chest, then smirked at me.

"A convincing woman who has very sharp teeth, and not much sense of humor." He nodded at me. "Though, Pedro, I think you would know that better than anyone. Doesn't she owe you a favor? Or you her? I've lost track."

"Morowen Waxbend," I replied with a heavy sigh, then rubbed my eyes. "*Mierda,*" I swore bitterly.

Lysander did a double take.

"Morowen..." he said hesitantly. "Short woman with dark black hair, black eyes, blue-gray skin, and a terrible temper? The *Sea Hag* of Port Royal? The town of Port Royal? *That* Morowen Waxbend?"

"Right down to her shark teeth. The very same, yes."

Lucien's smirk bloomed a bit more while he raised an eyebrow at the two of us.

"If one of the Daughters of the Deep kicks your door in, and tells you 'stop'," he shrugged, "by God, you stop. Especially after she's dragged more than one of your guildmates to the bottom of the ocean."

Then he let out a long sigh.

"Pedro. Lysander. If you two want to know about the *Codex,* and I mean really know about it, talk to Morowen. Everything I've heard tells me she has some personal stake in this." He shrugged again. "Hopefully, she won't gut you alive, drown you, or turn you into a writhing pile of sea spiders for asking."

I pursed my lips and stared into the air somewhere beyond us in the middle of the street while my thoughts churned. Sea gulls complained to each other while they staked out a few fresh fish in a net nearby. I watched a group of cargo handlers skillfully move a net of crates to the dock from a South China Sea merchant ship.

"There isn't much choice, is there?" I asked both of them in a low tone.

"Not that I can tell," Lucien replied with a sympathetic look.

"It makes a sort of twisted sense that there's a sea hag involved," Lysander mused with a thoughtful sigh. "I've heard the Daughters of the Deep are quick to drown anyone with a Dark Mark, or who plays with Etherwave necromancy, if they catch them."

"True." My expression darkened. "But then there's Joshua Argall. How does he fit in? Señor Argall claimed the *Codex* was a book of old maps. We're missing something very important, and I can't see what it is."

A thought hit me, and I shot Lucien a suspicious look.

"Lucien? What was the reason for all the secrecy with the note and meeting at Jasper's booth? Did something happen?"

He raised his eyebrows, then took a slow breath.

"You could say that," Lucien replied with a guarded expression.

The poisoner glanced over his shoulder, while worry lines deepened across his forehead.

"Once I got your note about the *Codex,* Pedro, I went searching Marquee guildhalls. I'll tell you, that took a few favors. Some of the Marquee Houses are a little touchy over who gets a look in their archives."

Lucien then gave us a half-shrug.

"You see, I was ambushed in House Jadescale's guildhall. Hired cutthroats, looking to beat out of me what I knew about the *Codex Luminari,* and that page you have. It happened again after I left House Frostsin's guildhall."

"You were attacked?" I scowled. "Twice? Once even *inside* a Brotherhood guildhall? Are you all right?"

"I was knocked around a little before help arrived, but don't worry, I'm fine," Lucien confirmed, voice brittle. "My ego took the worst of it, since they caught me off guard."

"Did they say anything?" Lysander was as alarmed as I was. "Or was it just asking about the *Codex* and Pedro?"

Lucien nodded.

"They did mention that their employer didn't want anyone looking into the *Codex,*" he replied before he glanced between us. "But..."

Suddenly, Jasper Finnegan was right there with us. There was a bombastic mention of 'amazing exploits' I hadn't quite paid attention to, but wished I had. The showman grabbed both Lysander and myself around the shoulders with a bright smile.

"Unpleasant company coming, gentlemen," Jasper whispered quickly under his breath.

A subtle jerk of his head alerted us to four broad-shouldered men behind the crowd at Freakish Delights. They stared at us with all the warmth a predator has for its prey. Methodically, they parted the crowd in our direction.

"Thank you, Jasper," Lucien said with a small, warm smile and a nod. "You're a prince among merchants, like always. I owe you."

"Think nothing of it!" Jasper replied with a bright grin.

"Until next time, gentlemen," Lucien said, then stepped away to vanish into the shadows beside Jasper's wagon.

"Now," Jasper told us with a tight hug. "Let's entertain the crowd, eh? Some rousing tales of exploration, while my associates toss out the rubbish."

The showman steered Lysander and myself toward his wagon of lotions and 'miracle medications'. He winked at his two acrobat employees. They nodded back, then slipped easily through the crowd to intercept the four cutthroats.

I swapped an uneasy glance with Lysander, as we found ourselves unwilling assistants of Jasper Finnegan's Freakish Delights.

To our credit, Jasper's sales of his rum-soaked elixirs were the best he'd had all week.

11

An Unwelcome Committee

July 26, 1722. On board the schooner, the *Silk Duchess*, in the waters offshore the newly rebuilt town of Port Royal.

"All hands! Port Royal off starboard!"

The muffled call from the spotter on deck snapped my attention back to the moment. At the foot of my bunk, Sebastian snored gently in his sleep. I watched him for a moment, then picked up my pen, opened my notebook, and recorded my thoughts.

Taking another dose of my 'medicine'. Hopefully, by letting it settle, that means it won't taste like toad sweat.

I set the pen down, then stared at the vial on the other side of the table. The small glass bottle was filled with an elixir based on Lyra Valtor's ingredient list. I brewed up a batch the previous night, before we set sail.

It was a thick, lime-green liquid that slowly churned on its own in the bottle. I watched it sway slightly while the *Silk Duchess* moved over the waves. My right hand felt warm, and the tattoo-like scars there shifted irritably.

I knew I needed to take a dose of my 'medicine', but I just couldn't will myself to drink it.

A few minutes later, that's how Elara found me when she walked into the narrow cabin. Sitting still, partly slouched, and glaring at the bottle with its dubious contents. I spared a glance at her as she walked over to sit on the side of the bunk.

With the ship underway, Elara didn't dress in what most believed a ship captain should wear. That was for stories and formal occasions. She was more practical than that and preferred function over fancy.

Today, she wore a plain white captain's shirt, blue vest, trousers, and boots. The shirt and vest had needed some alteration to accommodate her thayan dragonfly wings. But like she told me once, that's the challenge of having thayan ancestry in a human world. Most clothes fit fine, provided there were some adjustments made for wings.

I pressed my lips in a tight line, then looked at the 'medicine' I'd brewed with a sigh.

"You know," Elara said softly, interlacing her hands in her lap. "I'm just a ship's captain, and certainly no surgeon or alchemist. But I don't think you can drink that medicine by scowling at it, Pedro."

"It's vile, *querida,*" I admitted. "When I drink it, I feel something inside me tense and twist, almost into a knot." I took a frustrated breath. "Then there's the taste. I know I have to drink this to keep my 'affliction' under control, but still..."

"*Asa mvur*, you know it's necessary," she replied with a sympathetic look.

I rubbed my eyes while I clenched my jaw. There wasn't any good answer. She was right.

She clasped her hands, then shrugged.

"So, Durner and Skaldi finished building the part from the *Codex* page?" Elara asked. It was an obvious attempt to get my mind off the elixir, but I appreciated the effort.

"Yes." I pursed my lips, while I turned to face her, and not the bottle. "It's turnscrews, and part of a gearbox for a pump system. Not nearly large enough for a bilge pump, and a little too large to use in brewing. But I could make it work if I had to. They're convinced the pump is used to drain something, and I agree with them."

"Drain what?"

I shook my head.

"No idea, *querida*. But considering what has come from that *Codex* so far? I feel it's nothing good."

Silence filled the cabin, broken only by the distant sounds of waves lapping against the hull, and the crew on deck. I returned to my vigil, staring at the bottle. My own war of wills.

Finally, Elara walked over behind me to put her hands on my shoulders. When I didn't move, she reached over to collect the potion, then put it in my hands.

"*Asa mvur,*" she said softly. "Once upon a time, you helped me survive a bloody, mud-soaked massacre. You had every reason not to, but you did it anyway."

Elara tapped the cork on the bottle.

"So, take the medicine, even if it tastes bad." She patted my shoulder. "We all need you alive."

She paused for two heartbeats, then took a slow breath.

"I need you alive."

Then she gave my shoulder a gentle squeeze.

"The longboat drops in a few minutes, so we can put ashore in Port Royal to visit that horrible hag of yours."

I sat still, long after Elara had left. Her words stirred old, painful memories that I tried to blink away. I could almost feel the blood-soaked mud on my hands, and smell the powder shot from that day.

A spark of green flame on the back of my hand caught my attention. I scowled at it.

"Enough. I get the point."

The tiny flame vanished in a puff of smoke as I pulled the cork, and downed the syrupy liquid in one swallow. I coughed and clenched my right hand tight. After a moment, I reached for the pen and my notebook.

Letting it set didn't help. Now it tastes like toad sweat and despair. Remember to ask Lyra Valtor if I can add some mint...

I stuffed the notebook into my shoulder bag, then headed out the door with it, and my gray long coat. A sleepy Sebastian followed right behind me. With any luck, the visit to Morowen Waxbend would be uneventful.

Nothing could have been further from the truth.

The short trip to put ashore at Port Royal was calm and forgettable. Visiting Morowen Waxbend was anything but that.

Her home sat at the end of a gravel path behind four weather-beaten warehouses, a short walk from the docks. It was a two-storey cottage of gray stone, flaking wood, and salt-stained windows. Her heavy wooden front door was a sun-bleached shade of blue, reinforced with iron bands. It was her subtle way of suggesting she didn't enjoy visitors.

The place always smelled faintly of brine and old paper, and the moment we stepped inside, I had the uneasy feeling we were being watched.

"Elara! Behind you!" I snapped.

Three Death Whispers rushed in behind us through Morowen's front door. One of the ghoul-like fiends grabbed me by the shirt, then hurled me across a nearby table. I slammed into a window frame, then collapsed to the floor. Pain throbbed along my back as carved wooden figures rained on me from the shelf overhead. Sebastian barked, then spit tar at the fiend.

Elara stepped back, snatching her ghost blade free of its scabbard. A blue-white aura and hum chased the sword as she parried a slice from a Death Whisper.

"Where did they come from?" she yelled over the shrieking fiends. "I don't see any books flying around."

"No idea," I replied while I scrambled to my feet, despite bruises. "The woods? Nearby warehouses?"

The fiend that threw me rushed forward, ready to cut me apart. I snatched up a thick wooden chair and shoved it in front of me like a shield. The creature's cutlass slammed down, splintering the chair instead of my shoulder. Wood shards flew everywhere.

I shoved, knocking the cutlass to one side, then pummeled the Death Whisper with the chair. The wood splintered into kindling, but the creature barely noticed. Sebastian splattered tar spit across its face.

The Death Whisper backed away a few steps, then let out an ear-splitting shriek of rage. Eyes burning, its mouth stretched into a warped mockery of a human mouth complete with sharp, jagged teeth.

I hurled the ruined chair at it, but the creature batted it away like it was nothing. Wooden pieces tumbled in all directions across the floor.

Suddenly, lightning ripped the air with a peal of thunder, like a cannon. Bright bolts leaped from the far side of the room and speared the Death Whispers with a sharp sizzle. The three fiends convulsed, impaled on the lightning, while bits of their rotten clothing and withered bodies burned away.

Elara and I retreated while the lightning did its dire work. A short woman, barely five foot two, stalked across the living room toward the creatures. It was Morowen Waxbend. Her nailed boots added a percussion to the thunder, while more lighting jolted from her outstretched sea-blue hands.

"They're Death Whispers," she snarled. Solid black shark eyes scowled at the fiends. "They could've been made anywhere. Get ready."

The sea hag sneered at the Death Whispers, baring rows of sharp teeth at them.

"This won't wreck 'em, but it'll burn some of the fight out of 'em." She tossed another blast of lighting as she gave a tiny shrug. "Also, they'll be mad enough to chew nails."

Elara squared off against the fiend near the door, then nodded. I jerked my sword loose from its scabbard as green flames exploded to life around my right hand. Morowen arched an eyebrow at the flames before her eyes flicked to mine.

"Oh, well, don't we have a lot to talk about?" the sea hag rasped. "Wreck these, and we'll have tea."

Morowen slapped her hands together in front of her. A thunderclap to shake a ship threw the Death Whispers against the walls. Elara didn't waste time tearing into the nearest fiend with a vengeance. Her ghost blade a glowing hum of death.

The second Death Whisper moved to join its partner, but Morowen blocked its path. She was a grinning bundle of merry murder, wrapped in a cheerful, sky-blue calico dress. A charcoal vest was riddled with gardening tools that she brandished like an assassin.

Morowen tackled the fiend, knocking it—and her—outside the house. Ominous snipping and stabbing sounds followed. I didn't dare look.

Besides, I was already busy.

Once the lightning vanished, the last Death Whisper spun to face me and shrieked again. Its eye sockets blazed with burning blue flames of hate. The ghoul-like fiend closed the gap between us in a blur. Sebastian spit tar at it, but missed.

It attacked with a hot vengeance, cutting and slashing, but wary of my burning right hand. The fiend was relentless, its attacks getting faster than my eyes could follow. After each thrust or cut, the thing madly grasped at my shoulder bag. Each time, I danced out of reach, but I was getting tired.

"You will *not* get my notes," I growled.

I quickly put a small breakfast table between myself and the Death Whisper. When it lunged at me, I shoved the table forward and pinned the fiend hard against the wall. It shoved back, but I had already moved. The table flew end-over-end across the room until a bookshelf gave its life to stop it.

After a step to the side, I dove right for the Death Whisper. I slammed my burning fist, sword and all, into the fiend's ribs. It hammered a bony fist across my face. Stars exploded in my vision, but I kept punching. So did the Death Whisper.

Time was a bloody blur, mixed with shrieks and the feeling of hitting a bloated fish. Then I heard something snap in the creature. An odd wet sensation slid along my right hand, followed by a brief dizzy spell.

Suddenly, the Death Whisper exploded in a cloud of burned paper and cobalt blue lightning. A mist of black blood ink decorated the floor, my once white shirt, and gray coat. The green fire sizzled happily as I rubbed the side of my head.

A shriek from behind, and a bark from Sebastian, yanked at my attention.

"Elara!" I exclaimed, and turned for a fight. But she had it all well in hand.

Near the front door, Elara had taken flight to better avoid the Death Whisper's attack. I watched while she flew to the left, then slammed her ghost blade into the fiend twice. On the second stab, the creature exploded like the one from the bookshop.

The room went as silent as a tomb. Elara and I swapped a nervous glance, then looked to the front door at the sound of boots on the footpath outside.

Morowen Waxbend stalked inside carrying a Death Whisper's cutlass that trailed smoke. Black blood ink was smeared in a desperate streak across her calico dress. She hung the cutlass by the front door next to two parasols, then turned to face us, arms crossed.

"Now then," she said, jaw tight. "Someone grab those burnt papers fluttering around so I can ruin them. A ghost blade wrecks a Whisper, but the damn things sometimes reform. Then, we'll have tea, and discuss a few things."

The sea hag fixed me with a hard glare that made me fidget.

"Such as, why those things were in my own home after all these decades? Or how," she jabbed a sea-blue finger toward the green flames on my hand, "you wound up with that, Pedro? Let me guess..." I saw the reflection of the emerald flames in her shark-black eyes turn a poisonous yellow "...it has to do with a certain damn book called the *Codex Luminari*—doesn't it?"

I swapped a glance with Elara, then winced at Morowen.

12

Bruises, Tea, and A Bag of Hammers

July 26, 1722. Port Royal, House of the local sea hag. Tending bruises and battered furniture...

It took an hour to scrounge up all the loose, singed shreds of Death Whispers. I thought the bits were trying to run from us. Elara said it was my imagination; I wasn't convinced. Especially given how many times a piece would fly out of my fingers, then land as far under furniture as it could get.

The black blood ink splatters didn't seem to matter. Morowen thought they added character to the room for reasons I didn't want to know.

Once we were done, Morowen collected the stack, then stuffed it into a stained wooden bowl. Salt, soap, and a bottle of steaming purple liquid that smelled like anguish put an end to the sea hag's concerns.

In the meantime, Elara and I worked to bring some order to the chaos we created. We returned the small breakfast table and surviving chairs back to where they came from. The one I used as a club and shield? It was beyond hope and probably needed last rites.

I recovered my tricorn hat from where it had landed in a corner, then dropped into a chair at the table. The growing bruise around my left eye throbbed like a drum. But just peacefully sitting still for a moment felt good.

Elara checked the room once more, then sat down across from me. The worst she'd suffered was a cut or two along her right arm among a bundle of bruises.

I dabbed at the bloody bruise beside my left eye with a damp handkerchief, then flinched from a stab of pain.

"Those fiends hit like a bag of hammers," I complained softly, then touched the sore spot again. It didn't feel any better than last time, so I felt around at my belt loops for a healing potion.

Morowen swatted my hands with a towel. Water boiled on the stove behind her.

"They aren't fiends. You should've ducked, and you've a hard head. Now quit poking at it, and leave those potions alone," she snapped at me with a scowl. "I've got better."

Morowen turned her back to us, then rummaged through a set of overstocked cabinets near her stove. There were far too many stacks of bottles, dried herbs, and jars of orange mush I didn't want to know about. She sorted through it all somehow with a practiced hand until she found what she wanted with a pointed grin.

"What do you mean they aren't fiends?" Elara asked with a puzzled glance at me. "That's what Archbinder Lyra Valtor said they were."

Morowen rolled her eyes, as if she'd had this conversation a hundred times.

"That's because, like all of you, she's never really seen a fiend. Not a real one anyway," Morowen explained, closing the pair of cabinet doors. "No one has, for about a century. When you do, you'll know it."

A jar filled with a white-gold cream was dropped in front of me. The hand written label read, 'Slippery Witch Oil'. Morowen pointed at the bloody bruise and cut by my eye.

"Dab that on where it hit you," Morowen said, turning to the stove to check the boiling water. "Use it once a day. It'll stop the swelling, and you'll heal fast enough in a few days. Provided you quit letting things hit you there." She waved a hand at us. "Keep the jar. I've got plenty."

"What is it?" I asked, studying the jar.

"Helpful," Morowen replied dryly. "Coconut oil and witch hazel. My own recipe. Works better than a witch hazel or calendula tea compress." Then she pointed at Elara's cuts on her sword arm. "Works on cuts like that, too."

Elara gave Morowen a flat, calculating look while she dabbed at her cuts with a handkerchief.

"I've enough debts. A potion will do fine." The captain dug a potion out of a belt pouch, then took a long drink. The small cuts on her arm slowly knit.

Morowen shook her head with a snort. "Sea god's beard, you're stubborn. Suit yourself. There're no favors owed for the cream, anyway."

I opened the jar, then gently applied the cream as instructed. It stung, but to Morowen's credit, the ache eased off right away, or at least was more bearable.

The sea hag shot the bubbling water on the stove a sideways glance while she wiped her hands on a nearby towel.

"Like I was saying," she began, "Death Whispers are a type of golem. Rare and pretty nasty." She folded the towel, then dropped it on the counter. "Also, golems aren't what you'd call 'gentle'. That's why I won't bother with 'em, and especially not Death Whispers. Too many fragile things around here."

I glanced over at her collection of preserved squirrels on a shelf. One winked at me. I found something else to look at.

"Makes perfect sense to me," I replied dryly.

Elara narrowed her eyes at the sea hag. "Aren't all golems the same thing?"

Morowen unceremoniously plopped a wad of colorful tea leaves in a pot, then put them out of their misery with the hot water from the stove. Once their drowned ghosts rose with the steam and aroma, she brought the teapot, cups, and more to the table on a battered tin tray. The sea hag kicked broken bits of chair out of her path, then pulled over an intact chair for herself. A rusty iron bolt hit the floor in front of Sebastian. He gleefully pounced on the snack.

"Most are. These aren't." She poured some of the tea into a ceramic cup. A dubious, mist-like fog boiled over the side while she continued.

"You see, I call 'em a 'type', because when you make a Whisper, you do more than plump 'em up with arcane runes and Etherwave energy."

Morowen set the pot down, then slid over a dish of brown, finger-length cookies. They were as hard as wood, but softened fast enough in the tea.

"You have to stuff in a bit more to make a Whisper," she continued, snatching up a cookie for herself. "Like emotion and pain from the writer, cause we all know they've got plenty to spare. It gives the Whispers their strength. Also, it lets 'em travel between books, carrying whatever they grab."

I nodded a little, remembering that Lyra Valtor suspected Death Whispers could trap a person in a book.

"You certainly know a lot about them," Elara said, inspecting her tea.

Morowen shot her a suspicious look at the comment.

I cleared my throat to break the tension, then sipped at the fog-laden tea. It was peppermint, with something else sweet in it. The taste and warmth drove away more of my aches.

"You make it sound like a summoned spirit," I said, taking another sip.

"Oh, that's because you have to kidnap a specter, and stuff it in last." Morowen sipped her tea casually. "Fiends *can* work, but a specter's better. Like a specter of a murderer, assassin, or a pirate. Something desperate and angry. It just works better."

I nearly spit my tea. Instead, I coughed. Elara sat still as stone from morbid shock. Thoughts of Captain Storm and his crew flew through my mind.

"What?" I sputtered.

Morowen slapped me on the back until my teeth wanted to rattle for mercy.

Zombies aside, who were fairly rare and mostly considered 'living challenged', undead like specters were unpredictable and dangerous at best. Certainly not safe by any means. I knew of several stories where a single specter had slipped aboard a ship or into a town, then relentlessly wiped out anything alive.

What Lyra Valtor said about my curse, and that I 'consumed' Death Whispers, came to mind. I had an ugly idea of what my curse was really swallowing. I sipped my tea, trying not to think too hard about what that meant. At least this explained why Elara's ghost blade worked so well.

Morowen reached down to scratch Sebastian behind his horns and ears. He drooled happily at the attention. Across from me, Elara shifted uncomfortably in her chair.

"You said it's been decades since you've dealt with Death Whispers," Elara said to Morowen, voice slightly tense. "You also mentioned the *Codex Luminari*. We found it in a ruin about six days ago. Death Whispers appeared right after."

The sea hag looked back at her, lips in a tight line. All at once, the air felt thick, as it does before an approaching storm.

I've never figured out what put Elara and Morowen at odds. In Morowen's case, she's often at odds with everyone, like any other sea hag. But this always felt more personal. I was relieved it hadn't come to blows yet.

Then Morowen slapped the table hard enough to rattle the dishes. Sebastian leaped to his feet, gargoyle wings spread, while he looked for a threat. Even the mist over the tea retreated for a moment. The sea hag glared off at nothing in the middle of the room.

"How many of those assassins do I have to drown, to get it through their heads that when I say 'stop', I mean it?" Morowen snarled. "Not go get some privateers to go do it for them!"

For a moment, I thought I heard thunder roll in the distance. It was probably my imagination. At least, I hoped it was my imagination.

I shook my head, then held up both hands.

"Wait," I said firmly. "Yes, we've talked to the Brotherhood, but they didn't send us after it. A bookseller in Kingston did."

"Who?" Morowen demanded, her eyes sharp as a naked blade.

Elara's tense expression melted into a scowl.

"We're not telling you that," she snapped. "You'll go terrify them like you did the Brotherhood. They don't deserve that."

"Now you listen to me," Morowen snapped back, shaking a finger at Elara.

"Stop!" I interrupted, a little more harshly than I meant to. Both women turned a sharp glare at me. I hated to do that, but at least they weren't arguing with each other. I took a slow breath.

"This," I waved a hand in the air between them, "whatever this is, isn't helping. There are enough problems. We're trying to help someone, and people have been hurt." I picked up my tea, then took a sip, letting that sink in. Mostly, I wanted to steady my nerves. Yelling at a sea hag is an ugly way to die.

"Morowen," I continued with a sigh, "let me start at the beginning before you tear off to murder anyone."

I retold the events on San Andrés Island with the book, crabs, and Captain Storm. After that, I explained what we knew about my curse, the attack by the Death Whisper, Lyra Valtor, and more. I finished the tale with the ambush at Morowen's home. Joshua Argall's name was the only detail I left out. Elara added her own perspective through parts of the story, especially during the fight in the store.

The sea hag squinted suspiciously at the green tattoo-like scars on my right hand.

"The Marquee Brotherhood wants nothing to do with that book," I said, nervously running my fingers across my teacup. "But they were very clear that they believed you have a keen interest in the *Codex*."

"What do you know, Morowen?" Elara asked quietly. "How bad is this?"

Morowen started to say something, but thought better of it. She drummed her fingers against the table.

"If it were anyone but you two," the sea hag began, "I'd leave their bodies at the bottom of the bay." She shook her head slowly, then let out a deep sigh. “I want to talk about that,” she pointed at my cursed hand with a stern look, “but not yet.”

Morowen steepled her fingers and gave us a woeful smile.

“You could say I’ve a tie to that book.” The sea hag’s expression melted into a mix of memories, anger, and regret. “I helped write it. Well, most of it, including a lot of the notes on necromancy, with the former love of my life, Tristam Greenholm. At least,” she shrugged, “until he tried to kill me. Then I stuffed him blood, bone, and all, inside the *Codex* with a curse.”

She took a casual sip of her tea with a sad smile.

“I suppose I’ve got my own story to tell. Have a cookie.”

13

Dead, From a Certain Point of View

July 26, 1722. The small, weather-beaten, two-storey home of Morowen Waxbend, the sea hag of Port Royal. Where we learned more than we bargained for.

Morowen stared into her tea for a long moment before she spoke.

"Tristam didn't start out broken," she said quietly. "He was angry. Grieving. His sister was murdered by a necromancer, and he wanted to make sure no one else ever suffered like that again."

She took a slow sip, jaw tightening.

"He tried to raise her. Nearly died trying. After that, he decided necromancy itself was the enemy."

I leaned back in my chair, unease creeping in.

"Morowen," I said slowly, eyebrows rising, "are you saying Tristam wanted to 'cure death'?"

She let out a hard sigh, heavy with memories. "It was a mad, bold idea, and so very stupid. But he was a charmer and got me all excited about it."

I scowled a little, not sure what to say. My thoughts wandered while I studied the small kitchen and dining room. The plain rustic decor, from checkered curtains and dried herbs to her pickled squirrel and shark skull collection, was an interesting distraction. It helped me think. Sea hags were notorious for their hatred of necromancy. A chance to stomp it out would be an attractive offer.

One of the floating squirrels glanced at me out of its jar, then blinked. Suddenly, the curtains were very fascinating.

Elara's wooden chair complained faintly as she shifted position, then breached the silence.

"What went wrong?" she asked with a curious expression. "You left that part out."

Morowen pursed her lips. It looked like she'd licked a rotten lemon.

"He got obsessed," she explained with a ragged sigh, gripping the teacup like she might choke it. "Tristam thought he saw patterns to it all. There weren't any. It got worse the more necromancy he studied. I kept telling him it was just the darker side of the Etherwave whispering, but he didn't believe me."

She brushed at the air a little, as if to push aside memories. "Then he was stealing bodies from graveyards for 'practice'. By then, Tristam was convinced he could create life from the Etherwave, magic itself, and unlock immortality."

"That's when he tried to kill you and steal your power," I replied with a brief nod. "Pay magic's price."

Morowen smiled, but there wasn't any humor to it.

"Magic always comes with a price. Always."

The smile melted away. "He came at me one night with a pair of knives. There was a wild, sunken look in his eyes. Tristam didn't know me. I was just a thing. When he cut me, I lost my temper." Her voice was a growl. "I called down a typhoon right there. Wrecked his workshop, his assistant, just everything, as I cursed him."

Her shoulders sagged a little.

"Not my best moment with a curse," she admitted. "I should've just stuck to the classics and frogged him."

"Sun's breath," Elara sighed, wide-eyed.

"Tristam's not just trapped, he's haunting the book, isn't he?" I asked while I rubbed the bridge of my nose. "A book packed with necromantic rituals and enchantments primed to use?"

"Basically," Morowen replied with a small, half-shrug. "He really would've been a great frog."

Regret flowed over her expression. Tristam must have meant more than she wanted to let on. I felt a small sting of sympathy for her, and what she lost.

"I believed in his idea, you know?" she said mournfully. "Write the rituals down, then find a way to counter 'em. Not bury 'em, and hope they go away, like my sisters do."

Morowen poured herself more tea, then glanced at the two of us.

"The Tristam I knew? He's long gone. Necromancy took him." The regret in her expression turned sour. "Age doesn't always mean wise, I suppose."

Elara gave her a quiet, sympathetic look. "No, not always."

My thoughts tumbled over while I sipped my tea. There were a lot of pieces and they'd just started to fit into place.

"Now, if the *Codex* is so dangerous, why leave it in a library?" I asked after a moment.

Morowen's eyebrows knit at that.

"So, that's where you found it? A library?"

I nodded. "It's more a ruin now. The Library of Lësarilis on San Andrés Island."

The sea hag scoffed while she snatched up another hardtack-like cookie.

"It figures someone would stick it in a university library for just anyone to grab," she grumbled. "Idiots."

I gave Elara a confused look. She shook her head.

"The Library of Lësarilis was part of Fallohide University on Otherworld," she explained with a pensive expression. "At least, before our worlds collided during Crossing's Fall."

She idly tapped her teacup and raised her eyebrows at Morowen.

"It means someone found it, and that person made it to Earth," she added. "Which may be how knowledge of the *Codex* spread. Could it haven been another sea hag?"

Morowen soaked the cookie in her tea, then chomped down like a shark eating a fish.

"My sisters would've buried the book, then sealed me away if they knew," the hag snorted. "No, it's not them. The only other person I can think of is Casin Fairmont, Tristam's weasel assistant. But he was inside the workshop when it collapsed." She sipped her tea. "Good riddance, really."

I imagined an entire typhoon focused on just one building and anyone inside. A shudder tapped a tune along my spine.

"Pedro," Elara said thoughtfully, "I keep thinking about what you were told in the Kingston market about the *Codex* and that torn page. We should show that to Morowen."

"What page?" Morowen asked with a curious frown while I grabbed my shoulder bag.

"This one." I rummaged a bit before I produced the *Codex* page, then slid it across the table along with my notebook. "I was going to ask you about it."

Morowen reached for the *Codex* page, but hesitated, fingers not quite touching the yellowed, ancient paper. After a long breath to steady herself, she pulled it over. Slowly, her eyes drifted over the faded words and designs. The more she read, the deeper her sea-blue, freckled brow furrowed, and storm clouds rolled in her eyes.

"Señora, you helped write the book. Do you recognize this?" I asked. "Elara and I translated a little, but the rest is beyond us. I was told the current owner of the *Codex* desperately wants, even needs, this page."

"Tristam, you mad idiot," she spat under her breath, "and I'm an even bigger one."

My eyebrows shot up at that. I glanced at Elara, who shook her head a little, then shrugged with a confused expression.

"That's not promising," I said, leaning forward to look at the page. "What is it?"

Morowen fixed me with a stern glare while she jabbed a finger at the page.

"This? It's new. Tristam wrote this *after* I bound him in the book." She ran her fingers lightly along a set of words and numbers on the far-left margin. "But I know what it says."

"New? What?" Elara stammered, wide-eyed. "How even...?"

The hag shook her head. "Don't ask. It's necromantic. If I tell you, I'll have to kill you, and I sort of like you two."

I swapped an uneasy look with Elara.

Morowen shot a sideways glance across the kitchen at unsuspecting pots and pans hung on steel wall hooks. Suddenly, she snapped her fingers.

"You said 'haunting'. Haunting works." Morowen gave us a dark look. "You know how ghosts tend to move things around, harass librarians and all, just to be a right proper pain in the ass? It's like that.

Tristam's still doing his necromantic studies, but now he's trying to get free."

I nodded with a deep breath, understanding. But silently, I really wished I didn't.

"That makes a sort of unpleasant sense," I said. "But why is this page so important?"

Morowen's mouth curled into a sharp-toothed grin. It felt like a shark was about to invite me to be dinner.

"Most of this here on the page? It's called a 'soul anchor'." She shrugged. "That's what I call it, anyway. It anchors a person to the spot where a ritual gets acted out."

"Like anchoring a ship in a storm?" Elara offered.

"Just like," Morowen replied. "Only here? The storm is the dark powers trying to drag a person into the afterlife."

"Tristam," I replied, and she nodded.

The hag traced a finger over a series of numbers, then tapped the mysterious pump and gear design.

"Tristam so liked his toys. See this? If I'm reading it right, those are for an arcane engine meant to siphon him out of the *Codex,* bringing him back to life." She glanced up, eyebrows knit in thought. "Sort of summoning himself, in a way."

With that, more pieces slid into place in my mind. I didn't like the picture it made.

"Summon himself out of the book, like a Death Whisper?" I asked slowly, with a worried expression.

The sea hag chuckled dryly.

"A bit," she replied, then glanced over the page. "He'll need someone to do the summoning, though. Still, it might work, it's just real risky. I bound him—anchored, really—into that book. First, whoever performs this has to live through breaking my magic. Second, if this nonsense works, Tristam will appear outside the *Codex* in a golem body. If it doesn't?" Morowen snapped her fingers. "He'll get dragged into the afterlife. Either way, this stunt will rip a hole between here and the afterlife."

Elara and I didn't move, but I could tell we thought the same thing. Morowen raised her eyebrows at us.

"Exactly. All manner of specters and worse, come crawling out." Her voice took on a deadly tone. "Want to see a real fiend from the dark side of the Etherwave?" She tapped the *Codex* page. "There you go."

Elara shoulder's tensed as she jerked a hand at the yellowed page.

"Fine. If whoever it is needs this, let's change it. Better yet, burn it!"

Morowen's dark look in reply made me uneasy. Enchanted items are notoriously durable. It's part of how so many remained intact over centuries. But there were ways to disrupt or even break them, which meant they sometimes exploded.

The sea hag glanced at her stove, then reached for the page.

"This is why."

"No!" I snapped. Sebastian leaped to his feet and barked.

Elara leaped out of her chair while I lunged forward. Morowen pulled the page out of my reach, then thrust it inside the cast-iron stove, right into the flames.

Nothing happened.

There wasn't even smoke. It was like the flames moved *around* the paper. Elara rubbed her eyes in frustration and sat down. I sat back in my chair with a long breath. Morowen recovered the page, dropping it on the table. It wasn't even warm.

"Some warning next time, señora?" I asked. Morowen simply grinned at me.

"So," Elara snapped. "We started out trying to deal with a theft, but now we're what? Stopping some lunatic from turning all manner of ghosts loose on Jamaica? Not to mention raising a bigger monster from the dead?"

Morowen smiled as she patted the captain's hand.

"This is why I like keeping you and Pedro around," she grinned. "I'm too old to go running off like that. Bad for my knees."

Elara simply rolled her eyes.

Morowen held up the *Codex* page for a moment.

"Now, I don't have some magic compass that'll point out the *Codex* for you. A damn fool pirate stole my last one two months back. But," she tapped a finger against her blue lips, "this type of ritual needs space, and a plenty big source of power to pay the Etherwave's price."

"How big?" I asked uneasily.

"A typhoon would do it," Morowen replied thoughtfully. "You could also murder about a hundred people. That'd do it, too."

I bit back several sharp replies that tasted like bile. After I rubbed my eyes, I found Morowen staring holes into me.

"As for you," her voice brittle. "Your hand. That's ghostfire, and it'll kill you. Why is it bound to a corrupted curse? Why is it trying to protect you? Start talking!"

14

Catching Breaths and Inspiration

July 26, 1722. Walking along the Port Royal docks in the late afternoon to catch our breath, and maybe some inspiration.

Morowen had a lot to say about the ghostfire, my curse, and how one of them was killing me. Probably the curse, but she wasn't sure. Honestly, she sounded almost irritated that she hadn't been the one to curse me. I wasn't sure how I felt about that.

The conversation had been like the one with Lyra Valtor, but with a couple of new twists. First, I still needed to drink that damn purification potion, but there was a risk it would change the curse. How? No idea.

The second was more unsettling.

Ghostfire, from what Morowen remembered, wasn't a typical spell channeled from the Etherwave Arcana. It was a rare consequence, or side effect, of shaping magic. She said it was called 'spark touched' on Otherworld.

The way she explained it, this happened when victims reached out to channel the Etherwave for a spell. In return, something else, or even the Etherwave itself, reached back and refused to let go. A permanent, open channel formed, which flooded the spark touched with magical power. At least, until the spark touched burned up in a burst of magical flames.

I absolutely didn't like the sound of that.

But I wasn't dead yet, so I felt things were looking up.

"Hm, 'spark touched'?" I muttered to myself while I walked. "Just 'hit on the head once too often' would've covered it well enough."

Elara didn't reply, but gave me a rueful look.

The afternoon sun had reclined across the sky by the time Elara, Sebastian, and I left behind the path to Morowen's home. Bands of amber and gold were painted across clouds as we reached the rebuilt docks of Port Royal.

Music danced through the air somewhere to our left, deeper into Port Royal itself. It was most likely from a tavern. The town had several, despite its small size.

Most of Port Royal had been rebuilt after the hurricane in 1712 nearly wiped it out. Once it was a lawless pirate town, but now it had become a tiny haven for clockwork engineers and similar inventors. Ships often stopped to resupply here before they headed on to Kingston harbor.

Not that there weren't plenty of pirates and privateers around Port Royal's taverns. It's just that they'd learned to keep their antics under control. No one wanted to startle the gearwrights around town. That often made things explode with an ominous 'sproing' sound.

I stopped at the end of a pier, turning right to look out over the water. The *Silk Duchess* was at anchor in the harbor, along with a half-dozen ships of her class. Farther down the docks, a work crew unloaded a barge stacked with crates from France and other parts of Europe.

Elara stepped onto the pier next to me, clasping her hands behind her. A gust of wind blew in off the water with the scent of rotten seaweed, brine, and old dreams. Sebastian sniffed at the air, but didn't seem impressed. Elara's wings fluttered for a second, her mouth pulled into a tight line.

"I don't get along with Morowen, but I'm still sorry she went through that. No one should," Elara said with a frustrated sigh. "She didn't give us much to work with, though, did she? Other than just how bad Death Whispers are?"

I ran a hand through my unruly dark hair and sighed. Had she? It was hard to tell. Morowen told us a lot more than I felt she'd tell anyone else.

"Honestly? I think we did, *querida,*" I suggested, tapping the brim of my tricorn hat against my fingers. "Especially with what she didn't say."

Elara narrowed her eyes at me.

"What do you mean?" she asked.

Sebastian pounced on a piece of driftwood that had a fascinating smell. I glanced down at him, then out at the water. Just what did I mean? There was an idea in my mind. It just wasn't easy to put into words.

In the distance, past the harbor, the Southern Arcane Gate for Jamaica appeared in a brilliant flash of magical power. Lightning and fog curled around it in a brief thunderstorm that soon vanished.

Massive, shimmering stones of the archway glowed in the sunlight, while ancient runes pulsed along its sides. Two ships, a pair of frigates flying the League of Nations flag, sailed through the gate a moment later. They disappeared from view through the enchanted archway, on their way to somewhere else in the world.

I tugged on my hat, then gave a small shrug.

"For instance, the Death Whispers. Morowen said each one has a ghost or a specter in it. That's channeling a lot of magical power in a short time to make a golem, then trapping a specter in it so the whole thing works." I glanced over at Elara and raised an eyebrow at her. "So far, that's been what? Four? Three at once in one day?"

"I see what you mean," she said with a small nod. "This isn't just anyone who has the *Codex,* but probably a wavebinder."

I made an idle wave at the comment.

"One that's well-trained to the point of even being an Archbinder. Then there are the ghosts. This wavebinder has a ready-made supply of trapped ghosts just sitting around."

Elara gave me a dire, stern look.

"You mean Dryden Storm and his crew."

My expression went a little sour.

"The same. He made a point in the marketplace, when he haunted or possessed that merchant, to tell me we're 'connected', among other things. If he's a ghost, that would explain how he did that, and that he's haunting me." I shrugged. "It isn't a far leap from there to guess he's trapped in or near the *Codex* with his crew."

Elara wrapped her arms around herself while she shuddered a little, wings fluttering.

"So this wavebinder who has the *Codex,* forces one of Storm's crew into a Death Whisper. A Whisper that's then sent after us. We destroy its body, then what?" She asked quietly and gestured to my right hand. "You're using the ghostfire to send them back, and it starts all over?"

I glanced down at Sebastian, who had found a very interesting and forgotten sprig of dried out seaweed.

"Honestly? I don't know," I replied, words tense, pushing my hands into my coat pockets. "Archbinder Valtor said I was tethered to something through this... affliction. Morowen says I'm 'spark touched'."

I drew in a deep breath and watched the Arcane Gate out in the ocean sparkle under the afternoon sun.

"Maybe I'm sending specters to that place in the Etherwave? Maybe I'm just sending them on to the next life?" I shook my head as I felt a little helpless.

"I don't know," I said sharply. "The last thing I want is for them to wind up back at the *Codex*, even if they're wanting to kill us."

Elara pulled her lips into a tight line before she took a breath.

"I hope that's not where they're going," she replied bitterly. "Sending them back to the *Codex* sounds like the worst kind of trapped hell."

Bored with our conversation and the seaweed, Sebastian slowly crept away. Carefully, he stalked a quartet of seagulls arguing over a dead fish farther down the row of piers. I followed not far behind him. Elara kept pace while we talked.

"It's a good bet Captain Storm isn't in league with the spellcaster who has the *Codex,*" Elara said with a thoughtful expression.

"How do you mean?" I asked curiously.

"He's protecting, it like Lyra suggested," she bit a little on her lower lip, "along with demanding you put the *Codex* back to stop all of this."

"But would it, *querida?*" I replied with a pensive expression. "If I return the *Codex,* then I have to put this 'soul anchor' page back with it. Then the whole *Codex Luminari* is in one place, free for the taking."

She shrugged a little.

"It still might," she replied. "*Asa mvur,* think about it. If Storm and his crew are caught in a Bindweaver's Curse, they *have* to protect the *Codex.*"

Elara gestured toward me, tapping out her logic on her fingers.

"First you grabbed the *Codex,* so they harass you. Then our mysterious spellcaster steals the *Codex*. But Storm has to still harass or even kill you, because the curse has him aimed at you. If you put the book back, wherever that is, the spellcaster can't touch it, unless he wants to be the next target."

I knitted my eyebrows over a frown, then clenched my jaw while chewing on that idea.

"That's a lot of 'maybe'," I replied, then idly massaged the scar-like tattoos on my right hand. "I've a feeling Storm will come after us soon, whatever we do."

Elara let out a humorless laugh. "It's all moot if we can't find this wavebinder who has the *Codex.* We don't even know just how they'll fuel that arcane engine Morowen described."

In front of us, Sebastian leaped into the midst of the four seagulls. The birds scattered in all directions, squawking complaints at the gargoyle's sudden appearance. Sebastian trotted back over to us, tail high and wings flat against his sides, pleased with himself.

"Almost got the group," I said with a thin smile. Then ideas slid together in my mind. "Group. A crew," I said slowly, glancing over at Elara, who watched me curiously. "A typhoon. Storm. Elara, I think I know what's going to be fed into Tristam's arcane engine."

Elara squinted at me before her eyes went wide.

"Surely not," she said in a somber tone.

I rubbed my right hand, which now ached even harder. It felt warm on the inside.

"Elara. Just how large is a pirate crew?" I waved a dismissive gesture. "The average crew?"

"About fifty to one hundred..." Her words trailed off as she closed her eyes and set her jaw.

"Exactly," I replied, feeling my expression harden. "Captain Storm and his crew are bound to the *Codex.* Even if that's only fifty crew along with Captain Storm, it could be enough for this arcane engine to work."

I could see the green of her jade-gold eyes turned glittery hard like stone. Her shoulders tensed, like they did before drawing her sword for a fight, or boarding another ship during a battle.

"We still have no way to find out who has the *Codex.* What lunatic is going to try this," she ranted, voice brittle, "*bilge* of an idea."

A thought occurred to me, and I could've kicked myself that it was so obvious.

"Not quite," I replied thoughtfully, then pushed my hands back into my coat pockets. "We should've thought of this before. It was right in front of us. Joshua Argall."

"What?" she asked, shaking her head a little, confused. "Pedro, he's in the hospital. Lysander said the man wasn't in his right mind."

I arched an eyebrow at her.

"No. I don't mean Señor Argall himself," I replied in a matter-of-fact tone. "At least, not directly. I mean his office. The man's a bookseller, Elara. He has to keep accurate records of his business affairs, such as hiring us. If he's had dealings with this wavebinder who has the *Codex,* he might have a record of that, too. At least a name. It's worth a try."

Elara looked pensive over that. "The city watch would've locked his office up tight."

"True," I replied with a thin smile. "But didn't you once tell me that some locks beg to be opened? Especially if lives are on the line?"

She grinned with a twinkle in her eye.

15

Lockpicks and Ledgers

July 28, 1722. Kingston, Jamaica, after a short trip from Port Royal. Making a late-night visit to the bookstore...

"The man desperately needs a better lock," Elara muttered under her breath, fingers dancing with her lockpicks.

A tense few seconds passed before the lock surrendered with a sharp click. We waited, watching up and down the moonlit alley beside the Word to the Wise bookshop, in case anyone heard. No one appeared. Elara yanked open the wooden door.

"Go!" she hissed.

I darted into the shop's shadowy back hallway with Lysander right behind me. Precarious towers of boxed books greeted us with a dusty silence. I kept my fingers to myself, despite some idle curiosity. The stacked boxes also looked a little unstable. I lifted my lantern to raise its hood just a little, just enough to give us some meager light.

Elara remained outside, holding open the side door, while she kept an uneasy watch on the alley. Silvery, pale moonlight played over her face, casting the worry lines around her eyes in stark relief. Her dragonfly-like wings fluttered nervously.

"Don't take too long, you two," she said in a low voice. "I think I've a sense of how often the city watch wanders by here. We won't have more than an hour and a half at best."

I nodded. "Understood. We'll be quick. Let us know if you see anyone."

With a nod back, Elara shut the door, leaving Lysander and myself alone in the dusty gloom.

"Sail the high seas, ransack an office for old papers," Lysander quipped, then peered inside the nearest box. "Ah, the life of a privateer!"

"Not helping," I half-whispered back. Still, I grinned anyway. It was Lysander's way of easing the tension.

"Remind me when we started doing all this skulking about?" I asked quietly. My eyes discovered an intricate cobweb nearby from an ambitious spider. It stretched from the ceiling to an abandoned, empty wooden shelf. The mild clutter in the hallway didn't give me a warm and fuzzy feeling about a quick escape if we needed one.

"Oh, when we started getting attacked by ink-blooded golem things, and you went to talk to a sea hag," Lysander replied with a grin.

I shook my head, lifting the lantern to part the gloom a little.

"Argall's office should be this way."

The bookshop was as silent as an old tomb, and slightly less cozy. A faint, bitter odor of singed paper collided with the stale scent of dust. I wrinkled my nose at it. Both smells hung in the air like a fog while we hurried through the hallway to Argall's converted office. The decor, and the state inside, wasn't much different from last time.

Everything was still a scattered mess, but at least it looked a little less like a battlefield. Someone, probably his assistant, Miss Stewart, had attempted to organize the chaos. Argall's desk was back upright, but there were still plenty of papers and books that had been tossed around with wild abandon.

"At least we don't have to worry about leaving anything out of place," I suggested.

Lysander shook his head at the haphazard stacks, which seemed to trail off onto the floor like an escape attempt.

"If he's really as tidy as he seemed, while the Death Whisper didn't kill him, the sight of all this might," he quipped with a sigh. "We best get started. I'll take the desk."

I nodded, then idly rubbed at the bruise around my left eye. This wasn't quite like looking for a needle in a haystack. Most haystacks are bigger than this. I looked around for where to start as the bruise nagged at me with a dull ache.

Moonlight played through the lone grime-stained window, pulling out long shadows across the room. The curtains almost seemed spectral, while shadows from bottles, trinkets, and shelves stretched out like the long, grasping claws of a forgotten nightmare.

Lysander pulled up a chair on the other side of the wide wooden desk, carefully opening drawers to rummage through their contents. I picked a thick collection of papers and a few books on the floor to the right.

As I set down the lantern on the corner of the desk, I realized this was close to where I found Argall during the Death Whisper attack. My right hand felt warm, but I shoved the memory aside and got to work.

I sifted through the stacks of paper, while Lysander was busy with three well-worn ledgers. For a few minutes, the sounds of rustling paper filled the room. Ghosts of a bookseller's past slowly appeared in writing. We hoped it would whisper something useful.

After what felt like almost half an hour, Lysander shifted in the chair as he stretched.

"Anything?" he asked in a low whisper.

I sighed, rubbing lightly at the bruise around my left eye again.

"Nothing yet," I replied, while I set aside another meticulously marked invoice. "Señor Argall has an alarming collection of invoices. Not all of them are for books." I studied a handwritten list in the feeble lantern's glow. "This is a list of books to purchase."

A slip of paper caught my eye after setting aside the book list on an unbalanced stack of paper to my right. I reached over, tugging out the mysterious paper from underneath the unread stack. It was one of Kingston's news broadsheets, dated a few days ago.

"'*Dockside Horror! Another Petrified Body Found!*'" I read in a low tone. There was an artist's sketch of the victim. A lifelike portrait that would live in my nightmares for a solid fortnight at least.

"Lysander, have you seen this?" I asked, waving him over. "It was last week."

He dropped the ledger he had found onto the desk, then walked over to look at the broadsheet with me.

"Oh, I remember this," Lysander commented quietly while he skimmed the article. After a second, he tapped it with the back of his hand. "Like it says here, the murders have been mostly happening near where Harbor and Hanover street cross. Out past the east end of the docks, where they talk about expanding Kingston."

He handed the broadsheet back to me and shrugged with a sigh.

"Each victim felt as dry as a mummy but was petrified wood. Died screaming, they say, or at least looked like it."

"Petrified victims?" I shot him an alarmed grimace. "How did I miss this?"

Lysander shrugged, patting me on the shoulder.

"You were buried in your potion brewing that week. Something about cleaning elixirs and tonics for a Comtessa?"

I nodded, raising my eyebrows at the memory of the stench those elixirs made. It took days to clear the air, and some of it still haunted a few pots.

"Oh, yes. The Comtessa and her blood-cleaning elixirs. Now I remember." A series of handwritten notes littered the margins of the broadsheet. "Look at this. It looks like Señor Argall's handwriting."

Lysander turned the edge of the page toward the lantern for better light. Then he squinted at the mangled scrawl.

"'*Who profits from this?*'" he read aloud. "'*Check warehouse again.*'" There was a sudden, confused look on his face. "Warehouse? He has a warehouse?"

"It would stand to good reason," I admitted. "Especially if he happens to have more than one copy of a book to sell. A lot of booksellers are doing that lately."

"But what else would he have there?" Lysander asked, raising his eyebrows.

There wasn't a good answer to that, other than to go find out.

I tapped at another handwritten note. "There's another one. '*Coincidence?*'" There was a line drawn from that to the murders. "Why would a bookseller be so interested in waterfront murders?"

"A new pastime?" Lysander replied with a faint grin.

I ignored the joke.

"It's like he's been looking into the deaths." I folded the broadsheet page carefully, tucking it away into my shoulder bag. Something about all this seemed off, but still it felt like we might be on the right path. A darker path, but still the right one.

"This doesn't feel like a coincidence," I said, glancing around the room. "But it also doesn't seem like what we're looking for. There has to be something else."

We returned to our search with a fervor. I'd started to lose a little hope, until Lysander let out a small laugh. He produced a well-used leather-bound journal from the depths of Joshua Argall's desk. The spine was cracked with wear, but the leather had been lovingly oiled and repaired in places.

"His appointment book," Lysander said, then spread the book open on the desk. I peered over his shoulder while he flipped quickly through the pages.

"There, what's that?" I put my hand down on a page, running a finger over an entry underlined twice. The lantern had to be nudged closer to make out the words.

"'*Visitor from San Germán? Brotherly advice? Discuss illness agai n.*'" I read aloud. "It seems the señor has a brother."

"That was early last week," Lysander commented curiously. "Argall was sick? He didn't look like anyone recovering from being sick."

"No, he didn't," I replied, as I flipped a few pages forward in the journal. A torn, loose piece of paper caught my eye.

"It's an order for an elixir," I said, holding it up for better light. "Argall has written on the side, '*regrettably treatments ineffective*'."

"When was that?" Lysander asked, glancing at the scrap of paper.

I turned the page over twice before I shook my head. "There's no date. It's been torn off."

Lysander scowled, flipping through a few more pages in the appointment book. Then he tapped one with a surprised smile.

"Oh, here's something." He ran a finger over a series of handwritten entries on a new page. "Argall wrote '*Lunch at home. Brother insists.*

Perhaps more unconventional methods needed.' Pedro, this was the day before he hired us."

"How many doubloons would you bet we were the 'unconventional method?'" I asked in a grim tone.

"That's a sucker's bet," Lysander replied, giving me a wry look. "Now this warehouse he mentioned? That's a bet I'd like to take."

I hurried around to the other side of the desk for the stack of invoices.

"You know, if he's storing books, there could be shipping manifests among those book lists and invoices," I said, snatching up a handful off the floor pile. "They might have an address."

I read through the top five papers, then tapped the sixth with the back of my hand.

"Which is right here." I arched an eyebrow at Lysander. "It's on Water Lane, a block away from Harbor Street at the east end. Sound familiar?"

Lysander shot me a surprised look.

"The murders," he said with a humorless laugh. "Pedro, now I *really* want to see this warehouse."

A rapid series of sharp, insistent taps against the grimy window from outside shattered the conversation.

"Elara," Lysander exclaimed softly, words tinted with concern.

My hand suddenly felt very warm to the point it ached at the knuckles.

She burst into the office two seconds later, wings folded tight against her back like drawn knives.

"Time to go!" she said with an alarmed expression.

"City watch?" I asked, stuffing the invoices into my bag next to the folded broadsheet.

"No," she said with a quick shake of her head. "A Death Whisper."

16

Aggressive Negotiations With a Bad Decision

July 28, 1722. Running through the streets of Kingston, Jamaica, while being chased by a golem in a very bad mood.

Elara saw the Death Whisper before the thing saw us. That alone bought us a few seconds to slip out the back of the bookshop, then escape down the alley for Hanover Street. Elara wanted to ambush it, then beat it apart. Lysander enthusiastically agreed.

I had other ideas.

"Have you lost all your senses?" Elara snapped at me with a sharp look while we ran for the waterfront.

"No, I haven't," I shot back with a glance over my shoulder. "They can talk, and have talked more than once! Our timing just needs to be right, along with the right motivation."

Our footsteps echoed like drumbeats in the darkness. The cobblestone streets were damp from mist, and the tall lanterns lining the road had already burned dim. Between their feeble islands of light and the pale moon overhead, the road was washed in an unearthly glow. It was that same heavy feeling of a disgruntled graveyard at the first touch of fog.

The Death Whisper ran, if not floated, quickly after us. Its flaming eyes were like hell and brimstone that burned hateful holes in the night. But its shrieks were the worst. They clawed at my nerves, making me almost question my idea. Almost.

"This is the *worst* place to try this," Lysander panted while he kept pace with us.

"There isn't anywhere else," I replied between breaths. "The bookshop was too close and confined." I pointed frantically ahead. "Turn west onto Harbor Street, just ahead. Look for barrels, crates, anything stacked tall."

Lysander gave me a surprised look.

"Harbor Street? The murders," he reminded me with a sharp look. "Is no one worried about the murders? This is where they happen."

"Very," I told him. "But I'm more worried about the Death Whisper. Look for crates, we'll trap it there."

We hesitated at the corner of Hanover and Harbor to catch our breath. Doubt clawed at my gut, trying to cut a hole up into my heart. I didn't blame Elara or Lysander for their reaction. We'd barely stopped the last few Death Whispers.

"This better work," Elara said grimly before she vaulted a stack of stray barrels at the corner. "If there's even a hint it won't, Pedro, I'm cutting the thing to ribbons."

"Trust me," I insisted. An overwhelming surge of heat throbbed in and around my right hand. "I have a feeling about this."

Past the corner, Elara cut west. Lysander and I were right on her heels. Our boots skidded on slick cobblestone and Lysander nearly lost his balance. I quickly caught his arm, then hauled him back to his feet.

After a nervous glance behind us, I pushed Lysander ahead of me while we darted down the street.

The cool misty air was a strange balm in my burning lungs. There was a dim promise of rain to it. In the distance, we heard the distant clamor of ships in the harbor. A ship's bell tolled the hour with a solemn echo. It was an eerie contrast to what was trying to run us down. Then I let out a humorless laugh, threaded with relief.

Outside a carpenter's shop called the *Cobbler's Wager* sat a cluster of wooden boxes bearing markings from the League of Nations. I had no idea what was in them, if anything, nor did I care. They were stacked three tall to the right of the front door. That would do nicely.

I stabbed a finger in the air toward them and lengthened my stride. The others nodded and followed.

We skidded to a stop beside the boxes. The sharp stench of rotten seaweed brushed past us on the evening breeze, trying to steal our breath. A tortured rattle battered the air. We spun around, glancing back for the Death Whisper.

It wasn't there. Not yet. But somehow, I knew it wasn't far away. We were almost out of time.

"Here?" Elara asked, voice clipped. Her wings flared out behind her from the tension, which cut an imposing silhouette against the street lantern's sickly yellow glow.

"Yes," I replied in a low tone before drawing in a deep breath. "It will have to do."

A faint surge of warmth poured up from my hand. I pointed to the crates, then waved back at the corner while I talked.

"Lysander? You and Elara crouch behind the crates. Stay in the shadows. I'll be out in front. Slam the Whisper into the wall once it reaches for me. After that, I'll try to use the ghostfire to subdue it, so we can get some answers."

"I *hate* this," Elara growled, eyes bright with concern. "I hate letting you walk out there like bloody fish bait for a shark!"

"Elara, we could finally learn more about who is behind this," I replied, unable to hide my exhaustion.

She glared at me. I frowned back.

Lysander's eyes darted between me and the corner behind us. Almost as if the Death Whisper had just charged around the corner.

"Pedro," he sighed, jaw tight. "I'm telling you, this is the worst trap idea I've ever seen. It won't fall for this. Death Whispers *can't* be that stupid or single-minded. Worse, you're the bait. It'll kill you!"

A flare of heat from my right hand made me glance over my shoulder for the Death Whisper. It wasn't there. Somehow, I just knew we only had seconds left.

"I've got the *Codex* page. Obvious or not, I'm counting on murderous greed over common sense. It'll head right for me." I made a shooing motion. "We're out of time! Go!"

Lysander narrowed his eyes but didn't press the matter. Elara looked fit to strangle me, which I probably deserved. I fully expected to suffer the full brunt of her anger once she cornered me alone.

That is, provided we lived to see tomorrow.

They scrambled behind the crates while I stepped out into the middle of the cobblestone street.

I was alone. The street was as empty as a fresh grave. Pale yellow light from the street lanterns danced a dying jig over the damp cobblestones.

Despite the ragged scream from my nerves, I planted my feet and waited. No matter what, I couldn't run. None of this would work if I did. After a second's thought, I took a deep breath of the damp harbor air to steady my nerves, then drew my sword. I wasn't going to use it, but the Whisper didn't know that.

Just then, the ugly truth of our situation stalked around the corner.

A skeletal hand covered in a pasty, papery skin grabbed the edge of a building at the far end of the street. Then the Death Whisper stepped out to face me.

Its eyes burned with blazing green flames. They spewed a sickly smoke that slid over the Whisper's head and ragged, unkempt blonde hair. A knot clenched in my stomach, then turned over, making me regret eating lunch. Like always, the Whisper was dressed in the tattered rags of a drowned sailor. The only thing clean on it was its eerie, glimmering cutlass.

Then the Whisper paused at the end of the street and tilted its head, considering me.

Panic needled me, but I stood my ground, holding my sword at the ready. The scars on my right hand burned hot. I could almost see them writhing eagerly from the corner of my eye. They hadn't caught fire, at least, not yet. I had the strange sense they were lying in wait, too.

Without warning, the Whisper's face split into a nightmarish grin, teeth jagged as a broken reef, jaw distended and unnaturally long. It laughed. A low, gurgling giggle that echoed through the heavy night air and crawled along my skin, leaving shivers in its wake.

"If you're done laughing at me, señor, I'd rather we get on with it," I snarled, with a bit more bravado than I felt. "Neither you, nor your master, are getting this 'soul anchor' page."

That did the trick.

It rushed down the street at me, shrieking like a noxious nightmare come to full, bloody life.

The Whisper closed the gap between us in a flash, slicing down at my chest. I stepped left and to the outside while I parried, then shoved the golem's sword arm aside.

"Now!" I cried.

Elara moved fast, erupting out from behind the crates. Every inch of her was all coiled instinct and purpose. A corsair captain to the core.

With a fierce yell, she threw herself at the Whisper, wings fluttering just enough to take flight. She shot straight at the golem like a thrown harpoon, sword ready. Lysander was right behind her, darting in low. She soared in on the left. He moved in on the right.

Too late, the Whisper tried to back away with a shriek. Elara stabbed the point of her short sword into its shoulder. Ghost blade magic sizzled at the Whisper's clothing. Lysander slammed into golem's other arm with all his strength.

Together, they dragged it off the street, bashing it against a nearby wall with a bone-jarring crunch.

As soon as they grabbed the Whisper, I threw down my sword and rushed after them. Fear and doubt burned away while greenish-white fire erupted around my right hand.

"Be quick!" Elara shouted over the shrieks. Then she slammed the golem back so its mangled head bounced off the wall. "We can't hold it much longer!"

I slapped my burning hand against the Whisper's dry-rotted chest. Did I know what I was doing? No. But I had a guess, and that would have to be enough.

The instant my hand touched the Whisper, the world drained away. All the evening sounds—from creaks of wood, to ships in the harbor, and even my friend's voices—faded like fog in the sun. All that was left was an odd warmth, and a twisted, muted light in front of me. Hazy, glowing threads that burrowed into the Death Whisper.

I locked eyes with the thing.

"Now. You, señor..." I snarled.

"Pull," urged a deep voice from somewhere inside my head, interrupting me.

I twitched, nearly pulling away in surprise.

"No," the voice insisted. *"Pull!"*

Heat flared, and the hazy, glowing threads grew brighter.

Elara and Lysander yelled something, but I missed it. My entire world had narrowed down to those threads.

I flexed my hand into a fist, and my fingers pulled the threads.

The golem's screams almost shattered stone. It fought with a renewed frenzy, wild and manic. Desperation squeezed my throat, but I clenched my jaw before I took a shaking breath.

Then I pulled with everything I had.

A sound like snapping sails and cracking timber echoed in my mind. I felt white liquid fire roll through my hand into my heart.

Suddenly, the Whisper exploded into a steaming mess of burnt paper, black ink, and putrid dust. As the golem dissolved, I yanked a ghostly figure free of the maelstrom.

We scrambled back as the ghost staggered forward in confusion. He blinked and looked at us with a stunned expression. Bits of golem rained behind him.

The ghost was a human sailor, or had been when alive. He wore a faded red headscarf around his translucent head and sandy colored hair. The man's clothing was threadbare, if not stained in spots, along his shirt, trousers, and vest. It was all spectral, but real enough from the memory of the man in life. At best, or worst, he looked like he had been in his thirties when he died.

I clenched my right hand into a fist, extinguishing the flames, even while I felt that liquid fire settle inside my chest. A whirlwind of emotions, from shock to elation, rolled through me.

"It worked," I muttered wearily.

Elara glanced at me, then narrowed her eyes at the ghost, keeping her sword at the ready.

Lysander just let out a nervous laugh that hung somewhere between disbelief and amazed.

"Well, now what?" he asked curiously with a shrug.

I started to reply, but the ghost beat me to it.

He looked at us through storm-cloudy eyes that sparkled with a hint of amusement. Then his lips curled into a delighted grin.

"You've my thanks for this," he rasped with the echo of a dead man's voice. "I'm truly grateful, but," the twinkle in his eyes brightened, "I believe you three might have a question or two to ask of me?"

"One or two, señor," I answered with a small grin. "At the very least, one or two."

17

Ghosts, Golems, and Aggressive Gardening

July 28, 1722. On the damp streets of Kingston, Jamaica. Facing a glimpse of the future...

I had no idea who or what that voice was that I heard in my mind when I pulled the ghost free. It wasn't the ghost, and I didn't have time to figure it out.

"We should head for the harbor, or someplace near it, away from prying eyes," Elara suggested. Then she gave the ghost an uneasy look. "Those shrieks were loud enough to rattle windows. Someone is bound to come looking."

I recovered my sword, then the four of us walked down Harbor Street and turned south on Georges Lane for the docks. Any route at all would've been fine, so long as we put as much distance between us and the golem's remains as possible. The idea was to appear normal, or as normal as three people walking with a ghost could look. Obviously, that wouldn't be much, but I held out some hope.

Five minutes later, once we were much closer to the docks, I cleared my throat. Having any sort of conversation with a ghost was still rather new for me.

"Señor," I began. "Despite how we met, if I may? I am Doctor Pedro Sangre. These are my close friends and companions, Lysander Riverwind, and Captain Elara Blackwater of the *Silk Duchess*."

The ghost nodded, then touched two fingers to the side of his head. A blue-white corpse light flickered in his cloudy eyes with what might have been recognition at Elara's name.

"Renwick. Renwick Taggert," he said with a mild Scottish brogue. "So then, it was you who blasted me out of that thing?"

"Indeed, señor," I confirmed.

"Though, maybe not as planned as it should've been," Lysander muttered lightly, with a pained look in my direction.

Renwick rubbed the back of his neck absentmindedly. "Well, surprise or no, like I said, I can't thank you enough for that. Being stuffed into that thing weren't too much fun. It's nothing but anger, spit, and bile once you're trapped inside."

Then he gave Elara a pensive look.

"Blackwater. I know that name," he said warily. "Are you the Captain Blackwater that slipped the Trade Syndicate near Pearl Island? Making off with that load of timber, spices, and medicines?"

"Yes," Elara replied evenly. "That medicine went to the local towns to put an end to the fever burning through them. As for the rest," she shrugged, "just a finder's fee."

Lysander chuckled dryly. "It's not like the Syndicate missed any of it. Probably stole half of it themselves."

Elara crossed her arms and fixed the ghost with a suspicious stare.

"So, you're serving under Storm?" she asked Renwick. There was a faint sigh with some steel hidden behind her words, like a concealed dagger. "He put you up to this with the Death Whisper?"

Renwick's expression flickered with a mix of remorse and resentment.

"Was. Am," he replied in a sour tone. "I first served aboard the *Far Ranger* for the Trade Syndicate, the East India branch. Cap'n Storm took the *Ranger*, and I was a survivor. Seemed wise to join his crew when he offered. The alternative wasn't healthy."

He paused, glancing up at the night sky while we walked, spectral hands clenched into fists.

"So then, I became one of his gunners on the *Rising Eel*, Cap'n." Renwick's expression turned hard. "At least, I was, until they put the Choice to me."

"The Choice?" I asked warily, even though I had a vague, unpleasant feeling as to what he meant.

"Either be fed to that hell-cursed arcane engine, or shoved into a Death Whisper golem. I chose the Whisper." Renwick's dead voice echoed with a bitter tone. "Again, seemed healthier."

"Fed to the engine?" Lysander repeated slowly, with a concerned look. "You mean sent? What happens to anyone sent to the engine?"

Renwick didn't say a word. Instead, he replied with a small, thin smile that lacked any humor to it at all.

A morbid silence wrapped around us like a thick burial shroud for a few paces down the road. The ghost cleared his spectral throat.

"You've other questions, I take it?" he asked lightly.

I raised my eyebrows at everything that wasn't said, but still pushed on.

"What do you know about the *Codex Luminari?*" I asked. Just in case, I gave a rough description of the book's appearance. "Your captain, as best I understand it, is cursed to protect it. Is that same curse on you?"

"Not entirely sure," Renwick replied with a small shrug. "But I think all of us aboard the *Eel* are. As for having seen the book? I have. It's always in the hands of that little man out fretting on deck for one reason or another. He keeps it with him no matter what, reading some note, design, or something."

"This man, do you know his name?" Lysander asked curiously. "What does he look like?"

"Oh, short man. Human." Renwick cast a pensive look at the near-cloudless night sky. "Five foot four, if I put a guess to it. Light brown hair, going a bit bald. Blue-gray eyes. Mostly thin. Has a rough cough that comes over him occasionally. The captain calls him 'Argall'. No idea if that's his given name, or family name."

Elara's eyes glittered dangerously. "Joshua Argall?"

"The ledger in the bookshop mentioned a brother, and something about an illness," Lysander pointed out.

Renwick gave us an awkward half-shrug, voice rich with a dead man's echo. He raised his eyebrows, lips pulled tight.

"Brother or no, that one's mad as a hatter. Dangerous as a rattled snake, too." His eyebrows found a way to reach higher. "Whispers to that book like it's alive. Goes on about ending death, bringing the dead back to life." Renwick gestured to himself with a half-grin. "Not that I'm too much against that last one, mind you."

"I'd expect not, señor," I said, smiling at his gallows humor.

Elara frowned over all of this. Joshua Argall had rattled Elara from the moment they met. She told me later when we were alone, the look in his eyes was unsettling. I had a guess that all this about the man having a brother, who was likely twisted up in necromancy, shook her even more. I knew it brought back other bad memories for her.

"How do we even know that isn't actually Joshua Argall?" she asked with a strained look.

Lysander shrugged. "We can check again, Elara, but Mr. Argall's still in the hospital, last I saw. His mind's not really even there when you talk to him."

"But," he half-crossed his arms and rubbed his chin, "if he's really on the *Rising Eel*, that would be quite the trick. Mr. Argall would have to give the nuns the slip to escape the hospital. After that, steal a boat if one wasn't waiting for him." Lysander's grin was almost infectious. "I'd put my money on the nuns. They'd catch him at twenty paces."

Elara replied with a thoughtful hum, but kept the rest to herself.

The topic changed as Elara and Lysander peppered Renwick with questions about the *Rising Eel*, details and questions around her ship class, how many cannons, and the like. But I was still focused on Renwick himself.

This man, or rather ghost, was a stark contrast from the Death Whisper he had been minutes before. Grateful and helpful instead of murderous. I also caught the bitter tone about his service to Captain Storm. This wasn't entirely a surprise, since it sounded like Renwick had been press ganged into service. I had a feeling he'd overheard a great deal while aboard the *Eel* that he hadn't mentioned. When Elara and Lysander's questions slowed down, I jumped in with my own.

"Señor," I began. "Do you know of a warehouse? One this Argall might have mentioned?" Then I waved a hand idly back at the bulk of Kingston. "Say, not far from here?"

The ghost pursed his lips while he gazed up at the sky again in thought.

"No, can't say that I have. He's gone ashore a few times, even here in Kingston. But no one's ever mentioned a warehouse that I've heard."

"Where's the *Eel* now?" Elara asked. There was a hard edge like polished wood to her voice, as if preparing for a fight.

"No idea," Renwick replied as he shook his head. "Truly. Probably harassing the shipping lanes." The solemn echo in his voice broke a little. "Grabbing crews for that cursed engine, most likely."

Elara clenched her jaw a little. To be honest, I did, too.

"So not nearby?" Lysander asked with a disappointed frown.

"Doubt it," the ghost said. "When any Death Whisper is sent out, the *Eel* drops anchor close. Those golem bodies don't float, and walking on the sea floor isn't all that good for them. Once the Death Whispers are away, the *Eel* weighs anchor, then makes herself scarce."

Renwick stopped walking at the entrance to a barely lit side street that ran right to the docks. In the distance, ink dark water lapped at shadowed piers with a hungry sound. Slowly, he grimaced, almost mournfully.

"Overheard today that the work with that demonic engine is going too slow. Not enough people being sent to it. There had been a plan to grab the sea hag of Port Royal, and put her to the engine."

"We tossed some rum in those waters," Elara replied with a faint note of satisfaction. A small smile tugged at her lips.

"Cap'n Storm didn't take that well," he replied, grinning, but it faded fast. "Argall raged like a wet hen when that plan failed, demanding to step up the work. Grab something stronger. Even ordered the captain to open fire on a fishing town. I'll tell you, Storm didn't like that one bit."

The ghost was silent for a heartbeat, eyes clouded, before he shuddered just a little. The kind of shudder only Death brought when he passed by.

"Even that didn't help, or really do whatever he was hoping would happen."

The Death Whispers themselves came back to mind.

"Renwick?" I asked slowly. "We fought four other Death Whispers before you." A pause filled the air while I gave Elara and Lysander an uneasy glance. "Did whoever was inside those three golems return to the *Rising Eel?*"

The ghost's chuckle was humorless and hollow, like an empty casket.

"Oh, that they did," he replied in a low tone. "Each one came right back to the *Eel.* Argall had them put to the engine for failing."

Lysander's mouth pulled into a tight, flat line. Next to him, Elara looked away to the harbor while a string of bitter curses brushed under her breath.

As for me, I rubbed the bridge of my nose, then let out a slow sigh. Being sent back was just what I was afraid would happen. Only the truth was much worse. I wasn't sure knowing made me feel any better.

"Begging your pardon," Renwick said softly, breaking the silence. "What now? As I know it, I should've faded, but here I am."

I started to reply, but stopped, puzzled.

"I'm not sure, señor. Is that how it happens with the others?"

Renwick nodded slowly. "About like. They jerked back into their bodies as if struck by lightning, raving about the world fading."

"What?" Elara said sharply, wide-eyed. "Their *bodies?*"

The dead man shrugged.

"Aye, Captain. Bodies frozen by magic on Dryden Storm's ghost ship."

Suddenly the air felt tense as Lysander's eyes went wide in alarm.

"Pedro!" Lysander exclaimed, lunging forward.

He grabbed me by the front of my coat, then yanked as a shadow loomed behind me. At the same time, a hand latched onto my shoulder from behind with an iron grip. A quick twist to the side yanked me loose, while Renwick and Elara stepped back in surprise.

I spun around in time to watch an older man, dressed like any other dockworker along the waterfront, wither into a wooden statue. His face froze into a pleading, silent scream. A perfect carving of petrified terror. All around us, the air went heavy with the fresh scent of tree sap and rotten wood.

Another murder victim, just like from the broadsheets.

Only this one was fresh.

The killer had to be nearby. I yanked my sword free from its scabbard, looking around in alarm.

"We need the city watch," I said in a low, quick voice.

"On it!" Lysander raced down the damp cobblestone street to rouse the evening watch.

I met Renwick's worried eyes.

There was no way to explain him—if anyone could see him, that is—and he knew it.

"We'll need to hide you," I told him.

I just wasn't sure how.

18

Mostly Dead, Mostly Right

July 30, 1722. Brewed Gambit Alchemy Shop on Harbor Street in Kingston, Jamaica. Brewing potions and stirring my thoughts...

I gently rubbed a small amount of the yellow-white cream that Morowen gave me onto the dark bruise beside my left eye. It was cool and soothing, right until I felt a sharp needle of pain. I winced.

"A day," I growled to myself in the mirror. "We lost an entire day sorting out that murder victim."

I closed my eyes and sighed while I leaned against the washbasin.

There had been questions and more questions from the city watch. After a while, the sergeant's tone went from suspicious to sympathetic when the reality of what we said sank in.

We didn't kill the man, but just had the horrible luck to be there when he died. To be there and have no way to help him.

"I feel sorry for the man who died, but why do I feel like he was used?" I shook my head a little. "Maybe I'm simply jumping at shadows."

The rest of yesterday had been a blur. Our late night encounter with the dying man meant we had to spend most of the day with the city watch. There were questions, and still more questions—in particular did we know our new dead acquaintance and why we were nearby.

But after a lengthy study by two surgeons and a wavebinder, we were declared curse and petrification-free. Luckily, they didn't find a hint about Renwick, despite looking for ghosts. So, in this case, I assumed that perhaps not all ghosts are dead.

Still, we had lost an entire day sorting all that out.

"How much damage can Captain Storm and Argall do in a day?" I muttered under my breath.

The answer was as plain as the bruise around my eye.

"A lot," I sighed. "More than I want to think about."

I clenched my jaw, then rubbed a little more cream over my black eye. It faded quickly into my skin.

The sea hag's mixture had done its job well. The black and purple bruise had already started to fade back to the natural olive tone of my skin. I hated to admit that Morowen was right, but she was right.

A healing potion would've been faster, but that can only do so much. Potions, even enchantments, repair the cuts, stabs, and breaks, but the body always remembers the pain. That it *should* be in pain. Potions can't get rid of that, but the sea hag's cream did.

Sadly, neither could help my mood.

I rubbed my eyes as I walked back to the front of the shop. The scent of slow boiling potions met me at the doorway like a perfumer's soft kiss. Odors of garlic, clove and oregano drifted in the air, stirring memories of potions past. This one would be an elixir for bad joints, if I didn't overcook it.

Sebastian, awake from a nap, landed on a chair I kept next to the washroom door. The gargoyle's landing was a tumble of speckled sandstone bat wings and eagerness. I scratched him between the ears and horns.

"Happy to be home from Skaldi's forge?" I asked with a small grin. "Nibble on his blacksmith tools again? I bet I owe him a new hammer."

Sebastian rumbled cheerfully back at me, then jumped down to inspect his food bowl. I refilled it before I went to glance inside a pair of copper pots suspended in the fireplace. Blue-green liquid bubbled merrily inside.

"A few minutes longer will do," I muttered. "Maybe a little more diced garlic? More garlic and cloves. The miller likes garlic and cloves in his joint potions, anyway. Thinks they add a better kick to the magic."

I carefully measured out the herbs on a nearby wooden cutting board, then closed my eyes to concentrate. Under my breath, I sang a low shanty to center my thoughts. Slowly, I waved my hand in front of me, then pressed my palm down toward the herbs.

Between tune and concentration, I felt a flow of power, like a trickle of water, run from the Etherwave Arcana through me. The amber-gold energy felt soft, almost damp, like potter's clay. Quickly, I shaped the light into symbols to paint across the herbs.

My mind wandered back to the bookshop. Notes in a ledger drifted through my thoughts, followed by Captain Storm's laugh. Then came the image of a petrified dockworker that screamed with the shriek of a Death Whisper.

Also, there was that voice I heard when I freed Renwick from the golem. Solid. Deep. Yet it was a soft whisper that seemed to roar like distant waves.

The amber-gold magic evaporated instantly, and a small headache punched behind my eyes. My right hand suddenly burned, and the room swayed. Desperately, I grabbed a nearby vial of my lime green medicine that I had named the 'graveyard syrup', and downed it in one swallow.

It still tasted like toad sweat and despair.

"*Maldita sea!*" I swore in my native Spanish and scowled while I hammered a fist against the counter.

Jars and spoons jostled on the table. Even my shoulder bag I'd left in a nearby chair tumbled to the floor. Its contents spilled across the dusky stone floor tiles, including the *Codex* page.

There was a sharp scent of brine, followed by a fog of black mist, as Renwick materialized next to both the page and my worktable.

The page was where, and how, I hid Renwick in a fit of desperation. Fortunately, my guess was right that the man could 'hide' inside the page as a ghost. Especially since he was cursed to protect the *Codex,* even if it was just a single page.

Unsettling? Yes. But when compared to everything else, his entrance wasn't that difficult to deal with.

"Then again, I'm not sure 'normal' and my life are on speaking terms right now," I muttered to myself.

The ghost of the sandy-haired gunner's mate with the faded red headscarf yawned once, then rubbed his spectral-cloudy eyes. He gave the pots, bottles, and brewing apparatus a dubious frown.

"So, this is what you get up to when you've got yourself in knots?" Renwick said in his usual Scottish brogue.

"What?"

I gave him a puzzled look while I picked up my bag and spilled contents from the floor. Most I returned to the chair, but the *Codex* page went on the table.

"Brew and hit tables, I mean." He crossed his arms. "I felt that punch all the way inside the page. Most folks I've known just whittle when they're upset."

"It isn't like that," I replied, a little more sharply than I intended. A frustrated sigh later, I shook my head.

"Maybe it is," I corrected myself glumly as I ran a hand through my hair. After that, I reached over to stir the bubbling potions so they wouldn't burn.

"I just need to sort something out," I added. More than a little frustration underscored my words.

Out of the corner of my eye, I noticed Renwick glance at me with a sad, almost bemused expression. Then he nodded.

"Ah," he said in a wistful, haunted voice. "Well, you've no reason to trust me. Not a bit. But mark me, I've known others like you, Doctor. You're the kind willing to dive in on your own with both hands to save a life, or solve a problem. Good on you for it, too. They are too many in the world who don't bother. You saved me, and I owe you."

The ghost walked back around the table to run a spectral finger lightly across the *Codex* page.

"I've no love lost for Storm or his crew." Renwick's spectral eyes turned hard. "They press ganged me into service. My own crew? Storm and his people killed them." He shook his head sadly. "I have no crew."

Then he leaned over the worktable toward me and stabbed a ghostly finger in my direction.

"But you do," Renwick said in a stern tone. "It looks to me you're about to try to carry all this yourself. Don't do it."

The ghost lightly tapped the *Codex* page.

"I don't understand all of what's happening. After all," he grinned, "I'm just a man who's only 'mostly dead', with a body frozen by magic on a ghost ship." Then his expression turned serious. "But I do know when things get bad, you trust those close to you. You trust your crew. Otherwise it'll eat you up inside."

I met his gaze, then glanced down at the cutting board without a word, my thoughts in a whirlwind. After a deep breath, I hummed the same shanty as before, pulling down the Etherwave Arcana's power to me. This time, when I molded the magic into glowing alchemy symbols of growth and renewal, it worked. Both the diced garlic and cloves gave off a soft green light as I dumped them into the lightly boiling potions.

The burbling sound of the cooking potions filled the empty space around us.

"You have a good point, señor." A smile tugged at the corner of my mouth before I let go of a soft chuckle. "Lysander would accuse me of being dramatic. Elara would give me that 'stop brooding and get moving' look. Skaldi and Durner? Well, I won't even go there."

I reached over and pulled both pots away from the fire to let them simmer and cool. No one likes to drink hot potions. Well, almost no one, and those were potions with scorpion peppers.

"Think it through," I muttered. "I just need to think it through."

My thoughts churned like well-oiled gears, spinning in a clock. Pieces clicked and snapped while the portrait of a plan took shape. I glanced at Renwick.

Trust was hard, but it needed to start somewhere.

Ghost, half-ghost, or something else, I felt Renwick had been nothing but honest. Both relieved and honest, really. So, he deserved the same in return. Besides, he'd been around the source of the problem, so he might've heard something helpful.

"This started with Joshua Argall," I said, staring off at nothing in particular. "A bookseller here in Kingston."

"The one whose kin you're thinking is aboard the *Rising Eel?*" Renwick asked curiously.

I nodded.

"The same." I crossed my arms, leaned back, then tapped my chin. "Señor Argall mentioned a 'wood boned man'. That, and these murders that turn people to wood, don't seem to fit. So, setting those aside, the bookseller's ledger had notes about a brother, and mentioned an illness."

Renwick shrugged. "The man with the book aboard the *Eel* was coughing enough for two people."

I raised my eyebrows at that.

"If he's the brother, and is dying, it explains a few things." My expression turned pensive. "Such as why Señor Argall, the bookseller, wanted the *Codex,* and why he lied to us, saying it only held maps."

Renwick looked an equal blend of shocked and disturbed at the same time.

"Oh, well now. That explains the man's ravings about 'curing death' and 'freeing him'." His eyebrows bunched together. "Also, it means that hell-cursed arcane engine is some sort of necrotic engine, doesn't it?"

"Something like it," I confirmed. "Supposedly, it'll rip a hole right into the land of the dead to yank a very bad man free." I sighed a bit. "It'll also let out whatever nasty thing that wants to come crawling through, too."

I snapped my fingers.

"Captain Storm is after me to put the book back to stop this, because he can't. But the man you saw aboard the *Eel?* That's different." I leaned forward and tapped my worktable. "He's gotten desperate."

I counted off the reasons on my fingers.

"First, he tried to power the necrotic engine with Storm's crew. That didn't work, so he went after the sea hag of Port Royal. When that failed, he put a fishing town to the torch, but even that didn't give him what he wanted."

Renwick flinched at the mention of the fishing town massacre.

"True," Renwick said, then frowned. "You're going somewhere with this."

I gave him a thoughtful look.

"You could say that. The man with the *Codex* doesn't want power. He wants a certain *type* of power. Not victims, not anymore. He's looking for an *amplifier.*" I reached over and patted the yellowed, torn page on the table. "Probably because he doesn't have this."

An idea or two leaped to mind. I didn't like either one.

"I think I know where he'll strike next."

The bell at the front door jingled as the door opened.

I exchanged a look with Renwick, and he vanished back into the *Codex* page with a brief burst of dark fog and the scent of brine.

Elara walked briskly between the scant shelves and two lone chairs toward my worktable. Once she caught sight of me, her shoulders relaxed a little, wings looking more like a cloak and less like sharpened glass knives. A subtle, silent sign of relief.

"You weren't at the docks or merchant row this morning," she said, sounding a bit tired. "I was worried."

A smile tugged at my lips again.

"You're just in time, *querida.* I was about to stop myself from running off like an overdramatic fool."

19

Mysterious Maps and Bleeding Ink

July 30, 1722. Brewed Gambit Alchemy Shop, Kingston, Jamaica. Charting the truth, even though it hurt...

"You've been up to something," Elara told me suspiciously.

The captain raised a thin eyebrow at me. A dozen other silent expressions warned that I'd better explain myself, and quick.

I raised my hands in defense.

"I've just been brewing a batch of tonic for a customer while talking with Renwick," I explained. "Which, I think, helped decipher something about our current problem."

Arms crossed, Elara leaned against a nearby window with a skeptical look on her face. Next to her, the mid-morning light slipped by her side, casting her in a warm, half-light.

From shirt to vest to boots, she looked every bit the commanding captain, with just a hint of intimidating. The short sword and flintlock at her belt completed the look. But it was her raised eyebrows that told the true story. I'd definitely roused her curiosity.

It didn't take long to repeat the conversation I had with Renwick, along with my slightly wild theories. I did my best not to sound like a raving loon. The more I explained, the deeper she frowned. Finally, she pulled over a chair to the other side of my worktable and sat down.

"An amplifier?" Elara grimaced. "It sounds more to me like you're talking about a sacrifice."

I shook my head and shrugged.

"Maybe? It's hard to ignore, *querida,*" I admitted. "There's a trail of bodies already a good mile wide, and it's growing."

Elara sighed, then gently dragged a hand over her face.

"Well, it fits with everything else so far. Now I'm very glad I sent the others out where I did."

"What?"

She fixed me with an even, stern stare from her jade-gold eyes. There was a flicker of unease half-hidden behind them.

"I sent the others to the hospital to check on Joshua Argall, and also run down other things we've been trying to chase."

A small surge of frustration welled up inside me, and I sat forward in my chair. But Elara was ready and waiting. She raised a hand to stave off my tirade.

"Don't you even start," she ordered. "Yes, we've been hounded by Death Whispers, but even you have to admit they aren't lurking behind every corner."

I opened my mouth to reply, but closed it, then sat back with a silent, stubborn nod.

Elara narrowed her eyes at me.

"Pedro, you've looked like a ghost since Port Royal." A brief flash of concern crossed her face. "If left alone, you'll work yourself to exhaustion. I wanted to make sure you had a real chance to catch your breath."

She waved a hand at my workshop with its brewing and alchemy apparatus.

"At least, rest in your own way, that is. We all agreed."

This time, I raised an eyebrow at her.

"We?"

A mischievous grin flashed across her face.

"We. Lysander, Skaldi, Durner, and myself."

The silence hit like a cannon shot, sharp and sudden, before she broke it with a sigh.

"*Asa mvur,* we need you whole and alive." She pursed her lips, adding softly, "I mean that. Just like I meant what I told you aboard the *Silk Duchess.*"

I blew out a breath, then watched the sunlight through the window tease its way across a shelf of potions to my left. The rainbow of light cast through the enchanted liquids danced cheerfully against the wall. Renwick's words about 'trust your crew' floated back to me.

Words swung through my mind like loose rigging. Phrases like thick-headed, daft, hare-brained, and egotistical loomed large. Death-wish was also tangled up in there. I don't consider myself a brilliant man, but I certainly know when I've been out maneuvered for my own good.

"All right," I told her, holding up my hands, then letting them drop into my lap.

Suddenly, I felt more tired than I realized. Had I slept, or did I dream it? It could have been a little of both.

"My captain? I surrender. So, tell me, what did everyone find?"

Elara glanced around to locate a chair, then sat across the worktable from me. The smile on her face was one of a cat with fresh cream.

"I scattered everyone out to cover as much ground as I could," she explained. "Lysander and Skaldi went to the hospital to pay a visit with

Joshua Argall. Durner? I had him keeping an eye on the *Duchess*, but also ask around about that fishing town Storm attacked. There might have been survivors."

"And you?" I asked, crossing my arms.

She shrugged as if it was nothing, which meant it wasn't.

"I tracked down Argall's warehouse," Elara explained, then vaguely waved a hand at me. "But let me start back with what the others found first."

"Fair enough," I replied.

"Lysander and Skaldi sent me a message about our *lovely* employer," Elara said sardonically. "Mr. Argall was still mumbling to himself until Skaldi yelled at him. As it turns out, being accused of murdering a whole fishing town had an effect."

I pinched the bridge of my nose. "Skaldi isn't known for diplomacy."

Elara's smile twisted into a sly grin.

"He isn't, but that's why Lysander was with him." Elara interlaced her fingers in her lap. "It also worked. Our Mr. Argall had a lot to say between sobs and apologies. Turns out, he was trying to help his dying brother."

"So he does have a brother?"

Elara nodded, her grin brighter.

"Lucas Argall from San Germán. A skilled wavebinder who fell sick a year ago while working for the Trade Syndicate. No idea about the illness, but what Mr. Argall described reminded me of our dead dockworker."

That got all of my attention. My wooden chair squeaked while I shifted position and tugged at my chin.

"That could explain the 'wood boned man'," I mused aloud.

"I'm sure it does," Elara replied firmly. "I've a guess that our good Joshua didn't expect his brother to attack him with Death Whispers to take the book."

I tapped a finger against my chin while I added this to my theory.

"So Lucas Argall, dying and impatient, attacks his brother to get the *Codex,*" I recited slowly. "But Lucas found more than he expected, since Renwick said Lucas talks to the book constantly."

I glanced over and met Elara's uneasy expression. A jade-gold eyed mirror of my own thoughts.

"Driven mad by the ghost of Tristam Greenholm in the *Codex,*" I suggested. "It would explain some of this unholy taste for mass murder. What about Durner?"

Elara glanced at her hands, lips pulled into a complicated line of anger and sympathy.

"There were a few survivors. Ten at most. Durner found them hiding in Kingston's pauper graveyard out of terror. They've been rounded up and sent to the nuns at the hospital."

I winced from a stab of deep sympathy. A sad, dark expression clouded Elara's eyes.

"They said a brigantine sailed in close, opened fire, then sent in the fiends. Two volleys, then slaughter. When there was nothing but bodies and burning buildings, they left. The survivors hid in the nearby woods."

I felt a warm fire ignite in my right hand as I made a fist. A deep, low voice whispered in the back of my thoughts. I ignored it.

"Maldita sea," I swore low under my breath, eyes squeezed shut.

I pulled my anger under control with no small effort. Slowly, I tapped my clenched fist against my forehead. Finally, I met Elara's pained glance with a sigh.

"And the warehouse?" I asked, voice brittle.

She inclined her head.

"Those invoices you collected did have an address. Two blocks south of the bookshop." She let a heartbeat pass. "We met a dead man there."

I stared, wide-eyed, as that rang a nasty bell in my mind.

"The dying dockworker? There?"

"Yes, right outside it," she confirmed in a tight voice. "It's mostly filled with boxes of books and trinkets. But on the east side, there's a clear space near a locked door with some blankets and a small iron stove."

Elara gestured to my fireplace and my brewing tools. "There's even brewing pots and copper tubing like yours."

"What? Brewing?"

"Brewing," she repeated. "They looked recently used. But someone had taken pains to clear out in a hurry. There wasn't much to look through, and someone came in while I was searching around."

"Did they see you?" I asked, concerned. "Who were they?"

The captain shook her head, then brushed a stray strand of chestnut hair from her face.

"I've no idea," she admitted. Frustration stalked behind her words. "It was just one person, but I had to leave before I could see them."

I nodded, tugging at my chin again in thought.

"Has anyone mentioned the *Rising Eel* being in port?" I asked. "Storm has a reputation. People might notice."

Elara shook her head a little.

"Not a word," she said, then waved a hand in the vague direction of the docks. "That doesn't mean they aren't nearby. Heaven knows that they could be anchored out of sight, then come ashore elsewhere. Jamaica is an island."

I grunted a little in acknowledgment.

"Then it's likely not Lucas Argall, Captain Storm, or his crew." I frowned at where my thoughts went. "Ignoring the city watch, that leaves... who? Joshua Argall's assistant, Señorita Stewart? Why would she be there?"

"Other than it belongs to Mr. Argall? Possibly for this," Elara said.

She pulled an old piece of folded parchment from inside her vest. It was a map, or a part of one. Obviously torn, it was also a little burned where it had once been part of a larger map.

"This shows the waters and islands around Jamaica." She stood and unfolded the map across my worktable. "The map seems recent, and someone has been charting locations on it."

She tapped her fingers next to different numbers at locations near Kingston, Port Royal, and places in between.

"Look here," she added, tapping a finger to a spot outside Port Royal.

My blood chilled. Elara and I had been there only a few days ago.

"That's where the sea hag's house is," I said, alarmed. "At least close to it, anyway."

"Yes," Elara ran a hand through her chestnut hair, mouth in a tight line again. "That isn't the only marked location we've been to, either. Some are in Kingston, others not."

I sat heavily back in my chair, stunned, not sure what to say.

Elara threw up her hands. "How far ahead did they plan this? This could have been quick calculations, but... was it? It isn't like we can just look at what they wrote and tell when it was written to see what's coming."

"Don't be so sure," I said slowly, with a small grin.

I picked up the piece of map, then ran to the sunlight with it. Once there, I leaned close. I didn't care about the map or numbers, but the ink used.

"If this is iron gall ink," I explained, "it'll take on an oily or glossy sheen in the light if the writing's fresh. The older it gets, the more it turns brown."

Elara joined me, then leaned in close, squinting at the ink.

"They could've used another ink," she said.

"Could," I agreed. "But likely not. Iron gall's very cheap, and Joshua Argall would've had plenty given his profession. I see four locations that could've been recently written." I glanced at my potion shelves. "But there's another way to narrow this down."

I handed the map to Elara and rushed to the shelves. Quickly, I grabbed two potions, returned to my worktable, then pulled out the cork stoppers. Carefully, I mixed a portion of each into a new bottle. The final mix bubbled maniacally, giving off an acrid fizz.

"Dry ink is difficult to remove," I commented idly while I stirred the mixture. "Fresh? It's easier. A mix of watered-down wood alcohol with an acid I prepared yesterday might help narrow down the freshness."

Elara smoothed the map flat on the worktable. Using a narrow wooden stir stick, I dropped a bit of the potion at the edge of each suspicious number. Then we waited.

"I've not been to any of those locations," Elara admitted while my acrid potion fizzed on the parchment. "They could be anything from nothing, to a small fishing or pirate town."

I opened the *Codex* page, then tapped a set of faded numbers in the margin. Ones that had appeared during the incident in Lyra Valtor's workshop.

"Possibly, but one set of those numbers from the map matches this."

I grabbed a pen and ink to underline the faded numbers on the page. Then I copied the various notes from the burned map, just in case my mild acid was more than mild.

But the precaution wasn't needed. The nasty mix had done its work. Bits of ink bled away, the oily sheen easily apparent. I tapped the ones that stood out.

"So, we've two locations, *querida*. Also, I very much want to know what was being brewed at the warehouse. Maybe even see what's behind that locked door."

Elara crossed her arms, raising her eyebrows at me.

"So we go back tonight?"

I shook my head a little, folding the *Codex* page.

"There's no time. We need to go now with someone who has the keys," I replied. "We need to speak to Señorita Stewart."

Then I snapped a cork into the bottle with a pop.

"Especially before anyone tries to lock us out of that warehouse with fire instead of a key."

20

Murder Alleys and Bad Deals

July 30, 1722. Bennington Warehouses. A block from the Kingston docks. For some reason, I'm always there at night...

Keys rattled like a broken alarm bell while we unlocked the warehouse door. One lock click later, and I gladly left the alley and its wandering shadows behind. Prowling around dark murder alleys at night had become an alarming habit.

"The broadsheets reported the murders have been happening all along the street outside," Miss Primrose Stewart said nervously. "I told Mr. Argall this warehouse wasn't a good idea, but he insisted he got a good deal."

Her eyes cut toward the yellow, smudge-stained windows just past the forest of crates. Pale, sickly moonlight slithered in around the stains.

"I'm not certain how good a deal it really was," she admitted to us with a rueful look.

Miss Stewart had mostly recovered from the Death Whisper attack the other day. But while she hid it well, she was still a bit jumpy. I didn't blame her one bit, given the shrieking things had been trying to gleefully live in my own nightmares.

She wore a modest powder-blue dress, sleeves and hem smudged with a little dust. We'd interrupted her cleaning the bookshop for reopening to drag her into our dubious warehouse adventure.

Primrose cast a weary, nervous glance at the looming stacks of crates around us. Walkways wound between those stacks like narrow paths through a madman's maze. She shoved a loose strand of her light ash-blonde hair behind an ear with a trembling hand. A sigh slipped out of her a moment later.

Elara gave me a slightly concerned look, then put a comforting arm around the younger woman. Quietly, she whispered a reassuring word or two that I didn't quite make out. Primrose nodded, then straightened her spine.

"Those pots and blankets and all are this way," Primrose told us in a thin voice. "It's unthinkable that Mr. Argall allowed this, or never told me he had a brother! But now I understand why he didn't want me helping him with the inventory here."

On the way to get Primrose's help with the warehouse, Elara and I debated how much the young woman knew. Did she know about her employer's true interest in the *Codex* or about Lucas Argall, Joshua's brother? Did the bookseller keep his assistant in the dark about it all?

We never quite settled that debate. At least, not until now.

Primrose suddenly paused and fretted over a small box out of place among the forest of head-high stacked crates. How she knew that on sight was beyond me. Most likely it was the cryptic number system on the crates. Probably one of the many reasons I never opened a bookshop. Alchemy was complicated enough.

With great, concerned care, she moved the small box to a stack on her left, then hurried on ahead of us. I squinted at the numbers on a crate until Elara tugged at my arm to haul me along.

"I don't think this is an act," I whispered to Elara. "She was shocked and terrified in the shop when Señor Argall was attacked. I really think he kept her in the dark about all this."

The captain's eyebrows knitted together in a mildly skeptical look. We watched Primrose fret over yet another box.

"I think I'm finally convinced," Elara said at last, lips pulled into a tight line. "I suppose all of this has me jumping at shadows. Though I do think the neatness in the bookshop was her doing."

Primrose once more moved another small box of books. Then, after some consideration, turned the box until its label aligned with the others.

"Easily," I replied. "She'd either have a heart attack or a field day in my workshop."

"Heart attack," Elara replied with a wry chuckle.

We hurried down a winding path through the warehouse. Just before I felt hopelessly lost, we reached a small clearing between the crates.

It was just as Elara described. A small campsite with worn gray wool blankets, an iron stove, battered copper pot, tin cup, and more. The fact that anyone cooked in here without getting caught screamed that Joshua knew exactly who had been living here.

There was also the mysterious locked door on the far side of the squatter's camp. It was a simple wooden door with a modest brass lock. The door was as old and weathered as the warehouse, but its lock was clearly newer. Both were sturdy, which was a must for any warehouse in Kingston.

"More storage?" I suggested in a low voice, gesturing to the door.

"To another alley outside?" Elara countered with a shrug.

Primrose didn't pay us any attention; instead, she focused on the campsite. The fact it existed didn't sit well with her. She wrung her hands, then started forward, obviously to clean.

"Señorita?" I said quickly. "Before you get started, could we take a closer look? We can always help you straighten up after."

Primrose nodded hastily, then backed away, only to be scooped up by Elara, who asked about the locked door. A quick use of a key later, the ladies were past the door and into a hallway beyond. I was far too occupied with the tin cup, broken tubes, and the iron stove.

I squatted down next to the stove. It wasn't something I expected to see, much less in the back of a warehouse.

Iron stoves were rare, but this one matched others I'd seen before. It was little more than a battered iron box near a window. Filthy, with sinister scorch marks inside, and a pile of charred paper and wood on the bottom.

Near the top, someone had rigged a space for a wide-bottomed pot and tubing. The pot was missing, but there was still a pair of savagely broken copper tubes held in place. Even the baffles inside the stove were altered, to allow more careful control over the heat.

I recognized the adjustment. It was the same kind I had made in the fireplace for my workshop.

The idea was to draw more heat off the flames, directing it as evenly as possible while distilling. That is, if the potion even needed to be distilled, and not simply boiled like soup. I preferred the latter. There was less chance of steam-related explosions.

"An alchemy still," I murmured.

I tapped the metal tube. It rocked a little in the singed metal bracket on top of the stove.

"Whoever you are, you've been trying to brew something delicate."

Just then, a drop of dark blue fluid with gold specks trickled to the floor. The instant it hit, the wooden planks turned a healthy green, then quickly sprouted a tiny tree limb with three leaves. I stared at it, wide-eyed.

"Just what were you brewing?" I murmured. "The planks are dead wood..."

A thought hit me like a hammer to the head.

"No. No, it can't be."

I quickly knelt down next to the tiny plant and pulled out my folding knife. Cold anticipation slithered like winter slush down my spine while I worried over what that potion really was. I touched the blade to the stem, then a leaf.

Both were firm and healthy, as if it had spouted from a living tree. Then I turned over a leaf and winced.

"Mierda," I swore under my breath.

Where the top of the leaf was healthy, the underside was not. Black spore balls and gray blotches of decay riddled the plant.

Suddenly, one of the black spores lashed out with a tiny sticky vine for my knife blade. I jerked my hand away as a second, then a third, tendril followed the first. They were grasping, reaching, with a raw, quivering need. As soon as I was out of reach, they retreated to underneath the leaf.

I jumped back and nearly tripped over the stove. The urge to stomp a boot heel onto the twisted plant was overwhelming.

Once I put my knife away, I pinched the bridge of my nose. My heartbeat slowly returned to normal, and I shoved a hand into my bag. Renwick materialized in a blast of briny fog a second after I opened the *Codex* page.

The ghost blinked, glanced around, then crossed his arms, giving me a skeptical look.

"You look like something just took a year off your life," he said. "What happened?"

I raked a hand through my hair while I tried to calm my nerves.

"Necrotic potion," I explained, then waved a hand at the tiny tree limb, then the stove. The tiny leaves chose that moment to turn black and curl in on themselves. Renwick grimaced, and I rubbed my right hand when it grew warm for a moment.

"Check the door and windows," I told him. "Whoever left this will be back to destroy it. Keep watch while I find a way to collect what's left."

Renwick nodded, but stopped just as he started to turn away.

"If it's dangerous, why keep it?"

"To know what kind," I replied. "If it's what I think it is, then I've a guess that Lucas Argall was the one staying here."

"What about that young lady? Miss Stewart? I'm liable to scare a fright into her if I shout," he added.

I shook my head, quickly searching my bag, then belt loops, for an empty vial.

"Can't be helped," I replied. "We'll just have to explain, and apologize, later. Go!"

"Going!" The ghost dashed off into the forest of crates.

21

Rising Secrets and the Restless Dead

July 30, 1722. Still in Joshua Argall's rented warehouse. I doubt his rental contract covered this...

A haunted echo of Renwick's footsteps chased after him while he vanished into the warehouse.

I frantically patted myself down for an empty vial, then finally discovered one in the bottom of my shoulder bag. Carefully, I knelt down next to the broken tube. It was copper and curved in such a way that I was almost sure it had been part of a worm tube condenser from a still. Dangerous droplets oozed down, thick and syrupy, testing both my nerves and patience.

While the trickle pooled into the vial, I studied the campsite. Elara had found the remains of a burned map. The stove was the obvious choice where the rest of the map had gone. Alchemy notes as well, unless Lucas took those with him.

"I'll need to search that," I murmured. "There could be more map, or some discarded notes on this potion."

The broken remains of the still were a mess. There was the condenser tube, but the main pot? Long gone. I saw a bent tube on the floor that might have been a Lyne arm. More evidence of a former alchemy still. Anything else was just blankets, the tin cup, cooking pot, and an old wooden chair.

Finally, I was rewarded with a teaspoon's worth of the blue and gold death potion. That would have to do.

"You found something."

Elara had returned from the hallway with Primrose in tow. Neither looked happy, but the latter looked more rattled than before.

I corked the vial, then stashed it deep in my bag for safekeeping. At least I hoped it was safe. If not, my notebook might go necrotic and try to eat me.

"Yes. A necrotic potion." I made a sour face. "It could just be a very eager plant stimulant, but I think it's actually meant to try and raise the dead."

Elara sucked in a sharp breath at that while a deep scowl lined her face and her wings buzzed a little. Her people, like any thayans, had a long history with magic and the Etherwave Arcana. Death magic? That was worse than murder, in their opinion. Beyond that, Elara had some unpleasant personal history with the topic as well.

"Exactly." I waved a hand at the campsite. "My guess? Lucas Argall was trying to cure himself. Though I've a bad feeling something else happened. What's down the hall?"

"Another way out to an alley. Also? Nothing good." She rested her hands on her flintlock pistol. "There's a pile of bloody hemp rope in there with bits of bark."

"It looked rather fresh," Primrose said in a thin, brittle voice, face pale as a sheet. "Fresh as such things would be, anyway. I've seen bloodstains a'plenty on napkins when I worked as a housekeeper. Those stains can't be more than a day or two old."

"Two days?" I glanced down at the floor, then over at Elara. "Wait... the dead dockworker?"

My right hand suddenly pulsed with heat. I thought I saw a flicker of green-white light from the corner of my eye, but it vanished before I was sure.

"Doctor!"

Renwick's haunted shout from the stacks cut through the conversation like a hot knife. I had hoped sending a lookout would buy us time. Sadly, it only gave us a few seconds.

A gang of six armed men, pirates by the tattered look of them, stormed out of the warehouse stacks with alarming speed. Most brandished cutlass and dagger, but two drew flintlock pistols. Renwick ambushed one, diving onto him, which made the pirate misfire, screaming in sudden terror from the ghostly hug. The second pirate aimed and fired at me.

I was lucky. At close range, a flintlock could punch a hole right through someone. But the pirate's aim was off, and the lead shot sang past my left cheek to savage the wooden wall behind me.

On my right, Elara drew and fired her flintlock in one motion. The pistol belched smoke and stabbed flame at a pirate, who jerked as the lead shot knocked him flat. Her clockwork pistol could reload twice if she got the chance.

Sadly, she didn't. Three other pirates rushed at her, swords at the ready.

Three became two when Primrose let out a war cry worthy of a panicked banshee. She smashed a wooden crate lid over a pirate's head. He crumpled to the floor like soggy laundry.

No sooner had he hit the floor, than Primrose brandished her makeshift club with a wild expression for another target. The next nearest pirate backed off, wanting none of that.

Motion to my left caught my attention. I grabbed my sword and turned just before a cutlass stabbed me in the left shoulder through my long coat. The white-hot pain yanked both air and a yell from my throat. I staggered back, trying to pull myself off the blade.

It was Captain Dryden Storm.

I gulped down air, drowning in pain, and glared at Storm. He slammed a fist across my jaw, then stabbed again. Same shoulder, only deeper.

A yell ripped out of me as I fell back against the warehouse wall. I gripped my bloody left shoulder out of instinct and tried to move sideways out of the captain's reach. Storm just chuckled while a sickly glowing green vapor billowed out from the squirrel skull around his neck.

"You're sticking your nose where it don't belong, Doctor," Storm snarled at me in a devious, aristocratic voice. "You should've gone to find the book, like I told you. But, you didn't."

He twisted his bloody cutlass, the point still aimed at me.

"So now, Doctor? You had your chance. I think I'll have your life as payment."

"You're welcome to try," I hissed back between clenched teeth.

Storm lunged for my throat. I sidestepped as I threw a vial from my belt. The vial landed first.

Glass shattered against his chest. Fog billowed out to swallow the air, and Storm stabbed at nothing. The captain yelled in a rage before he was grabbed by a coughing fit.

Pain shot needles through me with each step. My vision blurred, and I nearly fell over, but I managed to keep on my feet. I hissed out in agony through clenched teeth while I drew my sword.

The instant my blade cleared the scabbard, greenish-white fire erupted over my hand. Those cursed tattoos on my skin writhed with life. A warm fire washed through me like hot water.

It wasn't just the heat of the fight. Something was suddenly there, next to me, watching. For just a moment, a deep voice whispered in the back of my mind. Before I understood the words, they were gone, but the warm feeling never left.

I pushed through the pain and off the warehouse wall to head for the door by Elara and Primrose. One of Storm's pirate crew burst through the fog and was on me before I took a step.

The man slashed, and I parried, then stepped aside. My head pounded slightly from the effort, but the pain in my shoulder seemed far away and muted. The pirate stepped in with a thrust, but I knocked away his sword, then rammed my elbow against the side of his jaw. He dropped like a stone.

I felt that same warmth suddenly pour along my arm. A soft heat that soothed my pain. It didn't remove it, but made it more manageable for the moment.

Then Captain Storm barreled out of the fog at me with murder in his eyes. He slashed. I stepped back, and my head throbbed. Our swords crossed once, then twice. Each time, the fire around my hand flashed bright, as if it wanted to climb my blade. With each parry, every cut, I took a step closer to the door and freedom.

Somewhere to the side, I heard voices, shouts, cries of alarm. I couldn't spare a glance. If I did, Storm would've run me through. I was an alchemist, fairly skilled with a sword. But Captain Storm was a corsair, a true swordsman, and it showed.

But while I blocked, and the ghostfire blazed, Storm's amulet dimmed. It didn't go out, but after a few seconds, I realized it wasn't nearly as bright as before. The captain chanced a look at his skull amulet, then shot a glare at me to curl steel.

"So, you think you'll break the curse? Think you might steal it from me before the strain of it kills you, Doctor?" he snarled, hate boiling in his voice. "Think again!"

Before I could raise my sword, he slammed a fist against the bloody mess of my shoulder. A yell tore out of my throat while I collapsed against the warehouse wall. The greenish-white fire sputtered, not quite dying out, as I tripped and fell to the floor.

Storm thrust at me with a wicked snarl. I raised my sword a second too late.

But the blow never hit.

Just before the captain's cutlass ended my life, a figure rushed in between us. The cutlass stabbed deep, almost all the way through, then stuck. There was a sharp wheeze and gasp of sudden pain.

It was Renwick. Somehow, in all the curses and twisted necrotic magic, he was solid enough to be stabbed in my place.

I watched, frozen, in complete horror.

Renwick clutched at the captain's coat, quickly looking over his shoulder at me. Agony was painted across his ghostly face.

"Get out while you can, Doctor!" he yelled.

I struggled to my feet, stunned, not sure what I was seeing. Elara shoved the last pirate off her sword, running to help me with fire and panic in her eyes.

How could this even happen? I had no idea. Renwick was a ghost. My thoughts spun like a whirlpool, unable to get any footing.

One thing was certain. From the look on his face, Dryden Storm wasn't surprised. He had done this, been in this moment right here, before. Murdering someone who was already dead.

"Miserable rat!" Storm snapped at Renwick.

The ghost tightened his grip, while a trickle of ghostly blood showed at the corner of his mouth.

"Shut it!" the sailor spit back. "I know you can feel the curse like I can! You can't have that page back for your wart of a master. You can't!" Renwick trembled. "Doctor Sangre has changed the page, made it his own. He's the owner of it now, not that madman, Lucas Argall!"

Captain Storm growled like a feral dog and tried to shove the ghost loose, but Renwick held on.

"Oh no. This is for my crewmates you murdered! I stand with the Doctor and his crew, not yours," Renwick spit out again. "You'll have to go through me to get that page, even though you know you can't touch it! I'm bound to protect the page by the same curse that forces you to protect the rest of that damn *Codex!*"

"No," I protested with a wheeze and tried to help Renwick.

"Stop!" Elara hissed in my ear, pulling me away to the door, then down the hallway. "There's nothing we can do. Storm's dead men are starting to move, bathed in that green fog or whatever it is."

I was too tired to struggle, but I tried anyway. Elara still half-dragged me along as Primrose yanked open the door to the outside.

"*Asa mvur!* Listen to me!" she snapped while we staggered into the alley. "I don't at all understand what's happening, but there's nothing we can do about this. Renwick, for whatever reason, gave us a chance. Don't waste it!"

Suddenly, a man's scream of agony echoed loud enough inside the warehouse that I thought the windows would shatter. I squeezed my eyes shut as I felt my strength ebb. The tattoos on my hand slid just an inch, and the flames burned low.

"Let's go," I murmured.

Failure tasted bitter in my mouth. Renwick's screams faded away as we ran.

22

Bitter Bone and Stirred Spirits, Served Cold

Aug 2, 1722. Somewhere east of Kingston, aboard the *Silk Duchess*. The safest port we had available...

"Somehow, I'm still not dead," I said to the wooden ceiling over my bunk. The ceiling didn't offer any comment. So, I yawned, pulling myself awake.

Morning sunlight poured through the cabin's narrow window, lighting the occasional dust motes over the table. Muffled shouts and calls of the crew working on deck filled the air. Seawater kissed the ship's hull with a sloppy slurp while the *Silk Duchess* pressed on through the waves. They were a comfortable, reassuring sound of normalcy, and right then, I needed that.

I thought about my alchemy shop and how it looked when we reached it after the warehouse. That hurt almost as bad as my shoulder.

"At least Sebastian found a cabinet to hide in," I murmured.

Visions of shattered potions and burned recipe books danced in my head. I groaned softly before I shoved the thoughts aside.

"Get up," I told myself with a sigh. "You've things to do, like taming a necrotic nightmare in a bottle."

That seemed like a reasonable and good thing to do until I sat up. At which point, my body reminded me of all the abuse I'd put it through. It wasn't feeling very forgiving, and let me know with a broadside of sharp aches. My shoulder? It was another story.

Sebastian then jumped onto the bunk, and also me. It didn't help.

"Good morning, Sebastian," I wheezed, then scratched between his horns. He replied with the usual purr that resembled a soft rumble of rocks in a barrel. After a moment, I pushed him onto my bunk, where he grumbled but curled up to nap.

Carefully, I reached for my bag on the nearby tiny table, bathed in the morning sunlight. I rummaged inside until I produced two glass vials of potions, one a dull red and the other green. I downed them both, one right after the other. A dual swig of raspberry-flavored healing potion and graveyard syrup.

I called the combined flavor 'raspberry despair'. At least it wasn't toad sweat. That was, in my opinion, a small improvement.

The healing elixir did its work, as a dull warmth drove off the chorus of aches. Gently, I rubbed the bandages around my left shoulder. I grimaced. Healing elixirs had repaired some of the damage, but there was a lot more healing to go. Once I changed into fresh clothes, I ran a hand through my hair, when something moved in my bag.

It was the *Codex* anchor page. For a moment, it looked like the faded letters shifted slightly.

"Renwick?" I said in surprise, then snatched up the page and unfolded it.

Nothing. No burst of fog, smell of brine, before the man's ghost appeared next to me. A dull, heavy feeling sank in my chest.

"I'm sorry, Renwick," I murmured with a sigh. "I should've never asked you to keep watch."

The fight in the warehouse roared back through my head. I pinched my eyebrows in a dismayed, sad grimace. I'm trained to heal people, help them. This time I failed. Dryden Storm had stabbed Renwick. Gutted him like a fish, really. I *saw* him bleed. How does a ghost bleed?

I shook my head. How is it even possible to murder a ghost? To make them bleed? A ghost blade, like Elara's, can't even do that.

A knock on the cabin door battered down my thoughts to kindling.

"Yes?" I called.

Lysander pushed open the door, with the usual halfway smile that bordered a grin on his dark, weathered face.

"You're up! Good. I thought you might be. How's the shoulder?" he asked, stepping inside.

With Lysander in the cabin with me, the little room almost seemed claustrophobic. Lysander was a lean man, but ship cabins weren't known for space. He sat down in the room's sole, small chair across from me. Sebastian immediately left the bunk and accosted him for attention with a wiggle.

I touched my left shoulder, then gingerly moved it in careful circles. At least, until I felt a twinge of pain.

"Hurts, but the elixir is doing its job. I've been able to move it since last night. So I doubt I'll lose the shoulder," I explained as I slipped my left arm into a blue, cotton cloth sling. "But I'm not about to arm wrestle anytime soon. If I'm very lucky, I might even get full use back and only have a scar. But I won't hold my breath on that."

Lysander replied with a deep chuckle.

"You wouldn't be the first in our line of work with a scarred limb. Just think of it as a tattoo with a better story!" His laughter faded as he pursed his lips with a serious expression. "I'm sorry about your shop."

I sighed.

"So am I, my friend. Señorita Stewart was far too kind to take on cleaning the mess. I hope she'll be fine."

Lysander shrugged. "I'm sure she will be. You told the city watch, and they'll check in on her. Also, you know, Buttons and his street rats will keep an eye on her, too."

"Yes," I replied. "They will. Seeing what Dryden and his crew did to my workshop hurt almost as much as getting stabbed. Renwick dying to save us?" I shook my head at a loss for words. "All just to find the damn *Codex* page."

"I'd say Storm was looking for both you and the page," Lysander countered, then crossed his arms. Sebastian huffed, then returned to the bunk for a nap.

I shrugged with my good shoulder.

"Maybe. It fits with his rant at the warehouse." Then I rubbed my face. "I'm wondering if there's more to it for Storm, though."

I gestured wearily at the *Codex* page.

"Yes, he's cursed to protect the book. Demanding I return it fits with what Lyra said about the Bindweaver's Curse." I scowled at Lysander. "But that last bit in the warehouse? About me trying to 'steal' the curse or whatever that was? I just feel that was about his amulet."

Lysander leaned back to hook an arm around the back of the chair with a thoughtful look.

"Could his amulet have anything to do with the *Codex?* Another trinket made by that Tristam Greenholm who made the book?"

I shook my head a little. Then I remembered that voice I'd heard more than once when my hand's been on fire. I frowned, eyebrows knitted, wrestling with the thought.

"Maybe? But not entirely."

For some reason, that felt right. I didn't know how I knew that, just that I did.

"There's far more to it than just some trinket tied to a necromantic book," I added.

Lysander arched a curious eyebrow at me. I sighed, then rubbed the bridge of my nose. This wasn't a conversation I had been looking forward to, but I needed to tell someone.

I started with the moment we freed Renwick from the Death Whisper and explained about the voice. From there, I told Lysander about the murmurs and half-understood words that crept into my mind whenever the tattoos and my hand burned. I didn't leave out the feeling of a presence beside me in the warehouse when Storm attacked.

It was a lot, and once I was done, it sounded addled, even to me. I was used to imbuing potions with power from the Etherwave Arcana. Speaking with a not quite dead ghost was new, but I could manage. Voices in my head? That worried me a little.

To Lysander's credit, he wasn't suspicious or judgmental. He took it in stride.

"A voice?" he said. It wasn't so much a question as it was a thoughtful statement. "It's talked to you. Have you tried talking back?"

I stared at him like he'd lost his mind. Then again, I worried I had. I just wasn't sure.

"What? So, you mean like another ghost?"

Lysander shook his head.

"Not ghosts. Spirits, Pedro. I'm talking about nature spirits. When I was a boy, the elders told me all about nature spirits, and how they sometimes talk to people." He shrugged at me. "Given everything that's come from Otherworld, why not nature spirits? At least a few, anyway? They could've survived to make it to Earth."

"A lost Otherworld nature spirit?" I said thoughtfully. "Like a water nymph?" Then my mind went to darker places of murderous oak trees that ate people alive. "Even, say, a *roblón?*"

Lysander's only reply was another solemn shrug.

I glanced down at the floor and frowned in thought. The fight with Captain Storm in the warehouse came to mind.

"Storm accused me of trying to steal the curse. His amulet even dimmed when I felt that presence next to me. Before that, both Lyra and Morowen said the Bindweaver's Curse was altered. Knotted up with some sort of magic that drains victims."

I squinted at Lysander with a suspicious look.

"This is a bit of a guess. But what if this spirit is trapped in Storm's amulet, and it's part of what's corrupted the Bindweaver's Curse?"

"Which would, in a way, make it tied to the *Codex,* wouldn't it?" Lysander asked. "Almost like a fish in a net, trapped by this Tristam Greenholm who wrote the book in the first place?"

Aches flared out of my left shoulder, and I rubbed at it absently before I waved a hand at the *Codex* page.

"Señor Greenholm was also stupid enough to try to murder a sea hag for her power," I replied. "So trapping a nature spirit would fit." I pursed my lips again with a frown. "It could just be coincidence, too."

Lysander leaned back a little in the tiny wooden chair.

"So, that bit of potion you collected in the warehouse? Just what is it?"

I sighed and rubbed my bandaged shoulder again.

"It's in the galley. Last I checked, there's a scent of old nightshade, what looks like powdered bone, bits of fool's gold, even some resurrection fern." I shook my head. "It's very bad mix, my friend. Very dark. It's like a fast poison that would kill you and heal you at the same time."

As I described the properties of the elixir, Lysander's eyebrows climbed higher on his forehead, eyes wide.

"It kills you while it heals you?" he said slowly when I finished. "So either you're a very pretty corpse, or it's a race which gets you first, the poison or healing?"

I nodded slightly.

"Yes, something like that. I'm running it through a distillery I cobbled together. It should be broken completely down in an hour. I'll know more about it then."

We both fell quiet. The soft sounds of wind in the sails, creaking wood, and the muffled lap of water against the hull kept us company. This was broken up by the occasional voices of the crew on deck while they went about their work. I broke the soothing quiet first.

"When we set out from Kingston, Elara set course for those locations on the warehouse map. Are we still headed that way?" I asked. "How close are we?"

Lysander's expression turned grim.

"Close enough to see. I'd say we'll drop anchor in an hour."

"But?" I added suspiciously as I narrowed my eyes. "What aren't you telling me?"

His mouth pulled into a tight line. "The location?" He hesitated for a heartbeat. "It's for another fishing village."

That hesitation sent an ice spider crawling up and down my spine. I suddenly had a thousand questions, but I kept quiet. Instead, I nodded a little.

"Go on," I said while tension sank claws into my shoulders.

"A lookout was able to get a quick look ahead at the village with a spyglass," Lysander continued, voice thick with emotion. "Nothing's moving there. Not even the animals."

I lowered my head for a moment, then glared at Lysander.

"Maldita sea," I murmured. "When do we go ashore?"

"We?" Lysander repeated. "Pedro, you're going nowhere with that shoulder. You're staying aboard."

Frustration and anger bubbled up from deep inside my chest. It wasn't Lysander's fault, but it came out before I could throw a rope around it.

"Like hell I will!" I snapped. "Lysander, I can't just sit here while there could be survivors that need help!" Anger got the better of me. Slowly, I clenched and unclenched my right hand while I felt the heat and fire build inside. "I'm going."

We locked eyes for a long, uncomfortable moment. Lysander blinked first, then sighed.

"All right," he replied. "Elara is going to be furious."

23

Village of Silent Voices

Aug 2, 1722. East of Kingston, at the tiny fishing village of Westmere. Stepping ashore to find the face of evil...

I jumped from the longboat the second it brushed limestone white sand. Seawater sloshed around my boots as I half-ran for the dry beach. Behind me, the others pulled the longboat ashore, then hurried to catch up.

White sand gave way to hard-packed dirt and a weathered wooden footpath into the village. Stray nets and bits of fishing gear littered the ground along the way.

"Not a good sign," I murmured, running faster.

Sinister storm clouds had rolled in as the *Silk Duchess* dropped anchor. The promise of fresh rain still rode the wind, and those marble-gray storm clouds hung over the village of Westmere like a burial shroud.

I stopped in my tracks once I reached the edge of town.

"We're too late," I murmured in dismay.

A headache nudged at the back of my neck while a breeze stirred my gray long coat. The wind hinted at misery, like lost souls begging to be seen.

Elara, Durner, Lysander, and the rest joined me. The sight of Westmere stunned them nearly silent as well.

"Cor," a gunner's mate swore under his breath.

"Exactly," I replied softly. "I'm surprised there isn't a kelpwitch here to gather up the lost memories."

Lysander shook his head slightly.

"If only," he said with a shadowed frown on his dark face. "We could ask her what happened."

"I think we know already," Durner said in a craggy voice. "I don't like a bit of it. Feels like we're walking on a grave, or into a trap."

"I'd take the former, not the latter," Elara added.

"Hm, I'm for neither," the rust-haired gearwright replied.

Silence fell on us like a wet wool blanket that smelled twice as rotten. Slowly, as one, we eased into town. No one spoke, or wanted to, for fear of insulting the dead.

Westmere didn't look that old, but Mother Nature hadn't been entirely kind. Caribbean sun and rain had done their brutal work. The town's buildings stood as motionless as gray wooden tombstones, but with peeling paint. Fortunately, none were on fire, but they also weren't the only thing standing.

Scattered across the dusty, grass-littered streets were the withered wooden statues of people—it was the villagers.

Only a petrified handful lay scattered between the well and the edge of town. Each villager was trapped in mid-run, with screams of terror frozen into their faces.

"I see four," I muttered to the others, or maybe just to myself. No one replied.

The sight of even that many petrified people was jarring. It felt like a ferocious wave of fear had rolled down the street, then crashed into us like an angry surf. Another gust of light warm wind played through the nearby grass with ghost children we couldn't see, but imagined.

Worse than the statues, in some horrific comparison, lay the bloody bodies of the dead. There were quite a few of those. Blood seemed to be pooled everywhere in the grass. A knot of emotion rose in my throat, trying to strangle me.

I shivered, and my headache throbbed along with my shoulder.

The tension shattered like thin glass when Elara softly cleared her throat.

"All right," she spat, voice clipped. "We need to get busy, and be quick about it. If this was done by Captain Storm and his cutthroats, they've not been gone long. Blood's too fresh."

Elara glanced around at the lot of us.

"Skaldi? Signal the *Duchess*, we need work crews over here to bury the dead. They deserve that much," the captain said in a somber tone.

"Aye." Skaldi's deep voice was thick with emotion. "On it."

"Pedro?" Elara said sharply.

I interrupted before she sent me back to the *Duchess.*

"I'll look for survivors in town," I said, my own words clipped and tight. "Then I'll check the petrified. Maybe there's something I can do."

"Be careful," she emphasized, then added, "Durner? Go with him."

The rust-haired grimling with the fire-copper eyes gave her a curt nod.

"I'll be with him," he rumbled in a craggy tone.

I started to object, but the sharp edge of concern in her jade eyes brought me up short. She was worried, and so was I. We all were.

Instead of words, I gave her a small smile I hoped was reassuring. A silent promise that I'd try to be careful. Elara inclined her head, just a fraction of an inch, to tell me she understood.

"The rest of you! Look lively!" The captain said. "I need sentries watching for Storm's ghost ship, and some to help gather the bodies!"

It was slow, grim work. For Durner and I, it was a long half-hour walk through the village of the dead. We checked each body and statue we found, barely saying more than two words to each other. Soon, we simply ran out of words.

Finally, Durner broke the deafening silence first.

"It's like a bloody graveyard where the statues stare at you," he rumbled uneasily. The brass veins along his tanned skin glimmered softly from tension.

"True, but I'm not sure they're staring at us," I replied.

With a hand on my sword, I glanced through an open door to a woodcutter's shop. The owner was inside, as wooden as his wares. Yet one more statue.

That made five.

It was five too many.

I eased inside. That petrified soul was in no better shape than the others we'd found. But that also bothered me.

"If the attack was so recent, why do all the petrified victims look like they've been weathering for years?" I mused.

Durner glanced inside, then glowered at the petrified woodcutter.

"Hm. Weathering don't work *that* fast," he stated.

"No, it doesn't," I agreed. Something didn't fit, and it nagged at me.

Still, I clenched my jaw and moved on for the town well.

Durner had checked the powder and shot in his flintlock pistol for the tenth time in as many minutes by the time we got there.

Two wooden statues stood south of the old stone well, while four bloody, cut up fishermen lay dead to the north. The blood splashed over the gray granite well stones had started to turn brown in the sun. My skin crawled as I rubbed the side of my head to chase back the headache.

Seven. That brought the total statues to seven. I'd lost count of how many had been cut down.

Durner knelt by the bodies and tapped a forgotten short sword with his pistol.

"Hm," he rumbled thoughtfully. "They were making a last stand. Facing down something from in town, not the shoreline."

I rubbed my eyes.

"That fits with the statues. They were all running from something in town."

A gust of wind rushed in off the waterfront, then stirred the loose sand and dirt around us. I rubbed my nose with a frown as anger tore loose from deep inside me.

"Why do this?" I snapped. "It didn't work last time! Why again?"

Durner shook his head sadly and shrugged. I didn't have an answer either.

"I'll check the statues," I said, mouth pulled into a sour line.

The gearwright nodded, then set to checking the dead fishermen for anything more that could help us.

I stalked over to the pair of statues with a sigh.

Neither one looked older than twenty. The young woman was human, and the man with her was thayan. She was taller, maybe five foot ten, and her young man was a few inches shorter.

They were entirely wood, from skin to hair and clothes. Wood that had splintered like old, weathered driftwood. They had held hands the moment the petrification claimed them. My eyes lingered on that for a long moment.

"How can I undo this?" I murmured. Using my folding knife, I picked at the wood that used to be their clothing. It flaked away like powder.

That's when I saw the tiny twig attached to the young man's sleeve. My breath hitched. I knew that twig.

It was the same sort of tiny tree limb I saw in the warehouse. One that the potion created. It had the same shape and leaves, right down to the decay. I didn't touch it, in case it might try to grab me.

"Mierda," I swore. "He's experimenting with cures," I said bitterly. "I just know it in my bones. He's dying from this petrification disease. So he infects others, then tries to cure them."

A terrible thought occurred to me.

"What if Lucas is having Storm's crew cut down any resistance to get at the ones he wants to experiment on?"

I ran a hand through my dark hair, blowing out a sigh through clenched teeth.

"This wasn't a massacre." I fought down a shudder. "He's *harvesting* people."

I felt a warm burst of heat, almost fire, from the tattoos on my hand. That didn't go well with my headache.

"You're more right than you know," Durner snapped.

I spun around toward him.

Durner had moved from where I'd left him. Instead of by the bodies, he was a few steps away, kneeling in the dirt. He gestured to the dead fishermen.

"Those were buying time to let others escape." He shook his head, tapping a calloused finger against the ground. "Didn't work, though. Lots of tracks here. Two got dragged off, and another ten were marched off in a tight knot."

I frowned sharply.

"To where?"

Brass veins in Durner's skin flared forge-hot as he nodded to a large, bone-pale stone building at the far side of the town square. A black brick chimney stabbed at the sky.

"Over there, to that smokehouse," His voice growled, rich with menace, copper eyes hard. "These tracks aren't that old, maybe a couple of hours."

Thoughts snapped into place like well-fitting gears. I glanced around wide-eyed while a spark of greenish-white fire ran along my hand tattoos.

"He's nearby!" hissed that deep voice inside my head. It was so loud it hurt. I realized too late that was the source of my headache.

From the corner of my eye, I saw a faint finger of smoke curl up from the smokehouse chimney.

"*Maldita sea!* They're still here," I snapped.

Durner jumped to his feet, pistol in hand, and glanced around in alarm. I cupped a hand to the side of my mouth.

"It's a trap!" I shouted at the top of my lungs to the others scattered across Westmere. We were easy prey.

The second I yelled, Captain Storm and his pirates boiled out from buildings lining the town square, swords and pistols drawn. Six Death Whispers screamed their way into view from behind a granary.

A cold knot turned over in my stomach. Elara and I barely managed three at Morowen's home.

Durner fired and dropped a pirate dead into the dirt. There wasn't time to reload his flintlock, so he turned it around to use it like a hammer while he drew his cutlass.

"This is bad, Pedro," he rumbled in a tight voice. "We're too spread out! They'll cut us down like wheat!"

I grabbed for my sword, but thought better of it. Instead, I tugged my tricorn hat low, then snatched a vial from a belt loop.

"Then let's give them something to think about!"

There was more than one way to fight.

I hurled the vial at the closest pirates and murmured a quiet sea shanty. The Etherwave Arcana rushed to my aid. I focused on the vial, forcing power into the potion. The vial hit the ground and exploded in a wagon-sized ball of fire. Pirates flew to either side like rag dolls.

The remaining pirates ran past the fire as they charged in, but not at us. They broke into small groups to run right at our shipmates. Steel hit steel, while pistols and screams shook the air. Even Captain Storm avoided us, but the ugly glare he shot me spoke volumes.

This wasn't his choice. He was following orders.

A lone figure followed the mob's wake, escorted by two burly pirates. The man was painfully thin, even bone thin by anyone's standards. He wore a ragged brown and green hooded long coat. Matching gloves covered his frail, thin hands. All the rest of his clothes, from cotton shirt to blue trousers, were as ruined at his coat.

The newcomer had his hood pulled up over his head against the sun. What little light made it past showed a face made of rotten wood, but pliable as soft skin.

A pair of spectacles perched on his emaciated nose. Orange hellish eyes, like burning coals in a forge, peered out from behind that glass with a bemused, predatory gleam. A stained Archbinder's pin glimmered from the lapel of his black vest.

Despite all that, I still saw the resemblance to his brother, Joshua Argall.

"Lucas Argall," I said in a brittle voice and inclined my head.

I tensed. All this time, I'd been chasing a wood wraith. It would've been safer to kiss a siren, or even a vampire.

A sinister smile slid over his withered, wooden lips. He tapped his walking staff of twisted driftwood, wrapped by rotten sailcloth, against the ground.

I felt the magic faster than I could move. It snapped around Durner like a glowing ghostly rope, and dragged him to the ground.

Greenish-white flames burst to life around my right hand. I snatched a glass vial out of my belt in a flash. Lucas raised a hand before I tossed it.

"Ah, Doctor Sangre." The wraith's voice was chilly and smooth despite the faint, dry rasp behind it. "It's good to finally meet you."

His eyes flicked to my burning hand, then met my glare.

"Ghostfire?" Lucas chuckled with the sound of bone scraping wood. "Delightful."

I narrowed my eyes and slowly tightened my grip on the vial of rolling gray smoke.

Lucas tilted his head slightly, as if amused.

"Let's talk about a little bargain, Doctor. Before your companions and crew become a casualty."

24

The Devil's Bargain

Aug 2, 1722. Fishing village of Westmere. Facing a wooden devil and his devilish bargain...

Shouts and screams of the nearby fighting echoed through my soul, while Lucas Argall's voice grated like a dull spoon dragged across a slate.

Never have I wanted to stab someone so badly in my entire life.

"No deals, señor," I growled, then turned away to free Durner from the enchanted ropes.

"Oh, I wouldn't do that, Doctor."

It was the smug tone in Lucas' voice that made me stop. He had something up his sleeve. I turned back to face him with a bitter glare. That smug tone was also spread over his face with a thin, superior smile.

I clenched my right hand and nearly shattered the glass vial I held. Ghostfire played over my fist and vial, bright and eager. Bottled frustration coiled inside me. Wounded shoulder or not, I stalked toward Lucas. Thunder rolled in the storm clouds overhead.

"Lunatic!" I snapped. "Stop this!"

"Ah-ah," Lucas chided, wagging a gloved finger at me.

Something about his manner made me hesitate. That, or the fact I was about to charge at a wood wraith who, if the stories were true, could wither a victim with a touch. At least something like that.

Still, the shouts and yells of pain from far behind me almost made me charge at Lucas anyway.

The wood wraith strolled a few steps closer, as if he didn't have a care in the world. Dire amusement twinkled in his burning coal eyes.

"I've worked far too hard to get you into this dead town, Doctor," Lucas said with a casual, meaningless wave at Westmere. "So the last thing I want is to see some idiot with more sword than sense run you through. I should know, since I've a lot of those idiots at my disposal."

Lucas nodded past the gray stone well toward the pitched battle over by the blue and gray houses near the beach.

"Besides, your Captain Blackwater seems to have things well in hand. Magnificent swordswoman and captain. She might even turn the tables on Storm and send him running."

Lucas replaced his smirk with something a bit more feral. I fought down the urge to slam a fist across his nose. This wasn't the time. Not yet.

"That is, if I don't set my Death Whispers loose on her and your crew here ashore."

I drew a long, slow breath. Whether it was to steady my nerves or my temper, I wasn't sure. Lucas gestured past me, and I decided to glance that way over my wounded shoulder.

The six Death Whispers were clustered together outside the pitched battle between the pirates and my crewmates. It was like watching a pack of ragged undead dogs eager to run into a fight, desperate to tear everything to shreds. I could almost see them strain at an invisible leash.

"*Mierda,*" I swore under my breath between my clenched teeth.

Past the Death Whispers, Lysander and Elara had regrouped with the rest of the shore crew. They had retreated with the wounded into a nearby, two-storey blue-trimmed house, and barricaded themselves inside.

On one hand, if Storm and his pirates were distracted, my crew could make it to the longboats at the beach and escape. But the pirates were already trying to find a way inside. Pistol shot, and too few pirates, frustrated Storm's attempts.

"So señor, Dryden Storm and his crew are disposable?" I gave Lucas a sideways glance.

The wraith shrugged.

"I use what's at hand."

It was a bloody stalemate. If this was a game of chess, that might have been 'check', but not 'checkmate'. Not yet.

Out of the corner of my eye, I noticed Durner slowly wriggle free of one of the enchanted ropes. He gave me a quick, solemn nod while he worked, trying to avoid attention.

I subtly inclined my head in return, then sighed after a deep breath to cover it up. The taste of rain was on the air from the forward edge of the coming storm, sharp and electric with anticipation. I glared at Lucas. The wraith hadn't seemed to notice Durner in the least.

"So all this? For what?" I snapped with a quick gesture at Westmere. "Bait for me, or another failed attempt to power your arcane engine? Another failed summoning?"

The wraith wasn't bothered in the slightest. He just shrugged.

"Oh, you've been paying attention. Very good. You know the rules, Doctor. The law of balance," Lucas explained casually. "All magic from the Etherwave comes with a price. I'm just trying to pay it. Only, this one is rather steep. I probably need something larger than a town, or even a city."

Shouts and clangs of metal on the other side of Westmere made me twitch. My crewmates, my friends, were fighting for their lives to save the surviving villagers, while I was stuck talking to a monster.

"Call them off, señor," I snapped. "Both your horrors and Storm's cutthroats. Then we'll talk."

"No," he mused in that bone-on-wood rasp. "I don't think so."

Lucas slowly shook a gloved finger at me again. That feral smile still spread across his rotten wooden lips. The two pirates with him, honor guard at best—given Lucas was a wraith—looked more uncomfortable with each second. I wasn't sure what bothered them more, Lucas, my hand being on fire, or something else entirely.

"You're quite the problem, you know?" the wood wraith said casually. "Your companions didn't worry me, but you did. You might read the *Codex Luminari,* and I couldn't have that. So, I hoped that the corrupted Bindweaver Curse would kill you in hours, maybe a day."

"I'm hard to kill, señor," I growled.

He nodded, then slowly paced in front of me.

"Oh, I noticed. I didn't expect you to be so resourceful." Lucas gestured to the ghostfire around my hand. "Neither did I expect Captain Storm's trapped trinket to latch onto you, either. It took some doing to convince the captain to just ruin your shoulder, instead of gutting you in the warehouse."

He knew we visited the warehouse. We had been set up from the start.

That fact shot a cold chill through my spine, but I fought down the shudder. What else did this monster already know? A part of me wondered if the posturing was to cover up that he knew less than he let on. I didn't rise to his gloating, but set my jaw and glared.

Lucas paused in his pacing with a disappointed expression.

"Now, Doctor, don't be like that. I'm past trying to kill you. You're far too interesting. We're both men of learning, yet here you are swimming in foul waters, playing with pirates and privateers. Come now, we're above that."

"He's stalling," whispered the voice in my mind, the one I suspected was inside the ghostfire.

I silently agreed with it and felt a brief pulse of warmth back.

Behind me, I could hear flintlock fire and the clash of metal. Each second, every sound, felt like a new needle in my skin. A cold breeze raced off the sea, while the first splatter of rain fell. But I needed to stall to give Durner a little more time.

"What do you want, señor?" I asked bitterly, emphasizing each word.

"Oh, nothing much," Lucas replied with a casual wave and another of those feral grins. "Just the *Codex* page, and you."

"Me?"

His smile widened, and I felt a sudden urge to bathe.

"Yes, you, Doctor," Lucas repeated. "You must've discovered my humble attempts at potion brewing in the warehouse. I did have to leave in a hurry." He sighed regretfully.

"No matter what else I am, I'm a master wavebinder. A spellcaster. But you!" He gestured at me with both hands. "You, my good Doctor, are a true alchemist."

"You want me to fix your potion," I guessed aloud as I narrowed my eyes at him.

The man waggled his finger at me again, pacing near his bodyguards.

"But of course," Lucas replied, voice as smooth as slime. "Give me the *Codex* page. Let me put it back in the book, then free Tristam

Greenholm. Between his knowledge of the *Codex Luminari*, my skill in channeling the Etherwave Arcana, and your mastery of potions, we can change the world."

The wraith's voice had dropped to an unholy whisper.

"Erase the disease of death itself."

Lucas stopped in front of his bodyguards, turned to face me, then gestured at himself.

"Even cure this," he said in a low, threatening voice. "In return, I call off Storm and his pirates, and dissolve the Death Whispers. All of it. Then once all this is over, and we've succeeded, you never set foot in my affairs again."

A whisper of movement caught the corner of my eye.

Just to my left, I noticed Durner slip free of the last enchanted rope. He held them close against his chest with the pretense of being bound. Thirty feet beyond that, Lysander crouched behind a barrel with Elara's flintlock pistol. Sweat gleamed along his dark cheeks, cutting streaks in marred smudges of soot.

How he escaped the house, and Storm's pirates, I've no idea. But I was so glad, I nearly cheered.

"If I refuse?" I asked carefully, raising my eyebrows.

In a blink, Lucas yanked off his right glove, then slapped each of his bodyguards in the chest. Both men tried to back away, but barely managed a step. They screamed, but their voices drowned in the sound of cracking wood. In seconds, they petrified in place, clothes and all.

"Simple. Your friends die, and then I have you ripped apart."

A pistol's lead shot punched Lucas in the throat the instant after he pulled on his glove and glanced up. Amber, resin-like blood coated his neck.

Shock exploded on the wood wraith's face. He tried to talk, yell, anything, but his throat was too savaged to work. At least, it was for the moment. Wood wraiths had a nasty habit of being diabolically durable, even from a mortal wound.

Lightning flashed, and the rain fell harder. We might only have minutes before Lucas healed.

Durner was on his feet in an instant. He recovered his own flintlock and fired at the wood wraith. The shot went high and to the right, but still slammed into the monster's shoulder. Lucas staggered back, hate boiling in his glowing orange eyes.

Nearby, the six Death Whispers turned toward us and charged, but Durner met them halfway. Even though he stood four foot six, he was three times stronger than anyone I knew. Brass veins glowed under the lightning, and his copper eyes flashed hot as he lunged.

The gearwright hauled the lead Death Whisper into the air, then slammed it against the rest. Some fell, others darted aside.

Over by the house, I realized how Lysander got free. Somehow, Elara and Lysander had led Storm and his pirates on a fool's errand through the house. While the pirates invaded the building, Elara led our crew out through a root cellar door, partially obscured by sand grass. I saw her wave her glowing ghost blade at me.

The lone pirate who stood guard over that door never stood a chance.

"Tell Elara!" I shouted to Durner and Lysander over the thunder. "Get the surviving villagers out of that smokehouse, then haul everyone to the longboats!"

"What about Storm?" Durner roared back in a craggy voice, grabbing another Death Whisper to pitch it down the town well. Then he jabbed a calloused finger at Lucas Argall. "What about that?"

"Leave Lucas Argall to me," I snapped, then smashed my vial on the ground.

Fog boiled up between myself and the wraith, like ghostly claws greedy for air.

I locked eyes with the wood wraith.

“No deals, señor!” I snapped. “You can keep your devil’s bargain. I’ve made enough on my own.”

A grin brushed my face as I tugged at my tricorn hat, singing in a low voice to call down the magic.

“I’m a privateer of the sea, of the waves and wind, with my ship and crew, I sail the ocean without fear...”

The Etherwave Arcana’s power replied before I barely finished the verse, then roared through me like a wave.

Lucas tried to scream in rage, but I clouded his mind. We vanished into mist before his eyes.

25

Bloody Passages, Bitter Remedies

Aug 2, 1722. Off the coast of Jamaica, and the dead village of Westmere, aboard the *Silk Duchess*. Facing down angry storms and death...

It was hard to say which hurt worse—the running fight for freedom through Westmere, or the people we lost along the way.

I stumbled out of the last longboat from the village, then slumped against the damp railing. The *Silk Duchess* leaped among the waves, riding them with a desperate precision. All around us, rain fell in sheets driven sideways by the wind, slapping anyone still on deck.

Both the storm and overexertion aggravated my shoulder wound. Needles of hot pain stabbed along my back, which was almost a distraction from the headache. Deck crews rushed by in their canvas waxcloth coats to secure longboats and rigging. Others helped the *Duchess* fight back against the storm. The ship's wood frame creaked in anger, as if snarling at the weather.

Meanwhile, the sea grabbed for everyone with watery claws. Waves crashed against the schooner, spilling over the railing to kiss the stained deck planks with each greedy attempt. It was like the sea herself churned, eager to drown anyone nearby as the price for passage.

"That's the last from Westmere, Cap'n!" Durner's craggy voice boomed to my right, cutting through the thunderstorm.

"Understood!" Elara barked over the wind, boots planted, back straight against the driving rain. "Secure that longboat! We don't need it thrashing the *Duchess*!"

I started to help, but Durner stopped me quick. He pointed at my shoulder with a stern look, then shook his head. With a resigned nod, I resumed my perch against the railing. Below decks would have been safer, but my tiny cabin felt miles away, even though it was only a few feet.

Elara stalked the deck midships close to me, wings fluttering with anxiety. The deck crew scurried around her in a hive of frantic activity while she scowled at the rolling sea and churning thunderclouds with hard jade eyes. Quick as a wink, she scaled the ladder to the helm and took up position beside the ship's pilot.

"Storm's getting worse!" she yelled. "Get the last of the survivors below with the others! Move!"

The ship lurched drunkenly to port, and I latched onto the chestnut stained railing with an iron grip. Once the *Duchess* righted, I pushed off with a hard groan, then turned toward my cabin.

"Small victories," I murmured, then wiped the rain and salt spray from my face. "But still, how many of the villagers did we lose? How many of our own crew?"

My thoughts burned hot over the events of the past hour. Recent memories had become a haze of blood, fire and fury, wrapped in a ragged wool blanket of loss.

"This *has* to stop," I said with a hard sigh. "If I could just find the next step Lucas and Storm are going to take, we could get ahead of them."

My footsteps echoed dully against the damp wooden deck planks hammered by the rain. It was a marching drumbeat for my thoughts.

"That or bait." I pulled my mouth into a tight line. "Bait. If I had the right bait, we could lure the wood wraith out. Lure both Storm and Lucas out." I shook my head, bitter thoughts crowding me. "I don't know nearly enough about dealing with a wood wraith."

I turned to face Westmere over the water one last time, drawn by an uneasy feeling that the storm hadn't swept everything out to sea.

Lightning ripped the clouds, covering the shoreline in a wash of bright white light. Three of the six Death Whispers stood together, a pace back from the rolling surf, mouths stretched wide in grotesque screams. Those who couldn't be buried had been burned—hasty pyres meant to keep them from Lucas.

Withering flames scattered damp orange light across the sun-bleached, peeling blues, greens, and soft grays of the buildings.

As for the Death Whispers, we'd burned two of the others, and I suspected the one Durner tossed down the well was still there. Those three on the shore steamed as if the rain burned them like acid. Rotten pieces dribbled to the wet beach with a messy splat.

"Renwick mentioned that." I narrowed my eyes. "Death Whispers can handle some water, but not a lot. It's something to remember. At least they won't walk under the ocean after us."

I adjusted the soaked sling on my left arm until the sharp ache turned dull. Then I pushed through the driving rain and exhaustion to my cabin in the stern. I almost made it, when someone grabbed my arm.

Instinctively, I reached for the last few vials at my belt, eyes wide, snarling. Lysander stepped back, hands up in a peaceful gesture.

"Pedro! Hold! It's me!" he said sharply.

"Lysander... saints and devils..." Anything else I might say collapsed under the weight of a ragged sigh.

"I'm sorry, Pedro, but you're needed," he explained quickly. "It's one of the survivors. A young man. He's... Pedro, he's dying. Slowly petrifying."

"What? Where?" Anger instantly swapped places with exhaustion, throwing it overboard.

Lysander led me on a fast run through the rain, then down a hatch to the schooner's narrow rooms below deck. We darted and dodged between crew, hammocks, and other spaces to the forward hold. It was one of the two places large enough to store anything, including drenched and battered survivors of a madman.

We came to a fast stop in a knot of villagers lit by battered lanterns. An older couple knelt down on makeshift bedding next to a young human man, really only a boy that wasn't quite an adult. I wasn't sure he was old enough to shave. His condition made me want to beat Lucas with a fireplace poker until the wood wraith was only haunted kindling.

I knelt down to check the boy's health, aside from the obvious.

Thin and wiry, he had a healthy tan from his life under the Caribbean sun. Light brown hair was drenched with rain and possibly sweat. His clothes were ragged and torn, littered with signs he had gotten too close to something with claws. I suspected Lucas Argall, given the state of the boy's arm. It had started to petrify into wood, outward from a shallow claw mark just above his elbow.

"What's your name?" I asked as gently as my abused throat allowed.

"Garvin," the boy whimpered in a small, pained voice. "Garvin Hall, sir."

I checked his eyes, then studied the wound. Panic screamed in my mind. What could I even do? Is there anything to do but make him comfortable in his last moments? I frowned and shoved those thoughts aside, diving into the work.

"It's good to meet you, Garvin. I'm Doctor Pedro Sangre. An alchemist," I replied.

"Doctor? I'm his mother, Felicity. Felicity Hall." She was an older, matronly woman, with gray shot through her light brown hair. "Is... is my boy going to be all right?" she asked in a trembling voice, moisture at the corner of her eyes. "What's wrong with him?"

The panic threatened to come back. I clenched my jaw, then shoved it away again. Before I could say a word, I felt a throb of reassuring heat from the tattoos on my hand. There wasn't a whisper, just a feeling. Then, somehow, I felt the fatigue and exhaustion drain out of me, like water over stone. Gently, my head cleared, at least enough for this.

My eyes darted to Garvin's mother, then at what I assumed was his father. I took a long breath, then let it out slow.

"Señora? Garvin's been infected," I explained carefully, leaving out so very much to not scare them. After a frown, I leaned down to study the wound and the petrification.

The skin wasn't petrifying like I'd seen before. It wasn't that fast, but it wasn't slow either. This acted like an infection, a horrid venom, or fast-acting gangrene. Healing potions could stop either, and if that failed, usually the limb was amputated. I decided on the first approach, even while my mind considered the second.

"Take this," I said, pulling one of my deep crimson healing potions from a belt loop. "It's a healing elixir."

I put a hand behind the boy's head, ignoring the pain in my hurt shoulder, then held the vial to his lips. He drank desperately. Immediately, I stared at the wound and the petrified skin.

It didn't heal to normal skin, but the petrification did slow ever so slightly. Inside, I latched on to that thought. This could be cured, just not with healing elixirs. Those only delayed death; they didn't prevent it.

"Delayed," I murmured. "Quieted. Purified."

I took off my tricorn hat, then ran a hand through my damp black hair. A desperate idea echoed in my mind like a deep toll of a bell. There wasn't any logic behind it, just a guess. A strong guess based on observations.

"Señor? Señora?" I said quickly to Garvin's parents. "This only slows the problem; it doesn't cure it. Still, I've an idea that could help. It's risky and may not work. But I think it could be worth the risk."

Felicity exchanged a fragile, wide-eyed look with her husband. Eyes damp, Garvin's father nodded at me.

"Do what you think's best, doctor." His deep voice was thick with desperate emotion. "We've lost our home. Please help us not lose our only son."

"So you both know, this could get worse," I explained in a solemn voice, feeling a sadness haunt my eyes. "He could die faster. Petrify completely." I glanced away a moment before I locked eyes with them both. "He could become... something else."

Felicity put a hand on my arm in the sling.

"Doctor, please," she said, eyes pleading.

Their look was a stab to my heart, but it put some needed steel into my spine. I made a mental note to carry a fireplace poker along for the next time we caught up with Lucas Argall. Then I pulled the potion of graveyard syrup, the bitter mix that kept my curse at bay, from my belt. It was my last vial until I had time to make more. Then I grabbed another healing potion.

"Lysander," I said, voice hard as stone while I pulled the corks. "Go to the galley and get for me whatever's left of Lucas' potion I found at the warehouse."

The navigator recognized the vials in my hand, then pierced me with a hard look like I'd lost my mind.

"Pedro..."

Muffled thunder rolled around outside, like rocks rolling down a hill. I set my jaw, then shook my head.

"Damn it, Lysander, do it," I ordered. "Go! We don't have time to talk it out!"

Pain blossomed from my shoulder, but subsided when I adjusted my sling again. I lifted the vial of graveyard syrup in my other hand, eyes fixed on the cursed tattoos there. Lysander raced back in a moment later with only a little of Lucas Argall's necrotic recovery potion in a small jar.

Tears streamed down Garvin's cheeks. He whimpered as the petrification started up his arm again.

After a deep breath, I emptied the vials into the jar. My eyes were fixed on the tattoos across my right hand.

"Spirit, ghost, or other," I whispered under my breath. "It's time we meet in the middle."

Then I cleared my throat and sang in a low voice.

"I'm a privateer of the sea, of the waves and wind..."

Green-white flames erupted up around my hand and engulfed the mixture in the jar. Abruptly, I felt the silent, golden power and presence of the Etherwave Arcana rush to my exhausted aid. I knew this might backfire, because all magic comes with a price. But, I had to try.

"Of course, Doctor," a low voice whispered in my mind.

I swirled the mixed potions until they blended into an elixir the color of fresh-turned grave dirt. Then I put the edge of the jar to the boy's lips. Silently, I offered a bargain—every ounce of my battered soul that this wouldn't be his last drink on Earth.

Garvin drank. Thunder rolled again, and I held my breath with a small shudder.

26

The Bait

Aug 2, 1722. Aboard the *Silk Duchess*, forward cargo hold. Absolutely dancing around death...

The soft crackle of abused wood faded to nothing as Garvin's arm slowly stopped turning into ragged driftwood. A tiny sprig pushed its way out just above the boy's wound. Carefully, I pulled out my folding knife, then turned over one of the oval green leaves.

"Alive and healthy," I murmured. A confused ramble of theories suddenly rolled around in my head. Nothing I could easily repeat out loud.

It was a perfectly healthy little plant. No gray spot of decay, or even a hint of greasy black tendrils reaching for my knife. That it had grown out of the boy's arm was unsettling, but nothing about this was normal. I let out the breath I'd been holding that entire time while I put away my folding knife.

To be honest, I was as shocked as anyone down in the cargo hold that it worked. I really thought for a moment that I might've accidentally found a new and unspeakable way to poison someone. Alchemists are mentored by assassins in our first year of apprenticeship, after all.

"Señor? Señora? We'll need to watch Garvin's wound for a few days. Just to make sure this infection isn't spreading," I told Garvin's parents, swallowing the last of my nerves about the potion. "But, so far, I think this mixture may have done the trick. I'll brew up another batch. He'll probably need to drink some once a day. Try to keep his arm dry."

Hugs and tears came in waves after that, with both parents almost too overjoyed to string words together. The air smelled of old salt, damp canvas, and best of all, relief.

This was fine by me, as exhaustion had slipped up to ambush me when I wasn't looking. I fought down a yawn that rattled my bandaged shoulder, then got to my feet and left the forward hold.

Lysander caught up to me before I was even ten paces away.

"Pedro? Was that your last... what do you call it?" he asked.

"That green potion? Graveyard syrup," I replied, rubbing my eyes. "Yes, it was the last dose I had on me."

The *Silk Duchess* rocked and bobbed through the waves, cutting her way forward. Her planks flexed and groaned while she sailed, wooden bones creaking, irritated over the storm.

I couldn't hear the hammer of rain against the wooden deck overhead, so I trusted the storm hadn't returned. We dodged and sidestepped crew and hammocks we worked our way to the stern.

"How long will it take to make another mix of that potion for the boy?" Lysander asked. "From what you said, it sounded like he'd need a daily dose."

"An hour, maybe two. The graveyard syrup alone isn't easy to make," I explained, then shook my head. "But it's all a guess. I'm treating it like an infection, as if Garvin got too close to Lucas Argall and got clawed for it. I just wish I knew why it infects some victims quickly, and others, like Garvin, slowly."

"Maybe it's the wound?" Lysander offered. "A shallow wound means it takes more time for whatever this is to take hold?"

That idea stirred up plenty of thoughts. Some of them were actually good. Well, mostly good. I squinted at Lysander.

"You may have something there. If that's true, then this is more like a venom or a poison." Tired or not, I managed a faint smile. "I know how to work with those."

We stepped aside as far as the crowded space below decks allowed to let four crew members move past us for their hammocks. They had just come down from above, dripping with rain and exhaustion.

Crew space, or space of any kind, was a premium aboard ship. Calling it crowded was an understatement. Most of the crew lived below decks with a hammock or nook fixed to the hull, not unlike a pantry shelf for people.

"One of those ingredients was that necrotic nightmare from the warehouse," I explained, while we continued. "I've an idea how Lucas made that, but I'm not entirely sure. So, I'll need to experiment a little. Hopefully I won't poison myself."

There was also the part where necrotic elixirs could corrupt the maker. Turning them into twisted depths of evil and all of that. I left that part out. It just didn't feel like the right time to bring it up.

"Will it be enough to last the trip back to Kingston?" he asked.

I couldn't meet his eyes. Instead, I stayed fixed on the narrow path through the *Duchess*. What I didn't say was that I barely had enough ingredients to make more graveyard syrup for one person, let alone two.

"Just enough if you open an Arcane Gate for us to outside Kingston. Outside the harbor," I said over my shoulder as I grabbed the ladder to the deck above.

"Though, I might be able to make it stretch if we have to sail back the long way." An almost inaudible sigh spilled out of me. "Either way, once back, I'll get what I need from my shop to make a large batch for the boy."

Lysander must've caught the part I didn't say, since his eyebrows bunched in a hard scowl across his dark, olive-skinned face.

"What about for you?" he asked solemnly, eyes stern.

"I'll manage," I replied, then started up the ladder.

Lysander grabbed my shoulder before I took a step.

"Like hell you will," he snapped. "I know what that means coming from you. Have you taken any of that green syrup today to stave off the killing curse?"

I didn't answer for a good four seconds, jaw tight. This wasn't a conversation I needed to have right then. To be honest, I wasn't sure any conversation about that topic was a good idea at all.

"No," I replied, voice a little harder than I intended. "The boy needs it more."

Lysander's grip tightened when I tried to climb the ladder.

"Pedro! You're not stalking your way out of this one," he said. "Elara said you were struggling over drinking the cure."

"It isn't a cure, and this isn't the time, Lysander," I shouted.

"Oh yes, it is!"

I spun around to scowl at him, and he matched me glare for glare. Anger bubbled up inside me like a bitter fountain of bile.

"The boy might have died!"

"He didn't!" Lysander yelled back. "But if you die, then who can mix the medicine the boy needs? Damn it, Pedro. It's like you're trying to kill yourself. You could make a new batch of that potion, and then what? What if he needs more and you die from that curse?"

I started to turn away, jaw set, but Lysander pulled me back around.

"Use your head," he continued sharply. "Treat yourself first, then the boy. What's gotten into you?"

A dozen thoughts crowded my head, each one competing for attention. I pinched the bridge of my nose, then took a long breath. The scent of stale sweat, canvas, and other ship smells I didn't want to identify helped me sort my words out.

Deep inside, my anger burned so hot, I thought the *Duchess* might catch fire. But in truth, I wasn't angry at Lysander. I was angry at me.

Everything inside me wanted to rant at him that I felt responsible. That when we first got the warrant for the job, I didn't research the *Codex* enough, as if I even could, to know that it was this dangerous. That every death so far was somehow my fault through all this.

But I didn't say any of that. Mostly because I knew that it wasn't entirely true, even if I wanted to take the blame.

"Mierda," I swore bitterly, glancing away.

"I'm a doctor," I said. "An alchemist. I try to save lives." My words had dipped down into a light growl. "But right now? I'm doing a terrible job of that. Lucas and his pet pirate are cutting a bloody swath through people like a scythe cutting through stalks of innocent wheat."

Lysander squeezed my shoulder, mouth pulled into a complicated line.

"Just remember that when you try to save lives, you're included on that list, my friend," he said in a low voice.

I nodded, then drew in a shuddering breath. It had been a really long day.

"Those bastards still stay a step ahead of us," I explained, or maybe complained. "We need bait. Good bait. Something to lure them out. Not money, but something they don't have."

"Like a cure? At least something they think is one?" Lysander raised an eyebrow at me as a slightly devious grin blossomed over his face.

There are times I miss the obvious. It happens. Then there are times the obvious is dancing in front of me wearing colorful silk veils, slapping me with a wet rag. This felt like the latter.

I scrubbed a hand down my face.

"Now I know I'm exhausted," I murmured, rolling my eyes skyward. "Yes, like a cure. Just like that damn elixir I threw together."

Lysander patted me on the back with a grin.

"Go get some rest, Pedro," he said. "Then brew up enough for you *and* Garvin. We'll figure out the rest later. I'll get to work on opening that Arcane Gate."

I nodded, then started up the ladder so I could cross more easily to my cabin in the stern.

Once on deck, things got far more interesting than potions, or me being too exhausted to have functional common sense.

"Ship inbound! No flag!" shouted a lookout.

Uneasy conversation rolled through the crew like a wave. No flag often meant only one thing... pirates. I only knew of one pirate that was close enough to be a problem.

Captain Dryden Storm.

That's when I heard the roar of a cannon as it fired in the distance.

27

The Gate

Aug 2, 1722. Aboard the *Silk Duchess*, when hell came to call...

A short, faint whistle was the only warning I had that things had just turned ugly. I dove aside, careful of my sore left arm, and promptly knocked two of the *Duchess'* crew to the deck.

The ship's railing exploded behind me into a storm of charred splinters as a small cannonball tore through it like dry paper. Dust strangled the air, while charred bits of wood battered at us like a hellish hail.

Some skittered across the deck, others pelted the nearby crew, and the rest collided against my wool long coat. A litany of new bruises along my back complained at the abuse.

"Maldita sea," I grumbled wearily under my breath, swallowing the pain.

Sadly, my coat gave its life for the three of us. The gray wool was ripped, and I could feel the heat from blackened holes. I yanked the ragged long coat off with a gasp as my shoulder flared hot with pain. Somehow, the sling around my left arm was still intact.

My coat wasn't the only thing battered. Of the two sailors I'd knocked flat, one was pale and trembling with a bleeding welt across his tanned forehead from stray splinters. The other, a young thayan woman with copper-gold eyes and short black hair, scrambled upright and lunged for my shirt.

"Down, doctor!" she hissed. Her dragonfly-like wings snapped open in alarm while she yanked me to the deck. I didn't argue.

We crashed onto the wet wood next to the still-stunned young human man with the curly brown hair. Another cannon shot split the air where my head had been a second before.

The iron ball smashed off part of a yardarm, cascading chunks of wood and shredded sailcloth onto the deck. A tangle of that wood and tarred line trapped a few of the unlucky crew on that side of the ship.

"Fucking hells!" the young man next to me wailed, hazel eyes round as saucers while he looked behind me.

I shook my head, ears ringing, pain from my shoulder dragging me down. But I still managed to look back in time to see stray bits of lightning. It danced off the shattered wood and metal bolts of the *Silk Duchess* in a race for open air.

"Mierda," I swore, punching the wooden deck.

Above us, Elara's voice was like an avenging angel, cutting through the chaos as precise as a sharp razor.

"Hard to port!" she howled. "Gunners! Make ready! I want that ship sent to the nine hells! Where's my Arcane Gate?"

Lysander hauled himself up the ladder from below decks. Quickly, he scrambled for the steps to the quarterdeck, and the bronze-colored metal platform bolted there.

"Coming, Captain!" he shouted as he ran. "Keep her on this course!"

"It's the *Rising Eel!*" I called out to Elara. "Storm's ship! She's using a lightning cannon, Captain! Not standard shot!"

On the quarterdeck, Elara gave me a quick nod, her jade eyes flashing with concern.

"Do what you can!" she shouted back, her thayan dragonfly wings fanned out for balance near the helm. Setting her jaw, she fixed her eyes back to the *Silk Duchess* and her crew.

Sucking in a painful breath of air, I crawled over to the soot-stained young man. Quickly, I yanked out a handkerchief, then pressed it to the sailor's bloody forehead.

"Press here," I said, drinking down acrid air while I guided the young man's trembling hand to the head wound.

He nodded, then promptly vomited onto the deck. I waved two of the nearest crew over.

"Get him below! I'll see to him when I can," I ordered.

Then I turned to the thayan sailor next to me. Dressed in plain, soot-covered clothes, the worst she'd suffered was a line of bruises along her right arm. Ari Fairhill, if I remembered her name right. She'd signed up only a month ago.

"Señorita! Go to my cabin. The one with the gargoyle," I told her. "There's a small leather case there. Bring it to me. Don't drop a *single* bottle!"

Ari nodded, racing off. I stood, ducked a flailing length of halyard, then turned for the port side cannons. I barely managed a few steps before I almost collided with Durner, who acted as the Master Gunner aboard the *Duchess*.

"Sling's loose, Pedro," he grunted, nodding at my healing shoulder. I reached over and tugged the knot tighter, using my free hand and teeth.

We flinched as another shot tore over us. The mizzen mast rattled from the near miss.

Ari raced back with my dark leather pouch. I flipped open the lid and three vials inside it glowed a gleeful orange-red, promising rich violence in my name.

Durner shot me a quizzical look with a raised eyebrow.

“Lysander needs time to drag open a Gate,” I growled through pain-clenched teeth. “We need to hit the *Eel* now. Give her something to think about!”

The grimling’s rust-red beard split into a toothy, savage grin that flashed into his copper eyes. He jerked his chin to the nearest cannon, and the head-sized iron balls stacked next to it like fruit.

“We owe them a punch in the nose for Westmere,“ he rumbled in his craggy voice. “Give them bastards something they’ll remember!”

I hurried to the cannon and its small crew. A young bunch, younger than me by a good six years, were scared, but determined to do their duty. They looked up, startled, as I hurried toward them.

“Wait!” I ordered as they reached for the first iron ball.

Healing shoulder numb from terror and abused by motion, I leaned against the cannon for support. Fortunately, they hadn’t fired it yet. I flipped open the leather pouch once more. Orange-red potions greeted me with their gleeful, malicious glow.

“I call it ‘Heartsfire’,” I explained quickly, pulling out the vials one at a time.

The glowing liquid hissed like angry fire snakes, eager to burn the world. I smeared the potion over the first four balls. As soon as liquid touched iron, the metal shivered in eager anticipation, then turned reddish-black, like Hell’s own fist.

I nodded to the gun crew.

"Now," I said and pointed at the *Eel*. "Aim for that spot with the lightning. It's a lightning cannon."

The young crew worked with smooth precision. Durner's relentless practice drills showing through in the crew's clockwork-like motions.

"Mr. Terrason!" Elara yelled. "Get that ship out of my sea!"

"Aye!" Durner roared like an avalanche. "You heard the captain! Make ready!"

The *Rising Eel* was nimble, but she wasn't a schooner. Neither was she rigged for tight, fast turns like the *Duchess*. We turned hard, port side cannons loaded briskly.

"Aim!"

Across the waves, crew scrambled over the *Eel* like angry ants on an anthill. They tried to turn, desperate to match us, bringing their guns to bear. But they just couldn't catch enough wind. Two cannons on the *Eel* belched smoke, stabbing the air with fire.

Shots blasted across our quarterdeck. Railing blew out in all directions as the ship's pilot, Angus MacFerson, was thrown from the helm. Bleeding and battered, he struggled to rise. The ship's wheel was still intact.

Elara lunged for the helm, gripping the wheel in both hands like she might strangle Hell itself.

"For Westmere! Fire!" she yelled in a war cry, her jade eyes blazing.

The orders echoed along the line, and cannons tore the sky. I kept my eye on one in particular. That cannon's shot roared out, red and eager for blood. Exhausted, bloody, I drew in a deep breath, then quietly sang my shanty as I extended my good, shaking right hand toward that cannon shot.

"I'm a privateer of the sea, of the waves and wind..."

Instantly, the power of the Etherwave Arcana rushed through me, then out to the potion-covered cannonball. What once was red, turned searing white with a comet's tail.

The now charged shot streaked over, slamming into the *Rising Eel* like a hammer of heaven. Storm's ship listed sideways, rearing up like a wild horse, desperate to buck her crew into the sea. White flames belched skyward on impact, eliminating the lightning cannon and two others, along with their gunners.

Those same white flames then chewed on the pirate's sails and rigging. I watched while her crew worked like mad to put out the enchanted flames.

I turned away, stumbling for the quarterdeck to see after Angus, wiping blood from my nose.

"There's your time, Lysander," I murmured, running at my best exhausted, fast limp. "Open the Gate." The last came out like a prayer.

Once I hauled myself up the ladder, I ran through sheer willpower, then dropped next to Angus. The black-haired Scotsman was bleeding out of a dozen cuts from shattered wood, but luck and heaven had saved him from worse.

Meanwhile, to my right, on the brass-bronze platform covered in nautical arcane symbols, Lysander had started his work.

Etherwave energy rippled up from the round metal dais, surrounding him in a golden wire globe of magical light. Yellow clouds shaped like landmasses and more drifted over its surface.

Inside the globe, Lysander reached for the nearest golden cloud and stretched it out. The surrounding view changed to show the *Silk Duchess,* the *Rising Eel*, and the island of Jamaica.

Lysander then thrust both hands into the glowing clouds, pulling out a man-sized arch. A mystical Arcane Gate. Outside the ship, just a little off port, storm clouds boiled to life as the real thing suddenly appeared.

A ribbed arch of thunder and livid light appeared in a crackling haze. It was as if a finger from heaven reached down to scribble an arch made of storm light and enchanted marble pulled out of the water. It rose 400 feet or more, taller than any terror of the sea, higher than St. Paul's Cathedral. The arch towered over everything like an enchanted mountain.

The surrounding air seethed, resentful at the intrusion. It was a slice of sky, both vivid and wrong. The thing looked impossible, but was still so very real, dripping with power. Rain fell upward, distorting the Gate's boundary.

On the dais, inside that golden globe of light, Lysander's face was sweat-slick. He shoved a hand against the magical image of the gate, tapping strange runes and compass markings along its face. After that, he leaned in to grab a pair of glowing doors, pulling them open with his very being, arms shaking.

I could almost hear the creak of wood as the magic resisted. But Lysander bent it to his will, muscles tight.

"Hold the heading," he shouted. "If we even shear the mast, we're all dead!"

Elara clutched the wheel so hard her knuckles turned white, staring down the Gate like facing a demon.

"I have it!" she yelled back. "Get it *open!* We *need* to Gate-jump!"

The *Eel* fired again, wild with fury to catch its prey. One shot hit us, two missed. The *Duchess* lurched from the blow, but still tore forward, battered but not beaten. Determined to be free.

I focused on Angus, ripping strips of cloth from my shirt as makeshift bandages. Then I pulled out an emergency healing potion from my leather bag. He drank, and a healthy color painfully returned as the enchantment did its work.

Then, I felt a charge brush over me like a heavy veil. A pulse in the air like a celestial heartbeat. I looked up in time to see the peaceful, storm-free waters off Kingston ahead of us. It was a sharp contrast to the gray thunderstorm and boiling sea.

Our bow touched the shimmering, watery image of Kingston at the center of the Arcane Gate. The world suddenly stretched into a blur of light and sound.

Then we were through.

On the dais, Lysander shoved the glowing doors closed. Magic fought back, crackling with resistance. The navigator pushed harder, jaw set. Slowly, the magic gave way to muscle and will.

Behind us, the view of the *Rising Eel* and storm-tossed waters squeezed shut. Then the watery portrait vanished in a blast of pure, white light when the Arcane Gate closed behind us.

I never saw what came next. Exhausted beyond my limit, I collapsed onto the deck. Crew shouted and ran around me, but I just lay still and breathed in the warm, salty air. Somewhere in the distance, I heard sea birds complain irritably at our intrusion.

We made it through.

By God's grace and a navigator's skill, we had made it through.

Slowly, a light drizzle of rain fell as I heard the rumble of the Arcane Gate returning to the sea. The tiny drops were a tranquil kiss of Nature herself, promising us peace. At least, for now.

As for me? I just closed my eyes and laughed out loud in relief.

28

A Privateer's Gambit

Aug 4, 1722. Brewed Gambit Alchemy Shop, Kingston, Jamaica. Brewing up plans and skullduggery...

I wasn't laughing two days later, as I started brewing for the day.

"Even my aches have aches," I murmured. "If any of them would just stay in one place twice in a row, I'd attack them with liniment."

They didn't, so I didn't. Instead, I rolled up my sleeves, brushed off my rumpled vest, then focused on the work and what needed to be done.

Bright morning sunlight filtered through yellow stained windows. Occasional dust motes danced with steam while light spread from wall to brown, weathered wall. My dark wood and gray tile worktable, once clear, was thick with papers, my journal, inkwell, and a wide collection of ingredients.

White-tan spindly roots, bright petals, metal shavings and more stood guard in jars. Light floral scents mingled with earthy notes of cinnamon, dirt, and more dubious dried ingredients. Some even originated from a graveyard.

"This has to be it," I murmured, rewriting previous measurements in my journal. "The color and consistency look right, and even the stain experiments agree."

I rubbed my tired eyes, then studied the boiling pots and alchemy still in my fireplace.

Memories of cannon fire echoed in my mind, along with Lucas' snide speech back in Westmere. I stood my mental ground, running calculations again to reproduce parts of Lucas' necrotic potion—at least the parts I needed—and avoid poisoning myself in the process.

So far, I'd not been attacked by these potions yet; or at least, not today. Fortunately, Elara had made sure I wasn't alone while I worked. I also suspected some ulterior motives, such as making sure I didn't run off and do something rash. Well, do something rash *again,* anyway.

A blue-trimmed white cup filled with steaming tea appeared in a soft clatter by my elbow on the worktable. Next to it was a white porcelain plate with a warm buttered biscuit. Scents of soothing lemongrass drifted lazily from the cup.

"I have a tea serving set?" I asked, with an astonished expression at both the teacup and plate.

"Yes," Primrose Stewart replied in a matter-of-fact tone. "In that disheveled pantry where you hid them."

Today, the young woman's hair was pulled up into the same no-nonsense ash-blonde bun she wore while working in Joshua Argall's bookshop. She wore a white cotton apron over her soft, spring-green dress. The apron was already stained by the odd potion ingredient.

"Now, drink up, and eat your biscuit, Doctor." She stepped back, then shot me a sharp look, shaking a finger at me. "Also! Drink that graveyard syrup medicine of yours. Captain's orders."

"Of course, señorita. Thank you," I replied with a thin smile.

With a nod, Primrose dusted her hands on the apron, then hurried away. I just knew she was about to attack some cluttered section of my shop until it surrendered.

"It's like watching a typhoon of organization blow through," I murmured.

After another sip of tea, I glanced at the bubbling pots and hot copper alchemy still in the fireplace. Scents of stale lime, abused lavender, and something that wanted to be cinnamon and pine hovered in the air.

"Good enough," I decided, pulling over a tan cotton stretch of cloth. "Time for a stain test."

I heard Primrose return before I saw her, boots clipping efficiently across the wooden plank floors. This time, she was armed with a leather-bound ledger, long feather duster, and a face of proper iron nerve. Never in my life had I met anyone who wielded ledgers with such military precision.

Quickly, I took a wide-eyed sip of tea to bolster my resolve.

"You missed a dose," she said firmly.

The ledger landed on the worktable with a thump. She flipped through the dated entries before tapping her finger on yesterday's date. Then she fixed me in place with a narrowed frown.

"I just noticed a potion bottle missing from the drying rack, Doctor. You're doing *exactly* what Captain Blackwater warned me you'd do," she declared in a flat voice.

"Hm," I said weakly in my defense. "What?"

She ignored me.

"Please tell me you've saved some of that new batch for yourself? That it isn't just for your..." she wiggled a hand at the boiling pots "... experiment?"

I pinched the bridge of my nose.

"Cure and Bait, señorita." A sigh fell out of me to the floor. "A stable cure for Garvin Hall, and bait for a very bad man."

Her expression didn't waver one inch, so I gave in first.

"Señorita..." I began, trying not to roll my eyes or let aches and fatigue talk for me.

"Primrose is fine," she replied evenly.

"Yes, Primrose," I corrected. "I promise I've saved some for me. That's what is in the smaller pot tucked next to the still. I didn't take yesterday's dose because I was distracted over getting the measurements correct for young Garvin." Then I shrugged with my best, innocent smile. "We doctors make horrible patients."

She slowly raised an eyebrow at me without a word. So, I reached over to a nearby shelf that hadn't been invaded in the name of organization, and grabbed yesterday's glass bottle of graveyard syrup. I pulled the cork, downing the green elixir in one drink.

After a customary grimace over the flavor of despair and toad sweat, I corked the bottle. Primrose scooped it up the instant I set it down. After that, she marked the date and time in the ledger.

"I'll scrub that and put it with the others to dry," she replied briskly.

I shook my head, glancing around my shop.

Despite my complaints, it looked better. My shop was the most presentable it had been in, well, at least a year.

"Primrose? If I may? I know Elara... Captain Blackwater... arranged for you to be here, making sure I didn't get up to mischief."

She dusted her hands on her apron again, then inclined her head.

"Yes, true. Why?"

I raised my eyebrows as I leaned against a nearby chair.

"Even you must admit, your current employer has been a bit... dubious... in his business arrangements?" I replied carefully. "Such as his brother murdering people, the shop attack and all? So, I was wondering, what would you say to giving your notice to Joshua Argall, then taking up full-time employment here? Work as my assistant?"

For a second she stiffened, then faltered.

"I..." Primrose glanced down and made a valiant pretense to check her notes. "Well, that is..."

"A proper position," I repeated. "Employment. Not watching me like a hawk to make sure I don't experiment on myself."

I waved a hand at my alchemy shop.

"We can even do a trial run," I offered with a smile, tilting my head slightly.

"You organize this shop better than I could, and haven't turned up your nose at even the most dubious ingredients in the pantry. To be honest, you're probably twice as capable as I am in keeping this place, and myself, from burning to a crisp."

Primrose frowned, concern and concentration mixed across her face.

"Doctor, I'm not an alchemist," she blurted out before losing her words.

I waved a hand at the objection.

"Primrose, you know what work I do as a privateer with Elara, Lysander, and the others. There are times I need to be away from here for days. If you were here, I wouldn't have to close the shop. You could take orders, and I'd teach you how to make the more routine potions people ask for."

The young lady was quiet for a long moment, staring at her ledger, before she replied.

"This place isn't entirely safe. The bookshop isn't safe," she admitted softly. "Wasn't entirely before, but then *really* wasn't safe at all."

Her brown eyes locked onto my hand, where the tattoos glimmered eerily.

"You've your own monsters here, Doctor, but I feel more confident about facing those, if they appear."

Seconds crawled by until the air felt thick with anticipation. Finally, she thrust out a hand to me.

"You have a deal, Doctor. I'll send notice to Mr. Argall, telling him I resign for safety reasons. He honestly didn't need much of my help, anyway." She cleared her throat while we shook hands. "But if this shop burns, I'm billing you for my ledgers."

I laughed so hard my ribs hurt.

"Fair terms, señorita. Welcome aboard."

Primrose squinted suspiciously at the bubbling pots, then back to me.

"Doctor?"

"Yes?"

Her voice dropped a note, almost like admitting heresy.

"This plan of yours... this 'bait'?" she shook her head. "It sounds like madness. What's your real plan? If you lure Lucas Argall out with the potion, then what? Didn't he nearly kill you before?"

I leaned over and brushed a hand above the boiling liquid, wafting the scents to me. The lime had mostly devoured the lavender, but the cinnamon was still lying in wait to hug the remains in an unholy embrace.

"Honestly? It's a bit of a privateer's gambit," I admitted. "He desperately wanted me to help him with an addled scheme to 'kill death'. If he murders me, I can't help him. But I know he's not above killing anyone else."

I leaned back against the chair, giving the ceiling a pensive expression.

"So, we spread word about the cure for Garvin. Kingston's city watch will keep the boy and his family safe, and really, I don't want to bring that monster here. His pet pirates have caused enough problems."

We both gave the last few piles of broken glass in the shop a perturbed glare. Primrose had swept those up, but had not yet taken the remains to the nearby glassworks.

"Yes. I've noticed they tend to make trouble," she said dryly.

I grinned.

"So, instead, we lure him to a different place," I explained. "Yesterday, Elara offered me a warehouse she uses occasionally. The idea is to set the potion bait there, ready for the taking. Which I'm almost positive Lucas Argall will send Captain Storm and his crew to steal."

Primrose narrowed her eyes. I could almost see her thoughts churning.

"That sounds risky," she said uneasily, fiddling with her ledger. "You could lose his trail. Is there a way to follow these crates? Boxes?"

I nodded and crossed my arms.

"Yes, a few. Elara has some enchanted dust she uses that helps Lysander track cargo if it's stolen," I said. "More than that, we'll have several eyes watching anything leaving that warehouse."

Primrose nodded sagely.

"I see," she admitted. "The pirates will have to use longboats, or barges, won't they? They can't use their actual ship, because people would notice and raise the alarm. But Captain Blackwater's ship is anchored here at Kingston."

"True! Despite the fact that the *Silk Duchess* needs repairs, we can still outpace a barge or longboat," I replied with a grin before my expression faltered.

"But this isn't foolproof. Lucas is trying to pull together a staggering amount of power for a ritual. It's part of why he's murdering people."

I shook my head with a sigh.

"We'll have to move quickly once the potions are stolen. I'm convinced Lucas' condition is in the way of his ritual. He needs the cure, and we can't let him take it, or complete the ritual. But the pirates will take the cure to where Lucas is, which I suspect is where this ritual needs to happen."

"Why not use a fake potion?" Primrose asked wisely.

"It'll be partially a fake," I admitted. "Just enough of a cure that it might work for Lucas, and pass inspection as enchanted."

I exhaled slowly.

"Also, so long as he's distracted with this 'cure'," I continued, "that will give us time to catch Captain Storm and the rest off guard." I gave her a tired shrug. "Time enough to get at the *Codex Luminari* and destroy it once and for all. That *Codex* is the root of the problem. Rip that out, the rest *should* wither."

"How?" she asked.

"I'm not positive yet," I admitted, glancing at my potions in progress. "But I've an interesting idea..."

It was also a dangerous idea that I wasn't too sure anyone would agree with. But first, we needed to set that trap.

29

Bait and Bloody Portents

Aug 8, 1722. Kingston, Jamaica. Following the bait, but feeling a little baited in return...

I had the potions ready in an hour. The trap was set in the warehouse after that.

Everything else was about spreading rumors concerning a working cure for the 'petrify murder plague'—a dubious title at best. One the broadsheets had recently settled on for Lucas Argall's murder spree in Kingston.

Soon enough, word of the cure had spread, along with Garvin Hall's astounding recovery. It, and the boy, were the talk of Kingston. After that, all we needed to do was wait.

It was a lesson in patience across four tense days, especially for me. I was done taking hits from Dryden Storm and Lucas Argall, and wanted to give some back.

But those four days gave us time to rest and bandage our wounds. We patched up who and what we could in that time, including the *Silk Duchess*. She wasn't back to full fighting shape, but near enough to matter. It felt like all of us, including the *Duchess,* were itching for another run at Dryden Storm and Lucas Argall.

We were up before dawn the next day, tucked into the shadows across from the warehouse. The lot of us were spread out, like so many trapdoor spiders waiting for the morning meal to wander by.

In the distance, a hint of sunlight woke the horizon with a lover's kiss, making the sea blush in reply. A sigh of gray-white early morning mist traveled over the water like a hushed promise, rolling in over Kingston's outer bay.

"Another quiet morning on watch," I murmured, hands stuffed in a new brown long coat. "At least it's quiet so far."

"It's too quiet, and this morning weather isn't helping," Lysander replied.

I watched the tendrils of that cool morning mist dance along the waves, wrapping ghostly arms around ships at anchor. It covered them with a soft embrace, like the fond memory of a blanket. Nearby, the steady roll of the dark sea sent waves lapping against both damp shore and empty, wet wooden docks. The air tasted salty with the tang of rotten kelp scattered along the water's edge.

Our warehouse with the potions sat at the far eastern end of Harbor Street where it crossed Lower East Street. Oddly enough, it was close to where Lucas had been killing people. The irony wasn't lost on me.

Lysander fidgeted in the doorway of an abandoned livery stable next to me, giving it a dubious look. Brown paint flaked off old wood, split and cracked from both sun and salty air. Mildew played freely inside, fed by long rotting hay, apples, and forgotten dried manure shoveled into a corner. Feeble, yellow-white light from a nearby street lantern caught the thin sheen of nervous perspiration on his dark, olive-tan complexion.

"Pedro, are you sure we couldn't just be inside the old livery? Maybe up in the loft?"

I raised an eyebrow at him before I glanced through the half-open door next to us. Thieves had broken off the rusted lock some time ago, and the owner never replaced it. I shook my head, turning back to watch the warehouse across the road.

"As sure as yesterday, but go ahead. That ladder looked a bit rotten, but you'll probably make it up there fine." I gently raised my left arm a little, still in its sling. "There's no way I'd manage it with this."

Lysander gave the moldy, dark ladder a longing look. But eventually, he let out a resigned sigh and remained where he was.

"How are you healing, by the way?" he asked. "Getting stabbed in the shoulder twice by a cutlass isn't a small thing. Most lose the arm."

I shrugged with my good shoulder.

"It was close. Storm nearly ran me through on that second thrust. But Elara and I had healing potions. It took all I had with me to get the bleeding under control and repair the cut to something manageable. I've a few stitches still there, and an elixir I took for infection the next morning helped keep that problem at bay."

A sigh tumbled out of me as I gently rubbed at my left shoulder. The stitches itched, ever so slightly.

"Lucky I'm right-handed, so I can fight with a sword if I have to," I admitted ruefully. "But it's still awkward. Then there's the pain. Healing potions never really dull that, even after the wound's healed and the stitches are gone."

I leaned against the stained, tan wooden crates, eyes searching the silent, dark warehouse across the road from us.

"They'll come for it today," I murmured.

"You sure?" Lysander asked.

I nodded toward a nearby dock, still draped in deep black and gray morning shadows. A longboat with five sailors hunched over the oars, silently slipped through the water. Wet oars glimmered in the half-light, rich with malicious promise. Those sailors were silent, but I could just make out the shape of flintlock pistols and swords.

"Positive," I whispered. Carefully, I waved a hand to Ari and Durner, hidden on the other side of the warehouse. After that, I moved deeper into the shadows with Lysander.

The longboat bumped lightly against the dock, and four of the sailors in dark clothes eased out. They raced along the wet planks through the light fog for our warehouse. I glanced at Lysander, who raised his eyebrows with a faint grin.

"This just might be them," he hissed.

It was.

The pirates were in and out in minutes, loaded down with two boxes of what I hoped was the fake cure. We had stored other cargo around them, just to sell the ruse.

Once back in the longboat, the pirates rowed for the bay. Lysander and I eased out of the livery, slipping across to meet with Ari and Durner.

"Did you hear anything?" I asked. "We were too far back from the warehouse."

Durner nodded, but he didn't look happy. Which was, honestly, fairly normal for him, but this time there was a harder edge to his burning copper eyes.

"We did," he replied in his usual craggy voice. "They were mostly cursing the new lock. But one was downright scared over getting skinned alive by Cap'n Storm. Seems they needed to be back within a few hours for the ritual."

Lysander looked alarmed.

"Ritual? They can't be thinking of putting another town to the torch."

"No idea," Ari replied sternly, fluttering her dragonfly wings irritably. "But whatever is happening, they're doing it today, in a few hours."

"It could be that ritual needs to be done at a certain time," I mused. "Probably has to do with the *Codex.* Why at a certain time, escapes me."

Something about that idea stuck in the back of my mind. It was like a splinter worrying the end of my finger. Scowling, I let my thoughts churn on that while I waved to the others.

"In any case, they have the boxes. Let's get back to the *Duchess* so we can follow."

We hurried up Lower East Street, then along Harbor to keep from being seen. After that, we ran to a waiting longboat from the *Silk Duchess* several docks away. Once away from the shore, we tried to keep pace with the pirates, but not draw attention to ourselves. We were partway back to the *Duchess* when my thoughts settled on a likely conclusion.

"Whatever ritual Lucas has cooked can't be close to Kingston," I explained. "It would be aboard the *Rising Eel* at the least, and we've not seen her at anchor in the bay."

"That being the case, that lot won't row out to sea," Durner rumbled. "I mean they could, but if they're expected back at a certain time, rowing a longboat won't do. They'll need something faster."

My thoughts were sprinting faster than I could catch them in words.

"That means there's a small ship waiting." I frowned, squinting into the fog. "Something quick and small to get them to the *Eel.* Lysander, is Elara's tracing dust still on those boxes?"

The navigator closed his eyes, humming a soft tune under his breath, while he traced a circle on the palm of his right hand. A soft blue light flowed into the flat drawing of a compass, like a tattoo. Lysander opened his eyes, holding up his hand. The compass spun, then went still, pointing a glowing blue arrowhead toward the pirates.

"Yes," he replied with a smile. "I feel the pull."

Since I couldn't row because of my shoulder, I looked to starboard. Past the dark water, through the thinning fog, stretched the brown, bleak, sandy shoreline east of Kingston. It was mostly undeveloped land and scrub trees, save for the local hospital and a few houses close to the water.

"Are they just headed down the shoreline?" Ari asked while rowing.

All of that land was owned by one Robert Dukinfield. A member of the Jamaican Assembly and former slave owner, nearly lynched when magic returned like a tidal wave in 1712. He was also an arrogant British scoundrel.

Dukinfield and I weren't on the best of terms. But I knew him well enough that he'd never tolerate 'filthy magic' on his lands. Especially since he regularly sent armed hunters to make sure it didn't happen.

Wavebinders had learned to avoid the place if they wanted to keep their skin intact.

"No. That's *Señor* Robert Dukinfield's land," I muttered harshly. "He'd never let a ritual go on there, no matter who was creating it." My voice turned bitter. "He has a deep grudge against any sort of wavebinder."

I left off the part where he hated alchemists, too. But we alchemists were a 'necessary evil' in his eyes.

"Then where the hells are they headed?" Durner growled.

We had our answer by the time we reached the *Silk Duchess*.

Out of sight of Kingston bay, I spotted a black-sailed sloop anchored past a small thumb of land to the far east of Kingston. Smaller than the *Duchess*, she was a sleek, trim craft with only one mast. Sloops were agile and fast, especially near coastlines.

By the time I painfully climbed aboard the *Silk Duchess*, the pirates had already moved their stolen cargo and set sail.

"Lysander!" I called out over the scramble of the crew around us, then pointed out the sloop.

He joined me at the bow, squinting at the black-sailed ship.

"That'll do it. Sloops are fast. If Captain Storm isn't much farther out than Port Royal, they'll get there quick enough. Easily before us."

He shrugged.

"On time? Can't say. It depends on how fast they were told to get back. Now, if that sloop has a portal platform?"

He shot me a worried look from the corner of his eye, pursing his lips.

"An Arcane Gate would be enough power to get them there in a blink."

That stirred an idea in my head I'd been trying to pin down for days. Icy fear prickled at my nerves.

Power. Raw, primal power.

Suddenly, I had a very nasty idea of where the ritual was being held. What exact, insane thing Lucas was about to try this time. The tattoos on my right hand flared for a brief second in response.

Across the water, a faint glimmer of golden light formed into a round ball on the deck of the sloop. I thought I could feel the light crackle of arcane power drawn down from the Etherwave Arcana across my skin.

"They're opening an Arcane Gate," Lysander snapped.

"That's it!" I ran for my cabin in the stern.

The *Codex* page in my satchel might have the calculations I needed to confirm this horrible theory. Aches rattled through my joints, especially my shoulder. I hissed from the nagging pain, but ignored it. There was worse about to happen.

"What is?" Lysander called out. "Pedro!"

I stopped partway across the deck and fixed Lysander with a haunted look.

"How Lucas is going to get the power for this insane ritual of his. What he's going to break down to get it," I said with a scowl. "It's a wild guess, but damn if it doesn't feel horribly right."

I gestured to the sloop and the first stirrings of an Arcane Gate appearing near the small pirate ship. Already, she'd started to come about for their temporary Gate.

"He's planning to somehow wreck the natural Arcane Gate off Port Royal to steal its power. Maybe even shatter it to pieces so he can rip away the veil between life and death."

Lysander scrubbed his hands over his face.

"Pedro, if he does that," he shook his head, "God, if he does that to a Gate... I'm not sure what would happen. Those pirates could be burned to pieces, but the Gate could also erupt."

"Yes," I snapped, words clawing at my throat. "It also means he might turn loose every nightmare from free roaming ghosts, specters, to the drowned dead... maybe even worse, to devour the living. I'm not sure how we'd stop them."

My frown deepened as I shook my head.

"We need to get to Port Royal's Arcane Gate."

I spun to face Elara at the helm. Her frown said she'd heard the entire conversation.

"Captain..."

"I heard," she replied, cutting me off.

In my mind's eye, I saw legions of the damned crawling out the sea. Undead horrors painting Kingston in sheets of blood.

Elara punched the railing with a fist, then took a breath, eyes blazing.

"Lysander! Open a Gate!"

She punched the railing again. The *Duchess* seemed to creak back with eager anticipation.

"Durner! Call to quarters! I want those cannons manned and ready! I'm done with subtle. Let's send a monster to hell."

30

A Quiet Place Between Heaven and Hell

Aug 8, 1722. Off the coast of Port Royal, Jamaica. Sailing through the gates of hell...

In a flash of power, we snapped through the Arcane Gate, expecting a fight. What we got was a private little war.

The world dropped out from underneath us before the *Silk Duchess* slammed down onto whitecaps and storm-tossed waves. Saltwater roared over the deck as we turned hard, cannons creaking ferally against their breech ropes.

"Fire!"

Elara's shout cut the air like a hot saber. The deck lurched, cannon thundering out a broadside. Smoke belched over the sea like an angry dragon's breath. Cannon shot tore over the waves, iron fists racing for the pirates.

Our broadside hammered the sloop's foredeck and bashed into her bowsprit. Wood splinters erupted like a furious geyser. Men screamed as waves broke over the railing. Next to the sloop, the *Rising Eel* lurched hard, timbers shrieking, while she took her own black eye.

"Reload! Those pirates won't sink themselves!"

Durner's craggy voice was a peal of thunder across the deck. Gun crews raced to comply. The *Silk Duchess* crested another wave, then plowed ahead.

Behind us, Lysander's Arcane Gate collapsed with a furious roar, winking out of existence. It gave the air a sudden sharp smell of spent magic.

Across the waves, the *Rising Eel's* crew came alive, stung from the hit. Sails dropped, catching the strong wind. Beside her, the smaller black-sailed sloop lurched forward, still in the fight. Past them both, a mottled, battered wooden cargo barge floated next to Port Royal's natural Arcane Gate.

Lysander's timing with the Gate had been perfect. The pirates weren't ready for a fight, but had unloaded the bait. I saw the boxes sitting on that barge.

Sea spray from shattered whitecaps jumped over the deck, spattering everyone like a sideways storm. The tang of burnt powder mixed with scents of mild terror and eager excitement, sprinkled with brine.

I clutched the gunwale until my knuckles turned dead white. The tattoos on my right hand pulsed and glimmered, eager for a fight like everyone else. I wasn't much different.

Dryden Storm had a lot to answer for, but I was focused on the greater of the two evils. The one I knew was the real problem.

"Where the hell are you, Lucas?" I murmured angrily, wiping the sea spray from my face.

A silent tug pulled at me, seductive and insistent. It was like dark silken spider webs picked at my heart, drawing my eyes to that barge. Then a devious siren's song of death magic quietly reached my ears over the battle.

"The barge." I nodded. "That's where you are."

I squinted at it while the pirate ships got underway. The barge rode low in the water, too low for the open sea. Its type was better suited for shoreline work. Battered and old, it'd seen better days. It was a miracle that the thing had survived sailing to the Arcane Gate.

Finally, I spotted Lucas. He was the sole occupant on the barge, vomiting his stomach out. The shadow of a familiar overturned box of green potions lay beside him. Elixirs with enough graveyard syrup to quiet a city-sized necropolis, with enough spiced rum and hot peppers to give it that little kick.

Too bad he couldn't hold down his rum, or the graveyard syrup.

"Durner!" I yelled. "The wraith! He's aboard the barge!"

The grimling Master Gunner's rust-red beard split into a bright grin of violence.

"Oh really? More for the fish!"

Then he was off, shouting orders to the cannon crews.

I glanced from the barge to the Gate.

Arcane Gates are basically a force of nature. Something like a contained hurricane that hates everything. The ones created by navigators like Lysander are only temporary, lasting minutes. The navigators could—and did—close them. If not, they collapsed on their own as the world expelled the magical invasion.

A natural Gate was different.

They weren't made by people. They didn't collapse, but lurked out of sight in the sea, rooted to tiny granite islands, until a ship drew near or they were summoned. Then they roared into view—like the one Lucas was standing next to.

I lost sight of both wood wraith and barge when the *Rising Eel* blocked it from view. The *Eel* dropped her gunports, stabbing the air with rage and iron. I ducked, pulling my tricorn hat low, shielding my eyes.

Pirate iron slammed into our deck, exploding wood in a storm of dying timbers. Splinters lanced out, eager for blood. Two cannons shattered while a snapped yardarm sailed out to sea. Shouts and screams of the crew filled the air, thicker than old blood.

I bandaged whom I could, then raced up the short steps to the helm. Anywhere to get a better look at Lucas and his barge. I nearly jumped out of my skin when Lysander materialized out of the powder smoke beside me.

"What is it?" he asked.

"Lucas."

I said the name like a curse coated in rotten meat. At that moment, the *Duchess* turned hard to port, rigging aching for release, as we returned fire.

Our shots slammed against the *Eel*, knocking her askew. Shattered wood and nails were a sudden storm of death aboard the brigantine, breaking rigging and crew alike. A smoldering cannon broke loose, tearing open a new hole in the hull for the sea as an afterthought.

While the *Duchess* and *Eel* circled each other in a dance of death, the barge edged into view. Past the smoke, the old hauler was intact, still moored to the Gate. I slammed a fist on the railing.

"One good broadside into that barge could end this, or most of it," I said, waving a hand in frustration in that direction.

Lysander scowled through the smoke. Two shots from the half-shattered, black-sailed sloop whistled overhead, missing our rigging by a foot. The navigator glanced between our cannons and the barge.

"We've turned too much. Nothing has a clear shot." He shook his head bitterly. "If I judge Elara's course, we'll cut straight, then turn hard-a-starboard. That'll put the barge to our port, just below our cannons."

The *Duchess* spit iron again, this time at the black-sailed sloop. Broken, wet timber belched up and out as the small ship's waterline vanished. The sloop almost collapsed in on itself while the sea slowly claimed her.

"That's one!" Durner roared and our crew cheered.

I didn't feel like celebrating.

"Clear and reload!" he called out. The order echoed down the line with crisp precision.

Then an idea hit me.

Ship battles weren't constant blood and thunder. They were duels. Deadly dances of timing, distance, and misdirection.

Right then? Neither the *Duchess* nor the *Rising Eel* were ready, since the angles were all wrong. That would change in minutes as both ships rushed to be the first to fire.

"Cannons aren't the only way to solve this," I said, eyeing the bow of the *Duchess,* her rigging, then the barge.

Lysander followed my gaze, reading me far better than I liked, then swore under his breath, slapping the railing.

"A boarding action? On that barge? Now? Compass and coin, Pedro, do you just enjoy dancing on a grave's edge? You'll die before you get there."

I scowled as repair crews scrambled around us, securing tattered rigging, knocked loose from the previous volley.

"No, I won't. Listen."

I pointed between the *Silk Duchess* and the barge.

"Our cannons won't be able to hit the barge, but I could swing aboard. The *Duchess* will shield me from anyone aboard the *Eel* with a long rifle. Once on the barge, I ruin the ritual, *Codex*, maybe even Lucas. All of it. End the nightmare."

Lysander's mouth pulled into a thin line. I could tell he hated this idea, but he also saw the meat of it.

"This is insane," he said in a brittle voice, rubbing his eyes. "I'm also insane, because it makes a kind of desperate sense."

He glared at the *Rising Eel* while her crew frantically made what repairs they could. The brigantine turned, trying to catch the wind. On the barge, Lucas pushed to his knees, trying to get to his feet.

"Lysander, we'll only get one chance at this," I said firmly. "Lucas shook off a shot to the throat, so he'll shake off those potions. I doubt he'll fall for this twice."

"Elara's going to hate this," Lysander groaned.

Given the brief lull in the battle, Elara had swept down from the helm in a mad blur of dragonfly-like wings to the deck. Her captain's coat was now unbuttoned, singed, with two new smoking holes along the hemline. The cream-cotton shirt she wore was stained with a little blood. None of it hers.

She had rushed over to help pull a trapped crewman to safety, or at least safe enough to get him bandaged.

I locked eyes with her, and she froze. The wind caught loose strands of hair from her chestnut braid, tossing them about in a wild flurry. A hard flicker touched her jade-gold eyes before she side-eyed that battered barge, then me.

If Lysander could sometimes read me like a book, Elara had me memorized.

She took one last check on the two bruised crewmen, then turned on her heel, storming over to us. Mouth pulled into a complicated line, she planted her boots, snatching me close by my collar. I nearly stumbled off my feet.

"*Asa mvur,*" she said in a low, hard voice, barely audible over the chaos. "If you die, I'll find a way to bring you back, then murder you proper. We clear?"

A lopsided grin tugged at my face.

"For you, *querida?*" My grin widened. "Crystal."

There was more, but it was said with a look. Memories of a bloody battlefield, mud-stained bandages, and too many spells from the Etherwave rolled between us. She glanced at Lysander from the corner of her eye.

"That goes double for anyone with him."

Never a fool, Lysander touched a hand to his forehead.

"Understood, Captain."

With a last silent look at me, along with words we didn't say out loud, she let go. It was completing a ritual we'd performed a dozen times before.

In the end, she was the captain of the *Silk Duchess*. I was just an alchemist. We both knew what we had to do.

Elara barked orders in rapid succession like a series of rifle shots on an icy day. As always, her confidence alone painted a fresh coat of polished resolve on the crew.

At the same time, I ran to the port side with Lysander, ducking errant bits of cord and sail. Physical pain in my left shoulder gave way to a bright burn of worry. There wasn't time to think, only to just keep moving.

Minutes passed like seconds. A half attempt at a broadside from the *Rising Eel* bounced off our hull. Our reply was better, cracking timber above her waterline.

Off to port, the old weathered barge was still moored to the Gate. Sure enough at the center sat the *Codex* resting on a cobbled together pedestal of former crates. But it wasn't just sitting quietly.

That book breathed with a dark power.

Soot-stained symbols traced around those crates writhed in the sun. A light haze, like an angry shadow, paced around the book. It reminded me of a wild animal caged too long. Finally, whispering black smoke curled off the *Codex* pages, rich with dark promise.

Next to the barge, the Arcane Gate loomed impossibly large. Each glowing rune, compass mark, and other symbols that lined the massive arch looked carved by a crazed titan with a ragged chisel.

I felt it staring down at me expectantly, primal magic churning along its length. But mostly the Gate waited. Watching. Wary.

Lucas, having heaved even the faintest memory of a meal to the deck, stared hate at me. I gave back double. He was five yards, if that, from the *Codex*.

Elara's sudden shout snapped the tension, shooting ice through my soul.

"They're coming in!" she bellowed, yanking her glowing ghost blade free of its scabbard. "Prepare for boarders!"

Somehow, the *Rising Eel* was right there on us. Ropes with grappling hooks flooded the sky. Some missed, others hooked the *Duchess*, and a dire few hooked crewmates.

Captain Storm was the first across. Elara met him as soon as the pirate's boots touched our deck, swords crossing in an ugly clash of steel. Lysander grabbed me on the shoulder, while Ari and Skaldi raced over to join my mad gambit.

"Now or never!" Lysander yelled.

The tattoos on my hand burst to life the instant I grabbed the rope to swing over to the barge.

"Yes, Doctor," the mysterious voice whispered out of those flames. *"It's now or never..."*

Over on the barge, Lucas shoved himself to his feet, stumbling for the *Codex.* Dark mist swirled around his hands.

I looked back at the *Duchess*, my friends, the crew, and finally Elara. Below me, the waves churned, boiling like a watery abyss of whitecap and salt spray.

With a resigned sigh, I stepped off the side into that quiet, empty space between heaven and hell.

31

Salt and Shadow

Aug 8, 1722. At the Port Royal Arcane Gate, dancing on the edge of my grave...

I was subtle as a kick to the head when I swung down on a rope to the death-stained barge. After all, I had slammed a boot heel across Lucas Argall's jaw when I arrived, knocking him away from the *Codex*.

Bloody screams and the shouts of the battle chased after me, fading back into the smoke while I landed in a deep crouch. Lucas crumpled to the deck, eyes rolling in pain, while he clutched his battered mouth. Amber, resin-like blood oozed between his fingers. He'd recover, but it'd take time.

With a wet, garbled scream of anger, he scrambled out of reach to the ship's bow. Lysander and the others dropped down next to me a second later.

The sea boiled around the barge, a cloudy, agitated soup of gray-green brine mixed with the dark blue water. Gray-black wisps of putrid mist clung to wood, hair, and more. It was raw, untapped death magic, whispering from the Etherwave Arcana. The power slid over my bare skin with a lover's touch, even as it tried to suck the air out of my chest.

I drank in the scent of salt air and decay while I stood. A sharp cough later, I caught Lysander's eyes, then glanced at Ari and Skaldi.

"Watch that one and stay out of his reach," I said quickly with a nod toward Lucas. "His touch is poison. Also? Wood wraith or no, he's also an Archbinder."

"Well, shit," Skaldi rumbled, sounding almost like his brother Durner.

Ari paled, while Lysander looked stoic.

The battered wooden boxes with the fake cure were still aboard. I turned one over, then scooped up the last few vials before handing them out.

"Use this. It's poisonous to him. While it won't kill him, it will slow him down. Don't be shy about using it."

Lysander eyed the fluid, then quickly coated his short sword with it until the blade turned sickly green.

"What about you? The *Codex?*"

I nodded, hand itching to draw my sword to join my friends. But not this time. This required a more complicated solution.

"Yes, keep him busy while I try to stop what Lucas was trying to start." I met their eyes. "Hurry. He heals, but not fast. Watch yourselves, my friends."

Then the barge suddenly lurched up under our feet, as if a wave had punched the keel.

"Look out!" I yelled, shoving Lysander aside.

Dark wooden deck planks rippled like brackish, splintery sewage water along the barge. We scattered, but the violent torrent was fast, crashing into us like an angry tide. Lysander stumbled out of its path, while Ari took flight in a flutter of wings. Skaldi and I weren't so lucky.

The warped boards hit us full-on, metal nails lashing out like crude pistol shots.

Skaldi dropped into a crouch, using his natural, squat grimling bulk to hold ground. I also knelt, but yanked my long coat over my face. We avoided the nails, but the planks were another story. They hit us like a hammer. We fell hard, slammed backwards across the deck.

The wave of wood passed. I staggered to my feet, shaking my head to clear away blurry vision. A new bruise warmed my forearm.

"Wood. Of course," I murmured. "Naturally, a wood wraith can control wood, and we're standing on a wooden ship."

Skaldi fared better than I did. The blue and rust-haired grimling gave me a quick nod that told me he was battered, but not out. He stood, yanking his faded dark green waistcoat straight, then scooped up his axe with an ugly scowl.

A crack of wood and a rasping growl snapped our attention sharply to the bow. Lucas was back on his feet, eyes blazing.

"I gave you a chance, Doctor," Lucas wheezed, voice like rough sand.

The wraith wiped amber blood from his lips, rubbing at his once-broken, mummified jaw.

"You could have joined me, joined *us*, in changing the world. One last chance, Doctor. Send your minions away. Join us, or die."

Lucas stood hunched like a feral predator at the ship's bow, eyes bright with burning hate and deranged hope. Overall, he looked about as he had in Westmere—an impossibly bone-thin man, wearing a ragged green and brown hooded long coat over tattered stylish clothes.

But this time his hood was tossed back, showing his full, terrifying face. The man's skin resembled paper-thin, poorly sanded wood, like a skeleton wearing a mummified skin-suit. Past the undead trappings, he still resembled his brother, Joshua, right down to the sandy hair and deep, watery blue eyes.

I shot a glare at him, taking a deep breath to steady my fraying patience.

"No."

The word snapped out like a whip crack. I packed the conversation from Westmere in that word, tying it up with a bow of final determination. Lucas' blue eyes turned ice cold.

"Then die," the wraith growled, a chilly smirk on his lips.

"You first, señor," I replied, tipping my tricorn hat.

Lucas flung out a withered hand at us, and the air bristled with corrupted Etherwave power running wild. Deck planks rippled again like a sickly sludge before they rose upright. The wind howled as sharp cracking sounds flooded the air.

In the time to breathe twice, wooden planks twisted, split, then reformed into spindly tree-skeletons, complete with ragged claws. They rushed at us in a manic clatter of dry, dead branches, eager for blood, desperate to slice through clothes, skin, anything in reach.

I could almost taste the corrupted enchantment, rancid as old cheese. Lucas caught us by surprise once, but not twice.

"You get the book, Pedro. We'll hold him off," Lysander called over the wind.

He darted around an animated murder-tree, then rushed for the bow. Nearby, Ari and Skaldi exchanged a nod as they fanned out, corralling the skeletons between them. Skaldi put his axe to good use, turning skeleton-trees to kindling. Ari darted to one side, then the other. But being thayan, above was always an option.

She shot into the air, dragonfly wings a blur, before she dove at the nearest skeleton. Several quick chops later, tree-skeleton parts clattered to the deck. Black smoke coiled off the severed, warped wood, as if she'd beaten a foul spirit out of them.

At the bow, Lucas Argall rubbed his hands with a feral grin. Dark burns, like hell's own tattoos, crawled over his face, with a death-lust in his bright eyes. The wraith slapped his hands together before yanking them apart. A knotted, soot-streaked staff of petrified wood grew into twisted life between his hands.

The bastard was actually enjoying himself.

Lucas lunged and blocked Lysander's cut, then swung for my friend's head. Inhuman, undead speed or not, Lysander gracefully danced aside, avoiding a crushed skull.

The rest of what happened with that fight was a mystery to me, since I was busy trying not to die.

I darted around one of the tree-skeletons, racing for the middle of the barge and the *Codex*. It was right where I remembered, perched on a maniac's pedestal of ruined crates, surrounded by those slithering, sooty alchemist symbols. That same dark haze still covered it like a mound.

Only now, it had stopped moving.

By the time I reached the symbols, the haze had condensed into a dark, shadowy silhouette of a man with the ragged memory of thayan wings. Its eyes burned like red coals in a starless night of choking soot. I reached for my sword, but thought better of it. That wasn't my strong suit, and I was tired of getting stabbed.

"Tristam Greenholm, I presume?" I asked casually, reaching for my potions.

"Yes!" he snarled, voice like a hollow grave. "I know you, thief. You stole a page from my *Codex*."

Morowen's former lover turned attempted killer blew out an icy breath, probably out of habit from once being alive.

"I can smell the kelp stench of the sea hag on you," he hissed, making my spine shiver. "You're one of Morowen's tools, here to ruin my great work."

"Your insane plan, you mean?"

I kept my tone casual, even though my heart hammered at my ribs. Tristam had to be centuries old, and I had no idea how I understood him. I blamed it on the necromantic magic wrapped around the barge like a diseased shawl. Before he ranted at me about his 'great work', I cut him off. Especially since I felt I'd get only one chance at my own insane plan.

"You're right, señor, I do know Morowen," I snapped back with a dark, pointed smile. "She sends her regards and hopes you rot in hell!"

I darted between the sigils, avoiding them all. With a free hand, I popped the cork from a vial and tossed a purified mix of garlic and St. John's Wart at Tristam. He shrieked, stepping back as the repellent hit him. It would only last a moment, but I hoped that would be enough.

Then I breached the charcoal-black circle of grime and realized too late what I'd walked into. A wall of shimmering power slammed into me. I suddenly realized I'd been wrong. Lucas wasn't about to start the ritual—he'd already started it.

A strange, twisted energy filled the air, like living lightning looking for a victim. As for Tristam? He was regenerating into a withered walking corpse, still connected to the damn *Codex*. The necromancer was *feeding* off the Arcane Gate like a vampire.

"Dios mío!" I gasped, my eyes drawn to the Gate.

Cracks ran along the massive structure. Dark, jagged veins of destruction stretched from base to top. Pallid mist oozed from every fissure. Where there wasn't mist, there were ghastly white skeletal and ghostly fingers, working to snap the Gate piece by piece. Through the widest gaps, I saw a bleak, ruined gray landscape—a twisted and blasted mirror of our own.

"My work must continue!" Tristam shrieked, rushing forward.

"No!" I yelled as I dove for the *Codex.*

We reached it at the same time, each of us with a hand on the book. Tristam screamed like a banshee and clawed at my face. I ducked before I lost an eye.

In a fear-induced rush, I desperately snatched a potion from a belt loop, popping the cork. With a smooth motion, I soaked Tristam's face and arms in a thick, lime green fluid. He spat out a scream from the depths of his rotten soul as the graveyard syrup did its work.

Tristam recoiled, clawing at his undead skin, while the syrup boiled him like hot acid. The sharp stench from the gray steam assaulted my nose, making my eyes water. He let go of the *Codex*, and I snatched it off the pedestal. But I stepped back too quickly and tripped. Off balance, I stumbled to one knee right onto the slithering dark symbols outside the circle.

I screamed as dark power drove burning spikes right through me.

In that moment, the primal power of the Arcane Gate pulsed through me and the ritual, all to feed the burning reanimated corpse of Tristam Greenholm. It was magic that no one could or should tamper with. It was as if I were trying to swallow raw lightning hurled from a thunderstorm.

Somewhere, Tristam laughed with a ragged cough as I collapsed to the deck. The symbols swarmed over me like a nest of stinging ants. The world slipped sideways, falling away, a loose mix of memories and fatigue as smoke curled out of my mouth, draining away my life.

"I... I'm sorry," I breathed low, apologizing to my friends, my crew, and Elara for dragging them into this horror.

"Oh, this," the Tristam rasped with a dark laugh. "*This* is what I needed. You taste *delightful*. Lucas has served me well. Just perfect. Goodbye, *thief*. It's over."

A sharp pain stabbed my heart. I felt myself spasm, as if my body wasn't even mine to control.

Suddenly, a bright, hot warmth burned in my hand, while anger smudged my thoughts.

With deliberate effort, I slapped a hand to the deck. The sharp crack sounded loud enough to break stone. I pushed to my feet while ghostfire burned over my hand, dripping like molten, green-white liquid, eager to chase the corrupt symbols like a feral cat. In my left hand, a charcoal steam rose from the *Codex*.

I sucked in a ragged breath.

"No, señor."

The sound of my voice shocked me. I sounded ragged, raw, and just *done*. It was deeper with an echo, as if someone else, far away, spoke with me.

"I may not have stopped your ritual, señor, but oh no... we are *just* getting started."

A grin tugged at the corner of my lips.

"After all, I gave my word to my captain."

We faced each other, silent as the calm eye of a hurricane. He tensed. I flexed the fingers of my right hand. The *Codex Luminari* pulsed angrily in my grip.

"You don't have a chance," Tristam sneered. "You're alone."

The wind shifted, sharp with the wet promise of rain. Overhead, I heard the whisper of leathery wings beat against the breeze, then a low hiss like an omen.

I let a sly smirk drift over my face, slow as the morning sunrise.

"Not quite, señor."

Blue-white corpse fire exploded from the necromancer's hands.

I moved, hand flashing for the vials along my belt.

Tristam never noticed the bobcat-sized tumble of purple freckled leathery wings, claws, and anger until it was too late.

32

By Ink and Will

Aug 8, 1722. Aboard the ruined pirate barge off Port Royal. Nearly swimming with the sharks...

Sebastian slammed into Tristam like an irate harpoon. Claws and teeth ripped into the necromancer like a savage whirlwind.

Tristam shrieked. The magic flames around his hands shredded away as he threw his arms over his face. With him distracted, I yanked my sword free of its scabbard, then rushed forward.

Before I got close, he backhanded Sebastian across the jowls with a fist, sending him tumbling to the deck.

"Damn beast!"

The necromancer turned on me with a glare. Sickly greenish-black vapors curled off his fingers as I felt him draw down the Etherwave Arcana. A second later, the acrid smoke erupted into spectral green fire. He lashed out with a burning hand as I closed the distance between us.

Morowen told me almost nothing could destroy the *Codex*. I hoped that story had been true.

It was.

The instant that the *Codex* touched the flames, it soaked them in like a dry sponge. Its cover was still steaming when I bashed the book across Tristam's jaw. His head snapped to the side before he stumbled against that solid haze of dark fog surrounding us.

I glanced at the *Codex,* the fog, then narrowed my eyes at Tristam.

"You're not free yet, are you?" I murmured.

Wide-eyed, Tristam lunged for my throat or the book, maybe both. Instead, he met my sword when I rammed it through his undead guts.

I shoved him off my blade with a shoulder, pushing him back against that boiling, foggy wall of darkness. He stood up and started to pull down more power, when Sebastian spat at him.

The gargoyle's spit-tar splattered across Tristam's face, while stray tendrils of it smeared over part of those rotten dragonfly wings. Tristam fell backwards again, then to my surprise, was stuck to that hazy mystic boundary. That was something I'd think about later.

Now tarred in place, I got my first real look at Tristam Greenholm. I really hoped it would be my last.

The necromancer was a twisted mockery of his thayan ancestry. Pasty, drawn skin was stretched over a too-thin body. He looked like every pallid, nightmarish drawing of a vampire come to unlife. Fangs? I had no idea, but his eyes were solid black, just like his ragged, torn dragonfly wings. His ratty clothes hung loose and threadbare, out of style by twenty years.

Last was the place where I'd hit him with the graveyard syrup. That had burned a line of scars over his sunken face.

"What *are* you?" I asked, horrified.

Tristam hissed back like a furious, maligned snake. I raised my sword, now decorated with a dark ichor from when I'd stabbed him, and backed up.

"Give it to me!" he spat.

Those ragged thayan wings tore like tissue as Tristam ripped himself loose of the tar. Once free, he reached again, skeletal hands clawing for both myself and the *Codex*.

I side-stepped and slashed, cutting away more of those ragged wings. The necromancer growled, but another hot blurt of tar from Sebastian stopped him in his tracks. I bolted for the edge of the hellish haze.

"Sebastian!" I called.

He raced over the wooden deck toward me in a scramble of manic claws. Tristam recovered, nearly flying at us like every bad myth of a vampire taken shape.

Icy cold fingers lightly brushed along my neck like the tender caress of Death itself. I shuddered, ducked, then half-turned for a quick swipe behind me. It wasn't a serious cut, but I still connected.

Tristam howled, falling to the deck with a thump while sporting a new, dark charcoal slice along his neck that he didn't seem to notice.

I ran for the ghostly wall of dark haze, betting on a guess that Tristam couldn't follow me. Behind me, he got to his feet in a half-crouch, like a deranged predator. He charged, even as I dove for the swirl of sooty fog.

That slam of power from before hit all at once and wrapped around me like a weighted net. I curled to my side, shoulder first, as the deadly enchantment draining my life tried to keep me there. Invisible threads with countless hooks tugged at my heart, trying to steal the air from my lungs.

Suddenly, I was through, still clutching the *Codex,* even as the sword slipped from my hand.

I hit the deck sideways and bit back a yell when I landed on my left shoulder. Needles of pain traced a manic path along my arm between back and fingertips. I groaned, holding my arm.

All at once, Sebastian was there to help. He immediately braced against my good shoulder and applied a sandpaper tongue and wet nose to my face. I coughed out a rasping, dry chuckle.

"Yes, thank you, Sebastian. I'm alive."

Quick as I could, I forced myself up and rolled to my feet. After that, I scooped up my sword.

Behind us, I saw the shadowy apparition of Tristam Greenholm pound spectral fists against that clouded mystic barrier. He screamed, but I couldn't hear a word over the wind and sea.

I glanced at Sebastian, who barked at me furiously.

"He's not a ghost, Sebastian." I shook my head. "Tristam is something else. An actual vampire? A revenant? I don't know. This is a problem for a fully trained wavebinder. I'm just an alchemist."

Sebastian scratched the deck with his claws, then huffed at me.

I sighed, looked at my sword, then at Tristam. At the other end of the barge, Lysander and the others were in a hard fight against Lucas and the last of his tree-skeletons. My friends were winning, but only just, and it showed.

"All I know are potions, poisons, and cures," I murmured. "They'll have to do."

I tensed as a cough wracked my chest and ghostfire flared around my hand. Once it stopped, I quickly tucked the *Codex* under my arm, pulling the last vials of graveyard syrup and undead repellent off my belt. Calculations ran through my head like a waterfall of numbers and ingredients.

"They should mix fine and last long enough on my blade to stab Tristam a few times. Maybe it'll act like a..."

"No," said a now familiar soft, deep voice in my mind. *"You hold the anchor. His anchor. Bind what cannot die."*

I shook my head, well past worrying that I looked addled for talking to myself, or the fire on my hand.

"What?"

I drank in another breath of salt-smoke air. Something nearby was on fire other than me.

"*His* anchor?" I echoed thickly.

Then the words sank in past the pain. His anchor. Tristam Greenholm's anchor. That *Codex* page wasn't just some scribbled formula with elemental symbols to anchor that misguided ritual.

It was a specific anchor for *him*, and I'd stolen it.

"He's tethered to that book because of what Morowen did, and what he did, but I have his anchor." I nodded. "I stole it by writing on the page, expanding what was there."

An idea swirled in my mind even as I reached for my satchel. But it wasn't there. A cold realization shot through me.

"Damn. I left it aboard the *Duchess*." I blew out a hot sigh. "There's no time to get it, I'll need to improvise. I'll need ink to draw a new anchor in the *Codex* based on what I remember."

Nothing nearby looked helpful, until my eyes settled on the rough ring of dark dust on the deck that held Tristam captive. Sea swells crashed up and over the listing barge, splashing against that dust, smearing the deck with a greasy sheen.

"Ink. That's ink," I snapped.

Sheathing my sword, I raced for the circle, Sebastian on my heels. I stayed outside it this time, but close enough to reach it. Past the thin, sooty fog, Tristam beat his fists against the mystic wall, screaming incoherent rage.

The strange symbols still slithered like wild snakes in a hypnotic pattern. Beyond those lay the ragged ink dust ring. My eyes snapped up to Tristam, then back to the ink. The panicked look on his face told me he knew what I was about to do. Desperately, the man stepped back, slamming fire enchantments against the sooty ink boundary.

It held, but for how long was anyone's guess. I'd fallen across that edge once, which may have weakened it.

"Watch him, Sebastian," I said gravely. "If he sticks even one undead finger out of that fog, tear it off."

Sebastian turned in a quick crouch, snarling at Tristam. The apparition didn't look worried, only more frantic.

I set the *Codex* on the deck, opened to a blank page, then pulled out three vials. One was graveyard syrup, another was the undead repellent, and the third was empty. I carefully scooped a small amount of the ink dust, then mixed it with the two potions. Green fluid turned brown, then a shimmering black.

"Do I say anything?" I asked aloud. "Maybe it's more what I write than what I say?"

Nothing answered beyond the roar of the sea, howl of wind, and the distant clash of nearby fighting. So, I went with what I knew.

"I'm a privateer of the sea, of the waves and wind..." I hummed softly.

A soft rush of the Etherwave Arcana flowed through me in reply.

Quickly, I snatched up a nearby finger of wood, a casualty of Ari's recent fight against the tree-skeletons. I shook my makeshift ink mixture once more, dipped in the twig, and redrew the anchor page as best I could from memory.

From symbol to formula, I hastily recreated that page, or most of it. I replaced parts I suspected might help Tristam with my own designs. They were desperate, untried calculations and formulas that I half prayed would work. While I wrote, a strange glowing blue mist rose from the words, reaching toward Tristam.

Sebastian suddenly barked. I looked up to see the fog fading, like mist under a morning sun. Tristam grinned savagely, then charged. Frantically, I inscribed the last words at the bottom of the page.

"With this anchor lies Tristan Greenholm, bound by ink, flame, and surest will."

Tristam yelled as he grabbed my coat, hands burning with more spectral green flames. I knocked his hand away, snatching up the *Codex* to defend myself.

Suddenly, wet ink shimmered. The letters burst to life, bright as a lighthouse beam. A blast of thunder rolled overhead as the purest white light I'd ever seen exploded off that page.

The blanket of white light snapped around Tristam in an instant. Glowing chains of lightning locked around him, trapping him before he touched me again. Then, with a blinding pop, those chains yanked him bodily *into* the book. He became nothing more than a lurid, chained illustration along the corner of the page.

After that, the *Codex* flew out of my hands onto the deck. The cover snapped closed like a spring trap with a crack of sharp thunder. A gentle steam issued up from between the pages.

Then, before my eyes, a symbol I didn't recognize burned itself into the cover. It was a thin circle, and inside it was what could've been a letter 'A', or perhaps the stylized shape of an Arcane Gate. That emblem glowed once with a soft yellow-white light, then faded away.

I sat down on the deck, wracked with exhaustion and pain. Sebastian insistently bumped my leg with his horned head.

"We're not done, I know," I gasped.

A scream, ragged with rage, split the air the instant I climbed to my feet.

"What have you done?"

It was Lucas Argall.

I snatched up the *Codex* and reached for whatever potion I had left, or my sword. It didn't matter which, as the barge's abused deck finally surrendered.

Wooden planks gave way with a groan underneath me and anyone nearby. I fell to the lower deck with Sebastian, while wreckage avalanched around us. My gargoyle scurried to safety in a scramble of claws and a flurry of wings. I covered my face, rolling out of the way.

By the time I stood up, Lucas had dropped to the lower deck with us. The wood wraith stood barely ten feet away, rage smeared across his mummified face. He still carried that gnarled, gray wooden staff, only now it was painted with a dash of blood at one end.

I quickly glanced up through the hole to the deck above, but I couldn't see the others. All I heard was distant shouts and possibly a fight, nothing more. Overhead, more cracks ran through the Arcane Gate. A wall of storm clouds swirled overhead, stabbing lightning against the mystic arch.

"That was my last chance to be cured!" Lucas snarled. "I'll kill you!"

"I'm sure you'll try, señor," I replied with a small, tired smile.

Lucas darted forward, but I was already on the move. I was nearly out of potions, but I still had a trick or two up my sleeve. Quick as a wink, I snatched a vial off my belt filled with a boiling, gray mist, then popped off the cork.

Smoke poured from the vial in a raging torrent. It billowed up and out, hungry to swallow the air. Gray clouds boiled around me as a dark grin spread over my face.

I melted into the rising fog with a deep, echoing laugh.

33

Splinters and Smoke

Aug 8, 1722. Aboard the ruined pirate barge off Port Royal, dueling for my life with a madman...

My alchemy worked as intended. That is to say, I vanished into the murky gray illusion, nothing more than a lethal puff of fog. It amplified my voice, lightly mesmerizing anyone who looked my way.

But it didn't keep me from getting hurt.

I watched Lucas's eyes dance in horror while I melted into mist. But it was my laugh that got him moving. Quickly, in a panic-driven rush, he closed the gap and looked around. I backed away, but there wasn't much room on the ship's lower deck.

"Where are you?" he screamed, eyes bright with rage.

Lucas swung wildly. I slipped aside, but his staff still clipped me.

A sharp, stabbing pain tore into my left hand like a dozen needles. Despite the ache, I clenched my jaw, and kept quiet while I darted around behind the madman. Sebastian followed my lead.

What I know of a wood wraith, any wraith, I could put in a thimble. But I knew wraiths were infectious. A brief look at my hand told me everything. The skin around the red welt where I'd been hit had already cracked at the edges and hardened like bark.

I was infected, slowly turning to wood.

"You're still here," Lucas growled while he swatted the fog twice more. "I know you are! Show yourself!"

A part of me wondered how much more abuse I could take. Would I make it back in time to get the real cure that I had ironically invented?

The answer was obvious. I had to.

So, I shoved those thoughts aside and focused on staying alive.

Quick and quiet, I pulled the last two vials of my poisoned, half-working petrify cure from my belt. I poured one along my blade until it dripped a sickly green. The other? That one I drank down in one swallow, followed by a healing elixir, then fought the urge to vomit.

I never lied about the tainted potion. It had a mild dose of the real cure, at least enough to work for a few minutes.

But the rum and scorpion peppers I mixed in made it burn off fast, and then let the infection run wild. The concentrated bloodroot I added? That was just herbal revenge. I just never realized it would be for me.

Lucas turned fast when the potion corks hit the deck, then jerked when I buried two inches of poisoned steel in his gut. The wraith sputtered, wide-eyed, then clawed at my face. I knocked his hand aside, careful to keep the sleeve of my long coat between his hand and my skin.

"Well, hello there, señor," I said with a devilish grin that I didn't quite feel. "I'm right here."

I withdrew my sword, then stabbed twice more in quick succession. Lucas sputtered and jerked with each hit. We separated, the wraith glaring raw hate as the alchemical fog swallowed me again. Amber-resin blood flowed in thick rivers down his midsection.

"Clever alchemy, Doctor," Lucas wheezed. "Your own invention? Let me show you one of mine."

His staff exploded in blue-white flames. Quick as a snake, he lashed out with his weapon. Spectral fire burned a line through my fog, parting it like a sharp knife. His staff slammed against the deck, and the barge shuddered in its death throes.

I darted back in shock, even as Sebastian spit hot tar into the wraith's face. Lucas scraped the steaming mess from his face and swung twice at Sebastian. My gargoyle danced aside both times, then retreated through the withering fog.

It became a tango of death. He swung, I side-stepped, the fog thinned, then we warily circled each other. My only cover evaporated from the assault of the wraith's enchantment.

Lucas healed each time I stabbed him. But, undead or not, the rules of enchantments remained the same.

First, magical power can heal a wound, but the body remembers it should be in pain.

Second?

Using the Etherwave Arcana—what some call magic—always comes with a price. The Etherwave gives, but it also takes. Sunlight suddenly flashed overhead once, then twice, as the clouds parted above us.

A desperate idea sprang to mind.

The last of my fog vanished, and I swapped glares with Lucas from ten feet away. All around us, the barge cracked and groaned, pounded to death by the sea and the unhinged power that bled from the Arcane Gate.

"You don't look so good, Doctor," Lucas sneered as he winced from another new stab I'd put in his side.

I dragged a shaking hand across my face to wipe away sweat. It stank of poison and death.

"That would make two of us, you lunatic."

Lucas laughed. It sounded like wood grating against itself. But his withered face looked gray, as the tainted mixture started to take hold.

His eyes studied me for a moment, then he lunged. I dodged aside, a bit too slow, as the bloodroot continued to torture me, even as the half-cure tried to help. But I still parried, turning aside the wraith's flaming staff before it touched me.

"I see you're petrifying, Doctor," Lucas growled. "No cure, just a slow death."

A cough rattled my chest, but I kept my sword on guard, pulling on a grin for effect. From the corner of my eye, I saw Sebastian stalk Lucas from behind on silent claws.

"Are you sure?" I asked in a raspy voice.

I raised the now-empty vial that had held the partial cure where he could see it. Then, I turned my left hand so he could see the wooden cracks in my skin slowly turning back to flesh.

"Maybe it's just no cure for *you,* señor."

The wraith's eyes went round and wide before he yelled in wordless rage. He charged, but Sebastian struck. First was a slash at the wraith's coat, tripping him. Second was another spit of hot tar to the side of the face when Lucas looked back in alarm.

He stumbled and fell to the deck. Even as he hit with a thud, Lucas yanked down more power from the Etherwave, then more still. Each time, he hurled spectral bolts of fire at either myself or Sebastian.

Sebastian, nimble as always, darted aside before he took to the air and shot towards me.

I used the *Codex* as a poor man's buckler to slap and block the blasts of fire. Each one hit the *Codex*, and the book absorbed it like a sponge in a burst of yellow-white light.

Exhausted, sweating my life out, I backed away until I was directly under the hole to the deck above. I risked taking my eyes off Lucas to glance at the storm-tossed sky.

Wall clouds swirled like a foul soup overhead, but a break had formed. Sunlight glimmered down in sharp beams like fingers reaching for the sea.

The Arcane Gate that towered over us shook like a mountain ready to shed an avalanche. Raw, white power fell in bright rivers of light while smoldering, broken stones tumbled into the sea.

Suddenly, my vision went blurry as the world seemed to slide sideways.

"What in...?"

Above and outside, I watched the Arcane Gate split in two.

The massive, abused archway remained where it was, but now it looked like a *second* Gate was trying to push out of the first. Cracked, gray-granite rock split open like overripe melons. Dark obsidian spikes speared through the stone, framed by what could only be countless bones.

Those cracked, white bones framed every crevasse and fissure. In between was dark packed soil, smeared with greasy stains that seemed to pulse with their own heartbeat.

It was like watching the mismatched skeleton of a mythical titan push itself out of a grave. All the while, a tattered veil of mist stretched between the two, like pale spiderwebs pulled too thin.

Then, in the middle of the archway, I saw a bleak landscape.

It was cast in shades of black, gray, and deep sea-blue that mirrored the world. Ragged, ruined ships, manned by bloated dead crews floated on greasy waves. In the distance, along a broken, gray shore, shadowy specters of half-people silently gathered.

A fleet of the dead, moving to flood the world of the living.

Lucas slammed into me when mysterious golden lines of power wrapped around the split Arcane Gate. I hit the deck, air knocked out of my lungs, as Lucas pinned me down with a shaking, withered hand.

"You have a cure, don't you? Not this sewage you tried to poison me with! A formula you've written somewhere!" he screamed. "I'll go through you, your friends, your loved ones, until I get what I want!"

He hammered at my face. I managed to block the blows, but it was a near thing. Before he could try again, I fought back with a quick right jab. I was rewarded with a sharp, wet crack, and a line of amber resin trickled from his broken nose.

"You'll never get that!" I snapped back. "You've murdered more than enough people!"

Lucas yelped in pain as mystic flames from my hand tried to turn the wraith into a flaming pyre. It didn't take, and before I could get off the deck, he grabbed me by the collar, then bashed my head backwards against the wood.

Sebastian clawed and bit Lucas, but only ripped away chunks of rotten cloth. It earned him a kick to the muzzle that sent him tumbling across the deck.

"Sebastian!" I coughed.

Stars exploded in my eyes as my vision swam in sickly waves. My stomach churned in reply between the pain in my head and the tainted cure I drank moments ago.

Then the sun split through the clouds over us. Golden beams of light speared down, even as the storm rotated in the sky like a gray whirlpool of destruction. Lucas had me by the throat then, slowly choking the air from me.

What little I knew of wraiths was as much rumor as truth. But all the tall tales mentioned wraiths despise the sun. Memories flashed across my eyes of seeing Lucas in a long coat, skin mostly covered. The only time he didn't seem to care was when the clouds were so thick, they blotted out the sun.

Except now, a few fingers of sunlight had broken through the storm to brush the lower deck of the dying barge.

I grabbed Lucas by the collar and neck, then shoved with everything I had. He was still weak from the poison, which cost him both his balance and his leverage against me. We rolled across the deck as he drew on the Etherwave to craft another spell.

Wraith or not, the strain in his body was obvious. His hands shook as he stole power from the Etherwave, more spectral fire curling around his fingers. But a strange glow filled his eyes, like an out-of-control forest fire.

The Etherwave Arcana was about to collect its price for everything it had given Lucas. Take it all at once.

He clawed at my face with burning fingers, but I rolled us into the sun a second before he touched me. The instant that the golden light touched him, Lucas let go of my collar. His screams could've shattered glass.

I scrambled away on all fours, then scooped up an angry and snarling Sebastian in my arms. By the time we reached the nearest bulkhead, Lucas had stopped screaming. I curled around Sebastian to protect both of us as best I could.

No more than ten feet away, the wraith had frozen into a driftwood statue. Then with a quick shudder, he exploded as the Etherwave Arcana shattered him like glass.

A foul stench of burned rot held onto the air with a death grip while wood rained around us. The barge lurched heavily. Abused planks snapped, then pulled back from the keel. Seawater rushed in like a dozen fountains underneath us.

"Come on, Sebastian, time to go."

I set him down and located the *Codex.* It had fallen nearby and, miraculously, survived the fight. Part of me wanted to leave it, let the sea take it. But something whispered that I still needed that book.

We scaled a ragged ladder to what remained of the upper deck. I saw Ari, Skaldi, and Lysander were bloody, bruised, but alive. None of them looked infected, but we had a larger problem to deal with.

Lysander had used his skills with the Arcana to connect with the Arcane Gate. Sweat poured over his dark face while he struggled to force the broken Gate together. But, right then and there on the barge, he lacked a portal platform to ground him against that power. So he was failing, and starting to die.

My stomach churned, but I fought back the nausea, looking around for a way to help my friend. I didn't see a portal platform, but I saw something else more important. The last piece of this evil puzzle.

There, nestled at the foot of the Arcane Gate, sat an Arcane Engine. A rare, pulsing device made of bone, wood, and metal, attached to the Gate like a foul blister. I could feel it churn. That was the source of the curse that wanted to break the Arcane Gate apart.

"No. I didn't come this far to watch it all sink now."

I drank down my last healing elixir, then stumbled off the barge toward the Arcane Engine and the heart of the storm.

34

Dire Arts and the Arcane Engine

Aug 8, 1722. Standing on the Arcane Gate's granite base. Knocking at Death's door, and hearing a knock back...

I dropped to my hands and knees on the seaweed-slick rock, gasping for air. A wave of nausea slammed through my stomach.

My gut clenched. I vomited hard. It was sour bile with a little blood. Then I spat, wiped my mouth on my sleeve, and blinked away tears.

"Potions never taste better the second time around," I complained, throat raw.

Wood crackled as the infection flared again. Pain shot through my left arm while waves broke against the Arcane Gate's granite base around me. Sea spray was everywhere.

It wasn't easy to stand. The entire gray stone base was slick with rotten seaweed and brine. Whitecaps slapped Sebastian and I like we deserved it. The storm winds howled, delighted to have two more victims.

I felt hollowed out, lightheaded, but not done. That's when I noticed I'd cut my hand on the rocks. It was just more pain layered on pain. The infection flared, clawing at me, but I was still bleeding red—not amber resin.

"Just put one foot in front of the other," I murmured, then forced myself to stand. Sebastian barked in agreement.

My legs kept moving after the rest wanted to give up. It wasn't willpower, but a bitter elixir of guilt and desperation, trying to set things right.

Beside me, Sebastian scrabbled for solid footing, claws clicking against the stone. Desperate and determined in his own gargoyle way, so I wouldn't face this alone. Together until the end.

"Come on, Sebastian. It's right ahead."

Over the wind, Sebastian whined, low in his throat. I guessed he felt what I did—an itch behind my eyes and at the base of my skull, along with a tightness in my chest. A sense that something impossibly ancient next to us was awake and furious.

The last few yards felt like forever, but we crossed the wet rocks to the Arcane Engine nestled against the Gate. I knelt down heavily for a better look.

It wasn't some mythical carved statue with glowing eyes. This was actually something even worse. A device of brass, bone, and quartz, but not clockwork like I knew it. This Arcane Engine looked more like an abused wooden sea chest whose maker had a morbid fondness for bone and brass.

Bits of bleached whale bone and other scrimshawed bones lined corners and seams. What wasn't bone had been layered in light tan leather and tarnished brass rivets. Black resin had been used to patch ugly cracks, edged with the singed remains of lightning strikes. A large, tarnished steel latch kept the lid closed.

Gears peeked out from gaps in the chest's bloated wood slats. Some were on the lid, others along the sides. They glistened with a dark, reddish oil that I suspected might have been something far worse.

I remembered the conversation with Renwick in my shop, days earlier. He had explained that sailors 'sent to the engine' never returned. Suddenly, I didn't want to guess about where the bones, leather, and oil came from.

"It's a pirate's pet abomination, or an engineer's fever dream of the damned," I murmured. "How do I stop this? Open it? What is it even doing?"

Just then, the storm winds receded. Behind the moan of wind, I heard the muffled sound of countless small gearworks, the crackle of power, and what sounded like stone being chiseled. I glanced at the Gate, then at the Arcane Engine, and quickly reached for the latch.

It moved, but the lid didn't. At least, not until I found a thumb-sized knob hidden behind the latch's strike plate. I turned the knob, and every visible gear came to terrible life, chattering like dozens of metal teeth. Gears turned, then slid like elaborate puzzle pieces.

I held still, braced for something to hiss and explode. But instead, the gears abruptly aligned. With a soft click, slide, and snapping sound, the chest's lid opened a sliver.

Quickly, I caught the edge with my fingers and pulled. It shifted only a few inches. Steam hissed out, thick and sour, reeking of hot sewage.

With a frustrated sigh, I gripped the lid with both hands, putting my full weight behind it. The chest creaked in protest. I winced immediately from fresh pain as more skin on my left hand steadily turned into split wood.

"All right, what do we have?" I grunted with a glare at the chest.

Sebastian pressed in close against my leg, gargoyle tail lashing the air like a whip. his horned head cocked as if listening to a distant sound. After a second, he hissed furiously at the chest.

I didn't blame him at all.

All at once, the stink of boiled rot and burnt copper flooded out so fast, my eyes watered. I coughed and wiped away tears as I peered inside. The smell was so dense, it ignored the storm that tried to blow it out to sea.

"Dios mío," I coughed.

Inside was an alchemical mess, but at least it finally explained why the *Codex Luminari* contained so many mechanical and alchemical designs. This Arcane Engine was an elaborate combination of alchemical stills, a Hauksbee battery, and a deranged engraver's tool.

Row after row of tiny, interlocking gears, some of quartz, others of shell or bone, drove the entire thing. They meshed together in clusters like barnacles on a hull at regular intervals along a trio of metal rods. Those drilled and chiseled into the Arcane Gate itself, carving navigation symbols and alchemy formulas into the base, or grinding rock to powder.

That enchanted stone powder was conveyed to a series of distilling pots. Containers heated by a cluster of glass jars filled with a shimmering liquid. It was the most elaborate Hauksbee battery I'd ever seen. The silver-blue blood of Etherwave power literally pumped from the Gate itself, like an open wound.

Now, it wasn't hard to figure out what this was doing. I recognized those carved formulas. They were symbols rumored to be tied to resurrecting the dead. I shook my head, then coughed again against the rotten stench.

"*This* is how they're opening a portal to the land of the dead."

Another wave of pain shot through me. I grabbed my left arm and nearly doubled over. Heat boiled out of the chest like a blast furnace. I wasn't sure if my sweat was from what I'd drunk, or the heat.

"The Hauksbee jars must be storing power pulled from the Gate, but also from what's boiling in those alchemy stills. If I can disconnect just a part of this, that drill will stop, and so will what's being done to the Gate."

I tried to reach inside slowly, but the heat was too much. Even my coat sleeve smoked.

"There has to be another way," I murmured.

Wind whipped around me like a mad ghost. I looked over my shoulder at Lysander. He had the Arcane Gate stable for now. But I could see he was losing the struggle. I glanced toward the *Silk Duchess* where the battle had died down, then at Lysander, and finally at the Arcane Engine.

"He needs one of those gear-laden portal platforms to ground out the excess Etherwave power."

I scowled at the Arcane Engine. Not that it cared. It sat boiling out searing heat, eating at the Arcane Gate, practically breathing, like some hell-born parasite. Then I scratched Sebastian behind the horns.

"We need to solve one problem with the other," I said to him as much as to me, looking around the gray rocks. "Where did I drop the *Codex?*"

Sebastian found it before I did and dragged the battered book over to me. I leafed through the pages, with their lurid details about necrotic formulas and rituals, until I found Tristam's designs for this devilish Arcane Engine. It didn't take long to find the passage I wanted.

"Of course, disconnect the chisels, but the Hauksbee jars have to be tuned? Did I read that right?"

Tension gnawed at the back of my head while I read the passage again.

"Tuned. Musically, like 'singing glasses'. This is tuned by sound."

My eyes cut back to the glowing jars in the searing hot Engine. I skimmed the passages again, then glanced over at Lysander. The idea made sense, even if it might burn me alive. That sent me back to searching the *Codex* for a way to bleed off the heat.

"There has to be a way to touch those jars," I muttered, flipping pages so fast I nearly tore them out.

Then I stopped on a page adorned with a familiar, horrific diagram of a thin and ragged figure, barely even human.

A Death Whisper.

Just like the kind I'd fought too many of, and never wanted to see again. I grunted as my stomach rebelled again, threatening to bend me over in another wave of violent nausea.

I didn't want to create one of those nightmares. Especially given what Renwick had said—they needed a living spirit. I swapped an uneasy glance with Sebastian, who whimpered back at me.

"It's what we have," I rasped in a tight, brittle voice.

I pulled out the vial with the last of the ink I used on the barge, along with a broken bit of wood. Then I flipped to a blank page in the *Codex* and scribbled a slightly altered version of the Death Whisper ritual.

Sebastian whined at me one more time, and I scratched behind his horns. He gently butted his head against my hand.

"Don't worry. It'll be over soon. It has to."

Then, I slammed my open palm onto the page hard enough that there was a sharp crack. Blood from the cut on my hand mingled with the hastily scrawled formulas in an ink just waiting for a spark of power. I wiped a tear from my eye, took a deep breath, then sang against the wind.

"I'm a privateer of the sea, of the waves and wind. With my ship and crew, I sail the ocean without fear..."

Green-white ghostfire exploded to life around my right hand. At the same moment, I felt the Etherwave Arcana rush to my aid. It flowed down through the Arcane Gate, then into me, like a torrent of water breaking through a dam.

Drops of fresh ink bled up from the page to dance in the air in front of my eyes. Every formula glimmered and rippled, while a dark shadow of ink and blood stained the entire page. Sebastian's whimper was swallowed by the wind.

"I just hope this Death Whisper listens."

35

The Death Whisper

Aug 8, 1722. At the base of the Port Royal Arcane Gate. Righting a terrible wrong, only to face the storm...

A fetid burst of warm air, laced with the scent of rotten fish and seaweed, caressed my face in uneven bursts. It was like warm air spit from a ragged bellows. But this wasn't the storm, a fire, or the Arcane Engine.

It was the Death Whisper I'd crafted from the *Codex Luminari* and my own blood.

Wind and sea spray beat against me mercilessly, almost tossing me off the rocks and into the waves. To my right, Sebastian snarled, hissing at the Death Whisper.

Seawater slicked the granite under my boots. The air around us felt fractured by the dying Arcane Gate, by all the recent events. My stomach clenched in rebellion, but this wasn't the time to suffer that.

Barely five feet in front of me, the Death Whisper loomed over us. The golem stood at least six and a half feet tall, maybe taller. Dressed in ragged clothes from some forgotten sailor, it towered over me like a bad decision. Which, given the situation, wasn't a terrible comparison.

It hunched slightly, clothes dripping from seawater and drizzled rain. The golem's eyes were bright orbs of literal fire, coiling out of hollow eye sockets. Withered, mummified hands dappled with tiny barnacles flexed like claws, even as its distorted mouth stretched wide like an obscene yawn.

I half-expected a blood-curdling shriek as it tried to rip out my throat. But it didn't. Instead, it tilted its head to the left like an addled, eyeless, undead bird, inspecting me.

The golem stepped closer, dry breath rattling inside its empty ribcage.

I fought down nausea and stepped back, tense, ready for a fight. The strange ghostfire flared to life around my hand.

The instant it did, the fire inside the golem's eye sockets coiled, guttered, then surged with the same green-white fire of the ghostfire on my hand.

It drew in a long, shuddering breath that was, at best, breath in name only.

"You called," it said.

The words were barely that. They were a low, grating sound that left the taste of ash and salt on my tongue. Each word felt thick with memory, obligation, and something that felt like regret.

I drew the back of a sleeve across my mouth, watching the thing warily. This was a dangerous, undiscovered country that I was in a hurry to leave behind.

"Yes," I replied, voice raw. "I did. You're needed."

Slowly, not taking my eyes off the golem, I knelt down and recovered the *Codex.* Its flaming eyes watched while I tucked the book under my arm. Then the golem glanced at the Arcane Engine, and finally the dying Arcane Gate.

"You," it said, drawing out the word until it snapped. "You want to fix the... mistake. Not finish the ritual."

Every word vibrated through my battered bones. But understanding dawned in my exhausted mind. Lyra Valtor's comments about a Death Whisper came flooding back—only now a missing piece slotted into place.

They were wildly destructive, along with a dozen other lethal things. But like she had said, they were also made from cursed ink, books, and the contents inside them. They were, literally, ideas made whole with a voice.

"You are correct, señor." My voice felt like cracked leather. "I do. With your help."

The golem's eyes cut to the Arcane Engine, then it shook its head.

"The Engine is self-consuming now. Its music can't be silenced."

Next to me, Sebastian barked again at the golem, more perturbed than angry. I straightened my back, trying to ignore the pain of the petrification lancing through my left hand.

"No." I said the word like a pistol shot. "But it can be tuned, señor. Harmonized with another," my eyes twitched while I searched for the right word, "song. Another song."

The golem tilted its head to the right, looking again like some curious, predatory bird.

"Change the tune," it said. "Rewrite its will? It still needs to end its song in a pure scream."

I didn't like the sound of that. But somehow, given all that had happened, I wasn't surprised.

Pain flared in my left arm, and I grabbed it with my right. I could practically feel ribbons of wood spearing through my veins, muscles, and tendons. The warmth from the ghostfire soothed the pain, but I could still feel the uneasy discomfort from the petrification infection.

I winced at the pain, took a deep breath, then stabbed a finger at Lysander.

"We need to harmonize the Engine with him, with the Gate."

"The navigator? How?" it rasped, voice a dry echo.

I took a deep breath. It felt like I was dancing with a hungry shark. I hurried past the Death Whisper and over to the Arcane Engine.

"The jars."

I pointed at the glowing jars, their fluid levels uneven, and leaned in as close as the searing heat allowed. Then I wiped rain from my face, and a little blood from my lips, while I looked back at the golem.

"Do you know what a 'glass harp' is? 'Singing glasses?' Each glass making a different musical note? You said 'music' so I trust you do?"

The Death Whisper nodded, then blinked in an oddly human gesture that made me shudder.

"We remember."

I narrowed my eyes. That was something to think about later, if I wasn't dead.

The golem joined me at the Engine, then flexed a ragged, mummified hand toward the glowing glass jars. Each gnarled finger looked like woven rope wrapped around driftwood. Wind tugged at its countless ragged parts, like shredded skin, which made standing near it an effort of willpower.

I flinched as more hot stones tumbled from the Arcane Gate. It felt like time was sifting through my fingers like sand.

Then, the jars rattled. But this time, not from the storm or the falling pieces of the Gate.

I pressed the back of my hand to my lips again. The taste of blood and brine hadn't improved.

"How much of you remembers music?"

A pause. Its ribcage expanded. A wet, hollow inhalation.

"All of it. All of us."

The Death Whisper's jagged teeth were short, like the broken stones of a reef. Its jaw was inhuman and looked too wide, too imprecise.

"We lived as conscripts. We died at sea, and again in the books."

Its right hand hovered near the Engine's overheated edge, immune to the scalding air. My gut threatened to rebel again at the rolling smell of boiled sewage that assaulted my nose.

I coughed then peeled open the *Codex*. Wet pages stuck together or bled ink, but Tristam's instructions made a perverse sense.

His notes listed frequencies, ratios of liquid to glass, along with more disturbing things like the 'humble arithmetic of the departed'. I breathed out a bitter laugh.

"Nothing like having a sense of humor when you're an evil bastard," I murmured.

The more I read, the deeper I frowned in concern. I chanced a glance back at Lysander.

He was hunched on the deck of the ruined barge, surrounded by the golden sphere of light. He clutched at two glowing light sculptures of Arcane Gates, each as tall as he was, trying to shove them together.

It hadn't worked, but the Gates hadn't separated any more, either. His jaw worked, murmuring some sea chant I couldn't hear. Sweat traced lines down his dark face.

"We're running out of time, señor," I muttered to the Death Whisper. "If I guide you, can you tune the jars? Change the fluids?"

The Death Whisper tilted its head again, like it heard me through layers of thick fog, maybe even time.

"Tell us," it rasped.

I nodded as I thumbed the weathered page, but also pulled down old memories of alchemical mixtures.

"All right. The jars, and their tones, correspond to intervals between notes, as much as they amplify or bleed off Etherwave from the Gate. Ratio of potion to the vibrating glass is what matters. That's the key."

"Intervals," the Death Whisper repeated, as if that word was a flavor it hadn't tasted in centuries.

I used the *Codex* as a rough guide, then went off formula immediately. One by one, I pointed at the jars, directing the Death Whisper what to turn, how much to drain. Several times, I had to reach deeper into the Engine than my skin wanted. Blisters started to rise on my skin.

"First jar," I grunted. "Drain it a quarter, twist left."

The Death Whisper peered in close, then miraculously obeyed. Brown, sickly liquid sluiced into a crusted catch-basin when the golem tilted it. Then, it turned the jar as instructed once it set it upright.

Suddenly, I heard a sound shift. It was soft, under the wind and storm, but there. The jar glowed a faint sapphire blue.

Excited, I moved between the jars, spitting out numbers and measurements at a rapid pace.

"Next two? Half-drain, turn one-fifth. Leave the fourth."

So, on it went, sweat and light rain streaming down my face. I tried to ignore the mild groans of pain from Lysander on the barge. Skaldi and Ari were there, but they weren't navigators and couldn't help.

Finally, a resonance gathered. A hum I felt inside my jaw rattled my teeth. The jars, now realigned, vibrated on their own, playing out a song that seemed to harmonize with the storm.

"It's working," I murmured. "I think... it's working."

To my surprise, the Death Whisper hummed along. It was a hellish, ugly attempt at a baritone scraped over rough stone. In front of us, the Arcane Engine itself started to shake.

I glanced at the *Codex* to determine what, if anything, was next, then squeezed my eyes shut.

The scream. It needed to scream, and I realized what that meant.

An imbalance. It needed a sharp, unreliable imbalance.

My vision turned black at the edges, fraying like old cloth. The world tilted sideways as I felt lightheaded.

The Death Whisper caught me by the arm and pulled me upright. No words, just action. Waiting.

"Right. On my mark, crack the last jar in line," I called out over the rising howl. "Not all the way, just a hairline split. Enough to let it shriek."

I glanced at the Death Whisper, then at the last jar.

"Now!"

Sebastian let out a whining yelp, then yanked on my trouser leg with his teeth. Meanwhile, the Death Whisper's rough hand seized the stained, yellowed jar and flexed.

A sharp crack split the glass, webbing it with fractures.

The Engine howled, its 'song' reaching a frantic crescendo, while I saw threads of golden Etherwave Arcana pour in from Lysander's direction behind me.

Wind slammed at me, but I clutched the *Codex* and stood my ground. My heart stuttered, knowing damn well the warning words anyone learns when dealing with the Etherwave Arcana and what people call 'magic'.

"Magic always comes with a price," I wheezed.

The jar screamed as it shattered. A crack sliced through the Arcane Engine like a knife.

Then my world became nothing but the pure, blinding heart of a sun.

36

A Debt Paid, A Debt Owed

Aug 8, 1722. Somehow aboard the *Silk Duchess.* A handful of minutes later, after Death stopped by for a chat...

I jerked to life at the smell of rot whiskey and the feel of rough wool against my face.

It shouldn't have been a surprise to wake up feeling half-dead. But there I was. It was even more alarming to realize I was in the crook of Dryden Storm's massive arm.

I struggled, but he kept a tight grip while the *Duchess* rolled hard to starboard as if she'd been thrown.

"Easy now, Doctor."

A cough sputtered out of me, and I glanced over. Storm was nothing more than a smear of limping, mild evil, wearing a captain's coat. His red-streaked black beard split into a grin when he saw my bitter scowl.

"You know, Doctor, I've long carried men in worse shape than you from far worse places."

His voice rumbled like the guts of a volcano, raw with cannon smoke.

"But! I'll be having you know that it takes a special kind of talent for a man to hand himself his *own* ass." He barked out a rough laugh. "What you and your crew did to save Port Royal's Arcane Gate? Killing that lich and all? Impressive. Just don't die on me yet."

A headache hammered at my skull like a crazed, drunken blacksmith. I pried my sore eyes from glaring at him to the chaos of the deck.

The *Silk Duchess* had taken a sound beating, but came through with her pride and spine intact. My vision was blurred, but I still managed to see the crew running past us, keen to repair what they could. Captain Storm's presence drew more than one look, mostly glares, but to my hazy surprise, no one stopped him.

"Not dying, señor," I grunted. The words came out in broken, raw bits. "I refuse. Made a promise to live. I'm growing attached to the habit."

Storm belted out a murderous laugh, probably the only kind he had.

We half-limped across the deck towards the ladder to the helm. Dimly, I wondered where Lysander, Ari, and Skaldi had gone. There was a memory of it that just wouldn't come clear for me.

"Good!" Storm roared. "You've my gratitude for freeing me from that hells-damned book, the wraith, and all of it. That was no small deed. But you and I? We've a reckoning waiting. The spirit you've bound isn't yours to keep. That debt will come due."

We stopped next to the ladder for the *Duchess'* helm. Storm propped me upright, and somehow my spine held, though it didn't like it. The man hammered my shoulder once with a scar-mottled hand.

"Now, stay put. I've other things that need looking after."

The ship lurched wildly over the sea. Gray-black clouds boiled overhead while wind clawed at the sails, threatening to tear them loose.

Memories then returned in a drunken haze. There was the whine of splitting glass and the hammer of rain. A golem of ink and despair sang a funeral dirge while it stood between myself and an explosion. Then I remembered being thrown into the sea.

There was also a lot of screaming; I realized might have been me.

Storm's words to stay put rattled in my head and roused my anger.

"Bastard," I swore under my breath. "I need medicine. It's in my cabin. Need that."

Firmly, I pushed away from the ladder holding me up, and took a step. That nearly sent me to the deck.

"Doctor!" Ari's voice pierced the chaos like the brass echo of a ship's bell.

She shoved two of the crew aside and darted across the deck to me, copper-gold wings fluttering.

"Don't stand! You're..."

She caught my right arm before I fell on my face and made everything worse. A burst of white ghostfire traced the tattoos along my hand and wrist. Then it sank back into my skin.

I noticed Ari's lips went tight, eyes framed by a frown, and she quickly averted her gaze. The woman ducked under my arm, holding me steady.

"Durner!" she shrieked, sending a broadside of sound across my ear.

"Coming, damn it!" was the craggy, perturbed reply. "Only one of me to go around!"

Just then I heard Skaldi's voice behind us, maybe to starboard. He stomped across the deck, pure fury on short, stout legs. The brass metal veins in his skin glowed molten yellow. I saw the dark cloud of a bruise around one eye.

The instant we locked eyes his face went slack with relief. It was short-lived when he caught sight of Captain Storm a few feet away, deep in a conversation with Elara near the helm. Skaldi's face pinched into a raging scowl, like a bulldog savoring fresh meat.

"Storm! You'll pay for that punch!"

Dryden Storm's eyes cut away from Elara to the ship's blacksmith. A mild sneer drew across his face.

"I'll be expecting your bill, Mr. Terrason," Storm snarled. "But first, we've bigger problems, and your Doctor needs to be seen about."

I screwed my face up at that. Bigger problems?

"Ari? Skaldi?" I wheezed, trying to keep the horizon in sight. "Last of my potions are..."

"I'll fetch 'em, Pedro," Skaldi said with a poisoned glare at Storm.

"Already done," said a craggy voice from a certain Master Gunner with a rust-red beard.

Like magic, Skaldi's brother Durner raced out of the haze of my vision. He shoved my battered satchel into Skaldi's hands, who rummaged in it for the potions at the bottom.

Fatigued or not, I instantly recalled the inventory in the bag. There was a pitifully small amount of elixirs. Silently, I swore that I'd be smarter about having more on hand in the future.

In my defense, I never thought an evil sea chest would try to kill me.

Skaldi shoved the first of two medicinal potions into my hand.

"Pedro. Drink."

I did, choking down one after the other, barely tasting them. I went lightheaded. How I was still on my feet, I had no idea. Spite, probably.

My vision cleared in time to see Elara lean onto the rail overhead with a look that would've cowed a seraphim. She'd turned from Dryden toward me, wings fanning a bit behind her to keep her stable on deck.

She looked like hell. Hair unbound, her jade-gold eyes were steel-hard, shadowed with worried concern. Blood stained her captain's coat, but I couldn't tell if it was hers, borrowed, or both.

"Captain," I said with a respectful, tired nod. "The wraith..."

She cut me off.

"Pedro."

The brittle tone in her voice sounded like a dire warning.

"Don't you ever..." Then her lips pressed tight. "Never mind. We'll discuss it later."

She scoured the busy deck and crew with a hard gaze, while the latter scrambled like ants madly repairing an anthill.

"Lysander! Where's Lysander?" she bellowed, voice cutting over the wind.

"Here!" he called back in a thin voice, frayed with fatigue.

The navigator ducked under a tangled mess of loose rigging, reaching the stained ladder to the helm. Lips blue, purple bruises framed the eyes on his dark face.

"Sorry. A bit winded, Captain. Arcane Gate's mostly together. It'll repair on its own. That's something the natural ones do."

I felt Ari press something thick into my hands. It was the *Codex Luminari.* She gave me a look, then wiped her hands on her trousers uneasily before she raced off, leaving me with Skaldi.

"Of course it survived," I lamented to a peal of thunder. "Renwick, and so many more, are dead and gone because of you. I should've tossed you into the Arcane Engine, or the sea."

I almost threw the book away right then, but changed my mind. Tristam Greenholm was still trapped inside, along with his vile formulas. Against my better judgment, I pushed the *Codex* into my satchel to deal with later.

The conversation between Dryden and Elara snagged my limp attention. I nodded to Skaldi while I stood shakily on my own.

"It's the only way I see it," said Storm. "By your leave, Captain Blackwater, I'll return to the *Rising Eel*, my crew'll be taking lead from yours, if the plan be the same."

"It is," she snapped with a short, sharp glare.

Captain Storm gave her a curt nod, aimed a sneer at me, then stomped off. I watched him head for the lines connecting the *Rising Eel* to the *Silk Duchess.*

I gave Skaldi a worried, dark frown.

"Plan?"

Skaldi ducked under my arm to steady me, jerking a thumb skyward. The *Duchess* lurched sideways like a death-loving drunkard.

Hurricane.

We were in a hurricane.

"Dios mío," I murmured, clenching my jaw.

Elara's commands shot out, quick and fierce.

"Someone cut those lines to the *Eel* once the pirate leaves!" she ordered. "If that Captain Storm causes trouble, cut the lines out from under him. Lysander!"

"Captain?" he said, still out of breath.

"Do you have it in you for another Gate? Maybe two?" She cast a worried look at the sky.

Lysander let go of a sigh as heavy as an anchor, closing his eyes. I saw blood splatters across his shirt, leftover from the fight with the wraith. The fatigue bruises under his eyes seemed to darken. At my look, he shook his head at me.

"Aye. I can manage one," he replied, voice tired. "Maybe two before I drop."

Elara studied him and then nodded. I saw the deep concern that hovered behind her eyes and in her stance. Worry for Lysander, for all of us.

"Make it happen, Mr. Riverwind. The *Rising Eel's* navigator assists once you've opened the way."

Lysander pinched his mouth into a thin line, his next words like cracked crystal.

"What course, Captain?"

"Port Royal," Elara said, then stalked back to the helm and ship's pilot.

After a quick glance, and clasp on my shoulder, Lysander hauled himself up the ladder for the battered portal platform behind the helm. Over the storm, I heard the myriad of tiny gears churn as the platform started up.

"Off to your cabin, Doctor. The captain's going to want you rested up and full of medicine."

I eyed the storm overhead. Skaldi nodded as he helped me across the deck.

"It'll be tight. Using a Gate to get out of a hurricane?" He shook his head. "Risky as kissing hell."

I winced at the pain from moving, but also at my thoughts. A hurricane was nothing short of a tavern brawl between land and sea.

"True," I replied hoarsely. There wasn't much else to say, other than a silent prayer.

Whitecaps and rain smeared the horizon, turning it ugly and wild. A sheet of gray sliced down from the wall clouds behind us. It looked like gray teeth eager to bite us in half.

Skaldi muscled me over the stained deck between knots of crew, all of us nearly soaked to the flesh. Under the salt air, the faint tang of unwashed bodies and fear slapped my nose.

I felt the pulse of power before we saw anything.

"Here we go," I warned Skaldi.

We'd barely reached the small stern door to the cabins when the golden orb of navigator enchantment burst to life. Sebastian skidded to a stop by my leg and barked.

The orb burst up and out. A bright, gossamer ball of power, like yellow stained glass.

Ahead in the churning, angry sea, an Arcane Gate shimmered to life. Then the Gate went as bright as sunlight, almost as if a second Gate had been set against the first one.

"Two navigators working in tandem, placing one Arcane Gate against the other?" Skaldi murmured as he turned his focus back to stowing me in a cabin. "Privateer's gambit if I ever saw it. Gates hate that, last I ever heard. If even an inch is out of place, we'll likely die."

It wasn't the Gates that had my attention—it was what lay through them.

I slammed a hand against the door frame to stop Skaldi from stuffing me away. A spike of white-hot agony shot through my side.

Past the Gate was Port Royal, but not as I remembered it. Before, it'd been a lively port town coming back to life from the last disaster from years back that had tried to swallow it.

Now? Death had come calling.

"Dead gods and live saints," Skaldi muttered. "How big is this hurricane?"

The sea had consumed the eastern quarter. Streets literally flowed like hell's own slurry. Brick, clay and loose sand dissolved, churning under the hurricane's surf.

To the west, Port Royal's proudest piers had stabbed shattered corpses of ships. Timber was bent and twisted from the rising maelstrom. People raced over buildings and what land remained, swarming for any higher ground they could find.

On one, a hill beyond the ports, I saw a shimmering dome. It was all sea green, fog and spite. In its center, pushing out the protective cover for the desperate, was a certain sea hag of my acquaintance.

"Too big," I told him. "Sea hag or not, it's a coin toss if even *she* can hold back a full hurricane."

I turned to shout to Elara, but she'd spotted what I had. We locked eyes. Deep concern shone between us, then out at the shimmering dome. Pain, and possible loss she didn't want to happen.

Her eyes snapped back at me, and I spoke, hoping she heard me over the storm.

"Get us there, *querida.* We'll save them."

I left off the part where we all might die together while trying. It wasn't worth saying. We knew that part already.

Elara scowled at the Gate.

"All hands! Look alive! Port Royal won't drown on our watch!"

Beyond the Gate's glimmering veil, the town itself thrashed like a drowning man.

37

To Defy the Sea

Aug 8, 1722. Port Royal, Jamaica, or what was left of it. Helping the desperate run for their lives.

I've never watched the weather try to murder a town before. But that was exactly what I saw.

"Head to the far western docks!" I yelled to the survivors, waving my good arm in that direction. "Longboats are waiting to get you to safety!"

I stood on what was likely the last stable wooden footpath between Port Royal and the docks. Ragged clumps of people shuffled along, ushered by crew from the *Rising Eel* and *Silk Duchess.* We were allies for the moment against what Mother Nature had sent to kill us.

Lightning flashed a challenge. I clutched my battered satchel a bit tighter, shaking my head. Soaked to the skin, hat long gone, I felt like the enchanted storm spawned from the nearly shattered Gate was trying to strip me apart.

"This day is getting longer by the moment," I murmured, before helping an elderly couple onto the footpath. With a weary smile, I sent them down to the longboats and safety.

Port Royal's streets were nothing but a memory. Broken wooden planks, mud, and rain washed through the town. Every avenue was a dangerous stream looking for victims. Blood streaked the occasional debris, a final marker for those already lost.

Durner joined me a moment later, and we waded along the edge of the dying dock, looking for any stragglers. Mud sloshed nearly to our knees, the wind lashing at us. All we found were sad memories, and certainly nothing left alive.

On the way back to the western docks, Elara marched through the weather, meeting us halfway.

"Any left?" she asked, pushing damp brown hair out of her face.

Suddenly, the storm shifted sideways, hammering us with a downpour. We hunched our coats and huddled together as the small torrent subsided.

"We hauled one fisherman out of the mud. He'll live," I said over the storm.

"Aye," Durner agreed. "That was the worst of it. The last found hiding in town are on their way down to the longboats."

Pain throbbed up my wood-infected left hand and into my arm. My brewed elixirs bought me time, but not much, and exhaustion wanted to steal the rest.

"Any others?" Elara asked, words clipped.

She studied the flooded streets off in the distance, and I saw a small shudder run through her. Without a word, she held her wings tight against her back, tugging her coat closer as if against the world.

I wiped more rain out of my face. The rising water in Port Royal felt like a ticking clock against our efforts. It'd already invaded some homes, scavenging furniture for the tide.

Durner shook his head, brushing water off his own face and beard.

"No, Cap'n. Not so far." He waved a hand at the slush rising around buildings. "That water's a warning shot from the hurricane. It'll get worse before it gets better."

As if to punctuate the mood, a building ten yards away gave a low moan. We watched, speechless, as the sun-weathered, blue-painted walls rippled. Slowly, the old woodcutter's home sank, swallowed whole by the loose, watery sand as if by a hungry snake.

The sand squeezed and the wood-frame collapsed. In seconds, the tortured wood pleaded with a lingering mournful wail, then vanished. For a long, trembling moment, none of us spoke, until Elara broke the drenched quiet.

"I, ah, see what you mean." Elara swallowed uneasily. "We should check one last time, then make for the longboats."

Durner nodded, wiping more water from his face, voice more craggy than ever.

"Aye, Cap'n. Won't take long. I'll grab a few to lend me a hand."

He tossed me a slight, sideways warning glance, and I shook my head a little. That earned me a tiny nod, before Durner stalked off to enlist help for the last search.

"Thank you for not volunteering," Elara said quietly. "I know it's hard, but you've been through a lot, Pedro." The typical hardness in her voice turned soft with a sigh. "I do appreciate it."

I could've made light of the moment, spouting some bravado or a light joke. But some moments shouldn't be tarnished by cheap answers. She deserved better.

"Of course, *querida.*" I gave her a thin smile. "It's the right thing to do."

She gave me a thin, rueful smile, then a gentle squeeze on my good arm.

"Then I'll see you back aboard," she said. "Don't stay too long. The weather has gotten bad enough, that this'll be the last trip with the longboats. They'll leave within the hour, so please be aboard."

"Yes, *querida.* Don't worry," I replied.

She arched an eyebrow at me, then headed for the longboats.

After she left, I hurried through the punishing rain to the end of the western docks. Skaldi and young Jonas Banderwood, a gunner's mate, were there with four other sailors. The lot of them were shepherding a group of Port Royal refugees along the damp steps to the shore.

"Skaldi? Is this the last here?" I called out.

His eyes snapped up to me before he nodded. He patted Jonas on the shoulder, then stepped over to me so I could better hear him over the driving storm. The brass metal veins along his skin glowed like hot embers, a sure sign of concern. Lightning flashed overhead to stab the clouds.

"These are the last from here. The only others I know about are up under the sea hag's shelter."

I sighed wearily, glancing up at the hill with its eerie green glimmering dome.

"No one's gone to get her and the ones with her?"

Skaldi laughed bitterly.

"A couple tried and got run off for it." He clenched his jaw, shaking his head. "Pedro, you know sea hags the best. The captain'll kill me for asking, but if you're able, we could use the help."

Skaldi pursed his lips, glowering at me under his thick brows.

"Just in case she argues."

I let out a wry, hoarse chuckle.

"My friend, I only know one sea hag, and yes, she'll cause you trouble. She does it to everyone. But... I'll do my best."

Once the refugees were off to the *Silk Duchess*, we made the slow, treacherous climb up the soaked hill to the glimmering shelter and its perpetually irate creator.

Sea hags tended to be protective of the towns they lived near. But this? It felt like something else.

It was easier to see the death of Port Royal from atop the hill. What buildings weren't already washed away, sank into the sand like scuttled ships.

I watched bits of roof, splinters of homes, and even a few raw, exposed ribs of small boats tumble along—a deadly soup churning through the town's corpse. The air turned foul, thick with the stench of a waterlogged coffin, fresh from a grave.

After that, I turned to face the problem at hand.

The misty, crackling dome was as large as a massive barn. Morowen stood at its center, attention split between the hurricane and her shimmering shelter. Every minute or so, she'd sweep a hand through the air, sending a fog of glimmering light up to patch a thin spot or hole.

Morowen herself looked like the storm had dragged her a mile. The calico dress and worn leather boots she preferred were mud-stained wrecks. A blue shawl hung damp around her shoulders, a deeper cast than her sea-blue skin. Her shark eyes looked tired and haunted.

A small group of fifteen refugees huddled near her. Men, women, and children were all wet and terrified. Some looked at her. Others watched while their town drowned a slow death.

I waved the sailors with me.

"Get them out. I'll talk to Morowen."

The instant she saw me, the sea hag's expression went darker than the hurricane. Her eyes snapped to Skaldi and the others, then back to me.

I saw tension war with anger, then something softer, before irritation masked over it.

"Pedro!" she spat, eyes hot with exasperation. "I have this. Go away!"

Skaldi hesitated, but I waved him on again, then sighed.

"You don't, Doña Morowen," I said flatly. "Not against a hurricane."

She replied with a derisive snort, then bared her sharp teeth as the *Duchess'* crew helped the refugees gather their belongings.

I stepped in the way again, risking her turning me into an equal volume of crabs. Her lips curled into a snarl.

The shelter she'd made, even if it needed steady repair, had cut out the abusive weather. It was a small relief. I glanced over my shoulder at the approaching hurricane crawling across the waves. It felt far too close for comfort.

Still, I stood my ground.

"You're a sea hag, yes. But even you have your limits, Morowen. You've told me as much." I frowned, with a pinched expression. "We're taking these people to safety. You too, if you'll come along."

She didn't reply, so I waited a heartbeat before I added a bit more.

"Do you really think you can out-stubborn a *hurricane?*"

Deliberate calculations ran over her eyes. She glanced past me at the storm, then back to me.

"Is it done?" she demanded, tossing another gossamer stream of glowing fog at the dome. "I felt the seals snap earlier, then Tristam pulling on the Etherwave. After that? Nothing. So, did you do it?"

I longed for a bed or bunk and a lot of quiet.

"Damn it, Morowen, this isn't..."

"Did you do it?" she yelled, cutting me off.

I saw the usual feral ferocity in her shark-like eyes, colored with irritation. But now there was also a wild desperation. A look that I expected from a gambler betting everything on the next throw of the dice, not a sea hag.

That stirred some new ideas I'd missed before. I heard the refugees being shuffled out of the shelter toward the shore.

"You rolled the dice on me, didn't you?" I asked, just loud enough to be heard over the howling winds.

Morowen clenched her jaw while her eyes flicked at the clouds, then back. It looked like her words were a bitter rind she couldn't quite swallow.

"Yes," she snapped. "After all our time together, he tried to murder me!" Morowen waved her hands in trembling, frantic motions, trying to express the horror of the memory. "Use me like ingredients in a stew! It took all I had to trap the bastard, and it wasn't quite enough. So yes, I bet on you!"

I drew a long breath.

The simple answer would've been to say I'd solved it. But the Daughters of the Deep aren't easily fooled. If I tried, she'd know. Better truth than trouble.

I withdrew the stained *Codex* from my satchel, holding it up for her to see as my answer. Thunder rumbled around us enough to rattle the world.

"It's changed," she muttered, scowling at the book.

Her eyes widened when she saw the engraving on the cover, then fixed me with a glare.

"What in the watery hells did you do, Pedro? The book's different, but I still sense Tristam."

"What I had to. He's in here. Locked in." I shook my head. "He's not getting loose anytime soon."

"A ghost trap," she muttered. A wry, predatory smile flashed around her sharp teeth. "You clever bastard. You rewrote the *Codex* into a ghost trap."

"I tried."

"Good," she snapped. "Now go away! Let me deal with this."

"I would if you weren't lying."

Morowen twitched angrily.

"What?" Her expression flipped to primal rage. "I could kill you right here."

"But you won't," I snapped back.

Slowly, I returned the *Codex* into my satchel.

"Morowen, I understand at least this," I waved a hand in the air between us. "You almost killed yourself trying to stop Tristam, and it didn't quite work. But this isn't right."

"You don't know..."

"Yes, I do!" I growled, cutting her off. "Because I've been making this same mistake since I found the *Codex!*"

Her eyes flashed angrily at me with a hint of pain.

"Not the same, Pedro! That town is what I have left! Without it, I'm just an old sea hag rotting in the tide!"

I thrust a hand at the dying town.

"Morowen, that isn't Port Royal! Port Royal is its people. Throwing your life away isn't a solution. Come with me and help those people... *your* people."

She sneered, but then her expression softened at the edges. The hag's voice growled, its edge softer, with old pain pushing to the surface.

"Your captain's not going to let me."

"Pedro!" Skaldi yelled from outside the shelter. "We need to go! Floodwater is rising!"

I nodded at him, then turned back to the sea hag.

"Morowen, I don't know what bad blood sits between you and Elara. But she won't refuse you safe passage."

I clenched my jaw.

"But if you stay? Neither of you gets a chance to mend this fence, if you want it. Do you really want the Port Royal survivors, or Elara, to watch the hurricane tear you apart?"

For a tense moment, I thought I'd gone too far. Then Morowen's shoulders sagged, hands dropping as she blew out a resigned sigh. I watched her eyes drift over the drowning town, clouded by quiet memories.

"Fine." Then she stabbed a sea-blue finger at me. "But this is on your head if she leaves me stranded!"

I gave her a lopsided grin.

"Accepted."

My grin evaporated at the sound of roaring water dragging the last of Port Royal bodily into the sea. Broken shutters sliced through the air alongside tree branches.

"Time to go," I told her. "Time to start something new, one way or the other."

38

The Price of Ghostfire

Aug 13, 1722. Kingston, Jamaica. Where Fate collected her due...

We cheated death. There wasn't any other way to put it. But really, all I dearly wanted was a good cup of tea, a bed, and a week without curses.

The Arcane Gate yanked us out of Port Royal's watery grave and into Kingston Bay with a haphazard flash of lightning. We shot through the Gate with the *Silk Duchess* in the lead, and the *Rising Eel* on her stern. The hurricane howled after us like a starving fiend as the Gate snapped shut.

But in the end, we survived, even if survival wasn't peace.

The next five days were moments stitched together in a loose patchwork of poultices, bitter tonics, and half-rest. For me, this also included ample doses of my graveyard syrup and paralysis infection cure. By the fifth morning, once I could walk without swaying, I returned to the familiar walls of my alchemy shop.

I'd been back barely an hour, caught up with helping Primrose with orders, when a courier arrived with a summons from Archbinder Lyra Valtor.

"Is it about your curse?" Primrose asked, pulling the goggles from her eyes.

I read the note, then grabbed my long coat off a nearby chair.

"Yes. At the very least, señorita."

Which was how I found myself trudging up the stairs to her office on West Queen Street, sore and still glowering at the world.

The Royal Academy of Arcanum and Science hadn't changed, but Lyra's office had. Walls had been repaired, leaving new panels next to the old. Books were back in place, secured up against seashell carvings, glass vials, and the shrunken skull that mocked the world.

Her yellowed notes about curses peppered the wall behind her desk in concentric circles, like a mad astronomer's chart. Sunlight through the single, dusty window cast a warm glow over everything. The air still held the scent of smoke and old parchment.

More important?

There were also two people there waiting for me instead of one when I walked through the doorway. I reached for my hat, then remembered I'd lost it at the Arcane Gate.

"Archbinder Valtor," I greeted Lyra politely. Then I glanced at the woman seated next to Lyra's deck. "Good to see you again, Morowen. You're looking whole."

"You're late," the sea hag replied with her usual bluntness.

"I was helping Primrose with the alchemy shop. Teaching her the business takes time," I replied dryly.

Morowen made a soft grunt that I decided was agreement. She wore her usual blue shawl over another calico dress. Shadow-dark curls and glimmering shark-black eyes were at odds with a grumpier than normal expression. Lyra was a happy contrast with her undead gray skin, powder-green dress.

"Archbinder? Your note mentioned something about my curse?" I asked.

Lyra gave me a bright smile.

"It did, Doctor. Please."

She gestured to a chair opposite her desk, not filled with books.

I flinched, sitting down, as a resigned sigh bled out of me. Lyra brushed a strand of gray-black hair over an ear, concerned. Morowen shifted a little, studying me like an unusual bug. I felt a bit cornered.

"Really, I'm sorry for being a bit late," I said. "A few too many burns and bruises made the walk from my shop slower than I like. I'm healing, but not whole."

"Keep using that cream I gave you," Morowen said flatly. "It'll take care of those burns. Won't be quick, but it'll work."

Lyra simply shook her head.

"Don't worry about the time, Doctor. Everyone knows what happened during the destruction of Port Royal. No one comes through that without at least some bruises."

She steepled her fingers, resting her elbows on the desk.

"But first, the good news. Ever since you've returned, I can't find any sign of the Bindweaver Curse on you. Best as I know, it's lifted."

"I don't feel it either," the hag grunted, glancing at Lyra. She adjusted her blue shawl around herself before indicating me with her chin.

"What I can tell, Pedro got clever when he altered the book." Then she fixed me with a piercing gaze. "But gone doesn't mean destroyed. It just means it changed when he wrote it in as part of a ghost trap."

Lyra's gray zombie eyes lit up with a sparkle.

"Ghost trap?" A grin played over her face. "Interesting! I'll want to talk about that with you later, Doctor. But right now, back to you and your curse."

I folded my arms over my chest, wincing over aches, as I narrowed my eyes.

"You both just said the curse was gone."

Lyra swapped a concerned look with Morowen. The sea hag's shark-black eyes pinched with a rare unease. That was new, especially from the sea hag. The Archbinder pursed her lips, concern crinkling the gray skin next to her eyes.

"What I know is that the corrupted ink of the *Codex* and the Bindweaver Curse had been poisoning you."

I shuddered a bit, remembering my conversation with the Death Whisper at the Arcane Gate.

"So you said."

The Archbinder nodded.

"Also, as Morowen said, you altered the formula in the *Codex*. Not the ink, but how it was applied."

I nodded at that, realizing what I'd done.

"The spirit anchor page I redrew."

"Yes. The same," Lyra replied. "Rewriting that page pulled the curse off you, giving it a new purpose. But it also exposed something else caught up in the Bindweaver Curse. A second curse that's killing you all the same."

I took a deep breath, pinching the bridge of my nose.

"What is it?" I asked. "Will the graveyard syrup formula still work?"

"It's called a Deepbind Curse, and I'm not sure if the syrup's effective," Lyra said. "I'm not that familiar with this one. There's barely three references in a book written by a Silvashar thayan wavebinder."

Lyra gave Morowen a meaningful look. "Though Morowen says she's very familiar with it."

I frowned at Morowen, tired of curses, and feeling like I'd been chasing my tail.

The sea hag smirked back, showing the points of her shark teeth. I saw the usual devious glimmer in her solid black eyes, but no humor. Instead, there was something else. I saw sympathy. She brushed a wrinkle from the front of her calico dress.

"The Deepbind Curse," she began in a low voice. "It's an old one. Not seen it used since, well, in centuries before that Crossing's Fall breach threw parts of Otherworld to Earth. Never expected to see it again, really."

She shook her head a little when I started to ask a question. There was sadness at the edge of her rough demeanor.

"I need to get something off my chest first. Thank you for yelling some damn sense into this old sea hag's head, Pedro."

Memories draped shadows around her eyes, deepening the wrinkles there in her sea-blue skin.

"Port Royal *was* all I had left. Not the town, but its people. I needed to hear that." Her mouth pinched like she'd sucked down a lemon. "I got too caught up in making sure Tristam wouldn't get out and run loose. Was worried no one could stop him."

It was obvious Morowen needed to say this, so I sat back and tried to keep quiet. But what she said prompted a reply. My words were brittle.

"No one? Right before Port Royal was destroyed, you said that you gambled on me."

An ancient glimmer of lethal mischief shone in Morowen's shark eyes, followed by that terrifying, bloody-minded grin of hers.

"Yes, I did. All because if I'm going to bet on someone over this, I'm betting on those damned souls walking the hero's path. People who do whatever bloody thing needs doing, but keep their honor." She stabbed a blue finger at me. "Someone like you, Pedro Alejandro Sangre. Because, powers of the damn seas help me, you'll do the right thing even if it kills you."

I squirmed at that little speech, scowling. The hag let out a rueful chuckle.

"What you did with the *Codex?* What you did *to* it? Pedro, you rewrote that anchor page to bind Tristam, really any damn spectral thing, into the *Codex.* Which meant the book had to use the Bindweaver Curse, since that was all it had. That was stupid, reckless... just sheer *brilliant.*"

Morowen cackled like this was the best joke in the world, slapping Lyra's desk. The Archbinder started in her chair, and I nearly jumped to my feet. But I'd dealt with the sea hag for a few years now. Morowen wiped an eye before she settled down.

"Which is why I'm calling in a few debts you owe me."

"Then I'll collect mine later," I said, raising my eyebrows.

"Fine. But some creatures escaped the Grayfall when the Arcane Gate almost snapped apart."

"What?" Lyra exclaimed, wide-eyed.

"So something escaped the land of the dead," I sighed.

The sea hag's expression lost its mirth, melting into something more dire. Her words were flat as a river stone.

"More than one something."

"Wonderful," I said dryly.

Lyra frowned, leaning forward slightly.

"How does this tie to the Deepbind Curse on the Doctor?"

She glanced at Lyra, me, then waved toward the tattoos on my hand. For a moment, I saw the tattoos glimmer as if they might ignite at that moment.

"It's related." She waved a hand at me. "Pedro's ghostfire on his hand? It's poison to those things from the Grayfall. But somehow the Deepbind is feeding off him."

Morowen shifted in her seat, waving a hand at me.

"He's spark touched. The ghostfire is a sign of that. Back on Otherworld, that was rare, because that constant connection to the Etherwave kills."

Lyra glanced at me, then tilted her head a little, considering Morowen.

"So this ghostfire is the Deepbind Curse?"

"No, it's what the Deepbind has its hooks into. Pedro's just the fuel."

Fragile silence filled the air. I broke it first.

"Lysander claims it's a spirit," I suggested softly.

The hag's feral grin returned, raising a calloused sea-blue finger at me. I scowled.

"Clever. He's only half-right. It's not just some ghost. Spark touched are connected to something bigger, older, from deep inside the Etherwave Arcana. This was a big deal when it happened. Think of it like getting bonded to a powerful being as your patron. That ghostfire? It's the seal."

I clenched my jaw until the muscles ached. At her desk, Lyra had pulled out a small stack of paper and was frantically taking notes.

"Why didn't you tell me?" I snapped.

"You wouldn't have believed me," Morowen snapped. "Now? Don't care if you don't. You need to know."

"I didn't consent to this," I countered bitterly.

Morowen jabbed a finger angrily at my tattoos.

"Neither did the one who made that bond, Pedro! Blame Dryden Storm's little trinket. That squirrel skull amulet you told me about reeks of the Deepbind Curse. That skull is a jail keeping something locked up so people like Dryden can use it."

Suddenly, I realized what she meant.

"Like what Tristam tried to do to you."

A sad, bitter look crossed her face.

"Yes." Morowen sat quietly for a moment. "When you touched that amulet, whoever's trapped tried to call for help. By accident or fate, it got it... namely, you."

I swapped an uneasy look between the two women.

"So I have to find Storm and break the amulet?" I asked. "Free whoever or whatever it is?"

A flare of soft warmth from my tattoos told me I was right.

"Yes," Morowen confirmed, then pointed at Lyra. "Only now, we've a twist on the Deepbind Curse and spark touched burning up like a bonfire. You, Archbinder, stumbled over an answer. Pedro turned it into a potion."

Lyra nodded. I saw her thoughts as plain as day.

"The graveyard syrup," I interrupted.

"It makes sense," Lyra said, tapping her chin with her feather quill. "It was meant to bleed off excessive mystical energy from a graveyard. So long as he keeps drinking it, he stays alive."

"Sort of like how a portal platform grounds a navigator?" I asked.

"The same," Lyra replied. "In the meantime, I'll look for a better way to ground raw Etherwave so it won't kill you. Mind you, this won't be easy."

Morowen adjusted her shawl with a regal dignity.

"Never said it would be. In the meantime, Pedro, track down Dryden Storm and shatter that amulet."

I scratched the stubble thoughtfully on my chin.

"Storm knows what's trapped."

At the ladies' surprised looks, I shook my head.

"He accused me of trying to steal 'it' or help it escape. Dryden knows exactly what he has. Swore he'd come after me to take back the part I have."

"Good," the sea hag said with a sharp-toothed grin. "That'll make this all the easier."

I folded my arms across my chest again.

"Easier for who?"

The hag grinned at me so suddenly, I thought she was about to bite my fingers.

"By salt and sea, it's like old times. You know, Pedro, back on Otherworld we had a name for stubborn, honorable, angsty spark touched people like you."

I drew a deep breath, then braced myself for the insult.

"That was...?"

Morowen's grin spread, showing all her sharp shark teeth.

"We called them... *paladins.*"

That made me blink before I barked out a disbelieving laugh.

"I've been called worse. Now I get holy vestments and shining armor?"

The hag's grin widened.

"No. Just more steel in your spine. You're going to need it!"

39

What We Keep

Aug 14, 1722. Proud Dog Pub. Kingston, Jamaica. Needing to pay respect where it was sorely overdue...

There's a ritual for the living to remember the dead that's as old as history. It didn't require a priest or incense. Just nothing more than close companions, stories, and a bit of rum.

In our case, it meant two-thirds of the *Silk Duchess'* crew filled the Proud Dog Pub, Kingston's second-worst tavern. There we told stories of those we'd lost, making them grander with each retelling, until even heaven didn't dare call us liars.

Hooded iron lanterns hung from stained wall hooks at tactical locations in the room. Their warm, orange flickering glow draped the air, showing every mar in the wooden walls, from stains to old blood.

A polished, dark wooden bar dominated one wall for the bartender to serve drinks on, and to shield the kitchen from unruly patrons. Round tables made from cast-off whiskey barrels dotted the wide-open space like wooden islands in the dusky room. Chairs and patrons filled everywhere else.

Stories flowed like rum. Nothing was buried. But the names of the missing were a roll call. Elara led the charge as captain.

"To Levi Cresswell!" Elara called out.

Mugs were raised with a hearty cheer.

"To Felicity McCoy," growled Skaldi, face decorated with a new splint over his nose and purpled bruise around one eye.

The crew roared again, louder now, sending the memories of our missing crew onward to glory.

So, on it went. Each name was called in turn, escorted by cheers that shook the walls. Everyone took a turn calling the roll until there weren't any names left. But I remembered one that wasn't on the roster.

I glanced across the crowd at Lysander, always the reserved, quiet island in a storm. He nodded once, as if guessing the name I had in mind. Quietly, I shoved back my chair, lifting my mug high.

"To Señor Renwick Taggart! Who didn't let death stop him from doing what's right."

Cheers shook the windows like thunder as glasses and mugs touched. After that came more stories, but no more names. Nothing else. It was all that needed to be said, since anything else would've stained the memories.

The tavern emptied after that in small groups. Some went on to the next pub, others back to the *Silk Duchess.* I stepped out of the door onto the wooden footpath and a view of the bay to clear my head. Solemn thoughts chased after me, along with the cheering echoes from the pub.

Outside, the sun hung low and orange, brushing warm lips against the horizon for the evening's last kiss. Seagulls chattered to each other a block away at the pier, fighting over fish or whatever else had washed ashore.

A gentle salt breeze drifted in like wandering ghosts from the bay. It carried scents of old seaweed, but also notes of baked bread from the nearby baker, and cheap tobacco from dockworkers along the pier. A murmur of conversation drifted up from somewhere farther down Port Royal Street.

Life moved on in Kingston, carrying shadows in its wake.

I caught my reflection in the pub window, a smoke-gray silhouette surrounded by the brilliant yellow-red flames of sunset.

"Only some carry those shadows closer than others," I mused.

Cheers from the crew still rang in my ears with too many memories when Elara found me outside. We stood quietly there together, her dragonfly-winged silhouette bathed in yellow-gold from the dying day.

I watched nearby vendors latch shutters and lock doors, calling their day done. Faint fiddle music from nearby danced through the air.

Elara took a long breath, folding her arms across herself. A silent second passed before she glanced at me, toying with the edge of her brown vest.

"After all we bled for, this is still happening." It looked as if every word tasted bitter. Her wings fluttered in the half-light, a kaleidoscopic blur of color. "You're *still* poisoned by a curse?"

Elara's hands clenched into fists. I took a weary breath before I replied.

"Sadly."

Her mouth drew into a tight, frustrated line at that. The late afternoon light cast hard shadows along her face. As if it sharpened the edge of who she was.

"I *hate* this," she spat, glaring at the amber horizon like a challenge. "The Archbinder is sure, very sure, the graveyard syrup will keep you alive?"

"Yes, *querida.* Like I told you yesterday afternoon, Archbinder Valtor really does think it'll work." I sighed, pushing my hands into the pockets of my long coat. "Provided we find Dryden Storm and break that amulet he has."

Elara clenched her jaw, grinding her teeth in frustration.

"Branch and leaf! I knew I should've killed that pirate when I had the chance." She hissed out a low sigh. "There was just a lot happening at the time."

"There'll be other chances, *querida.* Storm threatened he'll be coming for me." I gestured at nothing with my tattooed right hand. "For this. Probably to cut my hand off."

The look she shot me was pure edged steel, but it wasn't aimed at me, and I knew it.

"How many more chances?" she snapped, almost a snarl. Then she looked away, rubbing her eyes with a free hand.

Words failed me. I glanced at the ground, painted in gray shadows by the failing day, and simply nodded in reply. With a light sigh, I clenched my fists inside my pockets for a moment.

"The *Duchess* will be seaworthy again in four days," Elara said quietly, staring off into the air. "I've a warrant to ferry some cargo out to the Pearl Islands after that."

I nodded again, feeling like I stood next to a jade-eyed volcano.

"Primrose has been learning to handle the alchemy shop," I said casually. "In four days..."

"*Asa mvur,* this is insane!" She interrupted me, voice brittle as frustration flashed over her eyes. "You promised to be careful. No more stupid risks. No more refusing help."

"Yes, *querida*. Lysander yelled the same thing..."

"But, goddess' teeth, you're still..."

Elara shook her head, loose brown hair shaking a little while her words turned into a full rant.

"You can't always leave your shop when I take on a warrant for a job. You have the shop. I have the *Duchess.* Land and sea. I *know* that."

Her hands clenched into fists, ready to attack something if she could.

"The idea of sailing off, then wondering if you'll be alive when we return, just eats at me. It's like we've all staked you out as bait for Storm."

I sighed, not sure what to say. Elara was right, from a certain point of view.

Could the Kingston city watch try to stand off Dryden Storm if he showed his face? Most likely. But could the watch know every single pirate from the *Rising Eel?* No, they couldn't.

Then, there was the curse. If I didn't shatter Storm's amulet, I'd die, or live drinking a potion to keep me one step ahead of death.

I wasn't sure that was much of a life. It felt like waiting to die, even if Lyra discovered a better way to help other than the graveyard syrup.

For a long, painful moment, the reality of our lives loomed large. We stood together but apart, in silence, as if on opposite sides of a river.

"Maldita sea," I swore low under my breath, eyes squeezed shut. "Elara? I..."

"No, *asa mvur*," she interrupted me. "No words. We know the reality here."

The sigh that fell out of her almost burned my soul.

"Words are sometimes no better than yesterday's wind," she said softly.

The world suddenly seemed more broken than I'd ever felt before. More ruined than the days of bloody brush wars on Afalon Isle, where we'd first met years ago. Elara was right, there wasn't anything to say. Sometimes words do just cheapen a moment, no matter what they are.

But that didn't mean there wasn't something I could do.

I let the silence sail between us while the salt wind off the bay ruffled my dark hair. Then, I silently withdrew a leather-bound bundle of tan papers from inside my long coat. I held them out to her without preamble. She frowned, eyes darting from the bundle, to me, then back again.

"What's this?"

I shrugged lightly.

"Not yesterday's wind."

She untied the cord, giving me a wary glance, unwrapping the bundle. Dry paper crinkled as she opened it, eyebrows reaching for her hairline the more she read.

"Pedro? This is the deed to your shop."

"It is." I gestured to the papers. "My idea was to add Primrose to the deed. This way, she has legal power to handle the shop when I'm not here. A business partner with me, provided she agrees to sign."

The silence that followed was as fragile as a butterfly. I pressed on.

"So, with a little more training, I can leave her in charge of the shop, since she'll be my business partner. Then I could move some of my equipment and things aboard the *Silk Duchess.* We wouldn't be safe. Privateering is a dangerous life. But we'd be where we could look out for each other."

It took a moment for Elara to find her words, still staring at the deed. A ghost of a smile haunted her lips.

"No, this isn't yesterday's wind," she replied. "Not perfect, but real. If Primrose signs, I'll see your lab aboard the *Duchess* within the week."

She tapped the deed against her fingers thoughtfully.

"Pedro? After we find Dryden Storm and shatter that damn amulet of his?" Elara asked quietly. "What then?"

I shrugged as she handed the deed back to me. Quietly, I folded it up, then tied it closed.

"We'll land on that shore when we reach it."

I slipped the deed back inside my long coat.

The evening wind picked up off the bay in short gusts. It rustled my long coat around me, brushing Elara's shirt, vest, and hair. Strains of music—a soft, meaningful rhythm—skipped out of the Proud Dog Pub and then around us.

I turned to face Elara, a smile painted over my lips, one hand behind my back. The other hand, my tattooed one, I held out between us, palm up at chest height.

"My captain? Shall we?"

Elara tilted her head a little to the side, jade eyes glimmering in the evening light. A wry smile lit her face as she reached out to rest her hand on mine.

I gently grasped her hand with mine, lifting slightly. Then I closed the space between us, stepping in time with the music and with her. The first smooth steps of a dance.

The rest?

Well, that's another story.

THE ALCHEMIST'S APPRENTICE

prologue to THE ALCHEMIST PAPERS

C. B. Ash

A Tale of Errands, Etherwave, and Skullduggery

Aug 17, 1722. Merchant's Row, Port Royal Street. Kingston, Jamaica. Four days after the destruction of Port Royal. Nothing like some errands and escapades to get the day going.

People throw themselves into whirlpools of pain in all sorts of ways—from fistfights to shipboard sabotage. Take your pick.

For us, it was simply being near the wrong wagon at the right time.

It had been several days since we'd rescued the survivors from the Port Royal disaster. In that time, Elara had forbidden me from doing anything that smelled like heroics. This included nothing worse than a fistfight with fresh-baked bread, and even that was debatable. She wanted me intact and ship-shape to move in with her aboard the *Silk Duchess*.

Captain Elara Blackwater didn't take anything for granted. That's why she assigned an efficient bodyguard to the task. Someone not about to put up with my nonsense.

"Dr. Sangre? Stop brooding," Primrose Stewart said with a raised eyebrow. "The swelling's gone down, and you've barely winced from your bruises in the last day."

Primrose, my apprentice and business partner, didn't stroll the Kingston streets. She *attacked* them. A gust of harbor wind rolled around us—salt and sugarcane mixed with the faint rot of bilge water. Jaw set, her boots ticked a martial tempo against the glistening cobblestones. Ash-blonde hair was pulled back in a secure, proper braid against the Caribbean breeze.

Today she wore a proper, powder-blue dress, a color supposedly the most forgiving when it came to alchemy stains. Under her arm was her ever-present ledger. I strode a step behind, carrying a small wooden box. The potions stuffed inside rattled like irritable glass wind chimes.

I wasn't the picture of menace that day, not that I ever was. A Spaniard, just a bit lean from too many missed meals at sea, hair the color of burnt rum, with a tanned complexion to match. I was a man held together by habit and bruised curiosity, wrapped in a long coat as usual.

"Hm," I grunted, then drew a long breath. "I'm only considering new trade options.Like herb gardening."

Primrose snorted out a soft laugh as she stalked along the wooden footpath. With a quick step, she skirted around a stinking puddle of something mud-dark I didn't want to identify.

"Which means, as soon as you tried selling those herbs, someone would try to drive a stake through your eye for herb poaching," she replied wryly. "Captain Blackwater said you could find trouble anywhere."

I grimaced, practically hearing Elara's voice in those words.

"'Anywhere' is a bit harsh, señorita," I countered with a surprised look. "Elara may have elaborated a little..."

She spun mid-stride, brown eyes hard as baked clay but tinted with a sardonic glimmer.

"An old sea chest exploded, nearly burning you or drowning you. I'm not sure which; the story keeps changing. Also, given I'm your apprentice, you don't have to be so formal, Dr. Sangre."

"My apologies, señorita." I winced. "Um, I mean, Primrose. I'll try to remember your name as long as you remember to call me, Pedro, eh? Besides, it's an old habit, *mi aprendiz*."

"Like nearly being drowned?" she replied smartly while she marched along.

I sighed. "No matter what Elara says, it isn't like I open a door and a fight breaks out."

Primrose arched a thin eyebrow at me, mouth pulled into a flat, disbelieving line.

I flinched at the stare.

"Yes, all right. Maybe sometimes," I relented. "But it's not every day. I'm only human."

"Acceptable." Primrose nodded curtly, then turned on her heel to continue down the footpath. "Still, we'd best hurry if we're to make this delivery."

I blew out a weary breath. Medicines and healing potions or not, I was still sore from the past weeks. Primrose, however, moved through the world with the dedicated certainty of fire over dry kindling. I ignored my aches and hurried along beside her.

"Why does Mr. Gale need so much liniment?" Primrose asked. We sidestepped a small, heavily loaded wagon stacked with bolts of Chinese-made cloth. "It wasn't even the usual formula you taught me. This one smells like cinnamon and cloves?"

"Sirens," I replied seriously. "They bit him in the leg some time ago."

"What? But he's not missing a leg."

"True, but a siren's bite sometimes comes with venom." I nodded toward a fruit cart about to pull into the street. We skirted it, dodged three newsboys in a fight, then dove back into the crowd. "A bit of something to learn as an alchemist," I added.

Primrose gave me a narrow, suspicious look.

"So, venoms? Poisons? You make it sound like I'll need to know how to kill people," she said dryly.

I gestured at the sign for the Timeworn Tart Bakery ahead, past the midday crowds on our right. Primrose glanced over the teeming clumps of people at it and nodded.

"Oh, murder? More or less," I grinned. "That way we know how to keep them alive. Speaking of which, let's drop off Señor Gale's liniment."

Aug 17, 1722. Later that morning. Timeworn Tart Bakery, Port Royal Street. Kingston, Jamaica. Skullduggery and fine pastries—two tastes that surprisingly go together.

The aroma of fresh gingerbread danced with the scent of roasted nuts and melted butter as Primrose and I left the Timeworn Tart. Flour dust motes spun through the air like daydreams. Ghosts of fresh-baked bread, cardamom, and savory spices lingered like a warm hug, inviting us to stay.

Despite that, and the owner's grateful gift of fresh bulla flatbread, we left the shop behind. The two of us weren't done with the day, and it wasn't done with us.

Waves of murmured conversation washed around us like a high tide of sound. The crowds along Merchant's Row were never quiet, but this was different. There was a certain spark of energy to the air. Not quite excitement, but not dread, either.

Then I felt it. A shiver of the Etherwave Arcana, vibrating like a crystal at the brink of shattering. It lingered like a predator under the fragrant rot of tobacco and salted fish left too long in the sun.

"Primrose, wait," I murmured, holding off on another bite of the flatbread.

It turned out the warning wasn't necessary; she'd felt it, too. I'd only just started to teach her how to feel and use the Etherwave Arcana, what some loosely called 'magic'. Mostly this was for mixing potions with reality-bending enchantments. But it also meant she could sense ripples in the Etherwave like I did.

Her brows knitted as she studied the crowd, the air, and the city itself.

"Pedro? What is that?"

"I'm not sure," I admitted slowly. "It's heavily enchanted, whatever it is."

Thoughtfully, I took a bite of the bulla bread, and felt the sweet, spice cake flavor hit my tongue. Seeing nothing obvious beyond people going about their shopping along the Row, I walked a few steps ahead. I stopped at a crooked wooden stall with limes stacked like artillery shot, glancing around again.

Then the Etherwave hit me with the scent of something sharp and metallic behind the fresh tang of limes.

I looked for the source of the smell. Not far away, I watched the crowd part along one of the narrow roads to the docks in slow, reluctant waves. Between them, a quartet of dockworkers rolled a battered wagon with a light, irritating squeak over the cobblestones. It was thick with bales of barley and cotton, with an odd box nestled on top.

I realized right away that the box—or really what was inside it—was the source of the disturbance.

It was a device or a sculpture of sorts, half hidden in a wet, weathered wooden box partially under a damp tarpaulin. The box had seen better days and had bounced partially open, its lid askew. From what I could see, the thing in the box looked beautiful in about the way a poisonous spider might.

"Over there," I nodded with my chin. "It's coming from that wagon. Inside that box on top."

I couldn't see much, but what I saw looked compact and oval, with odd metal legs tucked in at its sides. In place of any iron or brass, I swore I saw a latticework of fused sea-glass and polished steel. The exposed curve winked under the Caribbean sun.

Either way, it bent the Etherwave around itself, like a haze over water.

"Whatever it is, the thing is humming like a hive of angry bees. I can feel the Etherwave Arcana leaking off it from here," I murmured.

"All the more reason to know what it is," she declared with a narrowed, suspicious look at the device.

"Primrose? Curiosity feeds the mind, but it can also empty the rum cabinet."

She gave me a side-eyed glance and snorted, gesturing past the crowd at the wagon.

"If it's dangerous, we can't ignore it. You know that. Especially not after what happened to Port Royal. Besides, it doesn't hurt to just ask."

I pinched the bridge of my nose, mouth pulled tight.

"As much as I agree with you, this isn't our problem—and it could hurt a lot. We don't even know if it *is* a problem. Besides, we're not working with the Kingston City Watch today." Memories of being questioned by the Watch for hours over the Petrify Murders flittered through my mind. "They don't much like volunteer help."

Primrose crossed her arms, giving me a flat look.

I sighed. "You're not going to let this go, are you?"

"No," she replied. "In any case, I know you want to know as badly as I do. I *saw* that look in your eyes just now."

I grimaced a little, but tried to cover it up by narrowing my eyes at her. Primrose didn't seem all that fooled.

"Fine. Yes, I do," I admitted. "But we can't go barreling over there to rummage through the wagon. It'll get the Watch called on us as thieves." I drew a deep breath. "Still, that aside, we can at least follow it from a discreet distance. Perhaps we'll learn something."

She gave me a firm nod before we headed after our prey.

Most wagons along this road drew curses and elbowing; this one left a wake of silence, and bone-white faces or unnerved glances. I was surprised no one fainted.

"It's like waves of power pulling at people. Draining them? If that effect goes off indoors? That could hurt a lot of people," I murmured.

Primrose agreed with a grim nod.

The laborers with the wagon looked little better off than the crowd. There were four men in all—one holding the reins of the mule team and three guarding the cargo. All but one carried a haunted look. Their shoulders were slightly hunched, and a brittle air of fear hovered around them, as if the work couldn't be done fast enough. The mules didn't seem to care in the least.

Their boss, or the one I assumed was in charge, was another matter. He was all neck and old muscle, and moved with the pricey swagger of a man trusted with other people's valuables. A gritty disposition hovered around him like flies.

I settled into a comfortable stroll next to Primrose along the street, barely a few yards behind the wagon. The Etherwave Arcana churned in the wagon's wake—a frothy mess of invisible power that broke around us. We waded through it like high tide, determined not to lose them, but careful to keep our distance so as not to be noticed.

Primrose touched my arm, concerned.

"They're turning down Orange Street for the trading company offices."

I frowned at the wagon, then at the road ahead.

"Now that worries me," I said. "It could be bound for any of the dozen trading companies with offices there, such as the East India Company and others. At least half are said to have ties to the Trade Guild Syndicate. More often than not, most are up to no good." I scratched my chin, then shook my head a little. "I really don't like the enchanted hum rolling off that wagon."

We slipped past a knot of sailors either racing to a berth or begging for one. There had been an overflow of them since the enchanted hurricane nearly destroyed Port Royal's Arcane Gate and left that town in ruins.

"It's giving me quite the headache." Primrose sighed, rubbing her temples. "What specifically don't you like about it?"

I shared the same headache she had. That hum was maddening, but that wasn't what bothered me. I gestured to the sailors we'd walked past, then to a trio of merchants deep in a debate over a stack of fruit crates.

"Notice how much louder and insistent the humming gets the closer that wagon is to people? Especially groups?"

She wrinkled her nose with a frown. "I thought that was just the headache."

"Not just," I replied as we walked quickly through the market crowd. After a long scowl at the lumbering wagon, I wiggled my fingers a little in front of me. "It's reacting to anyone nearby. The more people there are, the louder the hum grows; spilling out waves of power, reaching out like grasping fingers. Why or how? No idea."

Our slow chase continued until the wagon turned off Port Royal and down Orange Street. That's when we stopped at the corner just out of sight. I pulled out a black leather pocket notebook to give the pretense of discussing alchemy ingredients or shopping lists.

It wasn't entirely a ruse. We needed some of those for the shop. But it let us keep a subtle eye on where the wagon was headed. Primrose pulled out her own small notebook to compare her shopping list to mine. Casually, she peered over the edge to glance down Orange Street.

"The wagon stopped outside the Emerald Coast Company." She wrinkled her nose, squinting down the street. "They're unloading it all down an alley. Probably a side door for storage in the back." Primrose fumed. "I still can't see what's in that bloody box!"

"Probably because you're not supposed to, Miss Stewart." A deep, smoke-ragged voice grunted irritably next to us. "I'm surprised to see you here, Miss. Especially with the likes of this one."

Primrose jerked around, wide-eyed with nostrils flared, as she held her notebook in a white-knuckled death grip. I also tensed, but turned more slowly, then tilted my head at the newcomer, Inspector Ambrose Leigh of the Kingston City Watch.

"Ah, Inspector Leigh. Good to see you've found your way out from behind your desk. Anyone die today?"

The city watch investigator arched a narrow, sandy-blonde eyebrow at the remark. He studied me suspiciously.

"Not yet," he replied crisply, tugging his gray tweed coat into place. "But the day's still young. You're not up to your usual apothecary theatrics, are you, Dr. Sangre?"

I grinned, snapping my notebook closed with a small flourish. Then, I wiggled it in the man's direction.

"Inspector, I'm hurt. It wasn't theatrics when you asked me to refine that cure for the Petrify Murders."

He breathed out a soft growl, like a frustrated bulldog. Primrose cut him off, not a bit ruffled by the inspector's bluster.

"If you must know, Inspector, I'm apprenticed to Dr. Sangre." Her words were brisk and matter-of-fact, giving the man no room to maneuver. "We're out getting ingredients. If I remember our current orders, you've one for bruised knuckles?"

"Ah. Well." The inspector harrumphed, caught off guard, pursing his lips, which made his mustache wiggle like an agitated caterpillar. He reflexively rubbed his right hand, which showed bruises from a recent fight.

"That's true. But I know the trouble your new mentor gets up to, young lady. So watch yourselves. Also, as you two are out *just* shopping, drop a word to me if you hear anything... odd. Such as some unique cargo that requires a closer look? Something that might not have been on a legal manifest? Hm? Can't be too careful now, given what happened to Port Royal."

Primrose stiffened a little as the air went tense. After a careful breath, and another easy smile, I nodded again.

"Of course, Inspector. We're always happy to help."

Inspector Leigh studied us both, clasping his hands behind his back.

"Good. Right then."

The man nodded toward Orange Street.

"Also? Take care when poking your noses in merchants' affairs. Some names are untouchable." Then he lowered his voice. "Others sign my pay. Good day."

With a curt nod, the inspector casually turned, then strolled away down Port Royal Street. My smile melted away, and I swapped a sharp look with Primrose.

"That was a warning," Primrose murmured.

"It was."

"So, that's it?" Frustration laced her words. "We just walk away?"

I raised my eyebrows at her.

"Oh no, that ship has sailed. Instead? Well, *mi aprendiz*, we keep poking and see what happens when we kick over a few rocks."

Primrose narrowed her eyes.

"Now I see why Captain Blackwater said you could find trouble anywhere."

I waved a hand at the comment.

"Eh, it's a gift."

Aug 17, 1722. Late afternoon. Merchant's Row, Port Royal Street. Kingston, Jamaica. Sometimes, getting no answers screams the worst answer of all...

Gift or not, it took time and effort to learn anything about that cargo.

This wasn't a surprise. Most trading companies' cargo manifests were closely guarded secrets, and Emerald Coast was no exception. Pirates and thieves were a constant problem, but so were competitors. I wasn't sure which was worse.

To get any idea of what Emerald Coast shipped into Kingston would take a little work. So we spent the afternoon on Port Royal Street, avoiding the city watch, but not the merchants.

By late afternoon, Primrose looked ready to set something on fire. My mood wasn't much better.

"Your chicken feet," Primrose deadpanned with a mild grimace, handing me a wrapped package.

"Thank you," I replied, tucking it under an arm. "My graveyard elixir medicine—and my affliction—appreciates the effort. Did anyone at the booth know anything?"

"Nothing," she said, tone flat as a board. "Same as the half-dozen times before. Some herbs from East Africa at best. Mostly silence and fidgeting. It's like no one really does much business with the Emerald Coast Company."

I trailed a suspicious look along the booths that lined the brown and gray cobblestone road.

"Doubtful." A sigh spilled out of me. "Emerald Coast Company isn't the largest shipper, but they handle the rare and hard-to-find goods. Lately, it seems to be special bolts of patterned cotton from India, red teas from East Africa, and the like. I've seen their goods for sale here and there."

Primrose turned her perturbed look on the nearest merchant. To his credit, the man stood his ground. The fresh fruit dealer offered her an apple and a weak smile as a peacemaking gesture. Primrose flattened her mouth into a thin line, but paid the man two *reales* and accepted the fruit.

"So they're afraid to lose the source for their more expensive goods," she murmured, toying with the fruit. "That would explain why they won't talk about it."

I studied the footpath as my thoughts churned, chewing my lower lip.

"Yes. But that doesn't mean we're at the end of our rope. It just means we'll need to resort to some skullduggery to see if the Emerald Coast has brought something dangerous into Kingston. If we're lucky, it's just some odd clockwork toy."

Primrose raised her eyebrows. "Skullduggery? If this results in you getting battered again, Captain Blackwater will have my hide."

I chuckled and patted Primrose on the back.

"No, *mi aprendiz,* nothing so drastic. Just a conversation with an old friend." I grinned. "You'll like him."

Primrose fixed me with a deadpan stare and a raised eyebrow, but kept any other comment to herself.

With that, I sent a note to an old friend, asking him to meet us at the Proud Dog Pub that night.

Aug 17, 1722. Early evening. Proud Dog Pub. Kingston, Jamaica. It's good to have friends in shadowy places...

It was lively that evening in the Proud Dog Pub, despite its reputation as Kingston's second-worst tavern. The place was crowded with a motley collection of cutthroats, mercantile marines, dockworkers, and more. Settled here and there among the energetic evening crowd were those of even shadier professions. My old mentor and friend, Lucien Massena, was among the latter.

Somewhere near the back, a fiddle screeched against the roar of sailors arguing myth against theology over cards. It set a lively tune that was almost an appropriate backdrop for our conversation.

"Well, it isn't the oddest thing you've asked me about, Pedro." Lucien drained his polished teakwood mug, then stared balefully into it. "Once I got your note, I called in a few favors and looked into the Marquee Brotherhood's records on the Emerald Coast Company."

He gave us a wary look.

"They're quite the *interesting* read. Better than a chapbook."

Lucien was dressed as he always was, in dirt browns and grays, a forgettable smear of the ordinary in a busy world. They were shades that let him blend into most groups, from fishermen to dockworkers. He did so with such uncanny ease. Some swore it was enchantment—but honestly, it was only natural skill.

It was also because of his eye for detail, which was why I asked for his help.

"What do you mean?" I tapped the top of my half-filled wooden mug. The brown water inside it—what the pub called rum—smelled of regret and molasses.

Lucien leaned against our small, round, barrel-top table conspiratorially. A sly expression ghosted over his thin features as shadows veiled his eyes.

"Jonas Ketteridge." Lucien waved down one of the servers to order another rum. "Ketteridge runs the Emerald Coast Company. The man has steered them into and around more than one squall of trouble. Some of it he's caused himself, with—let's call it 'questionable business'."

Primrose leaned back, eyebrows knitted.

"You make it sound like the man's a pirate."

"No more than any other in the trade business," the assassin countered. "Pirates are simply more honest about themselves."

My mind still sailed around what Lucien considered 'questionable business'.

I held up my hands like balance scales.

"Pirate? Smuggler?" I asked warily. "My friend, so far I'm hearing 'smuggler'. Just what does your Marquee Brotherhood have on him, that you, of all people, call 'questionable'? You've left a lot of space around that word."

The server returned with a fresh mug of rum, then breezed away. Lucien took a swallow before letting out a deep, baritone laugh.

"Pedro, you know me far too well. Let's just say, Jonas Ketteridge is a bookkeeper with blood under his nails. The kind who hides bodies behind his ledger entries."

Lucien took another swig from his mug, then tapped the table, giving us a dark look. Woody traces of pipe smoke hovered around us, framing the conversation.

"Ketteridge has been involved in trading ventures that brush just outside the law. A little rum smuggling, a few attempts to resurrect the damn slave trade, things like that. But he's been careful, not treading on too many toes in the same place twice."

I nodded. "Which means the man stays one step ahead of being locked in irons. Especially since Spain, Britain, and the rest argue over what law applies where."

Lucien raised his eyebrows at us with a smirk, then raised a toast with his mug.

"Exactly. If something does turn up, it isn't enough proof for any local city watch or Royal Navy to bother him. At least, not much."

Primrose tilted her head a little. I swore I could almost see the thoughts churn behind her eyes. She wrinkled her nose as if she smelled something rank.

"He sounds like a street mugger turned merchant with the same ethics. Emerald Coast supplies luxury teas and more along Merchant's Row for resale." She tapped the table with a finger, like marking time.

"All this explains why no one wanted to talk to us about Emerald Coast Company—fear and profit. I'd say they were mostly afraid that this Mr. Ketteridge would send cutthroats to pay them an evening visit."

"Miss? You've got quite a fine eye for detail, along with a bloody bit of intrigue." Lucien arched an eyebrow at me. "Where'd you find this one again?"

I sipped my drink casually.

"There was an incident where she beat a pirate senseless with a crate lid."

Lucien's eyebrows reached for his thinning hairline.

Not to be outdone, Primrose cleared her throat.

"Well, I do know the doctor," she replied with a wry grin, nodding toward me. "He does try to blow himself apart occasionally."

I gave her a wounded look while Lucien barked out a belly laugh, wiping his eyes without comment. Then he waved a hand at us once he'd stopped laughing.

"Now, that's just the top of the sail on Jonas Ketteridge. You two haven't told me why you wanted to know." His eyes bored holes through the air at us. "So, out with it. This isn't a man to mess about with. It's like sticking your hand in a bag of snakes and hoping they don't bite."

I swapped an uneasy look with Primrose before I waved idly in Lucien's direction.

"Well, it could be something, but it could also be nothing." I drew in a breath of the tavern's greasy smoke. "The señorita and I felt a ripple through the Etherwave Arcana earlier today along Merchant's Row. Something unsettled."

"Unsettled?" Lucien narrowed his eyes at us. "That's a specific meaning for you, Pedro. You two best start at the beginning."

After a deep breath, I recounted the events so far. It was everything, starting after we left the Timeworn Tart, to the odd device and what we felt ripple through in the Etherwave. Primrose provided a particularly detailed account of how people reacted with surprised distaste to the wagon when it passed them. Lucien nodded along with an even expression, taking it all in.

He sat back once we finished, staring into the middle distance. Then he frowned, tracing the grooves of the wooden table with a finger.

"I was going to tell you the list of gutter trash and bilge rats that swim in the man's wake." Lucien pursed his lips before his eyes flicked over to us. "But that story about the wagon and its glass and metal parlor toy? It narrows the list considerably."

"To whom?" Primrose leaned forward, eyes sharp and hands around her wooden mug as if she might throttle it.

Lucien tilted his head, then sat forward conspiratorially.

"It isn't pretty." The assassin frowned, taking a swig of rum, then nodded at his own thoughts. "I'd say Bart Roberts, but I heard he was killed this past February in a fight off Cape Lopez against Captain Chaloner Ogle. Still, that leaves Captain Matteo Lucca, Captain Thomas Anstis, and Robert Dukinfield." Lucien frowned again. "Then again, maybe Aldus Fettergray."

I grunted half-thoughtfully. "That *is* an unpleasant list."

"Wait. I don't understand." Primrose narrowed her eyes, glancing between Lucien and myself. "Robert Dukinfield? The young landowner here in Kingston? Why is he one of them?"

"He's a former slaver who's as cutthroat as the rest on that list," Lucien replied bitterly.

"Not to mention, Dukinfield hates wavebinders and anything to do with enchantments, spells, and the Etherwave Arcana," I added, then gestured between Primrose and myself with a bitter smile. "The man partially tolerates alchemists. It seems we're useful."

"Still, he stands out from the rest." Primrose narrowed her eyes, as if the topic irritated her sense of order. "Mr. Massena? Did you happen to find out what Jonas Ketteridge typically smuggles for the people on your short list? Just enchanted items, or is it more than that?"

Lucien pursed his lips before taking another drink of rum. A few seconds, and a slow hum later, he offered a reply.

"There's some of the usual, like sugarcane, cotton, and clockwork semaphones—when anyone can pry clockwork like that away from Kelstani ships." Lucien grinned. "But, more to the point? Yes, relics. A handful in the past two months. What? No idea." He shrugged. "The man keeps his most recent records closer to him than his enemies or his friends."

I leaned an elbow against the table, tapping my mug with a finger.

"Any idea where he keeps those tally sheets?"

My old mentor gave me a wicked grin.

"His trading company office for one. Rumors are he keeps it in a hidden iron chest."

Lucien drummed his knuckles on the table between us.

"I'll tell you both though—if you're thinking of some skullduggery—be careful. Word in the Brotherhood says Dukinfield's got a new 'family venture,' and Ketteridge is smuggling some 'special ingredient'. My guess? It could be what you both sensed."

Primrose looked hooked on every word as she stared holes into Lucien.

"So, a sample of a new trade good?"

"Ah, now that's a sharp question. Rare as anything, I've been told." Lucien gave a sly grin. "But one set to turn the Dukinfield family another fine profit."

I took a quick swig of my rum. "As if they need another one. They're still drowning in blood money."

Primrose scowled at the air over the table for a moment.

"We need to find out what's in those records, Doctor," she said with a stern glance to me. "You saw what I saw. That wagon—the thing on it—was doing something to anyone nearby. That isn't normal."

I frowned, remembering how every person the wagon passed turned ghastly pale. Primrose wasn't wrong. Something unpleasant was brought to Kingston. This was a problem for the city watch, but they often showed deference to powerful families like the Dukinfields. Inspector Leigh would need something ironclad to work with, or he'd not work on this at all.

"We could tell the city watch?" I offered. "Warn them to look into it."

Lucien snorted, then sipped his rum.

I gave him a sideways glance, then continued.

"Beyond that? We'd have to pay the Emerald Coast a polite after-hours call, Primrose. You bring your ledger—I'll bring picks, chalk, and something that makes locks forget they're locks. But we'd better be sure this is worth the risk."

"Pedro..." was all she said, packing my name with a dozen suspicions about the smuggled relic.

I exhaled slowly. Trouble had a way of tracking me down no matter what I did.

Lucien chuckled.

"If that thing you sensed really is for Dukinfield, it'll be trapped six ways—two for thieves, four for fools. Best figure out which you two are before you arrive."

Primrose gave me a sharp, suspicious look. I just sat back with a grin.

Aug 17, 1722. Late evening. Emerald Coast Company, Orange Street. Kingston, Jamaica. Not all piracy takes place on the high seas. The same can be said of smuggling...

Primrose cast a wary glance at the evening shadows that lined Orange Street.

"I thought you said you could pick a lock?" she hissed.

A rough sigh fell out of me while I crouched in front of the side door into the Emerald Coast offices.

"Some have said I'm better at picking one if it's for sale on a shelf. But yes—I *can* pick a lock. Elara is just far better at it than I am."

I clenched my jaw, dribbling a copper-colored oil from a small bottle onto the lock. Drops oozed inside, and then came the lovely sound of metal clicking. Gently, I inserted my lockpicks and felt carefully. I grinned at Primrose, lifted the picks and tugged. There was a muffled click as the lock surrendered.

"As I said, I do know how to pick one." I stood, opened the door, and gave a small bow.

Primrose shot me a wry look as she walked briskly inside. I followed and eased the door closed behind us.

The side entrance was a stubby excuse for a hallway, rich with wood dust and desiccated air. It was a ragged scent; the sort of smell coming from an old coffin startled awake by the living. I coughed once. Primrose wrinkled her nose in sour distaste, but we moved on. The air deeper inside hit us warm and damp, as the wooden walls had sweated out the sea with a touch of peat.

"It smells like an old glasshouse in here, with overgrown plants," Primrose murmured.

"Ones that might be rotting," I added, wiping my nose.

Past the hallway was the usual arrangement for a shipping company. Space was always a premium in Kingston, so shipping offices were typically one part 'office' and another part 'warehouse'. This was the latter.

The only light streamed in from the smudged, front bay windows. Moonlight sliced shafts through the darkness, painting clerks' desks and more to our left in a ghostly bone-white color. I glanced at the warehouse proper to our right with its stacks of cloth, crates, and all manner of rare goods.

"I'm surprised Señor Ketteridge doesn't have more guards," I whispered, turning toward the offices. "That makes me worry."

"Why?" Primrose hissed, then glanced sharply at me. "You think that box isn't here anymore?"

We reached an office that had a brass plate on the door engraved with the words 'Jonas Ketteridge'. At the doorway, I paused, feeling the flow of the Etherwave Arcana around me.

It was almost the usual, warm undercurrent that flowed through the world. One that washed and ebbed around everything—except in the depths of that warehouse.

"No, it's here," I replied softly. "Stop and listen, Primrose. Feel the flow of the Etherwave."

She inhaled a deep breath, blinking slowly.

"It feels... stale? Wrong. Like a part of the Etherwave was caught in a tidal pool, and is now going stagnant." Primrose inhaled again. "I can't tell where. It's like... it's the entire warehouse."

I held out my right hand. My snake-like, knotted tattoos glowed and flickered with an emerald-green flame.

"Neither can I." Bitterly, I shook my head. "We need that ledger more than ever to find where they've stashed the thing. As for the guards?" A sigh breathed out of me. "Given the man's reputation, they're here. Either they're checking the outside or distracted. So we don't have a lot of time."

We each pulled out a vial filled with a milky-blue liquid and shook them. Dusky blue light glimmered from inside as the glowworm essence came alive. Then we stepped inside the office and got to work.

There were 'official' office records and shipping manifests in a tall cabinet. We ignored those, staying on the hunt for the real ledgers. Everything we moved or touched went back exactly where we found it.

It took some searching, but we found it a few minutes later—a key hidden in a bag behind a drawer. After that, a thin iron chest under a loose set of floorboards. It was a long, narrow elm coffer, bound in iron with a stout lock.

The coffer was barely big enough to hold a ledger. I went to work on the half-heart padlock with my copper oil and picks. It snapped open a few seconds later.

"Ah, here we have it," I whispered while we crouched on the floor, poring over the ledger. "Oh my, Señor Ketteridge, you've been a very bad man. Bribes to soothe nobles who have an outburst of morals? Poisons? Even necromantic relics to raise the dead and use them as temporary slaves."

"It's a wonder he sleeps at night," Primrose snarled, reading over my shoulder.

"He likely does. Men like him are what keep evil alive and well in the world," I replied, leafing through the dry, weathered pages. Then I tapped an entry. "It's also why my lovely Captain Blackwater raids their ships so often. Ah! There. Space twelve, lot twenty-seven. Not sure what the abbreviations mean, but one of the smuggled items is a box from San Germán, Puerto Rico."

"Smuggled?" Primrose looked offended by the concept. "It was right on top of the wagon!"

"Hidden in plain sight," I chuckled dryly. "But we've got the lot number; now we just need to find the box."

A rattle of keys in the front door lock shot ice through my nerves.

"Quick! Put it all back!" I hissed.

We did, and then raced out of the office through the shadows toward the depths of the gloom-covered warehouse.

The darkness was heavier than I expected—so thick that it felt like a wet wool blanket wrapped around me. Nearby, the thing we were hunting churned the Etherwave Arcana so deeply that it felt like we were covered in thick, spoiled milk. We located a tall stack of crates, covered our glowworm vials, then waited.

Jonas Ketteridge strode through the door, followed by two heavily muscled men and a thin, nervous, young thayan man. The latter clutched a ledger and envelope like his life depended on it.

Both the muscled men were a problem, but weren't the ones I focused on. That was their employer and the stiff-winged man at his side.

Ketteridge was an average-height man as humans went, no taller than myself. But what he didn't have in height, he claimed in bulk. The man was broad-shouldered, if not shaped like a brick. Every inch looked like old muscle gained from hard labor.

It was his eyes that gave me pause. They were sharp as a pit viper's, with five times less remorse, as if he'd had that sensation removed years ago.

The young thayan man with them was rail thin, with tawny hair and glimmering copper eyes. With each step, the young man's dragonfly wings would flutter nervously, as if he felt there were safer places than this. His clothes were in far better condition than the others. They looked better cared for, and cut from a finer cloth.

"Does Lord Dukinfield even know what time it is?" Ketteridge snarled low, stalking through the front room to his office. "Some of us need our beauty sleep."

"A century ought to do it," breathed Primrose next to me. I sputtered, grinned, but waved for her to shush.

The young, thin man's mouth pulled into a tight line, looking down his nose at Ketteridge—which was a trick, since Ketteridge was a bit taller.

"My Lord Dukinfield requests delivery of the item now. He feels that time is of the essence. The thing is... fragile. They've been known to die rapidly." Dukinfield's representative made a formal, stiff gesture at the Emerald Coast's warehouse. "So, if you please, I'll take it and bid you good evening."

Ketteridge looked like he had eaten something rotten, but still managed a smile.

"Of course. Anything for one of my regular clients. Provided he's willing to discuss a new contract? Exclusive rights to transport the results of his new family venture? My ships can easily smuggle a few slaves. Quietly, of course."

The stuffy young man nodded back and sniffed imperiously.

"Of course. I'm empowered to draw up those papers now, along with payment."

Ketteridge was suddenly all poisonous smiles as he waved a meaty hand toward his office.

"Then by all means—Samuel Goodsong, was it? Let's settle the proprieties, and I'll have my men get Dukinfield's precious little box. It'll be good to do business with your Lord Dukinfield in his new enterprise."

Once the quartet vanished into Ketteridge's office and shut the door, Primrose gripped my arm like a vice. Fortunately, it was my good one, not the one that had been stabbed and was healing.

"We have to get that box!" she hissed.

"Agreed." I gave the office door another suspicious glance, pulling out my glowing vial. "We'll need to hurry. There's no telling how long they'll be in there."

We silently raced over the battered floorboards, narrowly missing the loose ones in the dark by a hair's breadth. The darkness and stacked crates made the warehouse feel close. Tight. As if the building's timbers loomed over us, but it was the tension at being discovered that was suffocating.

The gray, weathered box was stashed on the shelves in the back right side of the warehouse. I pulled it down, careful of the fragile wood, cradling it in my arms. Holding that thing close made me lightheaded, as the Etherwave Arcana swirled around it like water in a whirlpool.

"Dios mío," I murmured, shaking my head. "What is this thing? I feel like a sponge being wrung dry."

The box *shifted* in my arms.

I froze.

Primrose rubbed her eyes, frowning—not at me, but at the box. Carefully, she peeked inside.

"Pedro... it's a plant, and it's twisting the Etherwave as its dying. Quick, we need to get it out of here. I'll guide you."

Naturally, we made it five steps before the office door creaked open. It also reminded me of something else we needed.

"They're coming this way!" Primrose hissed. "Run!"

"No! The ledger," I murmured back. "We need a page out of Señor Ketteridge's hidden ledger. Something that Inspector Leigh can use to foul up whatever that man and Señor Dukinfield are doing."

Primrose nodded, clenching her jaw, while she escorted me partway through the warehouse. In the gloom, Ketteridge's bodyguards strolled to the back, heading for the shelf we'd left.

But Jonas Ketteridge and Samuel Goodsong remained at the office door, backlit by the limp, flickering yellow glow of an oil lamp.

I bit off a sigh, glancing at the stubby hallway to the side door and freedom.

"We'll have to come back for the ledger. Hopefully, they won't move it before then," I whispered.

Suddenly, Primrose grabbed the box from my hands, nearly staggering when the odd effect from it hit her.

"What are you doing?" I scowled, reaching for the box. She stepped out of reach.

"No. I'm the better choice here, Pedro. You're still hurt and healing. I'm not. Once I get their attention, I'll lead them into the alley." She thrust her chin toward the warehouse office. "Get a page from the ledger. The whole ledger, maybe? I'll meet you back at the shop."

Tension shot up my spine.

I hated this. Hated it with all my spirit to leave her being chased alone.

But she was right.

"Agreed." I fixed her with a stern look. "But be careful!"

"I'll be as careful as the mentor I'm apprenticed to," she replied with a sly grin.

I swallowed a groan.

"*That's* what worries me!"

Primrose flashed me another grin before racing off to the side door as I ducked into the shadows behind some crates.

To her credit, she didn't make any dramatic speeches or taunts. Instead, she just paused once as she opened the side door—just long enough for the moonlight to outline her in the doorway. It drew out her silhouette in plain sight, showing all and sundry that a woman had grabbed the precious box everyone wanted.

"Hold there! You! Who are you?" Ketteridge roared. "That woman! Stop her! She's got the plant!"

Both bodyguards ran from the back of the warehouse. Ketteridge charged from his office with Goodsong in tow, wings humming. But, Primrose was already out the door—expression grim—before they even made it halfway.

Her plan to divide and conquer was delightfully simple—which was likely why it worked.

"Nothing like desperate greed to blind a fool," I murmured with a dark grin.

I made a mad dash for the office once the last of them were out of sight. In moments, I had the floorboards pulled aside and the iron chest open again. I glanced out at the dark warehouse, holding the ledger in my hands, weighing the choice to take it, or only a part of it.

"If I take it all, Ketteridge will run. Raising the dead as slaves? Opium?" I shook my head. "One less corrupt trading company, the better, even if most are corrupt."

I ripped out two pages from the ledger that held his signature. Not so far back that it wouldn't matter, but not close enough to the recent page that Ketteridge would notice. At least, he shouldn't notice right away. I stashed the ledger back where I had found it, then darted outside.

My intent was to help Primrose. She was outnumbered four to one—tall odds for anyone, no matter who they were. I made it to the start of the alley beside the Emerald Coast company, with a vial of acid to throw. But what I found eased my worries.

At the far end of that alley, Primrose had hiked up her skirts, and—with one arm tight around the box—ran like the wind. The two bodyguards raced after her, at worst hurling insults, as she was well out of reach. Ketteridge and Goodsong were even farther away.

Then, quick as a spark, Primrose spun on her heel, hurling the contents of a flask from her belt onto the damp cobblestones. It shattered with a splash of a muddy-brown oil I didn't recognize.

Her pursuers didn't slow down a bit, at least not until the cobblestones stabbed for the night sky with sharp spikes as long as a finger. Then there were more curses, each worse than the last, while the four men tried to high-step off the road through cries of pain.

"Barely learned the basics, and you're already making your own mixtures," I murmured proudly.

As the men retreated from the alchemical spikes, Primrose grabbed a second vial from her belt. She popped the cork, hurling the contents at her feet. An oily gray liquid covered the cobblestones.

Instantly, a smoky fog erupted, eager to devour the air. It blasted up and out into a chaotic whirlwind, swirling around her. Even as the thick, gray tendrils rose, Primrose twirled once, skirt rippling, letting out a wicked, daring giggle. I felt the gentle nudge of the Etherwave Arcana as the potion finished the illusion—making it seem she melted into smoke.

Her pursuers looked deeply horrified, jumping at every nearby shadow.

"So that's what it looks like when I do that," I mused, grinning with pride. "Well done, *mi aprendiz.* Well done."

It was then I realized Primrose didn't need protection. She simply needed a little instruction, and for the world to back away, giving her the room to run—which now, she had.

"The world won't know what hit it," I murmured, chuckling. "I can't wait to see what comes next."

With that, I turned away to the nearest shadows along Orange Street, then strolled back to the shop.

Aug 18, 1722. Harbor Street, Kingston, Jamaica. Brewed Gambit Alchemy Shop. Settling an unofficial agreement and smuggling a little bit of truth...

I opened the shop door the next morning just as Inspector Leigh was about to knock. He harrumphed at me, and I stepped aside with a dramatic sweep of my hand.

"Good to see you this morning, Inspector! Won't you come in?"

That earned me a narrowed-eyed scowl along with another grunt—though I thought I heard a chuckle, as well. Inspector Leigh adjusted his brown tweed waistcoat, then brushed at some imaginary dust while his mustache quirked.

"You said promptly at nine, Doctor. This had best be worth the walk."

I grinned, shutting the door behind him after he strode inside.

"Of course, but the proof's in the telling... or the seeing, wouldn't you say?"

The Inspector grumbled something wordlessly, which only made me grin a bit more.

I led him back to the workshop table, where Primrose was already busy brewing up a new batch of fog elixir. We'd used up our last supply the night before, so making more was essential, but also a learning experience. The Inspector found a chair and settled down as I walked to a nearby cabinet to rummage through a drawer.

"Doctor Sangre, your message mentioned something about the Emerald Coast Company and smuggling?" Inspector Leigh rumbled, folding his hands in his lap. "Care to explain? Smuggling's an ugly accusation to throw around. Quite illegal in most places throughout the Caribbean. It takes more than just one person's word that it happened."

I pulled out the set of hard-won papers swiped from Jonas Ketteridge's office, then shut the drawer.

"True, Inspector. I've seen more than one brawl start in a tavern over accusations of smuggling." I idly tapped the papers in my hands and leaned a hip against the workshop table. "You mentioned that if we heard anything involving the Emerald Coast Company to pass it along?"

"Starting with *it's run by a rather bad man who's often up to no good,*" Primrose bluntly added.

"Well, hm," he grunted. "As a member of the Kingston city watch? I can't officially comment."

"Unofficially?" I prodded with a wry smile.

Inspector Leigh rubbed his nose and then tugged at his mustache. "Ah, well. In that way? The man's a menace. Whatever horrible thing he's dragged up into Kingston has put several people in the hospital. It's running the nuns ragged."

My smile widened, wiggling the papers in the air between us.

"How would you enjoy running Señor Ketteridge ragged for a change?"

I offered the papers to Inspector Leigh. To his credit, he looked them over carefully, not missing a single entry. Once his eyes reached the signature of Jonas Ketteridge at the bottom, he glanced over at us under his sandy-blonde eyebrows.

"Well now, this is quite interesting," he intoned. "Do I want to know how you got this?"

"Ah, no," I admitted. "But it is authentic... and a quick way to bring a bad man to heel. At least a solid start, yes?"

The inspector gripped the torn ledger pages in one hand, tapping them lightly against a knee. His eyes traveled down the list of illegal goods once more.

"What about the... thing... he brought into Kingston?" Leigh studied us suspiciously.

"Dealt with," Primrose replied curtly. "It won't be a threat. You've our word on it."

Inspector Leigh narrowed his eyes. "We'll see, Miss. What was it, if I may ask?"

"A plant," I shrugged.

"What?" Leigh frowned.

I nodded, while Primrose recovered the odd, oval contraption with its almost spidery brass legs from a nearby counter.

"Just as I said, Inspector, a plant. A rare one." I paused a moment, folding my arms, as I considered him. "Tell me, have you ever heard of a tidebloom vine?"

"Rumor. Tall tales." The inspector pursed his lips, shifting in his chair, making the wood creak. "Made up stories about a plant that steals your memories."

I swapped a knowing smile with Primrose, who set the glass, egg-shaped chamber on the worktable. The brass cylinder attached to the wide end glimmered in the morning sunlight through the window, like a secret waiting to be told.

"No, Inspector," Primrose explained, with an excited glimmer in her eye. "They're real enough. But no one's been able to cultivate one.

They don't steal memories, but transcribe them. Store them. At least that's the story."

Leigh harrumphed.

"Sounds dreadful. Is that what put people in the hospital? Some vine bothering people's heads?"

His answer was gruff, but I heard a note of fascination in his words. That, and he leaned forward a bit out of curiosity to get a better look at the glass chamber.

"The same." I reached over, gently tapping the glass. "Ketteridge—or likely whomever he was dealing with—got his hands on one and tried to transport it. You know Kingston is picky about the plants brought here."

"True," Leigh said, still fascinated by the chamber.

I waved a hand at the device.

"Ketteridge tried, but it seems the vines sadly die off when taken from wherever they grow. We're no experts on the plant, but as alchemists? Our best guess is that the vine was dying and reaching out for help. Like a flower for the sunlight. It wasn't intentionally trying to hurt anyone."

"Ah." That one word seemed to cover everything the inspector could say. He eyed us both, as if extracting a secret promise.

"So, not a threat now though? Good. Best it stay that way. Less paperwork and explanation all around."

Inspector Leigh took another look at the ledger sheets, then stood while nodding to himself. I cleared my throat as he turned toward the door.

"Inspector?" He met my gaze before I continued. "You mentioned some names are untouchable, others sign your pay. But I know a man of honor when I see one. Someone who cares about doing the right thing—even if their honor may be a bit tarnished from swimming in foul water."

I gestured at the pages of illegal goods.

"Those might help polish the tarnish off. Make what's underneath it shine like new."

That earned me a scowl and another grunt. Only this one lacked any bitter glower—it sounded more like respect.

Once the inspector had left, I studied Primrose's work at the distillery. Satisfied her potions were brewing nicely—which they were—I arched an eyebrow at her.

"How's our new guest?" I grinned slyly. Primrose mirrored my expression.

"Oh, fine enough."

She strode with her usual brisk precision to the back of the shop, pulling aside a small veil from in front of a shelf nook. It wasn't one I ever used much, save for potion storage now and again. Primrose had found a better use for the space.

Behind the veil was a small clay window box. Narrow, it was filled with damp soil and moss, cradling a small sprig of vine with long, ribbon-like leaves. The moment the veil was pulled aside, a tiny figure walked out from behind the thickest cluster of leaves—a glass-eel nymph.

It—or he—was a little larger than my thumb. He was human-like from the waist up, but with an eel's tail and salamander legs. Four gossamer, stained glass-like insect wings extended from his back. The creature's skin held the pale shimmer of sea glass. Apparently, he'd fashioned a rough tunic from leaves and a bit of cloth.

He blinked at us with wide, watery dark eyes. Grinning, he took flight in a rush, wings blurry like a hummingbird's.

"The moment I gave the vine some dirt, healing potion and water mix, along with sunlight, he sprang to life—maybe roused from near-death?" Primrose shrugged.

She giggled as it landed on her shoulder to inspect the stray strands of ash-blonde hair that had escaped her bun.

I nodded thoughtfully.

"Roused from near-death is most likely. Glass-eel nymphs are rare, and said to die outside a tidebloom grove—" I shrugged with a light snort of amusement "—but so do tideblooms. Yet, you've got a tidebloom growing and a glass-eel surviving. This is the first I've ever heard of it being done successfully."

The glass-eel nymph took flight, soaring in circles around us.

"Salt and bone meal in the soil might have helped." Primrose added. "Nothing you wouldn't have done."

I hummed softly. "Well, perhaps. Still, the vine—and our little friend there—aren't twisting the Etherwave Arcana into a knot anymore. So, I'd say the problem is solved. At least, for now."

"For now," Primrose echoed.

Then the distillery hissed out a whine for attention. Primrose raced over with the glass-eel in fast flight behind her.

I watched her for a long moment—the glass-eel nymph circling her, curious about everything. She'd given me credit that this wasn't anything I wouldn't have done.

But really, was it?

Primrose had devoured the basics of alchemy in days. That's better than most do by far. Silently, I wondered if she was on her way to becoming something more.

A part of me wanted to call it legacy, but not how most abused the word. To me, a real legacy wasn't about shops, bloodlines, or deeds.

It's all about what we keep close, and who helps us keep standing when curses and storms want to eat us alive. I smiled, glancing at the shop, then back to my apprentice.

"Heading to the *Silk Duchess* next, then?" Primrose asked me over her shoulder. "Captain Blackwater mentioned moving one of your smaller distilleries there, yes?"

"Later today," I nodded, watching the glass-eel nymph sniff the bubbling potion, only to make a face. "But we'll open an Arcane Gate back here every few days, so I can still help a little with the shop and check your progress. You've still plenty to learn."

"True, but that's tomorrow," she said, checking her fog potion once more.

Tomorrow. I had a feeling that tomorrow—and the days to follow—were going to be something to see.

Dockside Glossary

Notes by Doctor Pedro Alejandro Sangre, alchemist, privateer, and reluctant curse-collector.

Arcane Gate - The first things that appeared in 1712 when the Otherworld crashed into our own. They're towering arches of raw Etherwave Arcana that only appear out on the open sea. Sail a ship through one and you can cross half the world—or slip into broken pieces of Otherworld—in a heartbeat. It takes a trained navigator to get you through. Everyone else? They're just kindling with good intentions.

Arcane Engine - An engine only if you like pumping regret. These relic contraptions are intended to perform an enchanted task rapidly, repeatedly, and flawlessly. In practice? You only get to pick two out of the three, and always get a side effect no sane person wants.

Asa mvur – A Silvashar thayan phrase Elara uses for me. She says it means 'beloved'. But I've my doubts. I think it really means 'stubborn fool'.

Bindweaver's Curse – A nasty enchantment that doesn't just kill you. It binds your life to whatever foul thing it's wrapped around. I don't recommend it.

Codex Luminari – A book of necromancy and rituals to play with the dead, written in corrupted Etherwave ink. Currently my least favorite piece of literature. Now? Some sort of ghost trap. I suspect Morowen will make me regret turning it into that.

Death Whisper - Some swear they're fiends. Others a walking nightmare. Really, they're a rare golem made from old books, ink, and the writer's spirit. A lethal problem in their own right, they can wax a little philosophical if you catch them on a good day.

Deepbind Curse – Older and worse than the Bindweaver. Instead of killing you outright, it ties you to something else. A spirit, monster, or a damn mystery you'd rather not solve.

Durner Terrason - Grimling gearwright and master gunner of the *Silk Duchess*. Brass veins, rust-red beard, and an unhealthy fondness for loud artillery. If it explodes, Durner either built it, improved it, or is arguing with his brother Skaldi about how to make it worse.

Dryden Storm – Pirate and a smug, murdering bastard. Wears a squirrel skull amulet that reeks of curses. If you see him, either run or bring a small army.

Elara Blackwater - Thayan Sunweaver and captain of the *Silk Duchess*. Expert with a sword, brilliant explorer, and entirely too willing to risk her life—and mine—for a good cause or a mad idea. Graceful wings, jade-gold eyes, and a personal loathing of death and necromantic magic that could burn a hole through lead. She is the guiding star to my heart.

Etherwave Arcana – The invisible tide of power left after the Crossing's Fall apocalypse. Alchemists bottle it. Wavebinders command it. Most people just curse it when it sparks lightning in their soup. Personally? I like a little spice in my soup on occasion.

Ghostfire – An enchanted tattoo stamped on you from something in the Etherwave that thinks you're very interesting. It marks you.

Sometimes to help, other times to chatter at you. Mine likes to glow at damn inconvenient times.

Graveyard Syrup – My own invention. A tonic brewed to bleed off excess effects of the Deepbind Curse, so it doesn't kill me. Bitter as sin. Don't ask what goes in it. Especially don't ask about the chicken feet...

Grimling - Stout folk from Otherworld, built like carved stone and twice as steady. Calm heads, blunt tongues, and eyes that shine like polished metal. Their skin carries faint lines of glowing alloy—birthmarks that shift as they live, craft, and occasionally set something on fire on purpose. Yes, really, they do. Unmatched engineers and smiths. If something explodes, cracks, or collapses, odds are a grimling warned someone about it first.

Lysander Riverwind - Human Navigator and occasional cartographer for the Royal Institute of Otherworld Studies. Quiet, sharp, and more intuitive than he admits. Claims I'm smarter than he is, which only proves he has poor judgment in some areas. Without him, we'd have been scattered across rocks—or worse—by the Gates a dozen times over.

Marquee Brotherhood - A secretive guild of assassins, bounty hunters, and alchemists who live and die by something they call the Marquee Code. Organized into Houses like Jadescale, Frostsin, and Hawkguard, and overseen by a Council of Five, they sell precise, unpleasant solutions to very specific problems.

Morowen Waxbend – Sea hag. Sharp teeth, sharper tongue. Owes me debts and swears I owe her more. Neither of us is wrong. Heaven help me, we're likely friends. But don't tell her I said that. She likes to turn people into an equal volume of sea urchins.

Primrose Stewart – Ah, my apprentice. Smarter than she knows, and better than she thinks. Likely smarter than us all wrapped together. Wields ledgers like weapons. I still assume she'll outlive us all, provided she stops blowing holes in the shop roof.

Silk Duchess – Elara's ship. Proud, stubborn, graceful, fast, and far too willing to get us all killed. Which is not far off from her captain in some ways.

Skaldi Terrason - Grimling arcane engineer and blacksmith. Brass-veined, blue-rust hair, and a mind full of gears and runes. He builds the portal platforms and other marvels that keep our ship in one piece—then lets his brother Durner test them, which ruins the effect.

Soul Anchor Page - A very rare use of the Etherwave Arcana that anchors a person by their soul to a place during a ritual—usually a dangerous one. If someone mentions they want to use one? Well, either help them question their life choices or find somewhere else to be!

Thayan - Winged folk from Afalon Isle in the mid-Atlantic Ocean. Human-shaped but unmistakably Otherworldly up close—dragonfly wings, bright jewel-toned eyes, and that faint dusting of mana powder thayans shed wherever they go. Scholars, explorers, mystics, depending on the culture. Elara is one, which explains the grace, the courage, and why she carries herself like she could outshine the sun.

Wavebinder – A mage who commands the Etherwave like a storm answers the sea. Dangerous. Exhausting. Half-mad. Good men to have at your back, better at your side.

Wood Wraith - Some might think they're a playful tree spirit. Maybe that's true if they're playing with your skull. Rumor has it, they're what happens when someone dies trapped in a sinking ship. Their soul fuses with the wreck, turning them into driftwood-skinned nightmares with ember eyes and a grudge sharp enough to cut canvas. If you ever meet one, run. A lot.

Acknowledgements

Avast there!

Well, now, who do we have here? Oh, never you mind that. That's not why you're here, is it?

If you've sailed this far, you've a deep fondness for books and for what makes a story tick like a wound watch. For that, my hat's off to you. This tale—like many others—doesn't sit alone and cold by itself. Neither are stories made that way. Bringing them to life takes strong arms and a keen eye for imagination. It's those hands that hold them steady until they catch the wind in their sails, and then—off they go, riding the waves.

It isn't something one does alone. Oh no, I'll tell you true—it's not. You need a good compass and a bright star to guide a story, especially in the dark of night.

The Officers

To start, you can't captain a story like this without a good crew at your back. First among them would be my mom, dad, Charlie Marschall, Pat Marschall, Jarissa, and Wookieegunner. You believed—and therefore, so did I.

The Quartermasters

S. E. Reid (sereid.com) is the editor who helped keep order as these stories set sail. Her steady hand kept the rigging ship-shape, even in chapters that weathered the worst storms you might imagine. I had questions, and her answers were thoughtful, insightful, and always kept me on course. Her glass-eel nymph is on its way to her—once I catch the stinker! Along with her wasUeraynne S. who designed the fantastic cover art—my hat is well and good off to you!

Gunner's Mates

Ann Kimbrough (of *Tell Me a Mystery* on Substack), Tepcat, and Deleyna Marr (of *Deleyna's Drift* on Substack) served as beta readers with careful aim and steady hands, helping me sight the target—especially when I found myself a bit lost.

The Swashbuckling Crew and Powder Monkeys

Here's the pack of scurvy dogs and loyal crew who always have my back—the ones who cheer me on and bear with me as I battled my way through storms to get these stories launched:

Shawn Carpenter (*The Tides of Magic* series), Graylion, Jenks, Chip Malinowski, Dr. Unity Walker, Sarah Lowery, Jaime Buckley (*Wanted Hero*), Richard Ritenbaugh (*Serial Production*), Rob

Mortell (*Stories Have Power*), Mercedes de Santiago (*Mil Y Una Historias*), Leanne Shawler (*The Môrdreigiau Chronicles*), Shannon W. Haynes (*Chapter by Chapter*), and Alison Bull (*Historical Fiction Stack*).

Last of all, to those of you who took a chance on these stories—you're the reason it's a joy to write them. After all, you're the ones who pull up a chair, sit at the table, and ask to hear me spin these tall tales. Thank you for that.

With that...
All Hands! Go Catch that Horizon!

As the good Doctor Pedro Sangre himself once put it...

> *It's never wrong to live your best life with the wind in your sails, the sun at your back, with a touch of mystery for fun... after all, a bit of mystery is the spice of life, is it not?*
>
> Doctor Pedro Alejandro Sangre

With all my gratitude,
C.B. "Kummer Wolfe" Ash
web: kummerwolfe.substack.com
web: www.cb-ash.com

About the author

Death Whispers of the Etherwave and *The Alchemist's Apprentice* are the work of C. B. Ash, who also writes as Kummer Wolfe and K.M.R. Wolfe.

C. B., or as most know him through the nickname and pen name of Kummer Wolfe, spends his days going in several directions at once.

With degrees as a Physical Scientist, Mathematics, and Computer Science, it seemed only natural that he started out rather young teaching martial arts. Well, it made sense to him. Beyond that, he's also dabbled as a musician, artist, and spent a good deal of time in tech working out web designs, engineering, and software architecture as a consultant. Traveling to view the world through its real lens... people.

No matter where he went, there he was with a notebook and pen in his trusty bag, taking notes. Sometimes even with a tablet, writing out stories and characters. Which is, at the core of it all, what he enjoys most.

But don't worry! He does sleep sometimes, or at least that's what he says. Otherwise, people might start to wonder about him...

If you're looking to find him, maybe even get a sneak peek at what he's writing now? Head on over to Substack! He's got serial fiction stories, worldbulding, and so much more: https://kummerwolfe.substack.com/

www.ingramcontent.com/pod-product-compliance
Lightning Source LLC
LaVergne TN
LVHW090549110826
845146LV00001B/84

* 9 7 9 8 9 9 4 7 8 6 1 8 5 *